D0199912

CAN
YOU
SEE
ME?

CAN YOU SEE ME?

LYNNE LEE

THOMAS & MERCER

This is a work of fiction. Names, characters, organizations, places, events, and incidents are either products of the author's imagination or are used fictitiously. Any resemblance to actual persons, living or dead, or actual events is purely coincidental.

Text copyright © 2019 by Lynne Lee
All rights reserved.

No part of this book may be reproduced, or stored in a retrieval system, or transmitted in any form or by any means, electronic, mechanical, photocopying, recording, or otherwise, without express written permission of the publisher.

Published by Thomas & Mercer, Seattle

www.apub.com

Amazon, the Amazon logo, and Thomas & Mercer are trademarks of Amazon.com, Inc., or its affiliates.

ISBN-13: 9781542014939
ISBN-10: 154201493X

Cover design by kid-ethic

Printed in the United States of America

For Rex

I know a bank where the wild thyme blows,
Where oxlips and the nodding violet grows,
Quite over-canopied with luscious woodbine,
With sweet musk-roses and with eglantine:
There sleeps Titania sometime of the night,
Lulled in these flowers with dances and delight.

A Midsummer Night's Dream,
William Shakespeare

Creatures of the dark, moths aspire to the light.

Leave a light on and you'll see:

They will find you.

Chapter 1

The sky has changed. And not for the better. I've been head down, paddling out, labouring under a misconception. That the peach dawn which had broken as I entered the foaming water would still be here – bright and brightening – as I sat up on my board. But it's not. It has faded to grey.

My mood darkens with it. This is a bad day to be surfing, and I'm much too far out. Not waving or drowning, just trying to charm waves that aren't coming. Trying to chase away demons I can't even articulate. Trying to prove a point to myself; that I'm not who I am. That I'm someone my dead husband would no longer recognise.

Despite my earlier hubris I also recognise my folly. I shouldn't have come down to Wales. I definitely shouldn't have come out here alone. The words come at me like seagulls, wheeling and screeching on the wind. *You should never surf alone because it's dangerous. You know that. Because you could drown – just like that – and who'd see?*

Yes, there are other surfers out here, if only specks in the far distance, but I know I should turn around and head back in again. Because what I belatedly recognise as a fog, and a thick one, is now rolling in with malevolent intent. *You're a fool, Julia*, it whispers. *What were you thinking?*

And it's fast. I can't even see any other surfers now, I realise. I can no longer see anything, full stop. I lean forward, grip the board, slide my legs up out of the water, slip my arms in, and paddle back to shore.

And I'm right to. Our cottage, to which last night I bolted so impulsively, is no longer distinct on the hill. It's now a pale smear against the washes of grey blue and rust green. A smudge of ivory above the ochre of the beach. And as I slither up to the shallows and roll off the board, it too becomes lost in the swirl of grey mist. This is sea fog. It can swallow whole hillsides.

I stand up and rip the Velcro to take the leash off my ankle, winding it round the board with cold, fumbling fingers. I feel cross with myself, too, for being so irresponsible. Like I'm a teenager again, bunking off an A-Level revision class. As if irresponsible is the worst thing I can ever be.

Except it isn't.

I'm fifty metres from the cliff path the first time I see him. Just a glimpse; a flash of colour that shouldn't be there. An incongruous pixel of hothouse-flower pink, bright against the rear cottage wall. I only see him because the building has been freed temporarily from the fog, which is now drifting almost lazily upwards.

I slow and stop on the wet sand, trying to pick out more detail. The higher Down rises some two hundred metres above sea level, and the cottage, set at the back of a wide grassy plateau, is around thirty metres above where I'm standing. Once I reach the bottom of the steps which will take me back up there I know both will be temporarily lost from view. But, once again, there it is – the same

2

flash of bright pink. There's someone hanging around at the back of our property. I hitch the board up and hurry on towards the steps.

It's only once I'm on the pasture above the beach, with the house back in sight, that I see him again. He's sinewy. Purposeful. Youthful. He's wearing a grey T-shirt and I realise that the flash of pink I saw is a pair of hibiscus-spattered board shorts. He's also moving in such a way around the back of the house that it's obvious he's up to no good.

I increase my speed across the expanse of grass that separates us. He hasn't seen me. He's got his back to me and is peering into the kitchen window, which looks out over the bay. And the fog, now moving sluggishly but more thickly upwards, ensures that even if he does turn around it's highly unlikely that he will spot me.

I'm right. Temporarily shielded by the jumble of outbuildings in the garden, I'm almost at the low garden wall before he turns around, scanning the horizon, and then finally notices me – a dark shape, growing larger as I jog up the last five or so metres of track towards home.

Our eyes meet. He panics. Then, immediately, he bolts. Runs around the corner of the house wall, out of sight and out of earshot, to emerge seconds later, incongruously higher on the hill. Heading up the Down, where I'd have expected him to run east towards Rhossili.

But no. Straight *up* the hill. Where there is no route to follow – not even a path made by the sheep. It's too steep. Why on earth would he do that when there are so many other options? Because he thinks I won't follow him? Because he thinks I can't?

Whatever's prompted him, he now looks like a frightened Gower pony, making astonishingly fast progress, albeit in explosive, skittish bursts, around and among the muddle of bramble and dying ferns. Is it that – that sudden turn of speed – that prompts me to follow? Am I trying to prove something? To him? To myself?

In the moment, however, I don't think; I just do. I sling the board down by the back gate, run round the side of the house, and hare off up the hill in pursuit.

'Hey!' I bellow. 'Stop!' And I know he must have heard me. And again, because he has, and has chosen to ignore me, on I go, powering up the steep, dewy Down, my legs impelled more by indignation than proper anger. But he's too young and quick, and too intent on evading me, and within moments he's lost to me again, melted into the fog.

The higher Down is pimpled with outcrops of exposed sandstone boulders, and I stop by one, my breath coming in rasps. The fog has swallowed me as well, and for a moment sense prevails. *Let it go. Whatever it is. Just let it go, Julia.*

And that's how life sometimes goes. Turns on a fraction of a moment. Because I linger there just long enough to hear him scream.

I rarely surf without boots on, even in summer. I trod on a weever fish once and I've never forgotten it. You tend not to when inflicted with that intensity of pain. (*Typical.* I remember David saying that, chuckling. *How many times have I told you? A zillion? A trillion?* My late husband and I were still happy then.)

That's what strikes me immediately after the spike of human noise. That my feet are encased in rubber. I would not have come this far without them. I'm responsible again.

I call out. 'Where are you?' But there's no answering sound. 'Hello!' I call again, heading on up.

Another noise then. This time lower pitched; more of pain than terror. And as I jog on up the muddy track, I hear it again.

'Where *are* you?' I yell through the murk as I run. 'Call again so I can work out where you are!'

As I rise even higher the belt of fog begins to thin. And as I reach the flat path that traces the spine of Rhossili all the way to Hillend, I hear him cry out again. I twist to locate the sound, realising that it's now travelling *up* to me. So I swerve off the path to my left into the heather. A stonechat – such nervy birds – clatters upwards in front of me. I'm not sure which of us is more spooked.

I press on to where the rocks mark a sheer, scary drop. Despite the fog, which now hangs in a gauzy haze below me, I can just about work out where I am. 'Have you fallen?' I yell down. Another stonechat breaks cover.

A ragged voice floats up to me. 'Help!' Then, 'Down here!'

By early autumn, Rhossili Down is more filigree than tapestry; the rocks on the steeper inclines, liberally mottled with yellow lichen, are now half-buried beneath bracken and greying gorse. Even in my wetsuit I can feel them trying to snare me.

I've never once tried to clamber down there. Who would? Though by autumn to fall a long way would be almost impossible – you'd be trapped by the mesh of branches as efficiently as in a drag net, which consoles me as I begin picking my way down the hillside, moving gingerly, trying to find the least precipitous route. The fog eddies around me, displaced by my flailing, but another cry – unintelligible this time – at least makes the boy's location clearer.

Mine, too, is increasingly precarious. And almost as I think that, my foot slips on a watercourse and I'm falling, desperately grabbing at a bush to stop me tumbling down to join him. But it's as sharp as it's strong and, as if to teach me a lesson, a thorn ploughs a furrow through the palm of my left hand.

Cursing, I flail for purchase with my other hand and find one. And there he is, bent and stiff, just below me.

His hands are fluttering in front of him. 'God,' he's saying. 'Oh, Jesus! *God!*'

Transfixed, I scramble down to him, all other thoughts now forgotten, bar the blood that is spewing from him, holding all his attention. Bright, urgent, thick arterial blood.

From that to this. In a fragment of a moment.

They say it just kicks in, a medical training. Which is why the standard response to a medical emergency is to start looking around for a doctor. In reality, without drugs and machinery and tech, what you probably most want is a first aider.

It's been a good fifteen years since I've done life-or-death first aid. My speciality is cancer, which is a serious business, but it mostly does its deadly work at a slower pace. So such kicking in as is going on is a kick of profound panic. We are a very long way from the nearest A & E. The boy is bleeding profusely all over the pink board shorts, from which wisps of pungent steam are already rising.

I inch my way down to him, treading carefully across the stream that has already upended me, realising that this might well be what has happened to him too.

'Oh, god,' he says, hearing me, then looking up, seeing me. '*Help* me!' His face is paper white. His hands round his left thigh aren't actually touching it. They're just quivering above it, like dying crabs, blood-soaked, stiff and hopeless.

The slope is steep, much too steep, and I'm grateful for the fog now. That and the fact that whatever has stopped him falling shows no sign of relinquishing him now. His legs are both bent, his feet rammed against a boulder. I edge down to him and manage to kneel awkwardly just above him. 'Don't move,' I tell him, as I lean in to see better, my view of whatever is causing so much blood to pump out of him now partly obscured by his T-shirted back.

'Help me,' he says again, his voice astonished as much as any-thing. 'God, please *help me.*'

'I am,' I say. 'I *will.* I'm a doctor.'

It sounds ridiculously pompous, even to my long-attuned ears. But you do it because, usually, it helps. I manoeuvre my right leg down beside him and shimmy myself around so I am at least half beside him. 'Stay still,' I command. 'And try to keep calm,' I add, though I am by now anything but. 'Let me see what we're dealing with here.'

And then I see, and I realise there is no time for reassurance. Only immediate, decisive action. He has a wound in his groin that I know without question could kill him in a matter of minutes.

The femoral arteries are among the body's blood super-high-ways. Driving oxygenated blood from the heart to the legs, they are also some of the widest and strongest. Part of a closed, efficient system which is central to life. Or, if severed, the route to complete exsanguination.

Watching the boy bleed out, I grope desperately for fragments of my early training; mnemonics and mantras learned by rote, like times tables. *If it's life or limb, choose life. Use a tourniquet. Otherwise, never.* I know if I need to do that then he might survive but lose a leg. But I refuse to believe I need to take that risk. And the wound is probably too close to his groin in any case.

Which means speed is of the essence. Access to medical equip-ment is, too. But I am in a wetsuit, high on Rhossili Down, lodged between a rock and a hard place. *Think, Julia. Think.* I have two hands, one bleeding. And that's *all* I have. My only tools to apply pressure to the wound.

But ten seconds spent now could give me many minutes later. What I really need is some sort of pad to plug the wound, and it hits me that at least I have my bikini top beneath my wetsuit, so I reach around my back and fumble for my zip tag. I yank on it too hard at first, and the teeth try to resist me, but then it gives and I reach up to free the flap of Velcro, then pull the wetsuit down at the front.

'Stay calm,' I tell the boy. He stares sightlessly at me. His brows are thin and pale, but his eyes are big and dark. The school-uniform blue of a newly born baby. Who is he? Where's he come from? Might Tash know him?

'Don't move,' I tell him. 'I'm going to make a pad to plug the wound for you, okay?'

My bikini top is an old, sturdy, functional halterneck, which pings open at the back with the lightest of touches. Wrenching it from the wetsuit's strong embrace, I yank it up over the top of my head, fumbling the wetsuit back up my arms as I do so. I feel a hot swipe of pain as my gashed hand catches the strap, and then I have it and can ball it into a solid scrap of useful fabric. Not sterile, but at least salt rinsed. And precious minutes gained.

Plug the wound with a pad. Smallest surface area possible. Both hands, heel on back. Direct, constant pressure. 'Right,' I tell the boy. 'Lie back. I'm going to try to stop the flow.'

Then, one leg straight, one leg bent, I lean in, gently ushering his trembling hands away. Then yank his shorts down to his thighs – a shock of blonde pubic hair, his genitalia soaked crimson – press the pad into the wound, place my right hand on top of it, press my bleeding left one on that, heel to back, and press down.

And then I begin shouting for help.

I shout so loud, and for so long, and with such dogged persistence that I think I end up scaring the fog back down the hill. Saving lives is not a quiet, decorous business.

But my persistence pays off. I have no idea how much time passes. It could be ten minutes, or twenty. But in a lull between shouts I hear the cough of an engine. And moments later a voice comes floating down to me.

'I hear you, lovely!' A man's voice. 'What's happened? I can't see you!'

'I need the air ambulance!' I shout up. 'Don't come down. Call the air ambulance! It's a life-threatening injury!' I add, to make sure.

'Okay!' he calls back, and in a tone that suggests my request is nothing out of the ordinary, which gives me hope. He must be local. A farmer, perhaps. Someone, at any rate, who knows the lie of the land here. Who already knows just how far we are from the nearest road. I hear the engine again then. A quad bike, I decide. They use them on the Down to help them round up errant sheep.

'It's okay,' I tell the boy. Though I know he's almost certainly unconscious. 'It's okay. Someone will be here soon. It's okay.'

I dare not stop applying pressure, so I don't know how I'm doing – any more than I know who the boy is or why he's come here, or who will have their own lives destroyed if I allow his to expire beneath my hands. His own hands are now motionless, palms up, as if nesting in the brambles, and on the inside of his skinny right wrist, smeared with blood, I can just make out the outline of a small butterfly tattoo.

I wonder – is he old enough to have one? He's so obviously still on the cusp of full manhood; all bum fluff and angles and creamy young skin. The T-shirt looks new. The board shorts are old. A pair of pale battered Converse – no socks that I can see – are on his feet. I wonder how many summers they've taken him through now. Where they've been. What they've seen.

The bracken glistens beneath his hair and I suspect he also has a head injury – perhaps equally life-threatening. Did he crack his skull on the rock just above us when he fell? I want to brush the hair off his face, but I can't because I dare not move my hands. Any clot that might have formed by now will be too fragile, too tenuous. One move and the flood gate might reopen.

And I have caused this. I look away, to keep the horrible thought at bay, to keep my whole focus on trying to save him. And as I do so I realise the fog has disappeared. As if, having done its work, it has swept away, remorseless. And on the beach, still a dizzying distance below us, I see the beginnings of a gathering, presumably drawn by my shouts for help. Matchstick-men surfers. A man with two dogs. Another waving his arms. A couple in fluorescent jackets. Several are holding up mobile phones, which wink bright hellos. Filming, I realise. Filming us. Filming this. Whatever 'this' might turn out to be.

The air ambulance can get to anywhere in Wales in twenty minutes. I already know that because it's the sort of thing I would know. It has delivered critically ill children to David more than once down the years. And just the once, when I was on call, as a very junior doctor in Cardiff, a haemorrhaging RTA casualty to me. That precious golden hour. We managed to save him.

It's much less than that, though, before all the faces on the beach are tilted skywards, following the whump of rotor blades as they carve through the air. And there is the helicopter itself now – hanging over us like a big benevolent insect, hovering momentarily before banking away again, towards the top of the Down. I can feel the misplaced air tickling my sweating face.

More precious moments pass before I next hear my farmer. 'Can you hear me?' I still can't see him, but he sounds a little closer. 'Stay put,' he shouts. 'Okay, lovely? They're going to land. See if they can get down to you. What's the injury?'

My voice is hoarse as I explain it's a suspected laceration of a femoral artery. I do it slowly, firing the words up individually to him, twice. 'He can't be moved,' I finish. 'Not without medical attention. Tell them I'm a doctor. Tell them they are going to need a haemostatic agent.' This is no time to worry about causing offence by telling professional colleagues to suck eggs.

He shouts the last two words back down to me. 'Okay,' he finishes. 'Got it.'

I wonder if I know him. Wonder if I've passed him on the beach, perhaps. There are even more people gathered down on the sand now. More mobile phones trained on us. It can't even be eight yet. Where have they all come from?

I wait patiently with my patient. Still pressing. Still hoping. Still watching for movement beneath his closed eyelids.

My farmer's voice again, straining as the helicopter rises a second time. 'Can you hear me? They're going to winch down a medic. Stand by.'

'Please don't die,' I tell the boy. My cut hand is completely numb now. 'They're coming now, okay? Please don't die.'

Life-saving modern medicine comes in many forms. It comes now in the shape of a young doctor, lowered slowly down to us on a cable as slim as a little finger, with a stretcher and a sling and a bag of medical miracles, which he manages to wedge alongside the rock by my foot. Far below us, the previously scattered crowd has begun to coalesce. The noise from the hovering helicopter makes the air vibrate.

'I'm Ollie,' he says, detaching the cable. 'And you're?'

'Julia.'

'So, how are we doing, Julia?'

His voice, which is slow and deep, calms me a little. 'Not good. I think he also took a bang to his head. And I think he'd already lost a lot of blood before I got to him.'

My voice is thready now. But neither of us need to ponder specifics anyway. The boy's pallor tells us plenty, the sodden bracken even more.

'Lucky lad that you did then,' he says as he unzips his kit bag. He nods towards my hands. My red-and-white determined knuckles. 'You all right there for a moment more?'

My shoulders are screaming in protest and my bottom hand is numb now. 'For as long as I need to be,' I promise him.

He pulls items from the bag and begins to unwrap them. A pair of scissors. A pressure pad. An applicator pack of Celox. Life-saving battlefield essentials. 'You know your stuff then,' he says as he lays them out on the bag.

'To a point. I'm a doctor.'

'Ah. Got it.' He picks the scissors up. Makes short work of the sodden shorts. Peels the sticky, sopping fabric away, exposing more flesh – shockingly white – beneath the flaccid penis and tight, youthful testicles. There is absolutely no dignity in such violent near-death. 'He's been even luckier then, I'd say. You know what happened to him?'

'He must have fallen. I didn't see it. It's some sort of penetrating injury.'

He chooses the Celox next. A fat tampon-like syringe. 'How about you?' he says, gesturing again towards my scratched, bloody hands.

'It's nothing,' I say. 'Just got snared by a thorn. I have no idea what went into him. If anything even did . . . It was too hard to see. Maybe he fell on a jagged rock or something? I don't . . . I can't . . .'

'Let's see then, shall we?' he says, raising the applicator. 'Ready?'

I take both my hands and the pad away with the greatest of care. The bloody mess begins forming a fresh pool immediately.

He becomes professionally taciturn then, his full attention on the job, while my hands, no longer occupied, begin shaking uncontrollably and continue to do so as I hug my bent knee, anxious to help but unable to be useful in such a small, perilous, complicated space.

I'm not needed anyway. As soon as he pushes the contents of the applicator into the wound, magic happens; glistening soup instantly turns to what looks like a pile of breadcrumbs, which he then covers, before applying pressure, just as I did. Then he tightly wraps it, binding both thigh and lower torso, and, even before I have full feeling back in my tingling arm, the boy is covered up, harnessed up, buckled securely to his saviour, and with a promise to come back for me – to which I manage a stuttering 'hope so' – Ollie is spiralling upwards towards the helicopter, holding the boy in his strong embrace as if they are characters in a James Bond film escaping the villain's lair.

So it's done. Death defeated. At least for the moment. But with the boy's fate out of my hands, I'm frightened for myself now as the blast from the rotors threatens to knock me off my giddy perch.

Ollie keeps his promise. He's soon back with me, harnessing me up with quick, practised movements while my hand drips blood onto the already sticky ferns.

'Sure you're all right, Julia?' he wants to know as he tethers me to him.

The cable jerks us upwards. 'I'm okay,' I promise him.

Which is a lie. But not the biggest I've ever told.

Lymantria dispar

The Gypsy Moth

I lie too, Julia. About all sorts. I'm rather good at it. I *like* it. I often lie, amongst other things, about who I am. It's a survival strategy I had to learn early.

I am, I fact, whatever I need to be, whenever. Pleasing though it is to pick a side, pick a team, pick a tribe, or an *identity*, I'm actually pretty fickle: now you think you see me, but now, in fact, you can't.

Which is how it has to be now, because stuff changes, doesn't it? Case in point. Stuff *has* changed. Right here. Right now. For you, Julia, but also for me.

What kind of moth might you see me as, Julia? Something fat-bellied? Bellicose? I can definitely do bellicose. Something ethereal? Gnat-like? Insignificant and squishable? Something workaday and 'common'? (Oh, I can do that, if I must.) Something idiosyncratic, perhaps? Eccentric? Rare and strange?

But you can't see me, not for long, because insects *metamorphose*. Know this, though, Julia. I am a moth for all seasons; I *travel*. I am a gypsy moth. I am *Lymantria dispar*.

Dispar, from the Latin; 'to separate'.

Lymantria, also Latin. It means 'destroyer'.

Chapter 2

I know all about medical emergencies because it goes with the territory. The scant resources, the financial box ticking, the justification for every spent penny. This is even truer when expensive resources like helicopters are involved. So I'm surprised to learn that we are headed not for Swansea, but Cardiff. It turns out that it's because of the Neurosurgery unit there, which only adds to my fears about the boy. I'm even more surprised when it becomes obvious that no ambulance has been mustered to ferry me to a local surgery for a once over, a clean-up, and a couple of stitches. That they're going to take me to Cardiff as well.

I couldn't be more grateful. I don't doubt it helps that they know I'm a doctor, but mostly I think they understand that there is no question of me leaving the boy willingly.

The onboard paramedic has a clipboard on his knees and, while Doctor Ollie kneels and ministers to his patient, he is busy talking to the pilot and writing things down. Hills rise and fall. The Bristol channel keeps pace. Cars on the M4 blink up at us.

'So, do we know who he is?' the paramedic says through his headphones.

I lick dry lips. 'I'm sorry. I have no idea.'

'Did he have anything with him?' He glances towards Oliver.

'Not that I know of,' he replies. He looks at me and lifts his brows.

'No, I don't think so,' I say. I hadn't even thought to check. Couldn't have in any case, both hands having already been deployed.

'Nothing on him? Phone or anything? Wallet?'

There is no need to pat the boy down. Ollie shakes his head. 'Negative.'

'So, no idea why he was up there?' That question's for me again. I feel horribly airsick, sweet saliva in my mouth. I squeeze the boy's hand. Can he hear us?

'He wasn't up there originally. I saw him hanging around my cottage. And when I got to him . . . I don't know. He just hared off up the hill.'

'No idea why he was there?' The paramedic again, busy filling boxes.

'No.' I suck air in through my nose and swallow. 'I have no idea why he ran away from me either. I followed him up there. But the fog . . .'

'Tell me about it.' The pilot. 'Proper pea-souper this morning. A John Doe, then.' He says nothing more.

I squeeze the boy's hand again. Who *is* he? *Is* he someone Tash knows from uni, come looking for her? Could that be it? I feel sicker still at the thought. God, is he one of her *friends*? But if so, why on earth would he run away from me?

The last time I was at Cardiff University Hospital – the day my husband died – I entered via the reception, not the helipad. We alight on it now with the grace of a bee settling on a flower, insulated from the chaos we are causing beneath us (the incredible noise, the air turbulence, the arresting nature of our presence) and

17

I note the irony in the fact that this most glamourous of entrances is reserved for a specific 'chosen few' – those most at risk of making final departures.

The airsickness gets the better of me and though I try my hardest not to, I throw up as soon as I climb out of the helicopter. Someone duly hurries off to find me a wheelchair and they insist that I use it. So while the boy is rushed down into Major Trauma to be blood-matched and stabilised for surgery, I'm pushed by a nurse into the main part of A & E.

'We've called the police,' she explains, dipping her head to talk to me. She smells of vanilla, and my stomach churns again. 'And I think they will want to talk to you. Nothing to worry about,' she adds, as she wheels me to the A & E reception desk. 'Just procedure when a patient is particularly poorly and we have no ID. Just so you can tell them what you know. All right, lovely?'

For 'particularly poorly' I read 'critical'. 'No, of course, that's fine,' I say, conscious of eyes once again on me, taking in the blanket, the wetsuit, and the mud- and blood-speckled black rubber boots. Of the startling sight I must seem in this big city hospital, many miles, nautical or otherwise, from the breakers.

Once we reach the desk I shuffle myself forward in the chair and stand up. 'Really, I don't think I need this,' I tell the nurse. 'I feel better now. It was just the flight.'

For a moment she looks as if she might push me back down. 'I'm absolutely fine,' I reassure her, pushing the chair away from me. 'I'm sure someone else can make better use of this.'

Though I feel my legs start to betray me even as she wheels it away. I have to cling to the counter as the receptionist books me in, and only just make it to the nearest empty seat before they give up completely and deposit me on the floor.

A & E is rammed; the LED scrolls a wait of ninety minutes. And as I close my eyes, trying to shut out the stares I'm attracting,

I recall something I was told when I did my own stint on the frontline. That, rather than the Friday or Saturday evenings of most people's imaginations, it's Monday mornings that are always the busiest in casualty.

I'm feeling clammy now, and dizzy, and while I suspect it's as much to do with my newly emptied stomach as the trauma, I also recognise that I might be in shock. I scan my image-bank of memories in search of escape.

Ridiculous, the things that stay with you. The little mind maps in storage. It's been years since I've worked in this hospital, and it was only for six months, yet there are still nooks and crannies I could find my way to blindfolded. Including a hidden staff toilet just behind the triage area.

I'm just about to head there, so I can splash some water over my salt-scoured face, when I hear someone behind me call my name.

'Julia! Oh, my god. So it *is* you!'

News clearly travels. I turn around to see a familiar grey-haired woman hurrying towards me, a pile of notes clutched to her chest, pinioning a lanyard and badge, and a pair of purple reading glasses on her head.

Sonia, not so very long back, was David's clinical secretary. I haven't seen her since his funeral six months back. And I barely saw her then. So many had turned out for it. Such an astonishing number of people.

But perhaps not so astonishing. He was young and well loved.

She sits down next to me. Every eye in the waiting room is again trained on us. '*Look* at you,' she says, as if I've misinterpreted the dress code for a party. '*Look* at you. For heaven's sake. Let me see if I can find you some scrubs or something. You want a tea or something too?'

I tell her no. 'I'm okay. But I really need a phone. Do you have one I could borrow? I need to call Tash to let her know I'm all right.'

'Gosh, of *course*.' She stands up then, so she can pull a mobile from a trouser pocket. 'Here,' she says. 'Passcode is 3625. Hmm. You do need that cuppa. You're white as a sheet. I'll go and get you one now. And I'll have a word.' She lowers her voice. 'Get you pushed along a bit.'

Her relentless kindness is beginning to make my eyes prickle. 'Could you find out if there's any news yet?' I ask her. 'On the boy?'

She pats my shoulder. 'I'll find that out too,' she promises. 'Pat's in today, so I'll nip up and have a word with her. Try not to worry. You know he's in good hands.' She squeezes my arm then, her hand pale and liver-spotted against the black neoprene. 'He's *been* in good hands. Just imagine if you hadn't been there.'

I already have. And the conclusion I've reached is as stark as it's inescapable. If I hadn't been there, then he wouldn't be *here*.

'So, who *is* he?' My daughter's voice is still thick with sleep as she answers my call. Which at least means the grim footage has yet to reach her.

'I don't know. I was hoping you might. He's about your age. Maybe younger. Curly blonde hair. Big blue eyes. Skinny. And he's got a tattoo of a speckled butterfly on the inside of his wrist. Does that ring any bells? Could it—'

'*Christ*, Mum.' I hear clicks and rustling. 'God, that's *you* up there? Ellie. Rewind it. No, no. *There*. That's it – god, Mum, have you *seen* this?'

'Seen what?'

'It's on YouTube. God, Mum. *You're* on YouTube. What the f— How on *earth*? Are you okay?'

'I'm fine,' I reassure her. I dread to think what the films on YouTube might look like. 'Just need a couple of steri-strips in my hand. I'm more worried about the boy. Think, sweetie – could he be anyone you know? He's in such a bad way, and no one knows who he is. So, if you can think of anyone – *ask* anyone – then let me know ASAP, okay?'

'God, that bad?'

'Yes, sweetie, that bad.'

'But you're *sure* you're okay? You're not just saying that, are you?'

'I'm *fine*,' I say again. 'Tell you what, I'll text you a selfie to prove it, shall I?' Then immediately regret it, because my hand – because *all* of me – is such a crusted, bloody mess. 'Look, and in the meantime, if you can think of anyone? Ask around? It's important, okay? Because he's really badly injured. Can you do that?'

'Yes, of course, but—'

'And call me back on this number if you can think of anyone?'

'Yes, course I will. Mum, seriously, you think he might *die*?'

I can hardly bear to articulate it. 'Yes, he might.'

'Julia, what can I say? Good god. What a Monday morning *you've* had, eh?'

My wound pulled together by a brisk, capable A & E nurse, I've swapped my wetsuit for the scrubs Sonia's found for me and drunk the tea, which has made me feel much better. And, still ridiculously clad in my blood-spattered rubber boots, I've now found my way, ninja-style, to temporary sanctuary. The office of a consultant paediatric surgeon called Jack, David's former colleague and, also formerly, our friend.

I haven't seen Jack since David's funeral either, and though I wrote to thank him for his card – one of more than two hundred – I haven't tried to make contact since. It just seemed easier that way.

Less need to pretend. A clean, decisive break. Better for everyone. Not least because, a year or so before David's death, Jack left his wife, Prudence, who is a GP in Barry, and with what was widely considered to be unseemly haste, got divorced and remarried within a year.

I made no such judgements. *Judge not, lest you be judged.* I just felt stunned that a life that had for so long seemed so stable could be dismantled and reassembled so quickly.

It's good to see such a kind, familiar face. He finds a seat for me, and a contaminated waste bag for my bloody wetsuit, then sits back on his swivel chair, long surgeon's fingers meshed together between his knees. I spot his new wedding ring, which is thick and, knowing Jack, almost certainly high carat white gold. A reminder of the life that has carried on in my absence. I wonder how success-fully he's disposed of his old one.

I find I'm twisting my own wedding ring, and wonder how long it will sit there. When – if – I'll take it off. Tell the truth.

'How are you anyway?' he asks. 'It's been too long. You still in London? How's Tash?'

'Yes I am, and she's fine,' I say. 'Goes back to uni next week.'

'Swansea, right?'

I nod. 'I'm helping her move into her new student house. I wasn't even supposed to be coming down till tomorrow. She's in Edinburgh at the moment, with an old school friend. She—'

'You've spoken to her, then – told her where you are? Because it's all over social media. You know that, don't you?'

'I do. And, yes, just now. But she didn't think it sounded like anyone she knows. None of her friends are back yet, and she didn't recognise anyone from my description.' I glance up at the wall clock. Is he still in surgery? Still alive?

Jack is determined to drop everything so he can take me back to the cottage. It will be a three-hour round trip for him, and a massive imposition, but he won't take no for an answer. In the face of my repeated refusals, he even becomes short. 'Jules, shut *up*. Let me *do* this!'

I know it will mean moving a whole mountain range of NHS commitments, so, grateful, and also chastened, I leave him to do so, while I go back down to see the policeman in A & E, where Sonia has buzzed a message to let me know he's waiting.

I already know there's little I can tell him that will be of use to him. In fact, he is already several steps ahead of me. The boy is out of theatre now, he tells me, and has been transferred to ITU, where they are going to keep him in an induced coma till he stabilises.

If he stabilises. I know his body could tip over into shock again at any moment. That, if it does so, one by one, all his systems could fail. I try not to think about it. 'And have you made any progress with finding out who he is yet?'

The officer shakes his head. 'But we've got a photo – if we need to use it – and the butterfly tattoo, of course. And at least we have a phone number—'

'You have a phone number?'

He gestures towards his hand. 'Written in marker pen on his palm.'

I hadn't seen that. But how would I have beneath all that blood? 'Thank goodness for that at least,' I say.

'Well, in theory. No luck so far. But we'll keep trying. Sure we'll get there. We'll be putting an appeal out right away. Try not to worry, Doctor Young. I'm sure someone will come forward soon. Young lad like he is . . . He's sure to be missed, isn't he?'

By who? I think. And *how* soon? Soon enough?

By the time I've finished with the policeman and made my way back up to Jack's office, he's sorted everything he needs to and has his jacket on.

'I've just been up there,' he tells me. 'And it's still touch and go, but Pat's promised she'll keep you in the loop. Well, at least till her shift ends. I've given her your mobile number – assuming you haven't changed it?' I shake my head. 'Good. So she'll be able to speak to you direct then. You all set?'

I'd really like to see the boy for myself, but I know that won't be happening, so knowing Pat's there – she's a senior ITU nurse who worked with David for many years – is both a reassurance and a consolation.

'That's really kind of you,' I say. 'And, yes. Yes, I'm all done. Though—'

'Enough! Jules, honestly, you are doing me a favour. Because this huge inconvenience' – he puts the word 'inconvenience' in finger quote marks – 'means I'm going to have to reschedule my annual appraisal. And if we spin it out long enough, I might even have to miss a Trust meeting as well. Plus, between you and me, a few hours to myself are a commodity in extremely short supply lately.'

Jack is as conscientious and hard-working a doctor as I know, so I don't buy his 'bunking off' spiel for a moment. But I'm grateful that he's so anxious to peddle it, even so. I am not good with accepting favours, and he knows it. But what he says about time off strikes a chord, given the messy nature of his divorce.

'So, how are the kids?' I ask, as we set off for the multistorey. He has two, both teenagers, to whom he is devoted. I wonder how he's adjusted to all the changes and challenges. Even more than that, I wonder how *they* have.

'You probably don't know, do you? I have another one now – Harry. He's – let me see now . . . he must be eight, no . . . nine weeks old.'

'I didn't. Wow, Jack. You don't let the grass grow, do you?'

'He wasn't *exactly* intentional. But you know Emma . . . there was no way she *wasn't* going to have him, was there?'

I don't know her, but because the NHS grapevine is a very long one, I do know that his new wife, a former radiographer at this very hospital, is not much over thirty. She was married too, but childless, and, as I recall, keen to crack on. So, no, I'd imagine there wasn't.

And as we pull out onto the dual carriageway, heading west again, I wonder. Had he not died, might this have been David's story too? Highly likely, I imagine. As it is, I've been spared it.

It takes forty-five minutes to get to the Gower motorway junction, most of which we spend in conversation about the boy; analysing, considering scenarios, weighing odds. For Jack, this is an everyday, business-as-usual business. But for me, it's beginning to really hit home. I can't stop thinking that I'm heading back here, having left him back *there*. That I've abandoned him. It feels wrong.

But by the time we're off the M4, we've exhausted all the various possibilities, and, besides, now we're out on the peninsular proper, Jack's swept up in memories of a life already lost. The life that matters more to him – that of his friend.

'I still can't quite believe it, Jules. What's it been now? Half a year? There are patients coming in for follow ups that don't even *know*, of course, and, it's so bloody . . . Well, I don't need to tell *you* that, do I? Just the *shittiest* thing to have happened. I'm so sorry I haven't been in touch more. I really am. It's just, what with everything . . .' he sighs. 'And you and Pru being close . . .' He tails off then, as if to let the thought arrive at its own conclusions. Then suddenly he thumps the steering wheel, which makes me jump. 'Sorry. But that's a load of bollocks, isn't it? I let you down. I should have done more. I should have called you.'

'Jack, please don't apologise. It was complicated.' So much more than he knows.

'No excuses, Jules. I should have made more of an effort.'

'You wrote that note. Which was lovely . . .'

'Christ, will you just stop letting me off? I'm guilty as charged and we both know it.'

'Jack, you are guilty of nothing,' I begin, but I can tell he's now distracted by the view that fills the windscreen as we round the last bend before Rhossili.

'Wow,' he says. 'Sorry, Jules, but, *wow*. Why do I always forget just how beautiful it is here?'

It's the place where everyone says the same – it's like a punch in the senses. The 'I can see the sea!' point, but on hallucinogenic drugs. Where the elements come together in such glorious disarray that it's as if they mud-wrestled one another for geological supremacy.

'It is,' I agree. Though now we're back here the knot in my stomach tugs itself just a little tighter. How long has the boy been out of surgery now? Two hours?

Jack has no such insistent neurons firing in his brain. 'And you know what?' he says, as he slows down to admire it. 'This is how I'm always going to remember David. Right here, where he was always so happy. So himself.' He glances across at me. We both know what he means. 'I can't imagine how tough it must be for you, Jules. You must miss him like hell.'

I leave that to hang there, because I don't know how to answer. A simple 'Yes, I do' is what I should say, I know. Yet the words just won't come. Instead I nod. Because what else is there to do?

When we arrive at the cottage, Jack won't stay. Not even to use the loo, let alone have a coffee.

'Better not,' he says. 'To be honest, I really should get to that Trust meeting.' His fingers brush my forearm, then he thinks better of it and hugs me. 'As long as you're sure you're okay? *Are* you?'

'Yes, I'm fine, Jack. But surely you—'

'No buts. You get on inside. You look shattered,' he adds, reaching over into the back seat for my wetsuit. 'Well, assuming you can get in. Can you?'

I nod. 'I left the key under the mat.'

And as I watch him drive away, it hits me that our past is all so much debris clinging on to the tideline; just like all the razor shells and dead crabs and seaweed and frayed fishing line, it is all destined, inexorably, to be washed away.

Whereas, in the present, a young boy is clinging on to something much more important.

A lifeline. Is he still hanging on to it?

Heterogynis penella

Ah, yes, the infinite joys of parenting. The mummy moth here (let's call her Penny. Or, just for the lols, Trudy) has a pretty short, pretty rubbish existence. Mostly because she's wingless and legless. She emerges from her cocoon, one assumes, full of the simple joys of spring, only to find she's lost the lepidopteran lottery, and still looks, give or take, like a caterpillar. (A bit like the lot of countless idiot millennials who spend money *they didn't earn* on teeth whitening kits.)

It gets worse. She is legless and wingless for good reason. It's so that once she's laid her eggs she is obliged not to leave them. She must, of necessity, hang around till they're caterpillars, as her one job once she's laid them is to provide them with their first meal.

As in *be* their first meal: make the ultimate maternal sacrifice. But she's a moth. She knows the score. It's her job to be martyred. Which is why she'd deem it rude to take it personally.

Course the key thing here is that she doesn't know any different. Class *Insecta* is not big on cognition. You live, you crawl, you grow, you mate, you suffer, you get eaten alive. But I wonder. If she could *see* she had options, would she act differently? See another moth, say – one with wings, legs, and choices? Bottom line, she might not have a choice – hard to run away without limbs, after all. But it's the knowing. The *awful* knowing. It would eat at you, wouldn't it? As voraciously as any number of hungry offspring.

I had a mother once. Briefly. Now just a shard of painful memory. And then I had a foster mother. I remember her SO well. Because she promised to take care of me forever.

And didn't. She went and flew. Which is how people like me disappear, see? Because we are *starved*, more or less. Becoming weak, frail, etiolated, will-o'-the-wisp translucent. Less and less and less of the thing we were supposed to be. Till we are no more substantial than a dust mote among millions, bobbing in the breeze from the office aircon. Just another speck of nothing in the system.

Oh, you, though. Oh, you two. You pretty, pretty things, you. You know why? Because you HAD been mothered. You know, that's THE thing that struck me the most when he died.

He went and DIED, dammit. When I had plans, yeah? *Arrangements* in place. I was like that Skittles ad: I'd tasted the rainbow.

And when I found out he'd croaked, I went – as had for a while been my habit – to the citadel of smoke and mirrors that is Facebook.

YOUR Facebook. HER Facebook. Your two-for-the-price-of-one virtual smorgasbord of beguiling, pretty-even-in-extremis delights.

And, oh boy, you did NOT disappoint. In bereavement, as in everything, you kindly *obliged*. The short, thoughtful eulogy. The carefully curated photo montage. The 'love' icon clicked, oh so dutifully, on some three hundred posts. Of sympathy, empathy, hugs, healing 'vibes' – some of which, okay, yes, may have been genuine, I'll grant you, but others of which, come *on* (and, *yes*, more than you know, Julia), were vapid, follow-my-social-media-leader, emotion-lite *shite*.

I did good, right? Made you look, right? Way with words, me. I SPEW them.

De nada, Natasha. De nada.

Chapter 3

Our Gower cottage is haunted. Or so everyone has always told us. And not just by the ghosts of a complicated, expiring marriage. By proper spectral beings, with their troubled, restless souls. An Edwardian couple have been sighted several times wafting gracefully through its hefty walls, and there has also been the usual raft of apocryphal tales. Tales of unexpected pools of icy air in its corridors, and whispered voices: *Why don't you turn around and look at me?*

I stopped believing in ghosts around the same time as I dispensed with Father Christmas, but for these ghosts, we made an exception. It was such a thing locally that it would have seemed churlish not to. Besides, Tash was always fond of them, even as quite a small child. Never fearful. Just thrilled at the prospect of having ghostly tales to tell at school. So we allowed them to stay. Even spoke to them. *Goodnight friendly ghosts!*

Though, up to now, they've never spoken back to us. Celebrated as they are, our Gower ghosts have kept themselves to themselves. Perhaps they're just bored by being the only ones in town.

Perhaps they're waiting for company.

I hope they don't get it.

The key is not under the mat. There is no mat. When I'm surfing it lives under the pot on the doorstep. The one that holds the dead dwarf conifer that was a long-ago cottage-warming present from David's older sister Laura – and which we should have accepted gratefully and taken straight back to London. As I found out early on, trees don't so much grow here as endure.

The key is still there. My surfboard, however, is no longer where I left it. It's been brought into the garden and propped against the low stone wall that runs around the perimeter. So someone has obviously thought to check all is secure. The man on the quad bike? The police?

Every bit of me is aching now, particularly my arms and shoulders, so once I've checked my phone for news, I go straight upstairs to strip the scrubs off and shower. Despite the best efforts of A & E, and my own attempts in the staff toilet, there is still a stubborn residue of coppery red around the base of my fingernails – as if I was fifteen again, picking at them furiously at the back of the school bus, having failed to remove my weekend nail varnish. Only this isn't nail varnish. This is evidence. Of a near-death or an actual death?

Not that being braced for death is new for me – we've been acquaintances for years. I know protracted death. Sudden death. Death by misadventure. Death by fair means and foul. Death outwitted. Death denied. I have encountered death in all kinds of permutations and situations. And every one of them has stayed with me, deathless.

David died peacefully. At least as far as we could tell. Died with me holding one hand and Tash holding the other, seven hours after being felled by a stroke – the same thing that killed his father, though at a much greater age.

And felled dramatically, as is so often the way of catastrophic brain malfunction. No warning, no moment of terrified comprehension. Was just chopped at the knees (or so it was gently explained to me) while in the middle of a busy outpatient clinic. I cling to that thought of such instant oblivion. To what I'm told – that one moment he was explaining an MRI scan to a fascinated teenage patient, and the next, he was folded on the floor at her feet. He never regained consciousness before he left us. They only kept his heart beating (that magnificent brain of his had already died) so we could kiss warm cheeks when we said our goodbyes to him.

And, at the same time, in my case, to say goodbye to so much more. To our scheduled separation, our divorce, our final parting-in-all-but-parenting. To all those rocks in the road, around which I was expecting to have to stumble. All of them gone. At – and via – a stroke.

Even before they switched David's life support off, the idea of coming clean with Tash, at least eventually, suggested itself to me. I was so stunned and distressed that I could hardly think straight, yet emotions flew at me with the unswerving trajectory of poisoned arrows. Mortification, consternation and disbelief, obviously, and vicious piercings of bitter regret. Had I *known* he was going to die on me – well, what then? Say some slow, crippling disease. Some cruel terminal cancer. Had we talked about that scenario, and how we'd rearrange our respective futures if it happened? Yes, we'd made our wills. But imagined death? Not really. We were both only in our forties, after all. We were also too focused on our civilised de-coupling, on making the best of a bad business. Where 'making the best' meant protecting our daughter from the coming seismic shift by keeping her in the dark till she'd finished her degree. Both trying to be the noble exception to a millennia-long rule of thumb; that 'friendly divorce' is almost always an oxymoron.

Even so, on the journey to collect Tash from uni (she'd been plucked from a lecture, her phone dutifully off – ever her mother's daughter) I collected myself sufficiently to weigh up the

33

ramifications of the new reality I could now visualise all too well. Honesty is almost always the best policy and, after almost two years of reluctantly accepting David's 'necessary deception', the idea of lifting the weight in honesty's name was extremely seductive.

But having collected her – my hysterical, devastated, screaming, thrashing daughter – all bets were off. To unburden myself was one thing, to burden her quite another. I could hear David's voice saying *don't you dare*. And I listened. Because what shred of comfort could I give her but the fiction we'd agreed upon?

So, reluctantly, I donned a new emotional wardrobe. That of widowhood. A capsule collection that I could mix-and-match at will, but all of whose pieces draped me in the same subtle finery. Loss without blame. Heartbreak without heartache. Of having had something taken, rather than having wilfully abandoned it. Of memories which, though painful, would always be cherished. All that, my apparent solace.

And all of it a lie.

My bedroom is cold and unkempt, just like me. In my haste to catch the early tide, I left the bed unmade, and the duvet is still slung back almost all the way on my side. It's a stark reminder of the day I've been denied.

On Gower days, I normally launch myself out of bed as soon as I'm conscious, a ritual I first began during those early days of widowhood, when the size of the bed still had the power to derail me despite the two years when it had already become a part-time norm. It's now more than a ritual. It's a statement of intent.

My mother's blanket, which I use as a bed runner, has barely shifted even so. I rarely make much of an impression in my half-empty bed. I sleep the sleep of the righteous, as David himself once remarked, and, despite the thrashings of my mind, particularly when I feel anything but righteous, my body sticks doggedly to its own tidy schedule. It feels almost like a failing.

I rearrange the blanket anyway. Mum was a deft weaver of wool. Despite her energy and ambition, and her disdain for domesticity, she nevertheless found peace in creating swathes of soft things. It's crocheted, but not in squares, like Tash's many cot and doll blankets – it's an exuberant, unapologetic, Nordic maelstrom of a blanket. *A paean to the Aurora Borealis*, she'd called it. (Among the many gifts she gave me in childhood, the greatest was surely words.) She finished it only weeks before she died – a house-warming gift for a second home she'd never see.

Tash had been inconsolable then too, and not just because my mum was the last of her grandparents. It was because grandmothers, as a *species*, just weren't supposed to die before their granddaughters grew up. I still nurse a kernel of resentment for exactly the same reason. Fifteen years on, and the waves of anger at her leaving us still throw themselves over me with the ferocity of a spring tide during a storm. I smooth the blanket by way of saying sorry.

The sun is spearing in now, as it sinks towards the horizon, bathing the room in warm, yellowy brightness. Both its blessing – a bespoke, perfect, window-pane-framed sunset – and its curse. The room is sunless for most of the day in the summer, as if providing a suitably gloomy haven for all those ghosts.

I've just pulled on some jogging bottoms when there's a sharp rap on the front door. Imagining a policeman – that fateful knock, bearing the worst news imaginable – I drag a T-shirt over my head and pad fearfully down the stairs.

It's a man. Not in uniform, but presumably still a policeman. Tall and fortyish. Clean shaven. Shirt, shoes and trousers. Looking business-like, in other words, but only just. In my experience, people who toil at the business end of the public sector don't tend to think 'sharp' in conjunction with 'suit'. I expect him to slide a hand under his jacket and produce his warrant card, but he doesn't. He holds a hand out to shake instead.

'Nick Stone,' he says as he takes my hand and pumps it up and down. 'I'm a journalist,' he adds, as if anticipating my unspoken question. His hair, I belatedly notice, just a shade or two off black, is a little on the long side for the police force.

I pull my arm away instinctively, even though I'm not sure where the instinct comes from. Whatever else I am, I am mightily relieved. 'I was on the beach this morning,' he carries on, nodding in the general direction. 'I watched the whole thing.' He pauses. 'I hope it's not too much of an imposition, Doctor Young, but I'm currently writing a feature on the Welsh Air Ambulance for the *Western Mail*. And what happened this morning, to put it delicately, is obviously highly pertinent. I've already spoken to a few witnesses and I'm rather hoping you'll speak to me as well.' He pauses again and raises his brows a fraction. 'Will you?'

It strikes me then that I only looked out of the landing window two minutes earlier and at that point there had been no one walking or driving down the track. So where has he sprung from?

'Have you been waiting for me?' I ask him.

'Yes, of course,' he says. He seems unabashed to be admitting it. 'I'm obviously keen to talk to you, since you're the one who found him. Not to mention the one who also saved his life.'

I want to correct him. Point out that it hasn't been saved yet. And that I didn't 'find' him. I chased him. Which was almost certainly why he fell. But I don't want to talk to him, so I shake my head instead. 'Sorry, but no,' I say. Instinct again. 'At least not right now. It's – look, I really don't want to talk to the press at the moment. I'm waiting on a call from the police and I think I'd prefer it if we left it at that for now, at least while everything's, well, up in the air the way it is, and with the boy's condition so—' I form the next words in my brain but can't say them.

'I know. And I'm sorry,' he says, leaning in a little. He doesn't look particularly sorry, but then he's a journalist, isn't he? It's a professional requirement to be professionally detached. 'I don't want to distress you further,' he assures me. 'I do appreciate what a day you've had. But there's also the business of the lad still being unidentified, as you've just pointed out.' I haven't, not exactly, but he's clearly latched on to it. 'So time's of the essence. The sooner something's out there, the sooner someone is going to see it, aren't they? And the smallest detail could matter, couldn't it? And as the hero of the hour—'

That awful word again.

'I am *not*,' I point out. 'If you're running away with that line of thinking, please don't, okay?'

'Sorry,' he says a second time. 'But, look, I'm not running away with anything here, seriously. I'm just here to cover the story, and if there's anything you can add to the picture – you know, rather than have other people start poking around, weighing in . . .' He shrugs, faux-apologetically. He knows exactly what he's implying. 'It's already all over social media, as you probably—'

'Yes, I *know*.'

He must have read my anxious look, because he now peels himself off from where he's been half-leaning against my porch, and I realise there's a string hidden beneath the lapel of his jacket. Which belongs to a small nylon backpack – the kind you'd use for swimming kit – that has been out of sight, behind his back. He slips it down his arm and holds it out. Though not for me to take.

'I also found this,' he says. 'And before you ask, there's nothing to identify the boy in it. I already checked.'

'Where did you find it?' I ask.

He swivels around and points upwards. 'About a hundred yards or so up there. Up on the track towards the trig point.'

He knows the trig point. So he's local? Might he have been one of the surfers on the beach? I ask him.

'God, me?' A flash of teeth. A glance towards the bay. 'Surf in *that*. No fear.'

In other words, too much fear. Fear is always the biggest hurdle. 'But you're a local?'

He nods. 'I live just up on the road towards Middleton. And, look, full disclosure. I already know you. Well, know *of* you. I knew your late husband. He looked after my son.'

This surprises me. It also silences me while my brain processes what he's just told me. David was a paediatric neurologist, his young patients sometimes very seriously, and often terminally, ill.

'In Cardiff,' the man adds helpfully. 'Three years ago. And if you can stomach me saying it again, he saved his life.'

As reasons to let a strange man into your house go, it's a random, if not reckless, one. But since it's becoming increasingly obvious that the piece is going to be written with or without my input, perhaps speaking to him will help with damage limitation at least. Plus, I can see there's something in the bag he's holding. What?

I stand aside to let him in and point towards the kitchen. It's just big enough, but would benefit from being knocked into the living room. Though that's out of the question. Ghosts need walls to waft through, after all. There is only just room for the square kitchen table and while I pull out a chair for him he does a full three-sixty appraisal.

'I always wondered what it was like in here,' he says. 'Not to the extent of creeping into the garden so I can peer into the windows, obviously. But lots of people do, don't they? I've seen them. It must drive you mad.'

'Mad's a bit strong,' I say. 'It's occasionally an irritation. But it goes with the territory in a place like this. So the odd rambler wandering into the garden . . . well . . . it is what it is.'

'Speaking of which,' he says, turning to the bag. 'Take a look at the booty.'

He places the contents of the backpack on the kitchen table, one by one. A small bottle of water, half full, condensation clinging to the sides, an apple, a tangle of wires and greying earbuds, a khaki pack-a-mac – little more than a handful of thin fabric – then, finally, as if all that came before was just foreplay, he reaches in for the last time and pulls out a watch.

I gasp as I recognise it. 'Oh, my *god*,' I said, reaching for it.

He doesn't stop me. Just observes me. 'A Breitling,' he says. 'Some watch, eh?'

So the boy *had* broken in. The thought fills me with mortification. No wonder he bolted. No wonder he dumped the backpack.

'I know it is,' I say, turning it over in my hand, and sliding my thumb across the familiar casing. Just as I had when I'd been given it by the bereavement officer back in February. 'It's my husband's.'

'I did wonder. Did you notice anything else missing? Anything disturbed?'

I shake my head. Though, in truth, I haven't even looked. It hasn't even occurred to me to. Perhaps it would have, had I come home to find drawers spewing contents, ornaments broken, chairs and tables upturned. But everything was exactly as I'd left it this morning, including my laptop, which is still sitting on the kitchen table. Shutting the lid was almost the first thing I'd done when I'd come in.

It had also been the last thing on my mind. It still is. Even as I hold the familiar watch in my palm. The boy could have died – could still die – over this?

'I should check,' I say, standing up and heading off into the living room, to David's long-dead mother's Welsh dresser. It's moribund itself now, its shelves sagging under the weight of all the books that have migrated here from London over the years. Cookery books, field and walking guides, worthy tomes on local history, plus at least a dozen photo albums which we'd created ourselves; which Tash and I would spend rainy hours (there were often rainy hours) arranging and captioning and augmenting with mementos. Full of ticket stubs, ice cream wrappers and carefully pressed wildflowers, they form a visual encyclopaedia of Tash's childhood holidays here. I never look at them. I find it too melancholic.

The dresser also houses a lot of David's personal stuff, which neither Tash nor I can stomach sorting. Out on view, his binoculars, his wind-up torch, a pair of sunglasses, plus various treasures from the sea, amassed over years of beachcombing, each with its own imagined story. A desiccated starfish. A sea urchin shell. An enormous crab claw. A mermaid's purse. And in the bottom, a load of paperwork, a mess of OS maps and pamphlets. And in the stickier of the two sticky, elderly pine drawers, a collection of smaller bits and bobs.

I know the watch lives there because it was I who put it in here – when I brought it back from the hospital in its regulation bag, along with his fountain pens, keys and wallet. Plus, the superman cufflinks he'd been wearing that day and, bitterly ironic, the plastic hospital-issue badge he wore daily, just as I did; there to indicate if he was exposed to an excess of potentially life-limiting gamma rays.

I pick up one of the cufflinks, feeling a sharp stab of loss. Then stir the contents around with my fingers. Though I don't really need to. It's a very small drawer; a Tardis of emotions. Did the boy yank it open, see the watch, grab and go?

The man raises his brows as I return to the kitchen.

'Nothing else gone,' I tell him. 'Not as far as I can see, anyway.'

'Stolen to order, then? That's my best guess, especially if there's nothing else missing.' He points at my laptop. 'That, for instance. Another open invitation. And it must be worth, what? A couple of grand?'

'The Mac?'

'No, the watch.'

Of course he means the watch. 'More like six,' I correct.

He whistles. 'And you leave your door key under a plant pot?'

'I *left* my door key under a plant pot,' I correct him. 'On this *one* occasion. Because I was only expecting to be gone an hour, wasn't I? I wouldn't any other time. I'm not *that* naïve.'

Not naïve, but perhaps too laissez-faire. I might be vigilant about locking up when I leave, carefully checking all the doors and windows, but am I vigilant enough about making sure Tash is? Clearly not, because immediately a memory springs to mind. A creepy one, which sends me into another unexpected spin. I'd come down to stay back at the beginning of the summer, on another last-minute, after-work whim, and having arrived late in the evening expecting the cottage to be dark, I'd found the bathroom window wide open, and the light in there blazing. As a result, the room was plastered with flying insects. It had obviously been left open with the light on for a while, too – perhaps days – because as well as all the still-living (some had still been turning pointless circles round the light fitting) the bulk of my nocturnal visitors were corpses. Moths, midges, June bugs, flying beetles, mosquitos – plus a few alien-looking species I couldn't even identify. Many, particularly the moths, had died where they'd landed, their bodies pinioned to the tiled walls by some invisible force.

I'd cleared up, somewhat gingerly – insects *en masse* freak me out – and chided Tash for not checking, of course. She'd denied having done it but as I knew *I* hadn't (I'm too well trained in being scrupulously meticulous) I had written it off; she clearly *had*, and had forgotten, or perhaps one of her friends had and she hadn't realised. I didn't make a big deal of it, because it wasn't a big deal.

Now I think again. Or was it? Might I have had a human visitor too? Might he have been hanging around the cottage before, waiting for his opportunity? Even managed to climb up and get inside? The bathroom faces the beach, after all – not the village – so it would be unlikely that anyone would have seen him, especially if it had been at night.

The knowledge that he might have – that this might not have been his first visit – is deeply unsettling. I say nothing to the man, though. Because it *is* probably nothing. More to the point, given his sarcastic tone, it's a point I'm not remotely inclined to let him score off me.

'How did you know anyway?' I say instead.

If he's aware of my growing irritability, he doesn't show it. 'Because I watched you let yourself in, didn't I? Seriously, you really shouldn't. Not even for an hour. Trust me, I know. I've spent years reporting on criminal cases and it never ceases to amaze me how people are always so trusting. How they—'

'That's probably because you've spent years reporting on criminal cases,' I fire back. The watch is warming up in my hand now, but my mood is growing frosty. 'Besides, it was six in the morning. And this is rural Wales, not central London. How could anyone possibly anticipate—'

I shut my mouth. Why the hell am I defending myself to him? I decide I'm not going to offer him a cup of tea, despite the superficial conviviality of our domestic situation. I'm not sure if I have any milk anyway.

'Sorry,' he says, raising his hands. 'That was out of order. The main thing's that you've got your husband's watch back. Look,

42

I'm not going to keep you. I just want to be sure I have the facts straight, and—'

Something sparks in me. 'It's not the main thing at *all*. Have you any idea how serious the boy's condition is? How responsible I feel? He could have *died*! He could *still* die!'

He is unruffled by my sharp tone. He is obviously used to being snapped at. 'I appreciate that. Of course I do. I just – look, all I want to do is report the facts, like I said.'

'Which are that I saw him by the house, and when he saw me he ran away from me, up the Down. And I chased him. Then I lost him. Then he fell. Then I found him. That's *it*. Those *are* all the facts. There's nothing else to know. Except who he is, and I don't know that either.'

'But perhaps that watch . . .' he nods towards it again. 'Specially given that it's the only thing he took. That might—'

'Don't say anything about it,' I say, visualising the watch as his headline. 'Please don't mention it at all. Suppose he does die? What then? Seriously, do *not* mention it. *Please.* In fact, forget you even saw it. I really don't want that on my conscience as well. No one needs to know about it unless there's a reason for them to know about it. Once he's identified, maybe. But only once we know he's going to be okay.'

'That's very generous of you. But, okay, fair enough. Deal.' He says it too easily. I don't really trust him. He looks too much like a man with a new angle.

'You promise?'

'Yes, I promise. Though you do need to think about finger-prints. Well, if it comes to it, obviously.'

I place the watch back on the table. He makes no move to take it back. Instead, he pulls a pad from his jacket pocket. A spiral bound reporter's notebook. Something I realise I haven't seen in many years. 'But let's hope it doesn't,' he says. 'Let's hope they've already found out who he is, eh?' He digs around in another pocket and finds a pen, then, as well. A lidless Bic Crystal biro. Old school. Don't reporters work with iPads these days? I trust him even less.

'Won't take long,' he says. 'I don't need much. But I do need to get your name correct. Dr Julia Young, right? And you're a Consultant Oncologist—' He is writing as he speaks, in what looks like hieroglyphics. And also, I realise, checking through a list of notes already made. 'MBBS. MRCP. FRCR . . . Based in south London, but you visit the Gower often, to stay at the family holiday home. And you sustained an injury yourself, of course . . . To your hand . . . which needed stitches . . . How many, just for the record?'

I don't answer. I don't need to. He has obviously not been idle. He knows everything about me already. Was that what he was doing while he was waiting for me? Googling me? And what was he seeing as he stood on that beach, looking up? The answer is starkly obvious. A *story*.

'Forty-seven,' I say eventually. I have no idea why, but out it pops.

He looks up from his scribbling and studies my grim expression. Then he smiles at it encouragingly, as if challenging it to do better. 'Tell you what,' he says, 'how about I go out and come back in again?'

'Tell *you* what,' I reply, overcome by a furious, defensive rage. 'I have a better idea. How about you just *go*.'

He's not stupid. He clearly knows this is a cause he's already lost, so, though he apologises, twice, and leaves me his mobile phone number (I don't reciprocate) he makes no attempt to placate me further. He's got what he needs, after all. And once he's gone I thunder up the stairs and into Tash's bedroom so I can watch him walk back up the track to the village. He has a long, purposeful stride, and talks on his phone as he walks, his giant shadow keeping pace as the sun begins to set. I wonder who he's talking to; what he's telling them about me. And it occurs to me that he's just left me with a six-thousand-pound watch without any evidence that it even belongs to me. He has simply trusted me. Doesn't that prove the very point I'd made earlier?

I'm tempted to open the window and yell it down to him. Even reach out towards the catch so I can do so. But as I move the curtain aside, a bumble bee wafts out. He's disorientated and angry, and I'm scared he's going to sting me. So I set about evicting him as well.

Lobesia botrana

The European Grapevine Moth

We all have our natural patch. I was taught that pretty early.

As Absent Gran (gor' blimey, love 'er) was fond of saying (and saying and saying . . .), nothing good ever came of not knowing your station. Which tells you all you need to know about my sainted granny.

She's wrong, of course. Because stations are places to travel from. And *to*. Not to squat, knowing your place, while perspiring with resentment – *boiling* with it, like a fat, angry toad.

And yet and yet . . . See, the people with the fabulously well-appointed stations have a powerful vested interest in keeping you out of theirs, and in *yours*. Which is why when the European grapevine moth went on a jolly to the Napa Valley, it got called a 'pest', caused significant distress, and led to the quarantining of some 162 square miles of vines. Till it was obliterated, annihilated (made to know its place and then some) and natural order was once again restored.

But whose natural order? And what right did they have?

And – small point – who owns the rights to define the word '*pest*'?

Baby European grapevine moth to mummy European grapevine moth: 'You know, Mummy, when I grow up I'm going to fly to America!'

Mummy grapevine moth to baby grapevine moth: 'I'm not sure you should, dear. They are different there. Not like we are. They might, sad to say, dear, look down on you. Dare I say, dear, they might even *swat* you.'

'But I thought you said Mother Nature made all of us equal?'

'Well, yes, she did, and she's right, and . . .'

'So why shouldn't I go, then?'

'Because. Enough now. Just *because*.'

Because *what*?

Because she's right, that's what she is.

But . . . come ON. Is there any contest between 'fluttering butterflies' and 'common moths'? No. The moth is the supreme lepidopteran.

I know more than you might think, you see, and, as a result of that knowing, I have no patience with the facile, overweening vanity of butterflies. All their preening. Their day-dreaming. Their sunny-day scheming. It's all surface, with butterflies. No *feeling*.

Selfish bastards, butterflies. So self-absorbed. So *lucky*. While we toil in the dark, they bask in the light. Yet we do have the moon. The milky, milky moon. Which we cleave to, with straight-line obsession.

We do it to navigate. To steer a course to what we need.

I have navigated hard to get here. I have shape-shifted to fit. I can hold my own in any company. My tongue, when I need to. But though you might not smell it, the stench still travels with me; of the little bit of shit I still have on my shoe, stuck to me for life, from the shit-hole I shouldn't have gone to, but, to all intents and purposes, I came from.

Chapter 4

Tuesday, another day I should have begun back in London, dawns very differently to Monday. Even with only a slim strip of blue to guide me, I know the view from the bedroom window will be tourist board perfect, the autumn fog driven off by a bright, determined sun and the shifting sea a molten sheet of glass.

There is no such serenity on my side of the blind. I'm stunned to find I've ravaged the bed. And as a consequence, my laptop, which I have no memory of having abandoned, is inches from sliding off and clattering to the floor. It's open just enough to form a clam-like, scowling mouth.

It instantly reminds me; is the boy still alive?

I reach for my phone to check for messages. It's washed up on the cluttered bedside table and I fish blindly around for it, to find that a text from Tash, sent two hours back, has pinged in unheeded. I must have been even more exhausted than I thought.

How you doing, Mumma bear? the text asks, followed by her usual string of random emojis. *Okay, I hope. Setting off soon, so I'll see you in seven/eight hours or so. I'll try to call once we get to the first services.*

'Try' being the operative word, since our signal is extremely patchy. Yesterday evening, we'd managed no more than half a dozen words before 3G became no G and she was lost to me again. I text straight back, telling her not to worry about calling, matching love youuuu with love youuuu, trading kisses for kisses, and conjuring my own string of cryptic emojis. A unicorn, a spanner, a shower-head, a poodle. An expression of love that always makes me smile, but which today makes me anxious and tearful.

Had I not made my impulsive dash to Wales on Sunday evening, I would not be in the mess I am now. I'd still be *en route*, laden with half of Tash's term-time belongings (the other half are here) and looking forward to spending a precious couple of days with her. Instead, I'm now carrying a hideous cargo; a young man, lying attached to a ventilator, fighting for his life. Which means I need to get up, get on, and fix my focus on the practical, so I head straight to the shower, then tackle the beds. First my own, and then Tash's. And though I'm hampered by my throbbing hand as well as my anxiety, I am soon soothed by the sharp snap of freshly washed sheets, the plumping up of pillows, the cool gusts of fragranced air.

I then move on to make up the singles in the spare room, since, there being a big pre-term beach party tonight, Tash's best friends, Jonathan and Verity, will doubtless want to crash here rather than camp out.

Jonathan is on Tash's course and they became friends immediately, and Verity, who's studying photography, is his amicably ex-girlfriend. I'm always happy to see them, for they are also soon to be her housemates. I determinedly count blessings. For the fact that Tash is still in university, astonishingly, despite everything. For two ordinary friendships, seeded in the fertile soil of freshers' parties, which have blossomed into something even more precious in the aftermath of her loss. That she's coped so heroically in such desperate circumstances is in no small measure due to those relationships.

I then tackle the other job that's been nagging at me since I woke. Sending a text of apology to the journalist, Nick Stone, who a night's sleep has made me realise I've treated unfairly. I do my job. He was only doing his.

He texts back. *No apology necessary. Any news?* And since I have none, I text again to tell him I'll let him know.

But with the beds made and my conscience (at least in that respect) salved, I still have a whole day to fill. One thing is clear, though. That until I know how the boy is (and, equally pressing, *who* he is) I will fail to get any work done; the PhD thesis I'm supposed to be marking, which failed to distract me last night, is no way going to distract me today. Thief or not, the possibility of his death is just too appalling a thing to contemplate. So once I've made coffee and eaten half a bowl of Shreddies, I return to my phone. It's now half past eight, after all. The handover will have happened, and my old friend Pat should be back on duty.

She is.

'He's still with us,' she says. 'Stats not too bad, considering. But they're going to keep him under till the brain swelling subsides a bit.'

'Oh, thank god,' I say. 'And has anyone managed to identify him?'

'Not that I've been told.'

'But you'll let me know if you do?'

'Course I will, sweetheart.'

'And if anything changes? Good *or* bad.'

'Good or bad. But, Jules, trust me, he's going to pull through.'

I console myself by believing her, because there's no point in doing otherwise, and then find the piece of paper on which the policeman back in Cardiff scribbled a number down for me.

The PCSO I'm put through to in Swansea already knows who I am, despite it having been a Cardiff PC that had interviewed me yesterday. Not that I expect him to be able to tell me anything.

But, still, I can't *not* ask. I have a strong need to stake my personal claim on the situation.

This is even more true since knowing about the attempted theft of David's watch, which is still a nagging complication. As is the fact of that open bathroom window, and the light being left on, which has taken on a new and worrying significance. Yet nothing in the cottage has been disturbed. I've already been back and checked again, delving into places I've not looked at in many months, pulling out nothing but painful memories in the process.

'But we're still hopeful,' the officer says. He has a kind voice, doubtless bevelled by long years of calming and consoling. 'We've put an appeal out on our Facebook page now, and on Twitter. And we've still got a picture of the lad if we need to use it. Though we're obviously loathe to – not the sort of photo you'd want popping up on social media, is it? Specially when you're family.'

He tuts. I agree that it isn't. 'What about the phone number?'

'Drawn a blank there, I'm afraid. Generic pay as you go. No voicemail.'

'But you'll keep trying.'

'Of course. We've also been in touch with all the local campsites, though we've drawn a blank so far. Early days, though. We're only just twenty-four hours in, after all. We'll obviously step things up if no one claims him today. Or if things take a turn for the worse. Not a lot else we can do at the moment, lovely, I'm afraid.'

Though he promises again that he'll let me know immediately if they hear anything new, I can tell he's anxious to get me off the phone. *But what if it was your son?* I want to ask him. To someone who loves him, and might lose him, another twenty-four hours could mean *everything*.

But who is that someone? And where did he come from? I eye the nylon backpack, which is still sitting on the kitchen table. And with so *little*. No money. No debit card. No phone.

My head's too full of questions to even think about the thesis. Perhaps I should try to find some answers for myself.

By the time I've thrashed my way up the Down, through the bracken, the noise of my breath as it rasps in my throat is enough to drown out everything else.

I press on up, heading to the place where I left the path yesterday, but have to stop to catch my breath at the same point I always do, high enough to turn the village into chocolate-box whimsy, but not quite far enough to reveal the western end of the beach.

To the east, Rhossili Down slopes gently down to the church and village, then snakes out to become a promontory called the Worm's Head. The worm isn't a worm, though. It's actually a 'wurme'. Wurme means dragon in Norse, the language of the Vikings, and that's exactly what it looks like – a Tolkien-esque dragon, slumbering in the sea. When the tide's out, you can cross a rocky causeway and walk all the way across the body, to the dragon's head. I have done it just the once, with Tash, to dispatch David's ashes. But it's extremely treacherous. I know I won't do it again.

Far below me now, the beach is striped with footprints and paw prints, all evidence of yesterday's crowd washed away by the sea. It was right to come up here – it's already doing me good. I carry on up, the blood pounding in my ears.

I'm breathing even harder by the time I reach the place where I presume the boy fell. I know precisely where I stepped off the path again to try and find him because I'd located it as we'd risen in the helicopter. Now, up on the high ground, the heather crackling beneath my feet, I can even see where I trampled it down.

If he'd had earbuds then he *must* have had a phone. I'm sure of it. What young person goes anywhere without a phone?

And if that's the case, which seems feasible, then he obviously dropped it, presumably when he fell. I take a couple of careful steps to the place where I ventured down to try and find him, and in the sunshine it becomes obvious why he probably went the way he had; over to my left there is a faint track snaking away from me.

There are hundreds of tracks criss-crossing the Down, some footpath-wide, some no broader than a hand-span. It depends who created them; rambling humans, Gower ponies, or sheep. The one I join now is an obvious choice; it begins fairly flat and weaves around several rocks. Had his intention been to hide behind one till I went away?

I crunch across the heather to where the rocks form an untidy cluster. In the brightness the terrifying drop behind them is now obvious. But in that fog, how would he know that? Especially if he'd already become disorientated and didn't know the geography.

I step up onto the lower of two adjacent boulders so I can peer over the other. Even from this distance, the place where he almost met his death is grimly obvious, because the exposed rock face is dark with dried blood. His cut-apart shorts are still there as well – a raggy mound that looks, and no doubt smells, like roadkill.

But why go down there in the first place? Even in the fog, he'd have known how steep it was. It's all but sheer and I'm sparking electric jolts in my legs just looking down at it.

So why not carry on, or just stay where he was?

Unless he *had to*. Could it be that he'd already dropped his phone? I'd been slithering about on the wet rocks even wearing my rubber boots. Was it dropping his phone that had made him blindly venture down there? If so, then I might have a decent shot at finding it, mightn't I?

I do. It takes all of five minutes. It's no more than ten metres below and to the right of me, sitting flat, as if sunbathing, on a swell of scorched heather.

Locating it hasn't even required much of a search. With the sun reflecting off it, I spotted it as soon as I edged around the furthest rock. It's also obvious that he set off down the slope to try and find it. And lost his footing; a trail of flattened heather still marks his passing.

It's easy to imagine his terror. Because I can now see another drop. A vertical, into space. So perhaps he didn't so much tumble down the hill as fall off it. That would provide enough force to explain the laceration in his groin.

But the phone is nowhere near there. It obviously pinged off the other way. Possibly off one of the nearby rocks. And, as I can see even before I clamber down, it has suffered a blow of its own. The dew-misted screen is smashed, the glass starred into shards right across it. I don't press the home button. I know I mustn't till it's completely dried out, much less try to charge it. But I know mobiles of old, particularly those abused by teenage daughters. I know their phoenix-like powers of reincarnation.

Slipping the phone carefully in my jacket pocket, I scrabble back up, but by the time I've reached the main path again, another thought has occurred to me. Even if it still works, there's no way I'll be able to access anything on it without knowing the passcode.

Which means there's little I can do with it, but because I have no desire to return to the cottage yet, I don't retrace my steps. Instead I continue on over the top of the Down, along the ridge, where I can see for many miles in all directions. There are ponies nearby, three of them, fat-bellied and shaggy, with two still summer-spindly foals between them. I can almost hear Tash's squeals of indignant childish protest that they would never let her come close enough to touch.

Then I drop down, past the ruins of the World War Two radar station, to the point where I'm rewarded with a different vista. Toytown caravans in tidy rows. Muddles of multicoloured tents and awnings. Burry Holm, a benign pimple compared to the worm's aggressive bulk. Broughton Bay, beyond which lies the estuary and Carmarthenshire, the latter blurred behind a swathe of torn tissue-paper cloud.

The land drops steeply now, to join the campsite below. Did the boy come from here? It's certainly the closest campsite to the cottage. But as I know I'm much more likely to attract unwelcome attention than achieve anything the police haven't, I opt instead to stop short of the campsite itself, and skirt around the base of the hill, and back towards the cottage, on the path that marks the lower edge of the line of fields. Unlike the ferns, four feet high and rusting by increments, they are green as a bowl of shelled peas.

I'm just climbing over the final stile when I see Tash's little cappuccino-coloured Fiat coming down the track. And as I raise my hand to wave, I see her headlights flash twice in quick succession.

I jog across the final pasture, scattering sheep in slow motion, and we are reunited in a matter of minutes.

She smells, as she always does, of perfume far beyond her budget. David was always the string to her little finger and would treat her to a bottle pretty much any time he had to fly anywhere, of whatever designer brand was currently in vogue. He'd get endless stick from his sister Laura for such paternal over-indulgences. She'd reached peak apoplexy about the time of the Eighteenth Birthday Fiat. *You're ruining that girl of yours, you realise? Ruining her.*

But now it's history. And I couldn't be more thankful for every one of those indulgences. For all those shelves in my daughter's memory banks that, just like his mother's dresser, now sag and buckle under the weight of them. Remind her beyond doubt just how much her father loved her.

My now adult daughter has a good three inches on me. And what short-to-middling mother wouldn't want that? So I only just manage to keep my footing as she hugs me, her hair – dark like David's, and newly washed – a veil of fragrance against my cheek.

'God, Mum,' she says, as she whumps hard against me. 'Are you *okay?*'

'I'm fine,' I tell her. 'Honestly, sweetheart, I'm absolutely *fine.*' I will be so in perpetuity where Tash is concerned. I'll probably still be telling her I'm fine on my deathbed. I decide, then and there, not to bring up the business with the bathroom window again. Not yet, at least, even though it's still bugging me.

She pulls away again then, so she can get a better look at me. 'Oh, Mum,' she says, taking my bandaged hand in her own. 'Look at the state of you. You can't be. Have you watched it?'

'What, the stuff on YouTube? Only snippets.'

'Mum, you have no idea, do you? Seriously, you need to take a proper look at it. You could have *died.*'

She's wrong. I have every idea. Specially since this morning. 'I think I'll pass,' I say, smiling at her. 'Right now I'm more concerned that he doesn't.'

She huffs again as she steers me back towards the cottage. I haven't seen her in two weeks, and having her back is like a balm because it makes her a temporary absentee on the things-to-worry-about list.

'So,' she says, linking arms. 'Any news on who the boy is yet?'

'Nothing. No change in his condition. No ID. Though there's something else. A journalist turned up yesterday, to get the story, and he found the boy's backpack.'

I explain about the earbuds and how I've just found the phone. 'But there's something else too. Dad's watch was in the bag.'

'God, Mum – you're kidding! You mean he actually broke *in?*'

I shake my head. 'That's just it. There's no sign of a break in. Which means he must have used the key. I mean, what are the chances? We're talking six, seven in the morning. It was hardly even light. And some random young lad in board shorts is just wandering around Rhossili Down on the lookout for something to steal? It doesn't make sense, does it? Unless he already knew there was something worth stealing *and* knew where the key was. Which is why I think the journalist is probably right. He thinks he must have watched me put it there. Thinks it might even have been stolen to order for someone else.'

'Mum, he could just as easily be some opportunist local dope-head. Plenty of those around here. What about the police? What do they think?'

I push open the gate. The over-priced heritage-appropriate paint David applied last summer is already beginning to peel. 'I haven't told them yet.'

Tash gapes at me. '*What?* Why on earth not?'

'Because if he dies, I think that knowledge should die with him. If he doesn't, then, yes, maybe. But right now, at least till they find out who he is, and I know he's okay—'

'Yes, thanks to *you*. Mum, if you hadn't been there he *would* have died, for definite.'

We've reached the door. Tash slides her own key into the lock and turns it. She's stopped short of adding that he'd have had only himself to blame, but I know that's what she's thinking.

'Tash, if I hadn't been down here, he wouldn't have gone haring off up there in the first place.'

'So that makes it *your* fault?' Her expression catches me short. 'You're not listening, are you? *You* could have died.'

'Seriously,' I say, squeezing her hand and making a mental note to watch the footage after all. 'So,' I add brightly. 'How was Edinburgh? And what's the plan? What time is the party starting?'

She checks her watch. 'Is that the time? I still have to pick Jonathan and Verity up from the station. And I seriously need to have a lie down before I fall down. God, I am stiff as a *corpse*.'

She frowns then and hugs me tightly before jogging off up the stairs.

I don't know why I'm surprised, because I'm hardly a technophobe, but typing 'air ambulance rescue Rhossili' into Google brings up hundreds of hits, and right at the top no less than three different links to YouTube videos. One I recognise as the snippet Jack showed me yesterday morning. I don't watch it through. A quick fast-forward shows me everything I need to see.

Or want to. And I'm doubly glad I didn't venture to the campsite office. From the vantage point of the beach, we might equally have been clinging to some high Himalayan rock face, a hair's breadth from certain death. I feel rebuked. No wonder Tash was so shaken.

'You need to put that in some rice or something,' she says, once she's back down after her nap. She's brought me shortbread. A whole tin of it. Dinner. 'You haven't tried to charge it or anything, have you?'

'No. I didn't dare.'

'Good. Because you'd probably short it.' She carefully peels off the black silicone case. 'Have we got any rice knocking about?'

I go and delve in a cupboard, shunting around half-packets of various value brand pastas, evidence of her numerous impromptu overnight visits over the summer, and her attachment to managing her meagre Student Loan. She went from high end to budget in the blink of an eye – a feat I would never have imagined her capable of. I decide that while the hungover partygoers slumber tomorrow morning I shall have a long-overdue clear out; make up a box of groceries for the new student house.

I find an almost full bag of basmati which Tash decants into a cereal bowl. She then completely buries the phone.

'There,' she says, twiddling her fingers. 'Abracadabra.'

'You really think that will work?'

'Absolutely,' she responds. 'And maybe then we can find out who the mystery felon is. But now I'd better get a shift on and pick up the others. I think we're meeting everyone at Hillend, so I'll probably leave the car over there for the night. That's if you're sure you're okay on your own?'

I am lightning quick, always. 'It's either that or share the shortbread. I'm absolutely *not* sharing the shortbread.'

She catches my eye then and throws her arms around me. And I can tell what she's thinking from the tightness of her grip. She didn't know him. Hadn't seen him. Hadn't chased him. Hadn't touched him. Hadn't nearly – and by such an infinitesimally tiny margin – watched him die. But she might have lost me.

Which can't happen. I'm the only parent she has left.

Geometra papillionaria

The Large Emerald Moth

Before we had science we had to make all kinds of stuff up to try and make sense of all the bad things in the world. Some of this nonsense survives to this day (hi, flat-earthers!) but the rest is collectively known as 'folklore'.

Today kids still get born with all kinds of things wrong with them – cleft lips, severe autism, cerebral palsy. But because we have science we mostly know what to call it. And because we have medicine we try to fix it.

Back in folklore, which was a dark place, full of trolls and evildoings, some of these kids had a collective name – 'changelings'. And once 'diagnosed' as such, they didn't fare well. Some didn't fare again, ever. Some were shoved into ovens, some smothered, some drowned. Because your changeling child, so said folklore, was *not in fact* your child. It was a cuckoo in the nest, in the form of a fairy. And this was at a time (this is key) before the big fairy 'brand' make-over; when they were shysters and ne'er do wells, tricksters and thieves. Like a teeny Cosa Nostra sect with wings.

Details differ, but their *modus operandi* rarely varied. Out of envy, or greed, or just sheer wanton malevolence, fairies came into bedrooms and stole human children, substituting them with one of their own kind.

And I wonder. Wouldn't you wonder? And I *never* rule stuff out.

I recently stumbled upon all this in a library, by the way. I've been thinking about it ever since.

For the longest time – eighty-three per cent of my life, give or take the odd percentage point – I knew nothing about anything of my – what word should I choose here? – yes, *heritage*. And, *hey*, fact! What you don't know can't hurt you! I had one set of memories, mostly shit, grim, and ugly, and one set of hopes, of necessity modest, because shit, grim, and ugly do their work so well. Modest hopes, like 'on a good day I will score sufficient chemical enhancements that I will not have to trudge quite so desperately sadly through the foul-tasting sludge of my psyche'.

And it was fine. No, no, *really*. You get on. You get by. What you don't do is let your mind wander. Here and now. Day by day. No scheming. No dreaming. *Carpe* that *diem* and stamp on its ambitions. Keep on butting that light bulb. Keep on *going*.

And then one day, I got truth. I got a lorry-load of truth. I got it poured, dark and steaming, from the nozzle of a tanker. Just think how that goes, Julia. How that messes with you, floors you. To know you've been lied to. To know you have choices. To know you'd have *had* choices, if only you'd known sooner. But at the same time – here's the corker, and ain't life pecoooliar? – to hold the keys, and the map, to the Emerald City.

Chapter 5

When Tash was two, we bought her a Jack Russell puppy. She called him Tigger, and he lived up to his name. He had just the two speed settings, and neither of them was 'stop'. Even when he was elderly and developed the kidney failure that we knew would end his life, he hung on just long enough for Tash to finish her GCSEs. He was that kind of dog.

I've woken early again, and I miss him, because if we still had him, I'd already be out in the fresh air walking him. As it is, I stay in bed for a bit longer, reluctant to start banging around the place so early. I hadn't heard the kids come crashing in after their party – I still don't even know how many did – and this isn't the kind of house that forgives. It creaks, groans and grumbles at even the suggestion of movement. Only its ghosts move around unremarked.

So it's an hour before I finally pad downstairs. There is a muddle of pumps and flip-flops in the corner of the hall, and, as I've done for many years now, I do a head count via a footwear count. It was once such an everyday ritual that the action is automatic. It's also, though I'm sure I didn't appreciate it then, a shot of emotional tequila.

I note the story I'm being told this morning. A slick of sheep shit on canvas. A crescent of toe-shaped indentations on pale rubber. A puddle of sand in a heel space. A knotted lace. I smile.

There are flowers in the kitchen. A spray of carnations in a cellophane wrapper, sitting in water, in one of my jugs, on the draining board. They are the colour of sugar mice, and I don't know where they've come from. Are they for me? I leave them be while I run the tap and fill the kettle. Further along the counter, the boy's phone is still tucked up beneath its basmati duvet, and I wonder if Tash's confidence in it will prove to be justified. Perhaps it will. Mobile phones are the epitome of a modern paradox, after all. Built-in obsolescence yet a half-life of centuries.

I'm just about to pull it out when I hear the bang of the back door, closely followed by the sound of laughter and shuffling feet.

The little room off the kitchen – the so called 'boot room' – was originally a scullery. An artefact from the days when there were maidservants doing all the dirty work. Skinning rabbits. Heaving coal. Strapping scallywags.

These days, it functions mostly as a wet room. Or, more accurately, as a mud room; a necessary staging post for the purposes of donning and shedding, after going out on or coming in from walks and swims. David's ancient waxed jacket still has a home here.

I push open the internal door to find Tash, Jonathan and Verity, the latter's turquoise hair providing a shot of welcome colour against the quiet, listed period-appropriate grey tiling.

I anticipated that it would be harder to get to know Tash's friends now, as they are part of her adult life, much of it now lived away from home, so I'm doubly blessed that the cottage gives me these opportunities to dip into it, and, as a consequence, to spend so much time with these two; twin pillars of Tash's emotional foundations.

Coming in behind them is Cate, the girl who's moving into the house with them later today. I've only met Cate once, so I don't really have a sense of her yet.

She smiles shyly at me. They are all busy draping towels over their wetsuits. Still glossy with seawater, they look like seals.

'Ah, you're up,' Tash says, grinning.

I blink at her, confused. 'You've already been out surfing?'

They all nod in unison. 'Well, bailing mostly, in my case,' Jonathan points out. His hair hangs in skeins around his face, like washed wool.

'I did put my head round your bedroom door,' Tash says. 'But you were, like, *properly* blotto.'

'I must have been,' I say. 'I thought you were all still in bed.'

'Mum, we haven't *been* to bed,' she tells me, laughing.

Once they're all showered and dressed, and (all bar Cate, who's apparently Facetiming her mother) back down for the toast and cereal I've one-handedly prepared for them, we return inevitably to the events of the previous two days.

I am much hugged, much interrogated, and much wrapped in love and sympathy by Jonathan and Verity. They have spent money I know they can't spare on buying me a bottle of Pinot Grigio and two bags of wine gums. Already dangerously close to emotional overload, their thoughtfulness almost moves me to tears.

'And these are for you too,' Verity says as she plucks the stems from the vase and shakes the water into the sink. 'I'm sorry they're a bit manky. They were all they had left at the station. It was these or a bunch of multicoloured chrysanthemums, so we had to plump for the least worst option, didn't we, Jon?'

I want to tell them that they are beautiful. That I'm touched beyond words by their kindness. But I am unable to get more than a couple of words out before my brimming eyes threaten to do the job for me instead. I'm clearly still more fragile than I realise.

Anxious to address that, I bustle about and pull up the police appeal on my laptop, to find they've now added the photo. I'm also heartened to see how many times it's been shared. It's grim viewing, though, given all the medical paraphernalia the boy is attached to, and it doesn't take much of a leap of imagination to visualise the effect it would have on anyone who knows him.

Even on those who don't. Because none of them recognise him. 'Jesus. Is he going to die, you think, Julia?' Verity asks me, leaning in to study the image more closely.

'I hope not. He's made it through the first forty-eight hours, which counts for a lot, obviously.'

'But he still could, you think?'

'Yes, he definitely still could.'

'Or have brain damage?'

'Conceivably,' I admit.

'Shit,' Jonathan says. 'Look at him. Oh, *man.*'

'But with every hour he hangs in there, the odds that he *won't* die obviously increase. I'm a lot more optimistic than I was this time yesterday. I just wish I knew who he was. The more I think about it, the more I'm sure he's got to be someone who either knows us, or knows *of* us. Someone local. At least, that seems the most likely. He must have already known the watch was there.'

'Not necessarily,' Tash points out. 'It can't have been hard to find it. And you don't know for sure that he actually *planned* on taking it. He might just have found it and be, like, ooh, that looks expensive. I'll pinch that while I'm here.'

'But if he wasn't here for the watch,' I say, 'why *was* he here?'

'Good point,' Jonathan says. 'But you know, someone's going to recognise him. Got to.' He's pointing at the screen now. 'Because that's a pretty random thing for a guy to have a tattoo of, don't you think? I mean, a tiny *butterfly*? More the sort of thing a girl would have, surely? And on his *wrist*? Double random. Someone's *got* to recognise him from it. Hey, though,' he says suddenly. 'I just thought of something. That creepy butterfly card you got, Tash. Remember?'

'Card?' I ask, turning to Tash.

'That Valentine,' Jon clarifies.

Tash nods. 'I'd forgotten about that. God, that poem.'

'The *poem*,' Jonathan says. 'Ick. Ex*actly*.'

'What poem?' I ask.

'That was pretty random too,' Jonathan says. '*Properly* out there.'

'Why? How?' I ask. I'm all ears now.

'Hang on, though,' Verity says. 'I thought we'd already worked out who sent that.'

'*Who?*' I ask.

'Oh, just some geeky boy in uni.' She puts a finger to her temple. 'Had a bit of a thing about Tash.'

'But not this boy.'

Verity shakes her head. 'No, just some weird IT nerd.'

Tash considers. 'Yeah, but we never knew for sure that it was him, did we? And Jon's right. All that stuff about me being a butterfly was pretty random. I mean' – she spreads her palms – 'I know it's tenuous, but it's a possible connection, isn't it?'

'Yes, but what about that necklace?' Verity says.

Now I'm lost. 'What necklace?'

'Oh, just this random butterfly pendant the IT guy bought me,' Tash explains.

'Definitely him?'

'Definitely him.'

'Yeah,' says Jonathan, 'but that doesn't mean for definite that he sent the Valentine's card, does it? Which you've got to admit *was* pretty intense.'

'Fair point,' agrees Tash. 'And what with him taking Dad's watch . . . Still, I suppose we're going to find out soon enough, aren't we? Someone's got to recognise him eventually.'

'Well,' I say, filing away all this new information that's coming at me. 'We can speculate all we like, but we have the means of identifying him right here, don't we? At least, potentially. Do you think we dare risk plugging it in yet?'

Tash goes across to the counter and plucks the phone out of the rice. 'I reckon so,' she says. 'Don't you, V?'

Verity's head bobs, half-hidden beneath the towel she's brought down with her, as she rubs the last of the water from her hair. Even in a wetsuit, she's a feast for the senses. When dressed, as now, in her usual attire of mis-matched charity-shop bargains (her standing joke when Jonathan teases her is that she's 'sustainably sourced'), she is like a rainbow in the rainstorm, both emotionally and literally, which could not be more welcome today.

Jonathan, on the other hand – according to him, anyway – is one hundred per cent 'metrosexual hipster'. Which was why, Tash informed me recently, he got five different types of beard oil for his birthday. Though, as beards go, it's got some distance yet to travel.

It usually tickles me, all these newly transplanted young adults trying their 'tribes' on for size. Right now, though, I am struck by both their youth and their innocence. That the loss of it is their business. That there are lines I can't cross.

I decide to probe Tash about the 'creepy' Valentine later, when we're alone. It might not be connected but it's clearly not 'nothing'. Is he still at uni with her? Is there something more I should know?

Verity emerges from the towel-shroud and nods. 'It's not like it was submerged. Just cold and damp, right? And it's been in the warm all night. I reckon you're safe to give it a go.'

I unplug my own phone and push the charger into it. Nothing happens.

'But not yet,' Verity points out. 'You need to charge it first.'

'Not that I'm going to be able to do much with it even if it does power up,' I say. 'Not without the passcode.'

'Verity might be able to help you with that, Mum,' Tash says. 'We were just saying earlier, weren't we? One of the girls on her course could probably unlock it for you.' She grins at Verity. A conspirator's grin. There's clearly so much I'm not privy to. 'She's really good with, um, that kind of stuff,' Tash continues. 'If it does come on, it might be worth us taking it with us later and seeing if she's around, mightn't it?'

'Thanks, Verity,' I begin. 'That's really kind of you, but it's okay.'

'It's no trouble, Julia, honestly,' she says. 'I'm more than happy to help.'

'I know you are, sweetie, but I really need to get it to the police and let them deal with it. And who knows? They might have an ID for him by now anyway.'

Though, privately, I doubt it. Pat said she'd let me know, and so far I've heard nothing. But once I've seen the kids off to collect the car, and then the keys for their simply furnished but ideally located hovel, I call her anyway. And she's at least able to confirm that the boy is stable. He's slightly better, even, she tells me, but they're keeping him under for at least another day to give his brain the best possible chance to mend itself. I know they can do so for up to a week if they feel it's necessary. I really hope they won't need to.

I call the police station in Swansea next, and leave a message with a dispatcher asking what I should do about the boy's phone. Finally, hit by another idea, I decide to extend a conciliatory hand – and perhaps achieve something useful – by calling Nick Stone.

It takes several rings before he answers, and when he does, he sounds breathless. 'Sorry. Out with my dogs,' he puffs. 'You've seen it then, have you?'

I'm immediately wrong-footed again. 'Seen your piece? But I thought you told me you were going to show me it before you filed it.'

There must be an audible edge to my voice. 'And indeed I *shall*,' he reassures me. 'It's currently scheduled for Friday. I was talking about the news report. Well, I say "news report". It's little more than bloody clickbait. But that's a conversation for a *whole* other time.'

I can tell he's walking. I wonder where. I wonder how many dogs he has. Is he the man with the dogs I had seen on the beach?

'So, seen what, then?' I ask him.

'The police appeal. They've upped the ante now – added the mugshot.'

'I know. I saw it earlier.'

'Bit grim, isn't it. But I guess they have no choice now, do they? Let's hope it gets shared and someone twigs, eh?'

But will they? With every passing hour it seems more likely that he isn't being missed by anyone. Which only adds fuel to the story I've already woven, of some modern-day Dickensian orphan. I can't get the battered Converse out of my head. Or, now, the idea of a connection with Tash. And not in a reassuring way.

'I hope so. But listen, I have news too. I was calling to let you know he's a little better. Still on life support, but stable. I also wanted to tell you that I found his phone.'

'Good god,' he says. 'How the hell did you manage that?'

'Amazingly easily, as it turned out. I knew he'd have had one, and when I retraced my steps it just seemed so obvious that no one in their right mind would have ever tried to go down that slope if they didn't have a pretty good reason. So I figured that he might have tripped and dropped his phone. You saw how foggy it was. He'd have been massively disorientated up there, and it would have been almost impossible to see. It was literally only yards from the track.'

'Good work, Sherlock,' he says. 'That's some impressive detecting. And is it working?'

'The screen's smashed, but we put it in some rice overnight anyway. My daughter thinks there's a fair chance it'll come back on. That's the other reason I'm calling. I'm obviously going to hand it over to the police, but I've had to leave a message, and I was thinking, in the meantime, if the phone *does* come on, that I might be able to get his ID from it myself, mightn't I? And you strike me as the kind of person who might know something about this sort of thing.'

He laughs. 'Do I? I must be slipping. But yes, I know a bit. What model is it?'

'An iPhone Six.'

'Even better. I have an old one.'

'That makes a difference?'

'Well, we might be able to cannibalise it, mightn't we?'

'I wasn't thinking of anything that drastic. I've obviously got to hand it in. I was just hoping you might be able to give me some advice. If it doesn't go into some sort of electrical fugue, is there any way I could access any information on it without the passcode?'

'Highly likely it'll short, I'd say. But, yes, if he's filled in his Medical ID, and it does come on, you might just be able to access a contact number via the emergency function. You know the one on the lock screen? Lots of people don't bother, but it's definitely worth a go. And, look, if that fails, I might be able to speak to one of my contacts and see what can be done.'

'That sounds suspicious.'

He laughs. 'As in a *police officer* contact. Seriously, I'm glad to hear he's better. Must be a huge weight off your mind. Anyway, it's worth a try. Let me know how it goes.'

So, after we ring off, I try. But though it comes on, it immediately goes off again. Just flashes a ghost of an image of a battery-shaped icon, without so much as a glimmer of a telltale stripe of red. It's obviously not charging, but I remain optimistic, keeping it plugged in while I pack up a box of groceries, and when my own mobile phone rings an hour later, I first think it's his, rather than mine.

It's a different policeman this time. He sounds younger. And as if he's already busy with more important things. They all are, apparently, because he says they can't spare anyone to come and get the phone at the moment. 'You might as well just hang on to it for now,' he tells me.

'No, it's fine. I can drive it down to you later today if that's easier.'

'Oh, there's no point in you hiking all the way into Swansea just for that.'

'But won't it help?'

'Is it charging?'

'It doesn't look like it.'

'Then I doubt it will. Unlikely that we'll be able to retrieve anything from it anyway. Your best bet might be to get it back to the phone company and let them deal with it. After all, it doesn't sound as if the lad's going to have much use for it for the foreseeable, does it?'

And as I disconnect, even though I know I'm being unfair, I can't help but think that if he *had* stolen the watch, and I'd reported it as stolen, it would become a numbered crime – and, as a consequence, their responsibility in a much more substantial way. As it is, he's a person, an adult, no one's property. And if he doesn't belong to anyone, then whose problem *is* he, then? No one's?

It's moving-in week, so the roads around Swansea University are choked with traffic, and when I arrive at the address Tash has given me – a hilly street of terraced houses just off the Mumbles Road – there isn't a parking space anywhere. There are cars double-parked, hazards flashing, doors gaping, their owners scuttling back and forth bearing boxes and bales of bedding, as the great annual migration gets underway.

I soon spot Tash's car. Having arrived early, she's managed to squeeze it into a space outside the house, and, since everyone else is doing it with seeming impunity, I summon sufficient courage to double park as well, defiantly but neatly, alongside her.

This will be the first time I've seen the house and I already know I'm not going to like it. And as I climb out of the car and look up and down the road, I know it's a position I'm unlikely to shift. Not that my maternal sensibilities count for much. Where I see squalor, all they see is parties and pizza deliveries.

This is a big student area and has evolved in the paradoxical way of student areas everywhere – as a cash cow of a shanty town. Old-fashioned nets have been replaced by bamboo blinds and tacked-up blankets, paper orbs hang from ceilings where frosted glass pendants were once suspended, and the tiny front gardens, which would have once been hedged and clipped, now grow black sacks rather than flowers. Bins run in an unbroken chain along both sides of the street, like the keys on a giant plastic piano.

The front door is wedged open by a dusty pile of junk mail, and I can hear thumps, scrapes, and female voices upstairs. I'm just about to put my foot on the barely carpeted bottom tread when a middle-aged man emerges from the other end of the hallway. I belatedly recognise him as Jonathan's dad – he was there when I helped moved Tash out of halls back in June. Another blur. To my shame I can't summon his name.

'Hi, Julia,' he says brightly. 'Just been trying to fix the garden fence. Well, I say "garden" . . . And the drain's blocked. Of *course*. I've just come back inside in search of something to poke around with. You didn't bring any bleach with you, did you? I've sent Jonathan off with a shopping list, but knowing him, he'll be ages. So if you have some to hand . . .'

This I can do. I've come prepared, because, along with lots of other parents, I have already been inducted – I helped Tash clean up before moving out of halls. I tell him yes, and I'm just about to nip out and find it when the three girls come clattering down the stairs, followed by a woman I don't recognise. So perhaps Cate's mum. Or maybe Verity's. I haven't yet met either. Although I think Verity's parents are away on some Austrian river cruise or other. So, Cate's then.

Introductions are made amicably enough – she arrived earlier and is just about to leave for home again – but the atmosphere is noticeably strained. And as Cate goes to walk her to her car, I clock Tash's irritable expression.

'*God!*' she says, once we're back at mine to start the process of unloading.

'God what?'

'God, *Cate*. She is *such* a bloody *princess*! Oh, it's nothing to do with me,' she says, obviously seeing my dismayed expression. '*I'm* okay. I get the front bedroom by default, don't I?' This is true. She's paying extra rent for the privilege, too. Once an only child, always an only child; she always needs her space. 'But we'd already *agreed* who was going where. She can't start trying to change everything around now just because she's decided she doesn't like it. *She* agreed to it!'

'So what's the problem?'

'*She* is.'

'With the room.'

74

'Oh, it's just a patch of damp. I mean, a *minuscule* patch. But she's banging on about her asthma and demanding that they swap – and Verity's moved all her stuff in already.'

'So surely the landlord should be contacted, in that case. If there's damp . . .'

'Oh, it's okay, Mum. Really, it's *tiny*. And Verity's agreed to swap now, so it's fine. She's away on placements half the time, anyway, so she's not really that fussed. It's just the *principle*. God, I hope this isn't going to be the shape of things to come.'

'Well,' I begin, already fearing it might be, 'there's still no harm in having a word with the landlord about it. If you want me to—'

'No, it's *fine*, Mum,' she says, glancing towards the house. 'Forget it. As you're always saying, it's just first world problems. Just—'

'Need a hand?' Jonathan's dad has appeared on the pavement. 'You look like you could use it,' he adds, nodding towards my hand, which I have bandaged temporarily.

'Just a slight altercation with a bramble,' I tell him. 'Nothing major. And I'm all right carrying.' I raise my arms. 'Just not so good at picking things up.'

'*Slight?*' Tash begins. But, thankfully, she sees my look and correctly interprets it. 'But, yes, good idea, Mum.' She hauls out the box of provisions. 'Maybe you could start putting this lot away?'

I find the bleach for Jonathan's dad and duly go back inside, past the front room, which is now Jonathan's bedroom, on through the narrow sitting room, and finally into the kitchen, where the units look like a job-lot from a sale of damaged stock.

I try to coax myself into an appropriately laissez-faire mindset as I start opening and closing cupboards to find one for the food. Cate has already stashed all her groceries away in one of them; I know it's hers because there is a Post-it note stuck to the inside of the door, on which is written 'CATE'S!' in big emphatic letters.

Verity joins me just as I'm running a cloth around the interior of another cupboard. 'Tea?' she asks. 'Coffee?' She plucks the kettle from its stand. She's donned an extra layer of clothing, I note. The kitchen feels damp and cold, and I wonder if Cate's room change will solve anything.

'Coffee, please,' I tell her. 'I've got a long drive ahead. You all right, sweetie?' I add, as I finish wiping the cupboard out. 'All unpacked?'

'Pretty much,' she says. Then she grins and rolls her eyes at me. '*Again*.'

She seems fine, though. Her usual unflappable self. Of all Tash's uni friends, she's definitely the most capable. The practical one. The one who quietly made sure Tash ate when sick with grief. I doubt a princessy housemate is going to faze her.

I point to the groceries. 'You okay with me decanting this lot into here?'

She peers into the box. 'Oh, wow, so this lot's for all of us? Julia, that's really, really kind of you.'

'Just expedient,' I correct her. 'Better you put them to use than have them mouldering back at the cottage. And, yes, of *course* for all of you. A little house-warming gift.'

She wraps her arms around me. 'Julia, you're the absolute *best*,' she says. 'Seriously. Hurrah! We can *eat*!'

I think about her parents, far away, chugging along the Danube. And I can't get my head round that at all.

I'm just about to ask her how they are, when there's another down-the-stairs clattering, and Tash joins us in the kitchen. I scan her and note the details; her pink cheeks, the plastic storage box in her hand, the way her chin's puckering.

'What's wrong?' I ask, going to her, because something clearly is. Cate again?

'I can't believe it,' she says, thrusting the box at me. 'Look!'

I take it and see, and also smell, and I'm horrified.

'How?' she's saying. '*How?* How can this have happened? I was so careful. I wrapped them all individually in kitchen roll so they wouldn't move around, and had the box wrapped in a blanket, inside *another* blanket, inside my duvet, in that IKEA bag. How can this have happened, Mum? *How?*'

There isn't much to see. It's just a box of broken glass; a highly scented box of shards and chunks of shattered glass. No sign of any kitchen roll. Just the remains of all those expensive bottles of perfume David had bought her, the last of them – and the memory makes me feel even more wretched – for Christmas. It didn't matter if they were full, half-full, or long empty, either. She kept the bottles. All of them. Always had. Every one. They could not be more precious to her. They could not be more broken. The only whole things in the box now are a scant half-dozen of the stoppers.

'Was the lid on it?' I ask her.

'Mum, I just took the lid *off*.'

'Still, maybe it was dropped,' I begin. Though even as I say that I concede that it would have to be from a great height.

'How?' she snaps. 'When? And by *who*? Mum, I packed these up three months back! You loaded them into the car with me! They've been in my bedroom in the cottage ever since!'

She's right. That's where they have been. Part of the haul left for me to bring here today. Secure in their plastic box, in their bedding. Protected. Unbroken. So she's right, isn't she? *How?*

Since I'm holding the box now it falls to Verity to hug her. To console her, as tears begin tracking down her cheeks.

I put the box down. Take over. 'It's just stuff,' Verity tells her. 'That's the thing to remember. Just *things*. It's the memories that matter.'

'Verity's right,' I agree. 'Come on. Deep breaths. It happens. If Dad was here now, you know exactly what he'd be saying, don't you? "No sense crying over spilt milk. *Specially* if it's skimmed milk.'" Which monstrosity he considered to be the drink of the devil. One of his bugbears. Which he would always go on and on and *on* about.

The memory at least produces a sniff and wan smile. Though I suspect she will cry over this for days.

I say nothing to her, because I don't want to upset her further, but she's right. Someone almost certainly did this deliberately. When though? Could this be related to that open bathroom window?

And more to the point, *who* did it, and why?

Isochaetes beutenmuelleri
The Spun Glass Slug Moth

I have no Christmas memories. Not a cotton-picking one of them. Where – note – 'Christmas memories' is defined as a specific place in the brain; one hung about by fairy lights, scented with faux pine and cinnamon, and where the light is always rendered in that Christmas-card palette of milky white, frosted sunset, ember glow. There, much be-glittered, be robins.

I lost a whole bunch of memories when my head hit the car roof, and after *that*, despite the efforts of people with *other* Christmases to attend to, Christmas, as a *thing* for me, never really happened. It was a thing that always happened somewhere else.

To *someone* else.

Oh, and who *cares*, even? Because what is it really? A bunch of tinsel. A bunch of lights. A bunch of kitsch. A bunch of whimsy. A bunch of meaningless. A bunch of valueless. A bunch of *temporary*.

A massive bunch of tat, all tied up with ribbon and dressed in cheap, metallic, violently patterned paper.

The caterpillar of the spun glass slug moth, it is said, is so named because looks like a spun glass Christmas decoration. A posh one. From Harrods, say, or Fortnum and Mason. And like any glass Christmas decoration, it has just two USPs. To be fantastically beautiful and dangerous. Treat with care and respect and it will delight eye and mind. Handle roughly and its needle-sharp filaments will hurt you.

That's glass moth caterpillars for you.

That's glass for you.

Oops.

Chapter 6

As soon as I'm on my own, driving off, I speak to myself sternly. Tash will be okay. Yes, it's a big thing, but, in the scheme of things, a small thing. Much as I hate to see her cry, I know she will be rational. It's distressing, but surely nothing compared to losing her father. Plus, she has her friends with her. They will support and distract her.

I also remind myself that it's unscientific to leap to conclusions. It could just be coincidence. It probably is. But I'm as anxious as I ever was to see the boy. Whatever he's done or not done, his life is in the balance, and until it's not, my conscience won't allow me peace.

I drive hard and fast to Cardiff and, having just about kept one step ahead of the evening rush hour, I'm parked up in the big hospital multistorey by 5 p.m. The light is fading as I walk up the covered walkway that links the car park to the main reception, hearing the familiar fuss and chatter of roosting birds. Some people hate being around hospitals, and I understand that; few places can be so freighted with bad associations, after all. But for me it's always a return to my natural element.

Hospitals are like intelligent organisms in themselves. Huge, complex organisms, running multiple functions; a web of people and processes, each connected to the other, some loosely, some closely, but all with a common aim. To do no harm. To try to make people better.

Of all the reasons I decided to go into medicine, that sense of being in border-country, helping to man the shifting frontier between life and death, was perhaps the greatest; something I discovered when, as a seventeen-year-old with a vague, naïve notion of 'doing good', I was granted a one-night-only residence in my local A & E.

I returned home that night galvanised, not just by the things I'd seen, but by the rawness, the shock and awe of it, the jeopardy, the physicality. The incredible ease with which a human life could end. It's a privilege beyond description to be in a position to help people when they are at their most terrified and vulnerable, but it was more than that; I was intoxicated.

The penny dropped then. A career in medicine often chooses *you*.

I have a work-walk, which I've honed over years of pounding corridors. As I stride through the main concourse, I instinctively adopt it, past the Costa, the information desk, the busy shop-fronts, the tired benches, weaving purposefully against the human shoals swimming out. If luck is with me, it will be Pat who I'll first encounter in ITU. If it's deserted me, then I will simply brazen it out. Doctor Young come to check on her patient.

Luck is with me. Pat is at the nurses' station, head down, making notes.

'Bless you,' she says, and I smile in acknowledgement. Pat has acquired both the age and the professional respect that allow her to anoint anyone she chooses.

'It's so good to see you again, Pat. Any news?'

'What, since your last text?' She winks as she closes a file. Then stands up, slipping a pen into a breast pocket beneath her plastic apron. 'Nothing to report. Still no response to the appeal, still no joy with the number. Though we began lightening his sedation today, and he's been showing signs of fighting the ventilator. So I believe the plan's to try and wean him off it in the next couple of days. He's quite the favourite.' She checks her watch. 'Though he'll be all yours for a while yet, so take as much time as you want. Poor boy. It's not like he's got visitors queuing up to see him, is it?'

I've done my time in ITU, although it would never be a career choice. Where life-saving in A & E often takes the form of a pitched, bloody battle, this is more pistols-at-dawn stuff; a duel with death. It takes a singular kind of medic to actively choose such a speciality.

There is also something spiritual in this kingdom of machines. This is modern medicine's Styx, with the nurses playing ferrymen. As a junior doctor, I found it reassuring to be around its famously calm, competent practitioners, and as I follow Pat into the ward proper, letting the door sigh closed behind us, I realise it's a feeling that has never left me.

The light is bright, the sounds purposeful, but the ward hums rather than thrums, untroubled by the disorderly conduct of human voices. It's a place of beeping monitors, sighing ventilators, and wheezing self-turning beds. When life needs orchestrating, these are the ultimate musicians.

It's a big ward. The busiest ITU department in Wales. And as with any organisation, there is a system for occupation. Patients are moved around for maximum efficiency, like pallets in a warehouse, like pieces on a life-and-death chessboard.

Pat leads me to a bed in a corner, by a window. Outside, the spikes of the stadium pierce the sky; a promise that life, in all its precious ordinariness, is still within reach.

'Well, here's our golden boy,' Pat says, lowering her voice, as is the custom. If they are reminiscent of anything, ITU wards are like churches. Not just out of respect for patients on the edge of life, but because they both, in their own ways, are in the business of defying the grim reaper, and that needs a measure of respect too.

Buoyed by Pat's news, I find I'm less nervous about seeing him than I'd anticipated. Though there is little to learn from examining his face. He looks rested and restful. Even more strikingly youthful, and I think how herculean a leap it must take to agree to have a young life disconnected from a support system. I remember my grandmother, who languished similarly in the last days of her life. She too looked peaceful, but it felt real rather than imagined; a settling to final sleep, after a long life well lived.

This is not that. This is just a life interrupted. Now he's made it this far, to think of it in any other way is inconceivable. Whoever – and whatever – he is.

Pat leaves me, and I automatically check the monitors arranged around the bed. His oxygen saturation, blood pressure, his pulse, his ECG trace; all are reassuringly where they should be. And all the while, at intervals, the bed heaves beneath him; a leg lowered, an arm raised, a shifting of his skinny torso – as if he's in a dinghy, bobbing gently in a bigger boat's wake.

I then pull up the adjacent chair. Red regulation NHS issue. Large and unyielding, its only purpose here is vigil. No flicking through *Hello!*. No administering of grapes. And as I gaze down at his closed eyelids, and the dense crescents of lashes below them, I'm taken straight back to Rhossili Down, with a stomach-flipping judder. He looks such an innocent. So pure and sweet and guileless. But appearances can be deceptive. Is he any of those things?

His mouth is slightly open, to accommodate an endo-tracheal tube, and he's obviously been given some mouth care very recently, as his lips, chapped and bruised, are liberally smeared with Vaseline. I can see his front teeth, one of which has a substantial chip. Did he chip it when he fell? He will hate that when he sees it. I just know it.

If he sees it. There is all the time in the world still for catastrophe.

I take his hand, which is smooth and dry, and as I turn his wrist towards me, I realise the little butterfly tattoo – that 'double random', as Jonathan put it – isn't what I'd thought it was. The antennae are wrong. They're fat and look like feathers. We've all been wrong. It isn't a butterfly. It's a moth.

Why? I wonder.

Because years of asking politely have furnished me with a simple truth. That tattoos always have a story. What's his?

Biston betularia

The Peppered Moth

It's not a *speckled* moth. It's a *peppered* moth, Julia.

It's Darwin's darling. The poster-moth. The little moth that could. It's the moth that launched a thousand ships – and, oh, they were fine ships. Hearts of oak, many-masted and billowing of sail. And each one was laden, as all fine ships should be, with cargoes of bright, beautiful evidence. That he, darling Darwin, was right all along. That evolution happens by natural selection.

Which is an interesting concept to try and get your head around, isn't it? That the theory of 'intelligent design' wasn't actually that intelligent after all. Just a best-guess, trying to answer unanswerable questions, till science came along and replaced faith with truth.

And so it is ordained. At the altar of evolution. We are born, live and die to play our part in the process. Our genes either perish with us or are *selected*.

For the individual, however, there is no masterplan. We are what we are due to an 'accident of birth'. We have no control over our genesis, so what else would you call it? At least that's what they always say, don't they? And how easily, how smoothly, it trips off the tongue. Like 'mind the gap', and 'unexpected item in the bagging area' and 'make my day, punk', and '*c'est la vie*'.

But it's wrong, and if there's one thing I especially despise it's that kind of lazy inaccuracy. Not that you'd know, because what are the chances anyone ever said it to you? Let's take a guess, shall we? Less than zero.

Yeah, you might have thought it. If you had a shred of insight, you might even have let the notion sneak under the crack in the Great Wall of your enormous, perfect RIGHT. But I'm not holding my breath because I *know* how these things go. It's been said to me how many times? Let me count them on my fingers. Oh, shit. I've run out. Hahaha. Course I have. Just like I'd run out in, like, a *heartbeat* if I had to count how many times I've also heard 'remember, it's not *your* fault'.

All your stuff. All your advantages. All your privilege. All your *empathy*. Just like all the stuff I didn't have. And don't have. And *should* have. None of it, trust me, is an 'accident of birth'.

Because here's the thing. No one's accidentally born. It's a standard nine-month process. Cause and effect. First you are conceived, and then, *ipso facto*, you are born.

No, just like you, Julia, I am an accident of *conception*.

Chapter 7

It's almost eleven by the time I'm back home in Clapham. And once I've closed the front door behind me, I stand for a moment in the cool, moonlit hall. It smells strongly, though not unpleasantly, of the stargazer lilies I'd forgotten to throw out before I left last Sunday evening – a gift from my next-door neighbour, Moira.

I throw my keys down by the vase, tug my arms from my jacket and decide, in that instant, that I need to get another dog. Just to hear the clatter of claws skittering across the black-and-white-tiled floor again. To punch a hole through the heavy cloak of silence.

It's an unexpected thought. One I haven't had in years. Perhaps it's just a reaction to having left Tash so upset back in Swansea and knowing that when I wake in the night – which I undoubtedly will – she'll feel so far away.

So much of parenting is about measurements once you're doing it remotely. Just as on planes David would count how many seat backs we'd have to pass to reach an exit, so these days I count how many hours it will take me to reach Tash if she ever needs me urgently.

I dump my holdall by the foot of the stairs and walk through into the kitchen. Sleek, white, and lab-like – not so much as a splinter of stripped country pine here – it now extends, as do several others in the street, well into our narrow city garden. Which, in its turn, continues on, flanked by brick and stone walls, beneath which the deep herbaceous borders we'd toiled for weeks to create are still heavy with drooping late-summer foliage. There was an Anderson shelter here once, and a small sunken area remains, perfect for the trampoline David had been insistent would not be coming with us from our old house. It's rusted now, its safety net pockmarked with holes, but still it sits there, defiant. An angry relic.

Our house – my home – is on the north side of Clapham Common, close to the border with Battersea. To paraphrase the estate agent's brochure, it's an imposing and generously proportioned Victorian terrace on a sought-after, prime residential road. It is perfectly located: close to good schools and transport. It has high ceilings, deep skirtings, and no ghosts.

Except, perhaps, for one apparition: the ghost of my own former self. It's almost identical to a house, not a million miles away, that I lived in during my second year as a student. And having been happy there, I had had high hopes for here. Here, where there was room for a family to grow, perhaps the miracle would happen, and we *would* grow.

The first thing I did when we exchanged on our house was sweet-talk the elderly lady three doors down into renting us her garage, so David wouldn't have to countenance having to park his beloved Jaguar on the street. Looking back, it had been one of many such desperate acts of cajoling and coercion, such was his ever-growing compulsion to go west. Had he not died, he'd be there now, I'm sure of it.

Correction, I remind myself. He *is*.

Because I cater for myself these days on a need-to-eat basis, there is little in the house to make a meal from. I find an unopened jar of salsa, some tortilla chips and a half-full pouch of olives, and though I know I'm short of at least one major food group, it feels strangely appropriate to my current mood that, where I've stocked Tash and her friends up with enough healthy foodstuffs to last them till Christmas, I am sitting at a kitchen counter, eating like a student.

A text pings in from Nick Stone just as I'm screwing the lid back on the salsa. He has dropped round to the cottage. He's sorry to have missed me. The piece – as in *his* piece – will be in the paper tomorrow. I might want to 'brace' myself. He has used me, apparently, to 'top it' and 'tail it'. He has also quoted me, 'well, sort of', and hopes that's okay. He also hopes I'll be happy with the 'tone'.

It's such a long, detailed text that I wonder why he didn't simply phone me. But then I realise the time, so I text back a thank you. And a promise to read it, even though I know I won't.

By the following lunchtime, though I'm bone-tired after yesterday's exertions (not to mention having slept so poorly, worrying about Tash), I'm helpfully distracted from thinking about the boy, and who he is, by the sheer volume of work I have to catch up on. But every day seems to have the capacity to deteriorate at the moment, and I know I have used up my current stock of luck when, having woken up my phone, I spot a missed call from my sister-in-law, Laura.

I press the return call button immediately. I have many failings, but avoidance of confrontation isn't one of them. It's the sort of skill that comes in with the free medical school milk.

'Ah, Julia.'

Laura's tone suggests I've just scuttled into her office for a reprimand. She retired from her headteacher's job two years back and claims not to miss it, being too busy on important projects like making use of her free bus pass, running story-time in her local library, and bending her vast, defiant garden to her considerable will.

What a big fat lie that is. She has one of those voices that's made for teaching, and however much it waxes lyrical about coppicing and wave-power, I know it misses bossing people about all day.

'Laura. How are you? Sorry I missed your call earlier.'

'I can't believe you didn't see fit to warn me about any of this.'

'I texted you on Monday evening.'

'Yes, and I tried to call you back.'

And had opted not to leave a voicemail. Laura doesn't return texts and Laura doesn't speak to machinery.

It's not my place to apologise for the deficiencies in network coverage in the greater Gower area, so I don't. 'What, then?' I say instead.

'The article in today's *Western Mail*. I assume you've seen it.'

We have a currency, me and Laura. One of delicate diplomacy. Though since David's death, the channels of necessary communication having narrowed, she has become North Korea to my South. 'No, because I'm at work,' I point out again. 'What about it?'

'Well, quite apart from anything else, they have addressed David incorrectly. They have him down as *Doctor*, not *Professor*. It's completely indefensible. I've obviously telephoned them to insist on a correction, and I suggest you do too. It's bad enough that he's dragged into the newspapers like this in the first place, but this kind of shoddy journalism just isn't good enough.'

In what way *bad*? I think. And *why* bad? And why use the term 'dragged'? There is a life at stake here, for Christ's sake. I also feel defensive on Nick Stone's behalf, about her use of the term 'shoddy journalism'. But it's knee jerk. In recent months I've felt defensive on behalf of anyone – and any*thing* – David's sister locks horns with. An emotion as useless as it's ingrained.

'I'm sure he wouldn't have taken it personally,' I tell her. Because he wouldn't have. David minded about a lot of things, but formal appellations were never one of them. When on holiday (and how Laura would blanch if she knew this) he habitually travelled as 'Mr', preferring to leave his professional and professorial persona back at home. 'I'm sure it was an honest mistake,' I say, 'but yes, I'll mention it if I get a chance to. But I can't stop. I have a full clinic this afternoon. We'll have to catch up properly when I'm down again, okay? Now Tash is back,' I add, self-flagellation also being so ingrained, 'we could perhaps meet up for coffee or something?'

'Oh, really?' A rise in pitch. 'In that case, I'll call her later. I have some books for her.'

Laura rings off then, the question of coffee neatly sidestepped. And I reflect, not a little wryly, that while she had nothing for me – no 'how are you?' because, of course, I don't matter – she always has something for Tash. For Laura, husbandless and childless entirely by choice, my daughter is the ultimate pupil.

So much so that, to Tash, she isn't 'auntie' but 'Mamgu'. In law, David's sister is my daughter's paternal aunt, but in life, in reality, in every way that really matters, she has always been something else to her – her grandma. Mamgu means grandma in Welsh.

Did I play any part in this? No. It just happened. Did I mind? Not at all. I embraced it. At one time, and for a long time, it had made me very happy. Not least because once both my parents died, and with David's long gone, what right had I to deny my daughter that precious connection? It wasn't as if she was exactly over-burdened with them, after all. Have I any right to resent it now? Again, no.

But, still, I do. How can it be that someone you love so much also has such a strong, enduring bond with a person who seems to take such pleasure in hating you?

Hate is a strong word, admittedly. On a good day, perhaps I'd describe Laura's feelings towards me as something more every-day-functional, such as dislike. Or tolerate. Or disapprove of. But this isn't a good day. This is a middling-to-bad day that still might get worse, and I have a powerful urge to just come out and ask Laura for her considered view on that very question.

I won't. Mostly because I have no business interfering in a relationship which is clearly beneficial to my only child. One of the salutary lessons in contemplating the divorce which never happened was that, had David not died, my own relationship with Laura would have withered on the vine, as is the usual way of such things. I think we'd both have been grateful.

Mostly, though, it's because I already know the answer. She has lost her baby brother and she holds me responsible; his death, to her mind, the culmination of a butterfly effect which began, as they do, with the smallest of actions. Him meeting *me*, as opposed to someone more suitable. A compliant, submissive female who would make him her whole world. Who would grant his heart's desire and provide him with more children.

Finding out that David had told Laura about us planning to divorce had been one of the grimmest, shittiest revelations in an already grim, shitty time. My husband cremated, but our secret disinterred.

Well, what I'd thought was our secret. Which we'd *agreed* would be our secret. Which had made the betrayal so much worse. And a fragile détente is now our only way forward. And only then – Laura was all for immediate, full disclosure – because David had made it clear he didn't want it. Forcefully, as it turned out. To both of us.

And even Laura can't bring herself to go against his wishes. So on we trundle, locked for life in a prickly embrace.

I'm just heading back to outpatients for my afternoon clinic when my mobile trills again. I think it might be Tash, responding to the text I sent asking how she was doing, but when I pull it from my pocket I see the name Nick Stone on the screen. I duck into a nearby linen cupboard to answer it.

'Okay, I have some news,' he says. 'Though I'm not sure you'll be able to do anything with it. The boy's name is Kane Scott. Spelt K.A.N.E. That mean anything to you?'

Kane. I roll the unfamiliar name round my tongue. 'No. But thank goodness they finally know who he is now. Though hang on. How do you know this?' As in, *and I didn't.* 'Has someone been in touch with the paper?'

'No, I think it came via the police Facebook appeal. Or maybe their Twitter one. Apparently a friend recognised him. Anyway, the main thing is that it got back to his mother.'

His *mother.* He has a mother, then. 'But when did this happen?'

'This morning.'

'And how do *you* know?'

'Via my contact in Swansea.'

'So do the hospital know?'

'They do. And it turns out he's from London.'

'*London?*'

'Yes. So not a local.'

'Whereabouts in London?'

'Don't know, I'm afraid. I can try and find out for you if you want.'

'No, that's fine. I'll call my friend at the hospital. I'm sure she'll know. Thank you for updating me. It's a huge weight off my mind.'

'I'm sure it is. And, hey, any time. Give me a shout next time you're down?' He laughs. 'Though preferably do the shouting from a place of safety, yeah?'

I promise I will. And I think I actually might now. He seems decent. And helpful. And I haven't forgotten what he'd said about his son. But I have patients to see and just enough time to do some digging. I know I can't speak to Pat because she's off for two days now, which means I'll be unlikely to get a lot out of them, but I can try.

So I do. To no avail.

'All I can do,' says the young nurse who has already explained at length how tied her hands are, 'is jot down your name and phone number and add it to his notes. I'm sure his mother will get in touch with you in due course. Though to be honest, I couldn't give you her details even if I was allowed to. We don't even know who she is yet. Or when she's coming, for that matter. Still,' she finishes, 'at least the mystery of who he is is solved now.'

Not for me, I think. I have a name now. And I want answers.

Artona martini

The Bamboo Moth

Fun fact! Though it's often spotted there, basking darkly among the cultivars, the little bamboo moth isn't native to New Zealand. History records that it is mostly native to Japan and found its way to the land of the *Lord of the Rings* (which, of course, it isn't) inside the bodies of imported second-hand Japanese cars. Which, as well as being fair warning not to import second-hand Japanese cars, technically makes it an immigrant. And a stylishly named one, too, don't you think? 'Hey, make mine an Artona Martini!'

My parents were stylish to a fault. Also: out there. Imaginative. Singular. Eccentric. Look!

See them whoop as they think outside the baby-name boxes. Watch them celebrate as they push back the baby-name envelope.

Note the glee on their faces as they discard the humdrum and common. Oliver, Jake, Thomas, Joshua, *David*.

Look at how thrilled they are when, like a pair of happy parental bumble bees, they land simultaneously on the perfect name – Kane.

'Kane! Our little Kane! Oh, so perfect!'

History also records that a number of alternatives were in the frame. Of which Cain, I must report, was the original favourite. 'Such a strong, masculine name!' 'Such a ring to it!' At least till my mama put her pale, dainty foot down, pointing out that Cain – as in the Bible (back then, people still lapped that crap up) – had turned out to be a bit of a bastard. Hence the change to Kane. A handy homonym, or homophone – whatever – which, by a blinding piece of luck, means 'intelligent warrior'.

Hmm. I think I'll just leave that here, Julia.

Chapter 8

As soon as I'm home from work I do an internet search for the boy, and though I recognise none of the Kane Scotts on Twitter, I find his Facebook page almost immediately. The hair is longer, the image grainy, but there's no doubt it's him, smiling out almost coquettishly from the centre of a trio of boys, all clutching plastic cups of beer and wearing lanyards round their necks. A massive structure rears behind them and also fills the cover photo space – a backdrop I recognise as Reading Festival. I know because the summer before David died, Tash had been up to its twin festival, Leeds, and I'd watched coverage of both on TV.

There are slim pickings to be found there, however. No workplaces to show. No schools or universities. No life events. No interests. No family. No music. No quotes. No check-ins. No groups.

And, no, he does not accept messages. Even by the standards of the security-savvy young, this is a Facebook account with a very private face.

Armed with what little I have, I text Tash to see if she can talk. She rings me immediately, and since she's at her laptop I direct her to his Facebook account as well.

'I still don't recognise him,' she says. 'And I've definitely not heard the name Kane Scott before. It's not the sort of name you'd forget, is it? But, Mum, I've been thinking. You know that

Valentine card we talked about? It might not be connected but I remembered I had another weird message not long after that. Just after Dad died.'

'Another card?'

'No, a text message. Which just came up as a number. I didn't think much about it at the time – I just thought it must have been from a friend with a new phone. I texted back and asked who it was, but I never heard from them again. I didn't think any more about it at the time, but now I'm wondering.'

'What did it say?'

'Just sorry about your dad and so on, but it was all a bit odd – I'll send you a screen shot of it, shall I? Hang on.'

She does so, while I wait on the line, and in it finally pings. And it does indeed say 'Sorry to hear about your dad.' But beneath that is an emoji. The butterfly emoji. Beneath that, 'But remember, every new beginning comes from some other beginning's end. Seneca.'

'Got it?' asks Tash. 'What does Seneca mean?'

'It's not a what. It's a who. He was a Roman philosopher.'

'Ah, I see. Bit weird, isn't it?'

'I think it's a pretty well-known quote. But yes, taken with everything else—'

'That's what I thought.'

'And what about that Valentine poem? What did it say that was so creepy?'

'I don't remember the exact words. I binned it when I cleared my room out. It was just really odd. Weird olde worlde language. I think it was some ancient love poem or other. I should have kept it, shouldn't I? It could easily have been that IT guy – he was mad about *Game of Thrones* and stuff – but then I thought about that text. Another butterfly. It's all a bit odd, isn't it? Do you think he might be dangerous or something?'

At this point I know I could mention the open bathroom window at the cottage again. It's playing on my mind even more now, because the box of perfumes was just across the landing, in her bedroom. But I don't want to frighten her unnecessarily. I could still be barking up the wrong tree, after all.

'No,' I say firmly. 'Not least because he's attached to a ventilator right now, and isn't likely to be a danger to anyone for a good while, is he? Assuming he even is, and we don't know that for sure. But I've asked the hospital to pass on my details to his mother. At which point, I hope she'll get in touch with me. Not a lot else to be done until he's woken up, is there? And then, perhaps, everything will become clearer. Don't worry, though, sweetie. I'm probably just counting two and two and making five – you know what I'm like.'

I know what I'm like. As anxious about her child as any other mother. As prone to flights of worry. But increasingly I'm getting four here, every time.

Over the next few days I wait, expecting every unexpected call to be from Kane Scott's mother. If nothing else, an update. Plus, hopefully some clue about what I'm dealing with. Was this a single impulsive act, the motivation I can only guess at, or the latest in a line of them, all premeditated? The police might have closed their file (they don't know about the watch, do they?) but, for me, the case of Kane Scott is still open.

If I'd been his mother. That's all I keep thinking. *If I had been his mother I would have called me.* Forget everything I might feel, forget my guilt at what has happened; if I'd been his mother, I'd have made contact, no question. Mother reaching out to mother, driven by a shared hormonal instinct. Don't worry. My son is found. My son is safe.

So why hasn't she? Because I *am* making four? Because she knows I will have done so? Because she knows something I don't? Because she knows her son?

But I've also spent my entire working life in the NHS and know there is a fair chance she would not have even got my details. And though I'd have dug my way to them like a dog looking for a buried bone, perhaps she would not have had the time or inclination to do so. Whether she did or she didn't have the means to get in touch, it's not inconceivable that she's decided not to bother. A case of least said, soonest mended. Let it go.

Several years back, I had been good at letting go. Which didn't go down well – not with my husband at any rate. David, who would not. And could not.

Families come in all shapes and sizes. Happy ones, sad ones, dysfunctional ones, obviously. And, of course, big ones and small ones.

Because I arrived quite late, mine had been small by default. And though I didn't upset the apple cart to the point that it crashed, as far as I know – and I had no reason to disbelieve my scrupulously forthright mother – I caused sufficient mayhem in two already busy lives that further progeny were ruled out at around the time I learned to walk, talk and break things. I was apparently, as a toddler, 'quite a handful'. It was one of the first things I ever knew about myself.

David, in contrast, came from one of those big, sprawling families, which number great aunts and second cousins among their loving inner circles, and hold bi-annual family gatherings with an almost religious zeal.

And I had loved it. Embraced it. Found it so much to my liking. For a time, to my shame, I even found myself thinking how a lack in my life had been magically made good; that I was part of something bigger, and maybe better.

We were also very much in love. So when I found out I was pregnant, there was never any doubt that we would keep the baby. Because, complicated though it would be, we were both can-do people. I worked right up until they had to stop me, for my health and their safety, while David, more trapped by now than I in the slog-study-slog wheel, daubed crazy paint patterns on the walls of our tiny spare bedroom every night, fearless, even gleeful, in the face of our landlord – an irascible, oily, unpleasant man.

'How will he ever know?' he'd protest in the face of my fretting. (How I fretted. I had been born, my mother always told me, with an F gene.) 'And when we go, I shall delight in restoring it to its former glory. A shit colour, with shit paint, applied very shittily. Seriously. It's no less than he deserves, Jules.' Then he'd laughed his deep laugh, mischief playing over his handsome features, and I'd had a glimpse of the wild proto-David I'd heard so much about; the bold, fiery medical student I'd never known.

But we could never have done it alone. And, true to form, David's family (for which the word 'extended' was an understatement) excelled. In contrast to my mother, who'd been characteristically reticent when I'd told her, there was no sigh of disappointment about our lack of forward planning. No wondering if waiting a while might have been more sensible. Just pleasure, and excitement, and cloudscapes of knitted things. It didn't take my own mother too long to catch the tide of joy, but the fact that she had needed to was always there.

And when Tash came along she was duly smothered in love, almost to the point of suffocation. And, freed from the burden of enervating maternal guilt, I was able to cherry pick all best bits of motherhood. Giving all to my job, which I loved, despite its many and frequent crises, and, energised by the liberating mental stimulation, able to focus the resulting energy on my daughter. I was a model of emancipation, of cake-and-eat-it womanhood. Emmeline Pankhurst had always had my back.

And the luxury of my situation wasn't lost on me. I'd see patients in all kinds of domestic situations, some of them really very hard. So I understood what it took for women to achieve some kind of balance; saw how many sacrifices they had to make that I didn't.

I was, in short, excused. Because I was the joy-bringer. And, in producing Tash, I was added to the family hall of fame, having added to the long line of expansions. And, as David was the youngest (of four, and by a span of a dozen years, Laura being the oldest) also the means by which babies – as in plural, no question – would once again fill the family head-space with their lusty cries.

Perhaps I should have seen the signs then, but I didn't. Because I couldn't know then that I would turn out to be such a disappointment. That, when fear became fact, and the truth became too painful, my 'letting go' would turn everything so sour for us.

By the following Tuesday I decide I will wait no longer, and as Pat, frustratingly, turns out to be on leave, I take Jack at his word that he wishes to be more 'there' for me and send him a text, asking for news. He calls me at half past seven that same evening. 'Still at work,' he says, 'as per!'

I know how this goes. 'Bet you're popular at home, then,' I quip. It's a genuinely off-the cuff comment, because, with a new baby in the house, it wouldn't be the first time that a job with long, punishing hours also becomes an excuse to linger at work.

He laughs, but it's a loaded laugh. 'Hmm,' he says. 'Not exactly. Slight variation in our respective opinions about what constitutes an appropriate time to get home.'

Jack has always been candid. Well, bar in the matter of his years-long affair. So it's no surprise that he adds that there's also a bit of a mismatch of opinion about the associated business of earning sufficient to provide one.

I wonder how his other kids are really doing. Jack's right about my ongoing relationship with his ex. But also wrong, because, for the most part, these days it's virtual rather than actual. Though we keep in touch sporadically, it's mostly on Facebook that I see Pru; where her posts, so often daubed with broad strokes of bitterness and recrimination, provide the bigger, much messier, picture.

'Anyway, enough of that,' he says, as if anticipating my unspoken question. 'The lad's no longer here.'

'He's been discharged already?'

'No, not discharged. They brought him out of the coma yesterday, and he was apparently transferred to a hospital in London so he can be closer to his mother.'

'Seriously?' I can't imagine why such a thing would have happened, even knowing that was where the boy comes from. This is the NHS. If you need hospitalising after an accident, you end up where you end up. The service doesn't have enough cash run to a courier service. I say so.

'My thoughts exactly,' Jack says. 'But it turns out she has MS. And it would be difficult for her to visit him in Cardiff, because she's apparently quite severely disabled. So, since he'll be in for at least of couple of weeks yet, maybe more, it got sanctioned. She obviously has friends in high places.'

So he's gone. In fact, long gone. And is no longer on life-support. Is now conscious. I wonder what's going through his mind now. Is he worrying about consequences? Is he anticipating I'm going to want to speak to him? Is he scared?

More to the point, should Tash be scared? Should *I* be?

The news about his mother sends my imagination into over-drive, too. Multiple Sclerosis is a ruthless and callous destroyer. Of myelin, of neural pathways, of basic bodily functions, and, as a consequence, of relationships, and lives. It also attacks twice as many women as men. There has been no mention of a father. A husband. A sibling. And in the absence of facts, by the time I've gone upstairs, changed out of my work clothes, and come back downstairs to forage for something edible, I have fleshed out her entire, tragic story. A single mother, strapped for cash, progressively disabled by MS, and – again, as a consequence of the complex needs she'll no doubt have – of a boy with a world of responsibility on his shoulders, creeping progressively towards rebellion. Then a near-fatal accident, a long way from home. A mother paralysed by fear and anxiety. Because she'd know her son, wouldn't she? Or at least have suspicions. Is that why she doesn't want to talk to me?

Hemiceratoides hieroglyphica

I wonder what you know about poverty, Julia. I mean, *really*. Oh, I know how it goes with all you well-meaning liberal types. With your Amnesty subscriptions and your donations to Shelter, and your endless virtue-signalling, and your enormous social consciences. Hashtag *lucky*. Hashtag *savethebees*. Hashtag *bigissue*. Hashtag *blessed*. I know all about you because I've seen you in action. But you don't know. You *can't*. Because if you did you wouldn't *be* you. Your blessed life wouldn't be an option on the menu. Because – hashtag *re-al-it-y* – that's how it works.

But for the moment, consider *Hemiceratoides hieroglyphica*, another moth that is so rare that it doesn't even have something as commonplace as a common name. It also has an uncommon means of finding nourishment. It feeds off tears from the closed eyes of sleeping Madagascan birds. I like that. It's kind of sassy. This is a kick-ass kind of moth. Sly, you might think, but what's a hungry moth to do? In this case, evolve a tool, and what a beast of a tool, too – a specialised, forked, barbed proboscis. With hooks in it. *Hooks.* To pierce holes in their eyelids. Because a moth's gotta do what a moth's gotta do.

Which is true of all of us, isn't it? If we want to live and thrive, we have to *work* it. But, for some of us, it's hard. We've got to work it *and then some.* Because – newsflash! – the start line of life isn't actually a line. I bloody *wish.* And the playing field – another newsflash! – isn't level.

Don't get me wrong. I didn't start off on the social care scrap heap. I started out like a stem cell – full of glorious potential. Great things were hoped for me. Great things were planned for me. Have you any idea how much it hurts to know that? To be so cognisant of the future I was denied? Still, I cope. Most days – at least these days – I even manage not to think about it. But not all days. That's just *way* too big an ask.

Which is not to say I blame them. (My parents, that is. Not him. *Obvs.* As is, I believe, the accepted vernacular, *he,* the man who killed them, can go rot in hell.) Because it wasn't their fault either. That's on record. That's fact.

It's also fate. Sometimes your card's marked, and there's an end to it. (So says Grandma. So *said* Grandma. There's an *end* to it. Good old Grandma!) Sometimes the giant hand of destiny – a bit like the one they use to advertise the National Lottery, only with more of a nod towards the grim reaper than Mickey Mouse – singles you out, scoops you up, and snuffs out your life.

Or, in my case, scoops you up and then flings you back down again.

Into another place. A bad place. Poor unlucky me.

However, luck is what happens when preparation meets opportunity.

Great quote, huh? That's Seneca, that is.

Chapter 9

When David was still alive, and life became complicated, I tried to get into the habit of going to bed without my phone. I had more than enough to keep me awake as it was.

But when Tash left for university my phone returned to my bedside. Because if she needed me, I needed to know she needed me. So if I ever find myself unexpectedly awake in the small hours, checking my phone is the first thing I always do.

And I'm awake now, unexpectedly, so the action is automatic. I starfish my fingers and pat down the surface of the bedside table till I find it.

There's been a text from her.

Call me if you're awake? NOT A CRISIS!

I text back to say I am, and Tash calls me immediately.

'Why are *you* up?' I demand, now I'm over my initial panic. 'Is this early or late?'

She drawls through a yawn. 'Bit of both.' Of course. It's freshers' week. 'Bit of a late night,' she goes on, 'and I couldn't sleep, so I was reading, and then it struck me. *Mum*, listen. About Dad's watch. Did you take it back to the cottage? Because this is just the weirdest thing, but I'm pretty sure – no, I am almost a *hundred* per cent sure – that it wasn't even there.'

My sleepy brain struggles to process what she's telling me. 'No,' I say. 'I brought it back here with me last week. I told you.'

'No, not *now*. That's not what I meant. I mean not there as in not in the cottage in the *first* place. Not unless you took it back there recently. Did you?'

'No. How could I have done that when it was already there?'

'That's exactly my point, Mum. That watch you found – I mean, I know you said it was Dad's, but I don't see how it can be. Because I don't think his was even in the cottage to *be* stolen. I could be wrong, but I don't think I am. I think it's in the desk drawer in the dining room. You remember when I needed his voice recorder for that assignment last term? It's in the same bag, or at least it was. In the drawer.'

I'm already climbing out of bed by this time, wriggling my feet into my slippers.

'But how could that be?' I say, padding out on to the landing. 'I never brought it back here.' Apart from the obvious valuables, such as the watch and David's laptop (also taken back to London after my ticking off by Nick Stone), I've bought almost nothing back from the Gower house. Not yet. A whole raft of David's belongings are still there. He lived part time in Gower. He died at work in Cardiff. Choosing where to hold the funeral had been a political decision as much as anything. Choosing how to deal with his possessions is one I'm still putting off.

'Mum, that's what I'm *saying*. *I* did. I put it in the envelope with his leads and chargers and stuff. Remember? The stuff I took back home? I don't know why I didn't think of it. I remember putting it in there. I remember *seeing* it in there too, only recently. Mum, I'm *sure*. Go down and look. I'm sure it's in there.'

I hurry down the stairs into the hall. 'That's what I'm doing,' I tell her, flicking on the light switch in the dining room. 'But how can it be? That doesn't make sense. How can it have been in two places at once?'

'*Exactly*,' says Tash again. 'It can't, can it?'

I slip past the chairs that stand like sentinels around the big oval dining table. When was the last time we ate at it? Well over a year back. Just the three of us.

The drawer is stiff. Not from age, but from being massively overburdened. One of many such spaces in my life.

Of all the simplifications I know badly need making, clearing my life of belongings is surely one of the most pressing. I'm beginning to feel constricted. As if in an increasingly tight carapace. One I know I need to shed to enable me to breathe again properly. To grow. What's the biological term? Instar. That's it. From the Latin. Meaning 'form'. I need to find a new one, and soon.

I put the phone on loudspeaker and place it on the desk, then force my hand in to push down the resistant wodge of stuff. Out through the sash window I can see next-door's cat sloping across the patio. He's a big cat, Moira's cat. A Maine Coon called Brillo. He glances in, his eyes igniting green.

He then pads away imperiously, there being nothing to see here. 'Big manila envelope,' Tash is saying. It's as if she's in the room with me. 'Can you see it?'

'I have it.' I pull the bulky package out.

I've barely tipped it up before the watch slithers out of it. 'Good god,' I say.

'You've got it?'

I pick it up. 'I've got it.'

'I *knew* it. So what's this all about, Mum? Isn't that, like, *so weird*?'

I pick it up, flummoxed. *Does not compute*, my brain tells me. 'What the . . .?'

'*Exactly*, Mum. How can Dad's watch be in two places at once?'

'Well, obviously it can't,' I say, wide awake now. 'Hang on.'

I grab the phone as well and pad further along the hall into the kitchen, where my handbag sits on the worktop, corpulent and collapsed; another tired, over-burdened place.

It takes a while to locate the watch, and I feel a stab of guilt as I slip my fingers round it. Such a valuable thing to be dumped so unceremoniously into the personal landfill in the bottom of a bag. I haven't even wrapped it up in anything. David will be turning in his grave.

But, at the same time, my mind rebels. If it's that great a feat of precision engineering surely it's designed to withstand such abuse? Isn't this a watch built to be *in extremis*? We had that conversation many times.

But is it even his? I have two now. I lay them beside one another. They are twins. Rare and unusual. Unquestionably identical.

'So, in the absence of any evidence to the contrary,' I say to Tash, 'it appears that Kane Scott has – *had* – a watch identical to Dad's one.'

'So what does that mean?'

'I have absolutely no idea. A connection between them?'

A connection to David that extends beyond simple theft? Where does that sit with everything that's been going on with Tash? I am struggling to understand how things might fit together even more now. 'If it *was* his,' Tash says. 'Perhaps he stole it.'

'That's also possible. But, if that's the case, who from, if not Dad?'

'I don't know. That's just it. Or I was thinking maybe Dad could have lost his ages back, and then replaced it with another one, and then the original one turned up? I don't know. And *then* he stole it, maybe?'

Which all sounds very convoluted and would also presuppose that had happened and that David hadn't told me. Is that possible? He'd have surely made a claim on the insurance. And it still doesn't explain why the watch was in the boy's backpack. Or why the boy was at the cottage. Or why he ran away the way he did. Or was he trying to return it to David when I intercepted him? And if that were so, why again? And why run away from me? Who *is* he?

I catch my reflection in the window. I look hollow-cheeked and pale, like a ghost of myself. I'm at even more of a loss. Nerves jangling. Why has all this been visited upon us?

'I'm even more confused now, to be honest,' I tell Tash. 'Listen, get yourself to bed, sweetie. Me too. Let me sleep on it. I'm sure I'll be able to get my head round it better in the morning.'

Except, of course, I can't. It won't let me.

I call Pat as soon as I have the time the next day and have her send me the photos they took when the boy was admitted, under cover of being keen still to trace him to check his progress. Thankfully she doesn't question it – even wishes me luck doing so. She's apologetic about not being in touch herself – she was not in work the day the boy was transferred.

Up they pop, one by one. His face. The moth tattoo. The phone number on his hand. The last of which, after calling it, despite knowing it's still probably pointless, I add to my contacts as 'Kane Scott???', the question marks added because why would he have his own number written on his hand? And if it isn't his number, whose is it?

I also check back on Facebook, which tells me nothing I don't already know, and with Tash, who informs me she's sent him a friend request, which (and this is reasonable, given that he's almost certainly still in hospital) he has yet to respond to.

Then, as soon as I've seen my last outpatient of the day, and before heading home, I decide to be proactive and call Nick Stone. 'Doctor Young,' he says immediately. 'To what do I owe the pleasure?'

So I tell him about the second watch, and that it's actually the original watch, which piques his interest straight away.

'Now that *is* a poser,' he admits. 'The same as your late husband's? You're absolutely sure?'

'I am absolutely sure. They are identical watches. And unusual models, too, as you saw. I mean, what are the chances of that?'

'So you think the watch in the backpack was his own watch?'

'Conceivably. Even likely.'

'Hmm. So perhaps he wasn't breaking in. Perhaps he never went in the house at all. Perhaps he had the watch all along and was *looking* for your husband . . . Which would suggest he didn't know that he died, wouldn't it? Maybe still doesn't know, for that matter.'

I have already dismissed this as a possibility. I have no rational reason for thinking the way I am, but instinct increasingly suggests to me that there's a longer-standing connection between Tash and this boy, even if she's not aware of it. The fact that he has an identical watch to David's surely makes it even *more* likely. But because I have no concrete evidence to back it up I'm not inclined to share that with Nick Stone. At least not yet.

'It could be that,' I say instead. 'Which is why I'm calling. I was thinking about the phone. The police don't seem to want it, so I'm thinking maybe you'd look at it for me?'

'I can try,' he says. 'When?'

'Would Saturday work for you? I'm coming straight down after I finish work on Friday evening.'

'Good god. That's some journey. How long does that take? Four hours?'

'It's fine,' I tell him. It's automatic. 'I was born on a Thursday.'

'Oh, I get it. Far to go. My, you're sharp, you are.'

Not that sharp, I think. I still don't have a clue what's going on. Only a conviction, and it's a strong one, that something is. Something that's becoming more disquieting by the minute.

Tineola bisselliella

The Common Clothes Moth

Ah, pests. Particularly, nits. I love nits. Such great levellers. The greatest signifier of Human Under, *ever*. Under-privileged. Under-nourished. Under-educated. Under*class*. What pictures does your mind conjure when you hear the word 'nits'? A Dickensian orphan, right? A tousle-haired artful dodger. A poorhouse. A workhouse. A tenement. A sepia-toned photograph of a child in brown boots, a glob of yellow mucus nestling sweetly in their philtrum, a rancid kerb their preferred place to sit.

A child which you cannot help but stigmatise: 'Ah,' your mind tells you (this is probably true of everyone). 'Poor little lamb. Poor little urchin. To be born to such privations.' But who you know (you won't admit this) at least knows their station. Hence the natural social order – thank *goodness* – remains preserved.

Which is why, once it rampaged through entire child populations (*god*, mixing with the proles, eh? Damn you, state education!), an infestation of nits needed an emergency rebrand. If you are middle class and get nits, you are a different kind of victim. You have unfortunately succumbed to an outbreak of head lice, carried in – so irresponsible! – on some chav kid's claggy head. And why, pray? Why you? Why poor Daisy and Launcelot? Because as *everyone* knows, nits prefer clean, pampered hair. So that's okay, then. You can deal with it. You can sleep shame-free in your beds.

But, FACT. They do not. It's a LIE.

I tell you what, though, I had nits once. I LOVED it.

It was, like, wahhhh! We have nits in the house! Danger! Danger!! Man the barricades! Commence chemical warfare!

Ah, but Trudy, blessed Trudy. How fondly I remember your ministrations. Those long, sultry sessions in your avocado bathroom. You with your 99p nitcomb, and your gentle, gentle hands. Making partings. Scraping eggs off. Catching living, twitching lice. Me holding the piece of kitchen roll on which we'd lay them out to die. In tidy rows, so we could quantify our precious haul and practise counting. Part, comb, deliver. Part, comb, deliver. Transcendence. Oblivion. A taste of purest honey. A taste – and such a sweet taste – of what it was to be *mothered*. So much joy. So much peace. So much hope in my heart.

So much incentive to hang around with the claggy-headed chav kids all day. So much . . . what's the word? That's it. It's *faith*.

I had *faith* in you, Trudy. Do you understand how much that matters? And, for a while there, I thought you had faith in me too.

D'you remember that day when we were in the park near your house? That day when we went out for that picnic? I know I was only small. (Was I six? I imagine so, because we didn't see my seventh birthday together, did we?) Go on, *you* know. When we got caught in that unexpected thunderstorm. And I told you I was scared of all the thunder and lightning, and you picked me up – and I was heavy, and you huffed and puffed as you did so – but still, you clutched me to you, smelling of cheese and onion crisps and peppermints. And you carried me all the way home. All the way home! Like the precious gift you had told me so many times I was. And when we got home, Will was there, and you both laughed at how wet we were, and you told Will how frightened I'd been. And you said – swear to god, I hope this haunts you FOREVER, bitch – that I would never need to be frightened about anything again, *ever*.

Ah, we live, Trude, and, *boy*, do we learn.

Unlike the nit, your common clothes moth is a pest with pretensions, its larvae mostly found in the best-appointed bedrooms. To nibble nightly, and richly, on your artisanal, organic, no-polyester-round-here-please fabrics. Your linens, your cashmeres, your silks, and your furs. 'Oh, Jeremy! We have clothes moths! Call the housekeeper! Find some camphor! Oh, fiddlesticks! They've made a hole in my beaver lamb shrug!'

But – another fun fact! – just like the head louse, the common clothes moth *is* a commoner. Because much as it favours Giorgio Armani over Walmart, what it likes most is dirt. Gunk. A little *essence de* human sweat.

It's also crafty. It can spin its own camouflage matting, only creeping out in the dark to acquire what it needs.

It knows what it's about, does the clothes moth. It understands social mobility.

Chapter 10

I'm about to throw my holdall into the car and make a dash for the South Circular when I'm accosted by Reg. Reg is Moira's husband. He is Brillo the cat's dad. He is thick-set. Early seventies. Ex-forces.

Ex-Special Air Service, to be accurate, so Reg has seen things and *done* things. And some ten years back, not long after we moved in, he sustained a major head injury in a road accident. For a time it was touch and go if he'd ever get home. And, though he did, some months later, after intense rehabilitation, it was clear, at least to Moira – it took the rest of us a while to see it – that it wasn't exactly Reg who'd come home to her.

Reg suffers from hyper-vigilance. He sees danger everywhere. Which means he spends much of his time in a state of high alert; either sitting in his van, watching, or at his bay window, watching, Or, on fine days, in patrolling the streets for us, watching. His brain won't allow him to stand down.

The term 'for us' is key here. He makes notes in our absence, about comings and goings. He is the self-appointed guardian of our street.

'You off away again?' he asks, holding his exercise book as a visor to shield his eyes from the setting sun, despite his sunglasses being perched on his head.

'I am,' I confirm. 'Just for the weekend. Back Sunday. You okay, Reg?' I add, as I close the car door. 'How's Moira?'

'Hmm,' Reg says, clearly imagining a weary eye-roll will suffice. He then taps the blue ballpoint in his hand against his nose. 'In that case, I'll make sure I keep a special eye out for you, Dr Young.'

Reg cannot bring himself to call me Julia because it goes against the 'natural order'. Laura would love him. He looks more serious, suddenly, which, for Reg, is a stretch, given that his default expression is Code Red. 'I've been wanting to speak to you,' he adds, tapping the exercise book. 'Did you get my note?'

I confess I didn't. Resist checking my watch.

'Popped it through the door,' he says. 'Couple of weeks back.'

'I'm sorry,' I say. 'Perhaps it got mixed up with all the junk mail. What was it about?'

'Loitering,' he says. 'Outside your house. Sixth and seventh September.'

'Oh, I see,' I say. 'Well, thank you. I—'

'Young male. Slim build,' he continues. 'No distinguishing features. No sightings since.' He taps his nose again.

Ours is an inner-city street. Densely populated. Busy. If Reg were to compile a book from his many, many notebooks, the chapter marked 'loiterers' would run to many pages. In any other circumstance, this would, therefore, be an everyday exchange, particularly since the house next door but one went up for sale, and a purple patch of 'suspicious persons slash unusual activity slash anomalies' filled half a notebook. In any other circumstance, I'd have treated it as such.

Today I don't. 'Sixth and seventh?'

'Affirmative.'

'What time of day?'

He consults his notes again. The tiny snail trails of close, jagged writing, the scribbling of which consumes much of every day.

'I've logged 18.26 on the sixth, for fifteen minutes, and 11.38 on the seventh, for ten.'

'*Just* outside my house?'

'He made several passes. But yours was definitely the house of interest, yes.'

'Thank you, Reg,' I say, noting his choice of words, and feigning a lightness I no longer feel – *what on earth is going on here?* 'Whatever would we do without you, eh?'

His sparsely whiskered cheeks spread and bulge as he smiles. The old Reg returned to us, if only for a fleeting moment. 'All part of the service,' he says. 'Drive on safely.'

Fair, I think, as I climb into the car. *Young male. Slim build.* It could be nothing. It could be no one. It could conceivably be Lucy at number twenty-four's stepdaughter's latest boyfriend. But is it? I don't think so.

With my chat with Reg losing me ten crucial minutes, it's an agonisingly slow crawl out to the M4, every inch of which I spend trying to dissect the constituent parts of what I've found out, line them up, and compare them with what I already know. But what I mostly know is David, which means there is no credible connection between what I know of what has happened and what I know of *him*. Every time I try to find one, I'm presented with a wall that's seemingly impossible to break down.

Once I'm finally on the motorway the traffic thins out, thankfully, though my tired Friday night brain is no less congested. What am I to try and make of Reg's revelations? Have I missed a trick? I know the boy lives in London, and I live in London, and the fact that he was hanging around our house, assuming that it *was* him, makes me wonder if I need to look at things another way. Was he in some way related to David's decision to accept his part-time post in Cardiff in the first place? Was David subsequently keen to put distance between them? If so, why? Which is when the most likely answer supplies itself; that there might well be a woman involved in all this.

Perhaps I've missed more than a trick. Perhaps I've lost the entire plot; could it even be that David had an affair early on in our marriage and had been supporting the boy (his boy?) and his mother ever since? And has the boy been stalking Tash because he knows who she is? What she *has*, that he perhaps doesn't, and resents her? Could it be that Kane Scott's mother is David's former lover?

Oh, come on, I berate myself. *Really?* It sounds like a plot line from a soap opera. And even if it happens – and I do know that it happens – nothing about that scenario seems remotely credible unless I rewrite huge chunks of our marital history. Which will, of necessity, involve reimagining the man I thought I'd known as an entirely different person. As a liar. An opportunist. A man without integrity. But I can't do that. Because David was none of those things. Was he?

Things were strained between us before he died, no question. Have I missed a trick here too? Was there more to it than just our impending separation? Had I been so focused on 'us' and on keeping our secret that I'd missed the subtle signs that something else was going on? I certainly remember wondering – more than once, in fact – if he'd started seeing someone else, and as soon as I'd considered it, I had also dismissed it. It was no longer my business, after all.

This, however, is, and I can't shift from my hypothesis. Every less damning theory I try on for size doesn't fit. The boy has a watch just like David's. He was hanging around our Gower cottage. He might have been *inside* our Gower cottage. He might well have been hanging around Tash for months, as well. He might well have been hanging around our house in London, too. And, despite having every reason to get in touch with me, his mother hasn't. *Ergo*, she might well have a good reason not to. A reason connecting her to my late husband?

I can barely accept my thoughts as credible. This is David, after all. And yet, and yet . . . David definitely had reasons to stray. It's an awful word. A cheap word. A word with tom-cat connotations. Yet it resonates, because I know it's the right one. Because, bottom line, I pushed him away.

If. The cruellest dagger in the lexicon, surely? If only we hadn't waited to try for another child. Though for 'we', here, read 'I'. If only *I* hadn't been quite so hell-bent on waiting. But I was still so young when Tash was born, and I was just trying to be responsible. Life was just like my handbag. Stuffed. Strained to bursting. There would be a right time, but now – as in then – was not it. I worked sixty-hour weeks as a junior doctor. I had barely time to eat, let alone mother my daughter. The prospect of having another yet was unthinkable.

But there is never going to be a right time. How many times did you say that to me, Laura?

Wrong times, on the other hand – I knew all about those.

I began my first miscarriage on the afternoon of Tash's fourth birthday, which had fallen that year on a Sunday. We had some twenty-odd for tea, and a cake, which I baked myself, as I did – and still do – every year. It was an Ariel cake, styled as the eponymous Little Mermaid, that being her favourite book (and film, and doll, and dressing up outfit) at that time. And Ariel's titian locks had stained my fingernails red.

122

Then more red. Just a spot of blood. Then a cramping. Then more blood. Then a lot more, accompanied by the sort of gripping, angry pain that made what was happening to me unequivocal. I was a couple of days shy of being fifteen weeks pregnant, and even as I asked my mum if she'd mind staying over – David had been on call, and had, as per, been called – it's my sense of astonishment that I remember more than anything. Tash had been an accident. And a happy one, no question. But as someone who'd since spent the best part of four years trying *not* to get pregnant, this kind of disaster – this startling, determined, expulsive, violent miscarriage – simply hadn't featured in my plans.

There was a great deal of hand-wringing as the party bags were doled out, but Laura, regrettably, couldn't stay. She had a school to run back in Swansea, and I was glad. Nevertheless, she couldn't leave the party without dispensing orders. Lie down. Get your legs up. Put a cushion under your bottom. And it was easy to run away with the idea that she knew what she was talking about. That if I did as directed the baby could be saved.

It could not.

Nor could the next. Five months later. Eight weeks.

Nor the next. Eight months after that. Eleven weeks, going on twelve.

Nor the next. Two years on. A scant six weeks in.

Then nothing. Not a glimmer.

So. Deep breath. Onwards.

To investigations, options, cost-benefit analyses. To the spectre of This Probably Being *It* Now. Or perhaps not. So (onwards and upwards! Where there's a will, there's a way, Jules!) to co-ordinating our diaries. To making time. Making efforts. To a period of excruciating, orchestrated sex. Then, for a time, no sex. Then resentment. Then rapprochement. Then complicated discussions about how old

123

was too old. And, inexorably, to the uttering of those three small-but-enormous letters. Those big, screamy neons: IVF.

And, all too soon, to the point – and I remember this so clearly – when the way forward finally revealed itself to me.

I had just come home from work after a long, difficult day, in which I'd been obliged to share anxiously awaited test results with a couple in their thirties. A couple with two children – a boy of five and a girl of seven. The test results confirmed what we all already knew. That her breast cancer, now spread to her bones and liver, was no longer responding to treatment. That the last straw had been snatched from their grasp.

There had been many tears. And, in their dignity and gratitude for everything I had tried to do for them, there was also a lesson. For me. We discussed options, palliative care choices, hospices, clinical trials – at least, any that had the merest whisper of single-digit percentage hope attached to them.

But they had come prepared. They were ready. The discussion was now academic. She'd glanced at her husband, and he'd responded with a nod. 'I think we'll just stop now,' she said. 'I think we'll just go home and enjoy our children.'

Hours later, I had come home as well. Irritable, strung out, exhausted. So tired that I barely had the energy to communicate with Aurelie, our then au pair, as she hurried off to her English class *tout de suite* – my over-running afternoon clinic had made her late as well.

And in the post was a letter; a first appointment for a second round of IVF. And as soon as I opened it, I started crying. At that point, I'd had no thought of the couple I'd seen that morning, because learning not to over-empathise is a crucial, crucial skill. But then Tash rattled down the stairs, having heard me come in, and, discovering me crying – I seemed unable to stop now – immediately burst into tears as well.

It was at that point that it hit me, as I tried to console her – to reassure her that, really, I was okay, just tired – that I realised my quest to create another baby had morphed into something else. A manifestation of the possibility – no, more than that, the fact – that the child I already had wasn't quite *enough*.

I threw the letter in the bin that night. I told David I was done with it. Became the lightning bolt that struck the family tree.

The moon has been tailing me since Chippenham, but by the time I reach the cottage it's overtaken me and parked up, ready to welcome me home. Except – the thought won't let up – has it ever felt like home? Can it ever be now?

When I let myself in, there's a less welcome story on the doormat, in the shape of the *Western Mail* piece Nick Stone promised to get to me, which has been removed from the paper, clad in a pair of slippery polypockets, and pushed through the letterbox onto the mat.

I didn't read the original news report, because I stopped at the headline, which was *Local doctor saves life in dramatic Gower rescue!* Click-bait, as Nick says. Fake news.

Though I know I should, I have no desire to read this one either. So I take it through into the kitchen and put it down, face down, on the table. Then, once I've made a mug of coffee, I head straight upstairs, saying hello, creak by creak, to the ghosts.

There is a ridiculous amount of paperwork in the house (this house which was always supposed to be an escape from it), particularly in the third bedroom, which is these days only used sporadically. The third bedroom, which it turned out we didn't need.

Despite the two single beds in there, it's very much an office – became more and more so in the months before David's death. I begin to realise just how much he'd taken ownership of it, in his olde-worlde, technophobic way.

Yes, at work he always used technology – impossible not to, in his speciality – but when it came to his personal paperwork he would no more go paperless than trouserless.

He had also, in his last months, clearly let it slide. Is this in itself part of a bigger picture?

With no pressing need to be scrutinised or sorted, much of David's post still lies unopened. Was he seriously planning to live out his life here? Alone or otherwise? I'll probably never know.

Spurred by pique that I know is, at best, unreasonable, I begin sorting briskly, methodically, page by page, bringing order to chaos. And I strike credit-card-statement gold quickly. It's then only the work of minutes to narrow down the search range. David had just the one bank account (our joint one) one debit card, one credit card, and there it is. On a statement from the previous December. A four-digit sum in a two- and three-digit landscape. A tall poppy among the daisies. Impossible to miss.

I sit back on the rug and swing my legs around from under me. There is no room for doubt now. David did buy the watch. For the boy?

Or, if not for him, who then? And if he did buy it for someone else, how did Kane Scott get hold of it? The more I find, it seems, the less sense anything makes.

Oh, the joys of paperwork! I text Tash, who has already chased me down and wants to know why I'm down and what I'm up to. While I'm crick-necked on the floor, trying to make sense of the inexplicable, she's already out with her friends. For which I'm glad. Because I don't want her fretting like I am. Which she clearly isn't. Should she drive over on Sunday? she texts back. Surf report's good then, apparently.

I tell her not to worry, because I don't want her feeling she must, but she counters that with a long row of sad face emojis. A unicorn. A wave. A sun. A surfboard. Then my phone trills to life and she's there with me, on Facetime. 'Mummmaaaaaa! You okay? Look, don't rush back. Stay later. Pleeeeaassse? We all want to come over and seeeeee you!'

She's bright-eyed, much-mascara'd. Already two or three drinks in. And I suspect what they want is just to surf, swim and party. Suspect that, were I not here, they'd have come over anyway. 'Okay,' I say. 'That would be lovely.' Because it would. Just as long as it's on her terms, not mine.

'So, did you find anything else out about the watch?' she asks.

'Only that Dad definitely bought it.'

'Aha!' she says. 'Ahaaaaa!'

At least half a dozen people are waving and gurning behind her. I spot Jonathan and Verity, plus another lad I recognise as having stayed at the cottage once, and another girl, half in shot, who I recognise as Cate. Perhaps they are getting on better. Perhaps they will all gel in the end.

'Say hellooooo to Mumma!' Tash is trilling. 'Hellooooo, Mumma!' they all parrot.

I'm glad to see Tash seemingly carefree, living in the moment, but as I trill back and wave, I'm thumped by a bolt of sadness. That it's Friday night, and that all human life is not here. That I'm sitting on a tired carpet, papers strewn all around me. Just me, a six-thousand-pound secret, and all the ghosts.

Eumorpha pandorus

The Pandora Sphinx Moth

People often get it wrong about sphinxes. Everyone's so used to the lion's body-human head combo at Giza, that they fail to realise that if you took the time to read up on your Greek mythology you'd know the original sphinx also had the wings of an eagle (or a gryphon, or, indeed, a *hawk* – see what they did there?) and, at the business end, a serpent-headed tail. Historical note: this was one badass creature.

On the other hand, who doesn't know about Pandora?

'Come on down! Open the box, folks! Bring on death and all the evils!'

But seriously, you couldn't make this moth up, could you? A whole handful of military chic. Ice cool in camo. Hidden in plain sight. So, what's your superpower? This is the Pandora sphinx moth's. This is mine.

It wasn't always so. For a time, there, I was the centre – no, the epicentre – of attention. A planet ringed by satellites of medical interventionists. Pierced by asteroids of needles, knives and drains. Not attention I craved (I couldn't crave something *less*, obvs.), but what's interesting, should your interests run to spooky coincidence, is that the man that killed my parents, and nearly killed me, was also hidden in plain sight. A not-at-all legal alien. A lorry driver from there, come to here, with his deliveries. A man with a plan to drive right through the night, so to get – or so his lawyers pleaded pitifully in court – home to his loved ones. *His* wife. And *his* babies. And the law of the tachometer be damned.

I have barely any memories, of either that, or my parents. I've had to work bloody hard to sleuth this lot out. It's taken years but no matter. It's been a labour of love. To blow a kiss to stir the stardust of their ashes.

Chapter 11

Nick's dogs turn out to be a brace of German shepherds. One traditionally coloured, the other startlingly pale, as if mislaid by a Norwegian sled team. He is standing just outside his front gate, having presumably seen me coming, and they sit motionless either side of him like mantelpiece ornaments. Only as I draw closer can I see the steady swish of their tails. He tells me their names. The pale one is Freda, the other George.

'Failed PDs,' he tells me cheerfully. 'It's kind of a thing with me.'

'Failed what?'

'Failed police dogs.'

I eye them warily. 'That's a thing?'

'It is with me,' he says, clicking the latch on the gate. 'My brother's a copper – a dog handler, down in Kent. Don't worry. They won't hurt you. They're obedient to a fault. And I only let them loose on felons, obviously.'

I extend a hand towards the pale one. 'Hello, Freda,' I say, as she sniffs and then licks it.

'Ah, she likes you,' he says. 'I hope you realise you're very privileged.'

'She's beautiful,' I say, stroking her. 'I'd so love to get another dog.'

'Well, I obviously know a source, if it's a shepherd you're after.'

'Perhaps I will. I rather like the idea of being shepherded.'

'You really should.'

He says it with such conviction that I expect him to give me a list of reasons. But he just adds the word 'seriously', and with a strange sort of half smile. As if he assumes I already know what they are.

'Well, we'll see. Anyway, these two. Why failed?'

'Dodgy knees, in her case. And he's just too dozy. Couldn't find a haystack in a haystack. Flunked out of training before he'd even got started. You okay if we walk them first since it's nice? Take the cliff path round to the worm? Maybe get a drink in the sunshine? Or are you all done with gradients for the foreseeable?'

It's a fine autumn day for a walk, windless and cloudless. So the lane back to Rhossili is busy with crawling traffic, hopeful for spaces in the already filling car park.

It's territory I know well, having walked every walkable inch of it, at all times of day, in all weathers, and all seasons. With David. With Tash and David. With relatives and friends. Latterly, just with Tash. Endless strength-sapping, sleep-inducing, necessary trudges, the wind knitting our hair into knots, and whisking sobs out to sea. Often solo, these past months. Just lately, not at all. I must get another dog, I decide.

I recognise and wave to a couple of neighbours – though neither of them, thankfully, are close enough to actually talk to; I know many will have seen or read about what happened, and the thought of dealing with misplaced plaudits appals me.

My companion, though, today dressed down in jeans and a down jacket, seems to know almost everyone we pass.

We head off down the lane that will take us through the fields out to the cliff path. He lets George off his lead, and he bounds away like a giant lamb.

He makes no move to do the same with Freda, however. She remains on her telescopic tether. 'I can only let her off in very specific situations. Very early in the morning, and very late at night. Essentially when the rest of the world's asleep.'

'Why? Is she dangerous?'

'God, no. She's a complete softie. But she's highly trained, so I really can't afford to take my eyes off her. She's obviously been *re*trained, but instincts run deep.'

'So she *is* dangerous.'

'*No.*' He looks like I just kicked her. 'No, but I take your point. It's more like Jason Bourne. You know the film? Given the right triggers, her instinct kicks in. Someone running, say. If she thinks she's had the nod, for whatever reason, she'll think she has to bring them down. Hypothetically,' he adds. 'It's never actually happened.'

He laughs at my expression. 'I said "bring them *down*". Not maul them to death!'

'Still,' I say, eyeing Freda just a little more warily. 'Quite a responsibility. Do the neighbours know?'

'Absolutely not.'

'So, how long have you lived here anyway?' I ask. 'You seem to know more people here than I do.'

'Only about eighteen months or so,' he says. 'But I'm one of those people who likes to "get involved". I help with beach cleans. I turn up and cause trouble at the odd council meeting. Though mostly, this summer, I've been busy surveying seaweed.'

'Seriously?'

He stuffs George's lead into a jacket pocket. 'Seriously. For the Marine Conservation Society. You have no idea how many varieties of seaweed there are down there. Well,' he corrects himself, 'you might, actually, being a surfer. I certainly didn't. I drag my son along when he's down.' He grins again. 'He pretends he enjoys it.'

'What's his name?'

'Nate.'

'How old is he?'

'Seventeen.'

'And he's okay now?'

'He's fine.'

'What was wrong with him?'

'Meningitis. Pretty terrifying.' He frowns. 'Correction. *The* most terrifying three weeks of my entire life.'

'I can imagine.' Then I catch myself. 'Actually, I can't begin to. I'm not sure anyone could, could they? Even saying the word "meningitis", it's like . . .'

'*Exactly*. I still find it hard, to be honest. Soon as I do, it's like . . .' He shakes his head. 'It's almost physical. All comes flooding right back again. Boom.'

'That doesn't sound mad at all,' I say. 'Probably PTSD. And not really surprising, given what you went through.'

He nods. 'They told me to expect it. Still catches me off guard, though.'

'So, enough about that, then. I'm just glad he's okay. Glad David was able to help him.'

'Trust me, the word "help" doesn't even *begin* to cover it. I could never have thanked him enough. *Never*.' He stops on the path. 'Such a waste. I couldn't believe it. I came to his funeral, you know.'

I stop too, examining his face again. Had I seen him there? I don't think so. Though I'd seen little that day. Everything around me seemed amorphous, out of focus. Only Tash was razor sharp. Tash, who, all the way into the church, I'd had to keep on her feet. Who collapsed into a screaming heap when the curtains closed in the crematorium.

Is there any pain as intense, as bright and blinding, as watching your child suffering and knowing there is absolutely nothing you can do to take their agony away? I remember someone once telling me – this before I had Tash – that once you become a parent, you are a hostage to fortune, because you can never be happier than your least happy child. So my own agony at losing David was visceral that day. I've have given anything to take that pain away from her.

'Really?' I say. 'I'm sorry. I didn't realise.'

He nods. 'It came through on the wire – I have my ear to the ground, as you know – and I read it and I was stunned. We both came, my ex-wife and I – we just had to. I remember seeing you. And your daughter . . . believe me, seeing *her* . . . Christ, that *really* brought it home to me.'

He stops then, his grim expression crumpling into a rueful smile. 'Sorry. You must think I'm some kind of weird stalker. But we weren't the only ones, were we? I mean, how many of his patients and families were there that day? Felt like hundreds. That must mean a lot to you. To both of you.'

'It does. It was—'

'*Shit.* George! Sorry. Sheep in the bloody lane. Hold up.'

He hands me Freda's lead and sprints away then. A blur of red, following a tail round a bend. And I stand there for a moment, among the corn marigolds and buttercups, lifting my face up to the sun, trying not to cry.

FFS, as Tash would put it. Trying not to *cry*. Freda presses herself against my leg and I crouch down to stroke her. She licks my hand again. 'For god's *sake*!' I ask her. 'What's *wrong* with me?'

Perhaps a bit of PTSD of my own.

Our trial-separation talk, just before Tash went to uni, was an impeccably polite conversation. We'd borne witness to several moribund marriages in our orbit – Jack's being a notable low-point – and just at the point when our own had begun to fray around the edges. We didn't want that. We would be kind to one another.

We'd gone to an Italian restaurant – a decision straight out of the Good Divorce handbook. Any flarings of temper would necessarily be tempered in such an intimate, public space. Though as it turned out, there'd been no need to guard against emotion, because the fiery exchanges that had characterised our early romance had long since been watered down by the drip-drip of infertility, then extinguished by the fire-break of separation.

So, textbook. Big tick. Gold star. I even remember us walking home in the rain, arm in arm, because we were sharing my umbrella – we were both pretty tipsy by that time, admittedly – then going home and making coffee and chatting about compost. After which, where, in the movies, we might have tumbled onto the nearest shaggy rug, we retired politely to the same, long-chaste bed.

And would continue to do, at least for three nights a week, till we'd seen our daughter safely settled into university. After that, we agreed (we were suddenly *so* good at agreeing) we would bide our time; wait and see how things went. What a fine pair of responsible celibates we'd become.

What the *hell* had we been thinking? What the hell had *I* been thinking? To just accept such desiccation. Such self-denial. I twist the ring on my finger now, as I set off in pursuit of man and dog, and am struck by a sudden revelation. It's time to draw a line in the sand. Then step over it.

'So,' Nick says, when I've caught him up and George is back on his lead again, 'enough about all that, eh? Where are we at? Have you managed to find anything else out?'

We're out near the cliff edge now, where the land stops so abruptly at the sea. There's a path, though, a narrow and well-worn one, which snakes its way around the top of the higgle-piggle coastline, tracing its contours to join the other side of the worm. The tide is almost fully out, and though it's still relatively early, there are already walkers out on the causeway, keen to make the most of the scant time in which they can cross it, to dabble among the rockpools, and, if they're lucky, see a seal or two.

The wind is blowing straight into my face, as if trying to scour off all my carefully applied protective layers. 'David bought a new Breitling watch – the one you found – last December.'

'For Kane Scott, you think.'

I nod. 'The question is, why? Which throws up other questions, obviously, such as who was the boy to him? What's their connection?' I pause to grab a breath from the breeze. In for a penny, I think. I *so* need to share this. 'There's another factor too,' I say, looking at him square in the eye now. 'Before David died, we were planning to separate.'

'Ah,' he says, without so much as a blink. 'Got it. I see where you're going. At least, I think I do. It does add an element of logic to the situation. So you think perhaps he's the son of . . .' he pauses. 'Unless . . . Is there a chance he's a former patient? Something like that? Might there be some work connection?'

'I did wonder about that,' I say, realising I need to share this too, 'but there've been other things happening too. Odd things. All things that can be explained away – I have no evidence, only theories – but taken together . . . I don't know. Mostly things to do with Tash, which are really beginning to worry me.'

'What kind of things?'

'Creepy things. Weird stalker-type things.' He acknowledges this with a nod. 'Some of them going back some time. Even before David's death.' I explain about the strange Valentine Tash received, the condolence text, the sea of desiccated dead insects in the cottage bathroom. 'I know it sounds silly but, given the other things, I can't help but wonder if the window was left open with the light blazing on purpose. As some kind of warning?'

He shakes his head. 'I don't think that sounds silly at all.'

I also tell him about the discovery of what had happened to Tash's perfumes. The fact that they were in the cottage at the time too. 'David was forever buying her perfume. So they were very precious – obviously deeply sentimental. And the more I think about it, the more it's clear. No way could they have been smashed to smithereens the way they were by accident. And now it turns out that my neighbour thinks he's seen him hanging around our house in London too, back in early September. I found that out last night, and now I don't know what to think. Except it all seems to point in the same direction. That this Kane Scott is somehow connected to all of it. And seeing as it's not beyond the bounds of possibility that before he died David was seeing someone else,

and—'

'You think the someone else could perhaps be Kane Scott's mother.'

'Possibly. Potentially. Though how that fits with anything else, I have no idea.'

'Or – forgive me for suggesting it – could he be a son from another, *older* relationship?'

'I've already considered that. Honestly, I have no idea. Maybe. I can't imagine it, but that doesn't mean it isn't true, does it? But if *I am* right, why? What's he after?'

'Money? I'm sorry. Just throwing that out there. Is it possible he's been using Tash to get to your husband somehow? I don't know. Threatening to reveal who he is to her?'

'But David's been dead nearly seven months now.'

'Sorry,' he says again. 'This must all be painful to try and process.'

I touch his arm. 'There's no need to be. *Really*. I've already been following the same thought processes you are. My only worry here is Tash. That I don't know what I'm dealing with. That's why I'm so desperate to get into that phone and find out what the hell is going on.'

'Well, you've come to the right place,' he says. 'Though right now, since I first need to tire these two out, how about we park this for the moment – skirt round the worm, say, then I take you down and educate you in the defining characteristics of bladderwracks and dabberlocks? That's not a chat-up line you're going to hear every day, is it? *George!* Sorry – George, do *not eat that*!'

By the time we've climbed back up to Rhossili it's started raining, so, with the prospect of a drink in the sunshine off the agenda, we instead walk the half mile or so back to Nick's house, where, after rubbing the dogs down, he sets about making coffee. It's a complicated business, conducted in respectful silence, while he pays homage to his spitting, growling behemoth of a coffee machine.

Nick's home is a typical flat-fronted detached Gower house. Four windows, one door, pitched roof, twin chimneys, small, open porch. The kind of house a child would draw. It has a small, neat front garden and a square of lawn behind it, which looks out across the ancient medieval fields to the south-east.

Inside, it is dog-friendly, shabby un-chic. And what it lacks in all the stereotypical 'feminine' embellishments, it makes up for in shelves and shelves of books. I remember the reporter's notebook and the swift, efficient scribbling. I suspect Nick, unlike me, has yet to embrace the e-reader. I find that strangely endearing.

One whole bookcase, I note, is devoted to the dark and danger-ous. Rows of crime books, fact and fiction, form orderly lines, the palette of their spines telling its own murky story; like much of the kind of life he's made his business reporting. They are uniformly black and charcoal, stained with red.

Beneath the tomato-coloured jacket he wears an elderly Linkin Park T-shirt. Beneath the T-shirt I can see that he's lean, tanned and toned. All that seaweed surveying, dog walking, beach combing, I imagine.

Then I check myself, embarrassed, because I recognise what I'm actually doing. Not making clinical observations. Just *seeing* him.

I'm seeing the colour of his eyes. When did I stop noticing such details? They are the palest, palest blue. As if chips from a glacier. I see his hands, which are outdoor hands; brown, scratched and worn. I see the contours of his thigh muscles as he crouches to pick up the dog bowls. The sinews in his neck as he turns around to smile at me. And I realise something's happened. I am seeing a man, physically. I don't know if it's somehow related to what I might have found out; to imagine David having perhaps embarked on a sexual relationship before he died – perhaps, even, years back – but something long buried has stirred in me. I *feel* again. And I'm not sure what to make of it. What to *do* with it.

Perhaps just run with it. Heaven knows I could do with a distraction right now. I wonder when and why he got divorced. I congratulate myself for having resisted the urge to google him. I know I'll google him as soon as I get home.

'Houston,' he says, once the coffee's made. 'We have a problem. I don't think I dare try to take this apart to get the battery out of it, not with the screen cracked the way it is.'

'Ah,' I say, sipping mine as he consults a web page on his lap-top. 'So we're stuffed, then?'

'No, not stuffed. I just don't think I dare risk trying to replace it myself. I don't have a small enough screwdriver, for one thing, and for another, I have these.' He waggles his thick-fingered hands.

'But I know someone who can.' He checks the time on his own phone. 'This afternoon, even, maybe, if he's in. He's only down in Penclawydd. I'll give him a call, shall I?'

'Would you mind?'

'Not at all. I have to head down that way later anyway, to pick up some dog food. Plus, you've got me on the case now. I want to know as much as you do. Tell you what,' he adds. I can tell he's already scrolling through his contacts. 'I'll see what I can do with this and call you when I know. And if you've no other plans, I'll stop by later on?'

Our eyes meet, over the laptop, and for just that fraction long enough to confirm that, as of now, I have no other plans. The thesis – the bloody thesis – be damned.

'Okay,' I say. 'Thank you. I'd appreciate that. And, in the meantime, I think I'll go surfing.'

He shakes his head. 'I do *not* understand the attraction. You any good? Do you hang five, or whatever they call it?'

'I'm pretty good,' I tell him, 'but sadly not that good.' Though I'm pleased beyond measure to have someone to tell.

Like most forces of nature, be they human or otherwise, the sea is a harsh, capricious teacher. Of all the sports – and I've skirted around the edges of several – there can be few so at odds with the medium on which they're practised. Few that set you up with such relish to fail.

But like any demanding teacher, the sea repays hard work and commitment. Grudgingly, perhaps – she'll toss you under soon as look at you – but the first time you pop up, and stand up, and *stay* up, it rewards you with a sensation so euphoric and intense that you are immediately enslaved to her.

So, you treat the ocean with respect, and you hope she will be kind to you. And for all that she's abused me, she has been that in spades. Though it was something I only came to appreciate years later, I'd spent a long time at loggerheads with my malfunctioning body, unable to see past my useless, withered womb, zooming in on the one thing it couldn't do for me. Surfing, at least in that respect, saved me. It helped us to make friends again.

I stay out for an hour, even though the sets are weak and erratic, finding more than adequate pleasure in the sea's caress. In immersion, in buoyancy, in spray on my face. In all the routines and rhythms of surfing's singular choreography; paddle out, duck-dive, emerge again beyond the surf line, wait, line the board up, catch the wave, repeat.

I usually leave the sea reluctantly on days such as these, but time is on my mind today, and when I reach the top of the beach steps, I see that Nick is already at the cottage. It's the red of his down jacket I see first, and from some distance. It's draped over the low wall at the side of the back garden, billowing in the breeze like a tiny downed parachute. He is standing beside it, scanning the beach, eyes shielded from the sun by cupped hands. It's gone five and, as I approach, I see his jawline is shadowed.

He turns and sees me and waves, then begins jogging towards me.

'Really,' he says, holding both hands out to take my board from me. 'You didn't need to get all dressed up on my account.'

Though instinct directs me otherwise, I let him take the board. I'm cold and wet, but I know my face is burning. A full-body wet-suit, particularly when wet, is both opaque and revealing.

'I wasn't expecting you quite so soon,' I point out. 'Did you have any luck?'

'Indeed I did,' he says as he follows me into the garden. Where I know he will now note another key left out, recklessly, in another place. 'Though he was up to his eyes, so I've had to leave the phone with him till the morning.'

So he doesn't have the phone with him. He's just brought himself. On the off chance, or on the on chance? On the 'on' chance, it seems, because when he reaches to grab his jacket he also stoops to retrieve a carrier bag, a striped blue one, which clinks as he picks it up. 'So, who is "he"?' I ask.

'Oh, just a techy friend. Website developer. We go back a fair while, and he's good at fixing stuff, so if it's sortable, he'll definitely sort it. I brought wine,' he adds. 'Thought I'd better come good on that proper drink I promised you. And an assortment of stylish nibbles. Well, as stylish as is possible given the constraints of the rural Gower retail landscape.' He gestures to the surfboard. 'So, where does this live?'

I find myself laughing. Warming to the forgotten rhythms of flirtatious conversation.

Once I've got the door open – no comment passed on the key under the boot scraper, I note – and I usher him inside, his proximity unsettles me again. But not in the way I might have expected, either a week back, or a year back. I'm unsettled by *myself* – by how powerfully my nerve endings are pinging.

Normally, when I'm alone, I sluice myself off in the sink after surfing. Wash the salt off, tug the zip tag, peel myself out of my wetsuit. Rinse off, grab a towel, rub my hair, head upstairs.

I grab a towel now. 'Go on through to the kitchen,' I say. 'I need to dry off first, then go up and get changed. Why don't you open the wine?'

'Red or white?' he asks. 'I bought both. Wasn't sure which you liked.' Then a pause. 'You need a hand with that zip, by the way?'

I say, 'White for now, please. And, no, it's okay. I'm fine, thanks.' But I know what he's hoping. He's hoping I'm thinking what he's thinking I'm thinking. And he's right, too. Not *no*. Just *not yet*.

After my shower, I dress again, more thoughtfully than I have in a long time. I'm remembering my mother. She'd married late, and had 'lived a bit' before that, and had sat me down one day, to run through 'logistics' and fill me in on her 'rules of engagement' regarding sex. 'Three main things,' she'd said, from across our vast kitchen table, habitually covered in toast crumbs and tented scientific textbooks. 'Don't mistake lust for love, don't do anything, with *anyone*, that you don't truly want to, and above all – above *all* – don't get pregnant.'

She'd reached across the table then, covered my hands with her own. 'Your body is your own, Julia. Yours to do what you like with. You are answerable to no one but your conscience. But if *any* of those things ever give you cause for concern, *tell* me. There is nothing you can tell me that will shock me or upset me. What *will* upset me, Julia, is if you ever think you can't.'

I feel for her wedding ring, the slim yellow gold band which has its home on the third finger of my right hand. How I wish I could talk to her now.

Not for help. Just to let her know I've ticked all the boxes.

A spritz of perfume, and I patter back downstairs.

The moon is up by the time we've finished our impromptu picnic. Which, shrouded in blankets, and warmed by cold wine, we have eaten on the patio, just outside the kitchen, the better to enjoy the spectacle of the sun going down, spreading a slick of liquid amber across the horizon.

'That is one enormous moon,' he says. 'What's it called? A harvest moon? A blood moon?'

'Just a moon-moon, I think.'

'But so close. So *huge*. It's almost like you can reach out and touch it, it's so big.'

'That's an optical illusion,' I tell him. 'It's really not.'

'Seriously? No. *Look* at it. Come on. It looks *vast*. That's got to be because it's close to the horizon, surely.'

I shake my head. 'It really isn't any bigger. That's your eyes playing tricks. No, your mind, actually. Your eyes see it right, it's just that your brain *interprets* it as being bigger.'

'No way,' he says. 'Seriously? He peers out, beyond the worm. 'No way,' he says again. 'That can't be right, can it? Once it's up there, fully risen, it's way smaller, surely?'

'Nope,' I say. 'It's just that you *see* it as smaller. People used to think it was magnified because it was seen through more atmosphere. But we now know it's not. It's just our brains playing tricks.'

He's opened the second bottle and pours wine into my glass. Then pulls a face. 'You know what my brain's doing now? Hurting.'

'It'll all make sense later, I promise. But it's getting chilly. Let's go inside. I'll bring some wood in and we'll get a fire started, shall we?'

It takes a moment for me to realise that I've said what I've said. Then another, to acknowledge that I *mean* what I've said.

'Hey, hey. Now you're talking,' he says.

Actias luna

The Luna Moth

Oh, for god's *sake*. You know, sometimes I listen to the things you say, Julia, and I think '*Christ*, this wants recording.' Setting down, for posterity. (Which I know *everything* about, obviously.) Seriously, you should listen to yourself.

You've never known that I've been listening, Julia, but I'm your biggest audience. Like a chrysalis on a plant stem, I hang on every word. And, boy, are there a lot of them. Your mouth's so stuffed full of words it's a miracle you don't choke on them. Bless.

The Luna moth, in contrast, doesn't have – or need – a mouth. It emerges for one purpose and one purpose only – to mate. And it has to get a shift on as well; it's a jungle out there, and it has but a week. Seven nights of *amore*, then (take this down, please) it *dies*.

For a couple of weeks, they all thought I was going to die. I was 'hanging by a thread', a source of bleeps and waves and numbers.

Was this high enough, was that low enough, were the wave patterns their multiple monitors created consistent with the continuance of life? Beep. Heartbeat. Beep. Heartbeat. Beep. Heartbeat. Uh-oh! Then the crackle of polyester as the uniforms descended. Tweaked this, altered that, stood and fretted, paddles poised.

By god, though, I was tough. 'Made of stern stuff, this little poppet!'

Tough as nails, me. I wanted life. And I nailed it.

For a few weeks after that, it was, like, 'okay, we can breathe out now'. Only a little, mind. I was not out of the woods yet. Not free of the damned *forest*. When's a shape not a good shape? When it's in *bad* shape, that's when. And that was me. Busted. Not the band, but the body. The body, mind. Take note of that. Just the body. *Not* the mind.

'*They fuck you up, your mum and dad. They may not mean to but they do.*' Oliver James. Noted psychologist. (At least I think it was him said that. Can't look it up right now, sadly.) But let's be honest. It wasn't just them. Yes, they're in the frame, but they're no way the whole picture. Actually, if you were going to take things right back to their molecular level, say, to the point of conception – to the place where my first pair of embryonic cells divided – you could argue that chemistry had a hand in things too. And edging forwards a little, to the point where my parents died, you could, if you chose to, pin some blame on them, I suppose. If Mum hadn't been driving just there, just then – if my sainted mama hadn't made the call to set off at that exact moment, to choose that route over another route, to insist they stop at that zebra crossing – well, of course you could blame them, because that's what people do. 'If only you hadn't been there at that moment! Then you wouldn't have died! You wouldn't have left me! How I HATE you for leaving me!' It's only natural, after all.

Less natural: Trudy and Will. As foster parents, I mean, in the business of fostering faith, hope and charity. But I mean – I think this still, often – what kind of people *were* they? What drove them? To be scrupulously fair, I think they never thought it through. Innocents. Naïve. Cursed by idealism. By optimism. By blind sodding faith with a fat dollop of 'worthy'.

There's a lot I don't remember (bloody epileptic fits – they tend to do that) but I do remember this. Him saying to her – chip, chip, chipping away, always – *Trude, I'm not sure we haven't bitten off a bit more than we can chew with this one.*

Me, a morsel. A lump of gristle. Indigestible gristle.

Eeuww. Which is why they spat me out again.

Chapter 12

When Nick Stone's name flashes up on my mobile the following morning, I'm shocked to find it's gone ten and I've slept through since midnight. Midnight, when he left, to walk home beneath the moon, which he'd grudgingly noted was indeed the same size as it had been on the horizon. It's the longest I've slept in a single stretch for years.

I have a headache from the wine. I have a slightly cricked neck. I've twinges in places I'd forgotten were places. What I don't seem to have is a shred of regret.

'So,' he says. All bright and breezy. 'Sorry, did I wake you? Only I've been and got the phone back—'

'What, already?'

He chuckles. 'I have dogs, don't forget. And – ta-da – I have numbers. Three of them. Got a pen and paper handy?'

I roll over onto my side and ferret around in the bedside table drawer. What is the etiquette in this kind of situation? I am forty-six years old, and I have no idea. I have ticked all the boxes, but I still have *no idea*. But perhaps that's the point. I am breaking new ground here. I have been – I am, I *feel* – wildly irresponsible.

'Pen,' I say. 'Hang on.' I grope around on the floor now, coming up with last week's *British Medical Journal*.

'Okay, paper. Hang on . . .' I shuffle up till I'm sitting. 'Okay. Ready. What d'you get?'

'So, the first one's his own number.' He reels off the digits. 'That's not going to work, but at least you know what it is now. Then this next one is "Mum".' Another set of numbers. 'And this last one is Lewis. As in L.E.W.I.S. A brother, perhaps? A mate? Anyway, I'll leave you to call them. Let me know, yes?'

'Of course.'

'And, well. So . . .' He falters. 'I'll pop the phone back to you later?'

It's a question. A tennis ball. Lobbed into my court.

'I have my daughter coming over, so—'

'Ah,' he says. 'Okay. No worries.'

'So not *too* much later,' I add.

I try 'Mum' first, because, as he says, there's no point in calling Kane's number. And get the standard-issue voicemail, the voice female and generic – where the owner's name is just inserted into a pre-recorded message. The name in this case is Lacey Harrison. Lacey, like a soap character. Harrison, not Scott. Which tells me nothing, but at least I have her name now. And, more importantly, a place to leave a message. I disconnect and reconnect, and this time I leave one. Saying who I am and that I have some things of Kane's. Asking, *please*, when she gets a moment, could she call me?

I then visit Facebook, where there are several Lacey Harrisons, all of whom live in the US. I'm not surprised, because I've already leapt to unfounded assumptions, one being that she probably doesn't bother with social media. So I turn to the other number, which also goes straight to voicemail. But in no more time than it takes for my message to be listened to, my phone rings, and I recognise a habit I'm also guilty of: not answering when the display says 'unknown number'.

But there's no reticence in the voice that says hello. 'It's Lewis,' he tells me. 'You just rang me? About Kane? Man, what's happened to him? Is he okay?'

He has a West Midlands accent and is obviously glad I called. He knows about the accident, he tells me, because his uni tutor told them. But nothing more than that. He was away on a family holiday when the accident happened, and none of his mates have been able to get hold of Kane since then either. Not on his mobile, not on Facebook, not on WhatsApp, not on anything.

'No one's seen him since we all went camping there,' he says. 'Back in August.'

Camping *there*. Back in August. 'What, in Wales?' I ask.

'Yeah, down the Gower. That's where we went. The same place he had the fall. I saw the YouTube. I couldn't believe it. I mean, what the *hell*? I didn't even realise he'd gone back there. Is he really going to be okay, then?

'So far, so good,' I tell him, because that's still all I know. 'Well enough to be transferred to a hospital in London now, at any rate. That's why I called you. Because I can't get hold of him either. And I have some of his things, so I was hoping you might have heard from him. I have his mum's number – at least I think it's hers – but she's not answering either. Do you know her, by any chance?'

'Yeah,' he says. 'Well, sort of. I've met her a couple of times. Been up to stay, like.'

At *last*. 'So where do they live?' I ask.

'Um, Cordon? No, that's not it.'

'Croydon?'

'Yes, that's it. Croydon. Just south of London?'

'Look, if you hear from him can you tell him I'm trying to get hold of him? Tell him I have his phone and watch? I'm sure he'd like them back.'

There's no pause. 'Oh, for sure,' he says. 'Oh, *man*. Shit. You sure he's going to be okay?'

'I'm sure he is,' I tell him, but my mind's already cantered off. Twice. This wasn't a one-off, then. He's been here twice. At *least* twice.

I've just come out of the shower when there's a sharp rap at the door.

Expecting Nick – oh, so *keen*! – I check myself in the mirror before I answer. Then check myself for doing it; I'm not entirely comfortable with feeling so painfully self-aware. But when I open the front door it's a neighbour on the doorstep. Megan, who runs the guesthouse at the Rhossili end of the track.

I like Megan. She is kind. She is capable. She is an extremely thoughtful neighbour. She is also fecund. She has four children, two of each, and the eldest girl is Tash's age. She is a brood mare to my skittish pony. A sunny maternal meadow to my cold, barren tundra.

Was that why I felt so pathologically averse to telling her of my own reproductive woes? Megan was pregnant with her third after I'd just lost my second, and when we bumped into one another (her own bump being so obvious) and she'd asked, entirely reasonably, 'Are you planning on any more?' I'd answered with a clipped, curt 'We'll see.'

Not 'fingers crossed', or 'I hope so', or 'with any luck'. Just *we'll see*. As if the thing that mattered more to me than anything at that time was just some low-priority option at the bottom of an agenda.

Why did I *do* that? Why didn't I just bloody tell her?

She didn't ask again. I'd made it impossible for her to do so without seeming intrusive, so what she can't know, for this error of judgement was entirely my problem, is that the births of her children – nascent planets to her sun – aligned so closely to the losses that punctuated my own universe that whenever their birthdays came around, I would die a little inside. Yes, I'd smile, proffer presents, and dress Tash in her frilly finest – play the 'just-the-one-for-me!' character I'd told myself I must inhabit. And all the while, I'd be brandishing my mental miscarriage calculator; *they would have been three now . . . they would have been four now . . . they would have been . . . they would have been . . . they should have been.* I hated that I did it, but couldn't seem to stop myself. My damascene conversion to acceptance was way too long in coming.

Megan is Sunday-morning sheeny because she volunteers at the village church. She has a cake tin in one hand and a small parcel in the other. 'How *are* you, lovely?' she asks. 'I've been meaning to pop over. You all right? What a thing to happen. Is the young man okay now?'

'I hope so,' I tell her. 'I haven't heard differently. But I'm a bit out of the loop now, to be honest. He's been transferred to a hospital in London – that's where he's from. But yes, last I heard, he was recovering okay.'

'And due in no small part to you, I hear. I read the article in the paper. These kids . . . When will they learn, eh? Still, I'm glad you're all right. Anyway, this is for you. Postman left it with me yesterday.' She hands me the box. 'I would have dropped it round sooner, but I've been jam packed – would you credit it? This late in the season! Group of walkers from Canada. Nice enough kids, but they're running me ragged. You never saw so much food put away at one sitting. Still, it's business. Oh, and these are for you, as well, lovely. You and Tash. Mars Bar brownies.' She hands the tin over with a flourish. 'Enjoy. And now I'd better dash or I'll be late for the repairs committee. Make sure you let me know when you're next down, lovely, won't you? We're long overdue for a proper catch-up.'

I promise I will, even though, to my shame, I know I won't, and take both the tin and the box into the kitchen.

I get very little post when I'm down on the Gower. I don't get much paper post, period. But down here, bar local flyers, mail of any kind's even more unusual. As is the package, which I wasn't expecting.

So what is it? Intrigued, I look for pointers. The label's addressed to me – *Dr Young* – but could it be something Tash ordered? Then, as I open it, a strange earthy smell mushrooms out.

The package inside it – the only thing in there – is triangular, a bit like a samosa made of bubble wrap. It's also sellotaped up, tightly, so I need scissors to open it. And when I finally manage to prise apart the layers of bubble wrap and clingfilm, the smell intensifies and a dozen miniature cotton wool balls come tumbling out.

They are the colour of dirty dishwater. Soft. Lozenge-shaped. Fuzzy.

I pick one up. Sniff it. Recoil at the smell.

Recoil, period. Because it dawns on me that what I'm holding in my hand is not a cotton wool ball. It's a cocoon.

Cochylis atricapitana

The Black-Headed Conch

Everything is connected. That's how it works in food chains. The flies eat the shit, then the spiders eat the flies, then the birds eat the spiders, then the foxes eat the birds. Then man comes along, with his dogs and his horses, and he doesn't eat the fox – he just harries it and harries it. To exhaustion. To near death. Then – just for the hell of it, for the sheer *fun* of it – he *kills* it.

The caterpillar of the black-headed conch is a specialist, its food of choice being the oh-so-common ragwort. It also pupates there, in the roots and the stems. Common ragwort, coincidentally, is poisonous to horses.

Nothing against horses, but you know what? I kind of like – no – I *love* that. In reality, it's just your typical internet hyperbole – no horse ever keeled over from munching on a bit of ragwort. They don't even like it. (Hey, they prefer hay!) So it's mountains and molehills. It's all first-world *fuss*. 'Oh, saints alive, Cecil! We have ragwort in the lower paddock! Oh, Peregrine! Oh, Posy! Oh, do something, do! Jeeves, call a man out! We have *ragwort*!' [*swoons*.]

That's the thing with the food chain. It has a top link and a bottom link. The flies who eat shit. And the shits who create it. People like *your* lot. Pardon me, because, you know ... but like *you*.

I was reconnected. That's how the system works with poor little orphans. You're spat out. You're picked up. You're cleansed and assessed, and then you're allocated, and then you're plugged back in and reconnected to the chain. Connected to a social 'service' (yeah, *right*), who connect you to a social worker, who's connected to a link worker, who's connected to another foster carer. (Or, in my case, a foster witch – cauldron, broom, and all.) Then you're dumped there (say 'Bye, Will, bye Trudy!' Come *on*. Say it *nicely*) and plonked in a bedroom with a shitty Disney duvet, and a stain on the carpet which you don't know, but *do* know, is where the last kid, the lucky kid, the *chosen* kid, pissed or puked. Before speeding off over the forever-family rainbow.

Chapter 13

'Jesus,' Nick says. 'You're right. That is *gross*. What are they? Butterfly pupae?'

He has breezed into the kitchen like a last breath of summer, wearing his tomato-red jacket, a Glastonbury T-shirt and a pair of mirrored sunglasses on his wind-buffeted head. He's brought the scent of the sea in with him. I inhale it gratefully.

'No,' I correct him. 'They're moth pupae. Cocoons. Butterflies make chrysalises. Moths make cocoons.'

'No shit,' he says. 'You know some pretty random stuff.'

'Not as much as you might imagine. I've been googling. I mean I did know, at one time. But I'd forgotten, so I checked. And these things are definitely moth pupae.'

'And sent to you in the post. *Weird*. No note?'

'No note.'

He peers into the open box. 'That is seriously creepy. I mean, it would be anytime, obviously, unless you're a moth breeder or something, but in light of everything else you've told me about, hmm.'

'Exactly.'

I slide my laptop around and click open a tab. 'I've done some research too, and I think they might be tiger moth pupae. See? Though there are so many species, they could be one of dozens. But they definitely sell these—'

He peers. 'Selling pupae is an actual business?'

'Apparently so.'

His fingers glide over the trackpad. 'Wow. It really is, isn't it? Who knew? And for who? I've seen some things in my time, but this is something else. And there's nothing in or on the box that might give us a clue? A postmark? A dispatch note? There's usually a dispatch note.'

I hand the box to him and he screws his eyes up to read the postmark.

'Derby.'

'Which means nothing. That's just the place that sells the pupae.'

'But they'll know who ordered them.'

'And won't tell us, obviously.'

Then we both say simultaneously, 'Because of data protection.'

I laugh, but in reality it's taken me all of the forty-five minutes or so between opening the package and Nick arriving to calm down, to take stock, to give myself a good talking to, and, using techniques that are so instinctive they're almost a part of my DNA now, to consider all the differential diagnoses. To start thinking analytically. To add two and two and find a way to make four. Yes, it *could* be some sick joke designed to freak me out (if so, mission very much accomplished) but equally possible is that I am simply the recipient of a delivery packed in faith and intended for somebody else called Dr Young.

But it isn't. It cannot be. These are *moth* cocoons. And the boy has a *moth tattoo on his wrist*.

I put the cocoons back in the box and close the lid, firmly. Just the thought of them all in there – all that DNA soup, quietly and inexorably recombining – makes me shudder. Means I cannot countenance putting them in the kitchen bin. Any more than I could do so with all those desiccated insect corpses back in June which, having swept them into a dustpan, I lobbed over the garden wall.

Nick picks up the box. 'This is sick, that's what this is. You want me to take them? Best not to bin them,' he adds, as if having read my thoughts. 'Better to keep them, in case, you know, you need to produce them in evidence.'

'Oh, god, this is *horrible*. Why would anybody do something like this? D'you think he ordered them off the internet?'

'From his hospital bed? Well, I guess it's possible. Though why? To what end? Speaking of which, any luck with those phone numbers?'

'Not with the mum one. I've just left a voicemail. But I've spoken to his friend Lewis, and he's as much in the dark as I am. He knows about the accident but he hasn't been able to get hold of him either. So all I've managed to find out is that he lives in Croydon.'

'So that should at least narrow down the hospital. Have you tried any there yet?'

I nod towards the box in his hand. 'Not as yet. Because that thing arrived, didn't it?'

I must have shuddered. Or at least something. Because he tilts his head and frowns. 'This has really got to you, hasn't it?'

'A little,' I concede. Even though I really mean 'a lot'. 'It's just the whole moth thing. The not knowing what the *hell* is going on. It's . . .'

'Come *here*,' he says, coming round the table and circling his arms around me.

'I'm fine,' I insist.

'No, you're *not*. You need a hug. Anyway, I'm spooked as well now. So *I* need a hug. And that's my absolute last word on the matter.'

Which it is. Until, 'Oh,' says another voice. 'Hello. Sorry. Um . . .'

We spring apart, turning around to see Tash's friend Jonathan, with a hessian shopping bag in one hand and a cricket bat in the other. 'Er, um, hi,' he says, placing both on the table with a noisy clatter. 'Just getting the rest of the stuff in!' Then he strokes his nascent beard, turns on his heels and bobs out again.

'Ah,' says Nick. 'So I'm guessing that this might be ever so slightly awkward?'

By the time Tash herself appears in the kitchen, along with Jonathan again (newly bashful), Verity and Cate, Nick has squirrelled the box of cocoons away. I can see the bulge in his jacket pocket, and I'm grateful. Until I've begun to make inroads into what's going on here, it's not something I want Tash to see.

Nick himself, though, is very much present, and I wonder if Jonathan's already told Tash what he saw (would he, though? Would he really?) because I can see she's already weighing him up, wondering why he's in my kitchen. I keep trying to tell myself that *it was only a hug*. That there's no reason why he shouldn't be here. That he could be here – in fact, *is* here – in all innocence this morning. But, given that Tash doesn't know anything about him either – at least, *yet* – there is every reason for there not to be the slightest indication that last night he was also in my bed. It's one thing to be wanton as a single middle-aged woman. Quite another to be wanton as a recently bereaved loving wife and mother.

And it makes me cross with myself, because it shouldn't be like this. But as I'm the only surviving architect of the construction David and I built with such care, I have to take responsibility for its equally careful demolition.

Not right now though. For today at least, what it needs is shoring up. So I'm grateful that, as soon as introductions have been made, the kids are more interested in hearing that we now know Kane Scott has been transferred to London and is apparently out of immediate danger. And that, now I've finally got a phone number for his mother, things will surely soon become clearer.

Nick leaves, bulge in pocket, soon after. And despite Tash's protestations on Thursday that she was so keen to see me, now she's seen me – and inspected my wound – she is happy, and they are not hanging around for long either. Just time enough to get the cool box, the ice packs, a couple of body boards and blankets, the windbreak, the beach umbrella, firelighters, and some kindling to augment the cheap disposable barbecue they brought with them. To make the most of the unseasonable sun.

Though I don't get away scot-free, because while the others go on ahead, Tash lingers on the step for a bit so she can interrogate me privately.

'So that Nick bloke, what's he all about?'

'I told you. He's the journalist who interviewed me for the paper.'

'Yes, I know *that*. But why's he here?'

'I told you. To bring the phone back. Plus, he's kindly said he's going to keep an eye on the cottage for me. At least till we know what's been going on with this Kane boy. Just to put my mind at rest while its standing here empty. It's on his dog-walking route anyway so it's no trouble for him.'

'Oh,' she says nodding. 'Okayyyy.'

Which, actually, I know translates as *Okayyy . . . yeah, right, Mum*. Plus a string of emojis. A pink heart. A blown kiss. A see-no-evil monkey. And the one with the moustache and the tweedy detective hat, who's holding a magnifying glass against his face. Which makes me realise she's already stopped worrying about the riddle of Kane Scott because she's too busy worrying about what's going on with me. Because of all the truths I've failed to tell her.

Once they've gone, I pack my stuff up, tidy up, close and lock all the windows, and leave another bag of groceries and a note for the kids. Then, as per the arrangements agreed via a series of text messages, I lock up and drive over to Nick's place.

And when I'm lying with him in his bed I think the same thoughts as my daughter: *this Nick bloke, what's he all about?*

I don't know yet. But with so many roads blocked to the truth named Kane Scott, I'm immeasurably grateful for the diversion.

Moth,

Fairy Servant to Titania

A Midsummer Night's Dream,
William Shakespeare

Enter Peaseblossom, Cobweb, Moth, and Mustard-seede.
Enter Peaseblossom, Cobweb, Moth, and Mustard-seede.
Enter Peaseblossom, Cobweb, Moth, and Mustard-seede.

Enter Moth.

When I stage it, which I will, I have shotgunned that part. I will be Moth – I will make a *stellar* Moth – and Mum will be Titania. (*In your dreams.* Yes, of *course* in my shitting dreams.)

Though don't run away with the idea that I 'believe' in fairies. I have fairies' measure now, of course. *Bastard changelings.* Nor do I have any truck with superstition, or Ouija boards, or tarot cards, or dowsing, or haruspex, or crystal balls, or any other crap like that. I don't believe. I don't believe *in*. Add whatever word you want to that. I still don't. Believing's for sissies.

Oh, the irony! [*Laughs.*] Because, get this: there was a poster in my new bedroom, above the headboard of my bed. It was whorli-fied, curlified, pale pink and purple, with fairies at the top and fairies at the bottom, and in between the duelling fairy factions there was a poem. About – yup – fairies. It was ripped around the edges and stuck there with Blu-Tack. It had a good bit of previous, I imagined.

(She was called Cherry, my new foster 'mum'. [*Laughs again, dryly.*] The cherry on the top of the fostering cake. Which was a cake with many layers to it. And stale.)

I could imagine her choosing it, too. Cooing, 'Goodness, what a *lovely poster*! How perfect! How sweet! Just the tickety-boo ticket to chase nightmares away from these poor deprived orphaned little childers!' (Because, like, fairies are *so* known for that.) Then hur-rying home to stick it up and make everything *nice*. As if *nice* ever made anything better. And every night she would perch at the foot of the bed, and even though I burrowed down (I was always a burrowing animal; burrowing away, burrowing inside, burrowing under, to escape the world) she'd sit there and read out the bloody poem. (I try not to – so hard – but I could still recite it blindfolded. Even though it's shit and scans so poorly.)

Believe in the Fairies
Who make dreams come true
Believe in the wonder
The stars and the moon
Believe in the magic
From the Fairies above
They dance on the flowers
And sing songs of love
And if you just believe
And always stay true
The Fairies will be there
To watch over you.

Then she'd coo, and she'd rise, and she'd trot up to the head end. 'Kissy kissy,' she'd chirrup. Then she'd bend down and kiss me, wafting wire hair and fag breath on my face. 'Sleepy tight, little one!' she'd coo. 'Sweet dreams!'

I didn't do dreams, sweet or savoury. I did nightmares. Though, if you want to be pedantic – and, of course, I often do – my records record (neatly, faithfully, often) that they were not common or garden nightmares, but night 'terrors'.

So, despite all the fairies, and all their disingenuous dancing, singing crap, I'd fall asleep and be transported. Into dragon-infested underworlds. Into dungeons and oubliettes. Into sky, without wings. Into oceans, without gills. Into the wild woods, without any grizzly bear-slaying gear.

Then I'd wake, in the small hours, the scary hours, the witching hours, the pitch-sodding-dark-because-she-had-a-sodding-lights-out-policy hours – and I'd be shaking, and screaming, and sobbing, and quivering, and in she'd lumber, nightie flapping, all mad-haired, like Einstein, going, 'There, there, what's up? Did you have a nasty, naughty nightmare? Come on, chuck, it's all right, settle down, it's all right now.' And she'd kiss me again, and, eventually, despite the lingering scent of insincerity, I would go back to sleep.

And then, the next day, she'd discover I'd wet the bed. (What, *again?*)

And, despite all the crap about the fairies watching over me, she'd pull down my pyjama bottoms and spank me.

Chapter 14

Once I'm back home in London, I set up camp at the dining room table. Not just because I'm still feeling so spooked by the bizarre package Megan delivered. It's also because to not sit in here is to leave the room dark and empty, and, increasingly, I'm finding certain dark, empty rooms difficult. Unlike my breezy relationship with the friendly ghosts of Gower, the ghosts in this room – our ghosts – feel oppressive and malevolent, and though I don't know of what, quite, I am scared.

So, with every light blazing, and all the windows shut against any winged things that might wish to join me, I sit down at the dining table and set to work. And as with the credit card statements, it proves stupidly easy to find what I'm looking for. I have itemised mobile phone bills going back to the previous autumn, and once I've gathered them together, I begin trawling through them, first for the number for 'Kane Scott???', which I have now reduced to just '???', then 'Lewis', then 'Mum'. None bear fruit. Which, at least in experimental terms, still constitutes a result – and which I mentally set aside to ponder later.

I then search for Kane's own number, which I've saved to check last. And immediately, like coal seams embedded in rock strata, I see clusters of phone calls, both made and received. They date back to the start of the period I have bills for: two here, three there, the odd single phone call. Then, last November, a glut; a run of seven calls, two of which run to thirty-plus minutes, which have pinged back and forth over a space of three days.

What, though – what the *hell* – were they saying to each other?

There's a gap, then. Most notably in December, where there's nothing. Which seems odd because December was when David acquired the second Breitling. I recheck Christmas, then New Year, then on through to February, where there is a nineteen-minute incoming call, taken one week and four days before the calls come to an end. One week and four days before the bill comes to an end.

One week and four days before David's *life* came to an end. I set the final sheet of paper down in front of me. And a wisp of a thought whispers darkly through my defences. Could David's death and this call be connected?

Then, *bam*. Something else hits me. Where there are calls, there might be messages. And though the contents of David's iPhone will now forever remain unknowable, his iMessages may be on the hard drive of his Mac, just like mine are. All I need is his password.

Which I don't have. Why would I? The laptop was bought six months post our covert de-coupling. I remember Tash laughing. 'Seriously, *Dad*? Getting a *MacBook*?' With the sort of withering-but-affectionate inflection to her voice that's achieved so effortlessly by loving daughters.

I choose to text rather than phone Tash, because it's almost eleven. And it's Sunday, which in my world, is late. I also text because to phone is to invite speculation, and I'm not sure I'm ready to field awkward questions. At least not till I have amassed sufficient knowledge to make an assessment about how awkward the answers to those questions might be.

Heyyy, sweetie, I text. *My laptop's playing up. Got the password for Dad's Mac, please? Have a thesis deadline crisis looming. Urghhhhhh!*

I add a laptop, a lightbulb, some paper, a pencil, a spanner, a thumbs up and a turtle.

She calls back immediately. 'Bloody hell, Mum – *stop working!*'

'I know,' I say, feeling chastened for both the lie and the truth. She might be ten again, tugging at my sleeve while I type. Mu-*um*. Come and *play*. You're always *working*. 'I will. Very shortly. Just this one thing to get finished off and I promise I will. Bloody computers,' I add, for effect.

'Okay . . .' she says. 'Hang on, let me . . . *Hang* on. Where are you?'

'In the kitchen.'

'As in home?'

'Yes, of course. Where else would I be?'

'Oh,' she says. 'That's okay, then. Just when you said you wanted to use Dad's laptop, I thought you must still be down the Gower.' A nine-month pregnant pause. 'For some reason.'

'Ah,' I say, taking note of it before pressing on. Oh, she's sharp. 'No, it's here. I brought it back with me last time I was down. After my dressing down the other week, I decided it maybe wasn't such a good idea to leave valuables down there. Anyway, have you found it?'

'Hang on,' she says. 'Just got to find the right note. Here we are. Right. 'kay. So, ready? It's meaningoflife. All lower case. All one word. No spaces. Then a question mark, then it's number—'

'—forty-two.' We say it simultaneously.

'Then another question mark,' she adds. Then, 'Hang on. How did you know the number?'

'It's from a famous quote,' I say. 'From a very famous book. *The Hitchhiker's Guide to the Galaxy.*' David's favourite ever book in fact. Why did he never read it to her?

'The what?'

'I'll tell you when I see you. You'll have to read it. It's good. And now I'd better scoot, sweetie, or I'll never get to bed, will I?'

And we ring off and it's fine. But I don't go to bed. I lift the lid – the scary maw – of David's laptop.

It takes a good while to sift through David's iMessages. An eerie, unsettling and heartbreaking business, not least because the last one on the list, from a close colleague, reads *Dave, you free? About that patient. Can you call me urgently?* It had landed on his phone at 11.07. Half an hour after he collapsed. Half a day before he died.

I'm also surrounded by photographs of him and when I dare to meet his gaze, it hits me in a way that it has never done before. That he really is gone. That he is never coming back. That he will never walk into this room again, on a quest for some man-thing or other, and roll his eyes, and say, *really,* Jules, yet *more* bloody photos?

There are more similar messages, from contacts both known and unknown to me.

Dave, I have the scan result.

Okay, mate, in the diary.

Me again – sorry! – how about 3 p.m. Thursday?

And among them, from Tash, just the day before he'd died, the most heart-wrenching of all of them.

Daaaddyyyyy, re Friday, how exciting! Yes, indeed I can. Shall I book Jamie's Italian? Can't wait to seeee you! Proseccccccco times! Woop! (Smiley face. Pizza. Balloon. Italian flag.)

I'm scanning through tears by the time I finally find what I'm looking for. Just a number, which matches – Kane was not saved with a name – and an unbroken chain, the most recent at the end of January, which I scroll through in reverse, last to first. Then first to last, but, whichever way, they tell me almost nothing. Few in number. Mostly factual. I take screenshots of them all.

I'm on the Waterloo train. See you at 11.

OK.

Coming into Paddington. Train delayed. Might be late.

OK.

Meeting has run on. (This is David.) *20 mins.*

No rush! Have a copy of the New Statesman to keep me busy lol.

On they go. One, two, three, four, five, six, seven exchanges. Brief exchanges. *Male* exchanges. No kisses. No emojis.

But then, in November, corresponding to the call glut, there's one from Kane, which simply says: *I'm sorry* ☹☹☹☹☹.

Then, almost immediately, from David: *Not your fault. I'll sort it. Don't worry. We'll talk.*

About what?

Then a gap. Then, come late January, ten days before that lengthy phone call, their final text exchange:

On Waterloo train. All OK so far!

OK.

Just made it. Phew! See you soon.

Good. OK.

See him *where*? Was this their final meeting?

I could weep when I read the words *New Statesman*. The magazine had always been David's political bible. He'd read it every week since I'd known him. Latterly, had subscribed. Had tried to get Tash interested as well.

But had singularly failed to ignite the flame. *We'll get there*, he'd say. *Give it time, and a fair wind, and we'll get there.* He was like a puppy about politics; an excitable debater. He'd have so loved to inspire Tash to engage.

A worm of pain wriggles through me. For the wind that cannot blow now. But this boy . . . this secret project . . . this filial chimera . . . this willing new devotee to the bright hope of socialism? I don't know how I am supposed to feel. But it hurts.

The main puzzle, however, is what was he sorry for? What needed sorting? Was he *blackmailing* David? Was the watch not a gift, but a pay-off? But the tone . . . the emojis . . . the New bloody Statesman. I dismiss the errant thought process immediately. No. He *liked* David. And David liked him? Again, that *New Statesman* says it all.

But what does it *mean*? All this clandestine texting? The two people who do know manifestly can't tell me. And the one person who might hold a key to the puzzle is ignoring my message. Perhaps I need to abandon polite reticence and chase her.

It's with the word 'chase' still very much in my head that I pull my phone out of my bag on my way to the car park at the end of the next day. Why the hell shouldn't I chase her? I have a perfectly valid reason to, after all. Six thousand-odd reasons, in fact. Which is why, while I'm finding the number, and there's an incoming call from Laura, my thumb hovers uncharacteristically over the 'sorry, I can't talk right now' option.

It's not only that. I am tired, and I don't want to talk to her. But my sister-in-law shares qualities with the notorious Japanese knotweed. If I don't deal with her now, she will only come back stronger.

'Laura. How are you?'

'I'm fine,' she says. Sharply. 'Julia, I'm sorry, but you really need to tell Tash the truth.'

Sorry not sorry. But I'm caught off guard momentarily. Then remember Tash mentioning she was meeting Laura for coffee. So, today? Yes. Why else would she be phoning?

'About what?' I say.

'About you and David, of course.' Her tone is waspish. 'She's not stupid, Julia. She knows something's going on.'

Since I don't know what Laura knows, I'm not sure how to answer. But I don't need to. She supplies it. 'About the business with this *boy*.'

'What about him?' I ask, more to play for time than anything.

'Who he is. What he's got to do with David. The son of someone?'

'Ahem, *clearly*.'

'Why must you always be so *flippant*?' I feel the static coming off the phone. 'The son of someone who's got something do with *David*. She came right out with it, you realise. As if *I'd* know anything about it. She thinks he was having an affair.'

I'm caught off guard. Is this why she was so twitched about Nick? 'Why?' I ask Laura. 'What did she say?'

'Oh, just suspicions. This and that. Things he'd said, odd things. That he was keeping something from her, basically. She's very perceptive, you know, Julia.'

'Er, I think I know that, Laura.' Of course I bloody know. I'm her *mother*!

She ignores me. 'So, *was* he?'

I'm keen to point out that, since we were separated – well, as good as – to call it 'an affair' would not only be inaccurate, it would also, if true, be none of my business. But to do so would be to play into her hands, which, almost on principle, I don't want to do. 'I have no idea,' I say. 'To be honest, Laura, I'd have imagined you'd be better placed to answer that than I can.'

'*Me?* Why would I know?'

'Because you knew about the rest of it? Because he might have confided in you, perhaps? But, yes, you're right,' I carry on, leaving the question to settle. 'There is definitely a connection between him and the boy. They were in touch with one another for several months before he died. Whether that means there is a woman involved as well, I don't know. But it doesn't seem outside the bounds of possibility.'

There is a silence while she recalibrates her world-view. Her David-view. Which I imagine is difficult, because his pedestal is lofty. Not to mention slippery, from all the polish she applies. 'Good grief,' she says, finally. 'So there might be?'

'Yes, there might be.'

I'm tempted to also point out (the watch and secret meetings notwithstanding) that there is no law I'm aware of that David has fallen foul of. That if he was seeing someone, it's history now anyway. Except what I won't say, but increasingly think, is that there *will* be more to it. That David and Kane Scott go back a *lot* further. No, I don't yet have evidence, but, equally, I'm not an idiot.

But perhaps I am, damn you, Laura. Tash must have known full well that I was lying about why I wanted David's password.

Laura huffs. 'Well, can't you ask him?'

'How, exactly? I don't know where he is, do I? And till his mother returns my call, I have no means of finding out. And the fact that she *hasn't* . . .'

I almost think I can hear her swallowing her bitter pill.

'Well, whatever,' she says, rallying. 'But you still need to speak to Tash. Whatever did or didn't happen with this boy, *or* his mother, the fact remains that this whole charade about you and David has gone on far too long now. It's all very well airbrushing the past if there's some benefit, but in this case there clearly isn't. She knows you're not being straight with her, and you need to put that right.' Half a beat. 'Julia, it's a question of *trust*.'

And I'm not sure how it is that I come off the phone thinking it's me who's done something wrong here, but, damn it, I do. Damn *you*, Laura. Lecturing *me*? About *trust*?

And damn you too, David. How could you leave me with all this to deal with?

And then, of course, I feel worse. I signed up to it. So I'm as guilty as he is.

There's been some sort of demonstration going on in Fulham, so it's almost eight by the time I'm finally on the home straight to Clapham, still fretting about my conversation with Laura. Though it's mostly me I'm at odds with because, irritating though it is, I have to accept that she's probably right. Tash will have been chewing over the same questions as I am, and my batting them away will not have altered that fact. Plus, she's a psychology undergraduate. She's supposed to read between the lines and ask questions, isn't she? As should I. More robustly. So while I'm stationary in a line of traffic on Albert Bridge Road, I bring up Lacey Harrison's number and try it again. And, once again, it goes straight to voicemail.

But ten minutes later, my phone rings. Lacey Harrison's name comes up on the dashboard display, just as I'm manoeuvring into a parking space four houses down the road.

Reg is standing sentinel in his bay window, making notes. I wave to him. Smile. Thinking, *finally*.

Anxious not to miss the call, I keep the engine running so I can leave it on loudspeaker, and when I say hello, a sonorous female voice fills the car.

'I'm so sorry I haven't called you back sooner,' she says. 'I've been out of credit.'

'That's absolutely fine,' I say. 'I'm just so glad you called. You have much more important things to be worrying about. How is Kane?'

It feels strange to say his name to her. It feels strange to finally talk to her. She has the same south London accent that my gran did.

'He's doing okay, thank you,' she says.

'Off life support?'

'They took him off the ventilator before they moved him. Well on the mend now, fingers crossed. Still got a way to go, but definitely better than he was.'

'That's good to hear,' I say. 'I've been worrying about him.' Not to mention worrying *about* him, which I have already decided not to mention, because I'm terrified that if I do I'll scare her off again. 'And, as I said in my message, I also still have his phone. And his watch. Assuming it *is* his, that is. It was in a backpack, which I think he must have dropped? Did he mention it?'

'Yes, of course it's his,' she says, almost cutting across me. 'Who else's would it be?'

She's brisk, this female stranger, but there's no note of challenge or defensiveness. And it's a rhetorical question anyway, so I treat it as such. 'Oh, of course,' I say. 'And I'm keen to get it back to him, obviously. I'm hoping you'll be able to solve a mystery for me, too. Because it seems my late husband bought it for him. And I'm at a bit of a loss to know what the connection was between them. I—'

I'm drowned out by the blaring of a car horn. 'I know he did,' she says. 'Look, I'm sorry, but I really can't talk to you at the moment. My friend's just arrived to pick me up and she's on a yellow line, so I have to go.'

'Later, then?' I try, anxious that now I've found her she still might slip through my fingers. Did she even hear the last bit of what I said? Or is she actively ignoring it? 'Or perhaps I could meet you somewhere? At the hospital, perhaps?' I hear shortness in her breath. She's presumably off to meet her lift now. 'Or I could come to you if that's easier?'

'That would be better,' she says, 'as long as it's not too much trouble for you, Dr Young. I have MS, and I'm not very mobile.'

'I understand completely,' I tell her. 'And it's no trouble at all. How about tomorrow, perhaps? Early evening? I'm only in Clapham.'

To which she agrees, giving me an address in south Croydon, and asking me to ring when I'm on my way. Just like that.

And it all feels too easy. Too relaxed. Too unlikely. Too entirely at odds with every scenario I have imagined. *As long as it's not too much trouble for you, Dr Young.* As if I'm making a home visit to a grateful patient.

Reg has emerged onto his path now. He lifts both eyebrows and a thumb. I raise my own thumb. *All okay*, I mouth at him. But is it?

I have no idea, but at least it's progress, which I decide to run by Nick. I'm just dithering, however, about whether to phone or text him, when my phone buzzes again, with his name on the display.

'You must be psychic,' I tell him. 'You won't believe what's just happened. Kane Scott's mother has finally called me. David *did* buy the watch for him. She's just confirmed it. I'm going to visit her at home tomorrow evening and, fingers crossed, get some answers.'

'And he's still in hospital?'

'Yes. He'll be there for a couple of weeks yet. I'm going to ask – no, demand – to be allowed to visit him.'

'Sooooo,' he says, drawing the word out as if thinking. 'That definitely puts paid to one theory, then. Which was admittedly a pretty unlikely theory, and not one I much subscribed to, but . . .'

'But what?'

'I'm just back from taking the dogs out. I went to check on your cottage—'

'Thanks so much for doing that. But what?' I'm growing anxious. 'Was everything okay there?'

'At the cottage, yes, as far as I could see, but listen. That's why I'm ringing. There's been something else.'

He goes on to tell me that he was just crossing the stile when he noticed something odd down on the beach. So he tramped through the ferns, to where the plateau meets the cliff, and saw that on the stretch directly below the cottage, something had been written in the sand.

'Writ large, too,' he adds, 'in enormous bold capitals. Left to right, this is. Facing the house – not the sea. In a place where you'd see it if you were looking out of the windows. It said – brace yourself – NOW YOU'VE GONE AND RUINED EVERYTHING, JULIA.'

Just in front of my car, Reg is standing at the kerb, making notes.

'My actual name, then.'

'Yes. Macabre, isn't it?' Nick says. 'I took a picture. I'll send it. Fortunately, it's a clear night so you can just about make it out.'

'No doubt that it was meant for me to see, then. Not this time.'

'That was *exactly* my first thought. Or for me, to pass on to you. I've been tramping this route for several days now, don't forget. And you've just confirmed my second thought as well.'

'Which was?' I ask, even though I already know the answer.

'Which was that Kane Scott couldn't have written it, could he?'

Pterophorus pentadactyla

The White Plume Moth

You know what they say about white moths? A *lot*. That they embody the soul of someone dear and departed. That they embody the soul of someone dear but not departed. That someone dead's trying to speak to you. That someone's ill and going to cop it.

That *something wicked this way comes . . .*

Flitting in on its ghostly five-fingered wings.

According to Hopi lore (folk tale territory again, folks!) the cocoon stage is symbolic, denoting change. It's the pause, in the silent darkness, where metamorphosis happens. When the one thing – that crawling caterpillar, with attendant lowly world view – transitions to the new thing it's now destined to become. A flying thing, a thing of beauty, with all of nature now in reach. With a new view, a view from on high, from the night sky. Cocoon as watershed. Cocoon as catalyst. Cocoon (oh, aren't I just the sneak?) as fair warning.

Anyway, make of that what you will, Julia. When it comes to myths and symbolism you pays your money and you takes your choice, see? That's how it always, always works. Literally anything you want to read into anything, you got it. It flitters in, you think 'Aha – what can this possibly *mean*?' Then you pretty much make it up as you go along, to suit your need. Which is why you shouldn't believe everything you read.

Which is why I don't. (And I have now read a lot. A *lot*. A LOT.) And which is why I am so *incandescent* with fury that they did. That she did. That Laura P. Middlemiss, BSc (hons), Supervising Social Worker, believed every last evil thing that vile harpy wrote. About *me*.

I'm sad to say [no, you aren't] *that this child presents with increasingly aggressive and challenging behaviours.*

I have to say [no, you don't] *that there has been a regrettably marked increase in a tendency to tell alternative truths.*

It seems to me [well, of *course* it would] *that this is a child with a) a profound attachment disorder, b) a lack of empathy, and c) sociopathic tendencies.*

It's difficult to imagine, going forward [why? Damn it! WHY? Why not use your imagination?] *that a family situation is going to work in the longer term.*

I confess [yes, you should, on your knees] *that I am no longer able . . .*

People sit round tables. In houses. With cups of tea and biscuits. And read shit and talk shit and make shit decisions. They are called 'strategy' meetings. I'm not allowed.

'You mustn't think it's your fault, kiddo.' This is Sam. As in Samuel. As in Samuel R. Williams, BSc (hons), Social Worker. (Not 'Supervising' just yet. Apart from me – at least in theory.)

We're in the park just round the corner from where the bitch lives. Where I live. Where I have lived for a full seventeen months and six days now. Where I have a sodding fairy poster, and get slapped about a lot, but where I have at last – at last! – made a friend in school.

Where a friend in school *matters*.

He is called Amir, from Pakistan, so he gets called a 'paki'. And he hates being called that. Wouldn't you hate being called that? And because he's my friend, I hate him being called that as well. I'm a good friend. A loyal friend. I *understand* the rules of friendship. And half the reason the old cow thinks I'm such a problem is that she called him a paki, and *I heard her*. I heard her, over the fence, yabbering on to her nosy neighbour. And I called her a new thing I learned from Amir's older brother. I said, 'There's a name for women like you, you know: racist twat.'

I still have the bruises. I could 'disclose' them. I won't bother. I like to hang on to stuff, just in case.

We are in the park, and I'm riding the bike I brought with me. As in it's the bike I brought with me when they brought me here. The bike Trudy and Will bought me as a 'little leaving present', so when they spat me out, my 'little leaving' wouldn't leave such a big bad taste in their mouths.

'I'm taking it,' I tell him stoutly. 'It's mine, she can't keep it.'

'Of course you are,' Sam puffs. He is running alongside me. Until he is a supervising social worker, this is the sort of thing he has to do. 'Don't be daft. It's your property,' he says. Then adds '*Obviously*.' Though there is nothing obvious about it. She 'confiscated' it (her favourite word) for a whole month last month. She could confiscate it again. Why doesn't he *get* that?

We are on one of our 'little bike rides'. (*'Tell you what. Shall we go for a little bike ride?'* Why don't they buy Sam a bike? That's what I'd like to know.)

'I *hate* her,' I tell him. 'I'm *happy* she's getting rid of me. She's a *liar*.'

'Now, come on, kiddo,' Sam says. 'She's not getting *rid* of you. You *know* we've already spoken about this. Now then, how about we stop for an ice cream?'

Things I want:
A Tamagotchi
A rat
A bigger bike
My parents back

Things I do not want:
A bloody ice cream

Further gems from the treasure trove that is the Freedom of Information Act! I am (was, already, even *then*) 'academically able'. I have 'untapped potential'. I have a 'remarkably high IQ'. (Why is that so bloody *remarkable*? WHY?)

But I am also 'of concern'. I am 'volatile'. I am 'worryingly prone' to having 'flights of ideas'. Peter Pan. He can fly. Peter Piper. He can't. Peter Piper is a picker. He picked a peck of pickled peppers. (I can keep this up all day. You might have noticed.) Or should that be poppers? No, in this case – pahaha – not *those* poppers. But I *am* a druggy – always have been. A state-sponsored druggy. I've been popping pills for years, me, to keep the real me at bay. The unmedicated me – all seizures and attitude and dangerous preoccupations. Me Who Must Not Be Seen Or Heard Or Else. I've been on Tegretol for epilepsy. On Ritalin for ADHD. On Melatonin for the sleep necessary to enable the night terrors.

Drug, drug, druggy. Hardly surprising that I now have quite the taste for it.

Chapter 15

Lacey Harrison lives in a short, balloon-shaped cul-de-sac, just a handful of streets off the Brighton Road. It's one of those residential spurs, snaking steeply uphill, with a bus stop and a row of tired shops. I see a newsagent. A chemist. A building society. A Sainsbury's Local. Driving past, it occurs to me that if she no longer drives herself, the word 'local' means nothing in practical terms. Without willing friends and neighbours, or some kind of care package, she's almost as isolated as we are down on the Gower. Whatever assumptions I've made about her, one thing I do know. I'd find it excruciating to be so dependent. Dependency makes you vulnerable. Is she? Just how much, or how little, does she know?

A quick recce makes it clear that I'm never going to be able to park there. It's the time of day when commuters all come home to roost, squabbling like starlings over the scant space available. So I drive past the cul-de-sac and squeeze the car into a spot beside a row of railings, long since colonised by spears of dusty buddleia. A plastic undergrowth blooms in the dust beneath.

Hers is one of the two end houses, a flat-fronted semi, with a low hedge and a cracked concrete pathway. Dying bedding plants flank a small lawn, but it still looks respectable. Cared about and cared for.

The half-glazed front door is painted a bright cornflower blue. I press the bell to the side of it and wait. It's a long time before there is any sign of life from within, but eventually a dark shape appears and draws nearer, and I imagine her slow, tortuous progress to the door. And something occurs to me. Has David stood on this very doorstep? I wish I had a clue what I'm dealing with. Who her son is. If he's seriously mentally ill.

The door finally opens, warm air billowing out. And Lacey Harrison is not what I expected. She is tall and large, and a good deal older than I imagined she'd be. She looks to be in her late fifties, perhaps even early sixties, with bobbed salt-and-pepper hair that ends just above her shoulders, and, as my gaze makes an inventory of all the symptoms I've anticipated, her smile of welcome makes it clear that she is doing the same with me. Even knowing that surnames mean little or nothing, I simply cannot imagine her as Kane Scott's mother.

And David? I think. *David's lover?*

'Well, this is a bit of a business, isn't it?' she says. There is no hint of guardedness or tension. She steps back to make space for me. 'Come on in.'

I step into a narrow hall which is hot and smells of toast. It's wallpapered in blowsy florals, but almost the first thing I notice is that almost every usable inch is covered in photographs of children, clustered randomly, in a variety of frames. I spot Kane more than once as I follow my host down the hallway, my eyes drawn to a series of school portraits that dominate. It's deeply unsettling to see his face again. Even more so to see it as it should be, rather than an adjunct to a host of machinery. Does a warped mind lie behind that innocent face?

There are also pictures of many other children, several of them as babies. Though instinct and observation tell me she must struggle financially, it's a home obviously rich in all the important ways.

There is a black cat halfway up the stairs, which looks down at me from amber eyes; stairs which are dominated by the ugly, utilitarian presence of a stair lift.

Lacey walks awkwardly ahead of me, with a stick, which she eventually parks by the kitchen doorway. 'Come on in,' she says again. 'Excuse the mess.'

There is no mess. Just a room full of things. Pot plants on the windowsill. Ornaments on shelves. Two clocks. A pair of coat hooks. A plastic-bag holder. A red three-tier veg rack. And on the front of the fridge there is a jumble of plastic letters, seven of which spell out the word *dentist*.

'Thank you for agreeing to see me,' I say, as she pulls out one of two kitchen chairs for me, and insists on making tea. Even though I don't want tea, I find it impossible to deny her, but it's difficult to watch because it's such a complicated and painful business, every small feat of co-ordination made so obviously herculean by the neurological ravages of her disease. I want to help her but sense I mustn't – pride emanates from her like an aura – so I sit down and stay down, while she moves around the kitchen, finding mugs, getting milk out, taking teaspoons from a cutlery drawer, plucking saucers from a still-steaming dishwasher. Finally, she lowers herself heavily onto the other chair. A lazy fly repeatedly headbutts the kitchen window.

'How is Kane doing?' I start with. 'I've been worried about him.' And as I say the words I mightily wish they were the whole truth. That I could come clean now and add that I am worried about what he *is*.

'*You've* been worried about him?' she says mildly. 'Tell me about it.'

I sense no anxiety in her voice or her manner. In fact, she looks sympathetic, even strangely serene. What she absolutely doesn't look is guilty or defensive. Neither does she look even remotely reminiscent of any of my stereotypical stock images marked 'mistress'. But what does (what *should*) a mistress look like anyway?

She smiles as if aware of the story cards I'm shuffling. Or perhaps not. 'He's going to be all right,' she says. 'Or so they tell me. And I've no reason to disbelieve them. He's coming on better than expected, in fact. Specially since he's been reunited with his flipping laptop.'

Ah, I think. So he could definitely have sent those cocoons. But not written that message. So who did? 'And his head injury?'

'All okay too, it seems. Thank goodness. Just brain swelling. You'd probably know more about that sort of thing than I do, but his CT scan today was apparently normal, so that's one less thing to worry about. Just his leg now. I'm hoping to have him home in two weeks. Well, I say home. He'll be off back to uni then, of course.'

'That's really good to hear,' I say. 'And I'm so glad I managed to track you down.' I pluck my bag up from where I've parked it on the floor beside my chair. 'I have Kane's phone, as I said. And his watch, of course . . .'

I slip a hand into one of the side pockets, and retrieve both, aware of her silent scrutiny as I place them on the kitchen table. She looks at the watch as if greeting an old enemy.

'And you must be wondering just what the heck is going on, I imagine.'

'Just a bit,' I admit, as she hauls herself up again to fill the teapot. 'Look, please, can't I do that for you?'

'No,' she says, smiling. 'You can't.' Then she pats me as she passes, a warm, friendly weight on my shoulder. And her manner is so unlike anything I had anticipated, that I have absolutely no idea what she's going to tell me, far less how I begin to tell her of my multiple concerns about what her son might have been up to. Will she have any idea?

'I'm not sure where to start,' she says, once she is back sitting opposite me, the tea made and poured. The cat wanders in and tries to climb up on her lap, and she spends a moment fussing it. Tendrils of steam rise in commas between us.

'Well, with this?' I suggest, pointing to the watch that glints on the table. It's probably worth more than the combined contents of her kitchen, yet, within it, it's diminished. Too showy.

She looks at it again, with distaste. 'He should never have accepted it,' she tells me. 'We were fine as we were. We *are* fine. I don't even know what he was thinking giving it to him. Guilt, I imagine. But that's ridiculous, isn't it? He owed him nothing. And we certainly don't need or want his charity.'

She doesn't try to disguise her irritation at David. 'Is that what this was, then?' I ask. 'Charity?'

She relents and hauls the mewling cat up onto her lap. 'I dare say he wouldn't have called it that – your late husband, I mean. I'm sure he gave it to Kane with the best of intentions, just like everything else, but I knew it would cause more problems than it was ever going to solve. All this raking over the past – I just knew it wouldn't end well. And for what? Look where we are now. Can you imagine if you hadn't been there that morning? It doesn't bear thinking about, does it?'

I agree that it doesn't. 'But why did my husband buy it for him? That's what I don't understand. I mean, it's such an expensive watch. It's—'

'I'm well aware what it cost.' Irritation pinches her face again. And this time it's directed at me.

I feel my own hackles rise. 'I didn't mean anything by that,' I point out. 'It's just – well, it's a pretty bizarre thing to have discovered. And it's exactly the same model as his own watch. Did Kane tell you? So I'm sure you'll appreciate that this has all come as a bit of a shock to me.'

She is about to raise her mug to her lips but she stops and places it carefully back in the saucer. Where it wobbles, which it would, because it doesn't belong to the saucer. It occurs to me that the saucers are there solely for my benefit. Who puts a saucer under a mug? I realise I've already been allocated a pigeonhole; one marked 'posh'.

But her eyes are again kind – almost as if she can read what I'm thinking.

'It was for his birthday,' she says. She shakes her head slightly. Winces as the cat kneads her knees. 'You really don't know anything about all this, do you?'

'No. Only what I've been able to piece together, which is precious little. That there is – *was* – obviously a relationship between them. That much, at least, I do know.'

'But you do know he's Kane's father.'

A statement. Not a question. Which is interesting in itself. And no, I didn't, but I did. So there's no element of shock. No gasp of incredulity. I've turned the possibility over in my head too many times for that. But something still turns over inside me when she says this.

'I thought so,' I say. 'And you're obviously his mother, so—'

'Foster mother,' she corrects me. 'I'm Kane's *foster* mother.'

Now I *am* shocked. Because that's a dynamic that has never even occurred to me.

'Oh, I *see*,' I say. 'Right. That explains a great deal.'

'I thought it might,' she says.

'But what happened to his birth mother, then? If David's his father, then—'

'Long dead,' she says. 'She died only days after he was born. Awful road accident. Fatal. That's why he came into care. He was only a couple of weeks old when they brought him to me. Premature, too.' She smiles fondly now. 'Just a scrap of a thing.'

My mind clunks into another gear, grasping for a cog to hang on to. A baby. Just a baby. So . . . 'How old is he?'

'He'll be twenty-one in January,' she says, cupping her hands around the mug again. 'Oh, I see what you're thinking. But it's nothing like that. Your husband didn't know anything about it. Yes, he knew Kane's mother, but he didn't know about Kane. Not then. Well, I say he didn't. I could be wrong on that. I obviously only know what social services told me.'

There is nothing obvious about any of this, at least not to me. I scroll through a mental calendar, trying to work dates out, trying to make sense of what she's telling me. So did David have some tawdry one-night stand with someone else? *Christ.* When I was pregnant with Tash?

And who now might be stalking her?

Lacey stretches a hand out, touches my fingers. 'You're barking up the wrong tree,' she says. 'Yes, your husband was Kane's father but only his *biological* father. He just donated the sperm. I'm sorry. I thought you knew that much at least.'

I am rarely lost for words. I am rarely lost, period. But I am totally lost for words now. I am as lost as I can be. 'But—'

'Hang on,' she says, sliding her tea slightly away from her. 'I'm just confusing you even more, aren't I? I've brought his box down. Let me – actually, why don't you grab it for me. It's just there.' She points behind me. 'That big blue box on the worktop. It'll probably make more sense if I show you.'

I push my chair back and do as instructed. It's a shoe box. One of the ones where the lid levers up. And covered not with paper, but with a thin denim cloth, and with the name Kane neatly appliquéd in felt letters on the top. It's old and worn, and obviously precious.

I take it back to the table and place it between us.

'This is what's known as a memory box,' she explains, turning it around to face her. 'Lots of children in foster care have them.

They're encouraged to. It's where they keep all their special things. Keepsakes and pictures, letters, postcards and so on. I made it,' she adds, running a hand across the lettering. 'To take with him when he was adopted. Not that there was a great deal in it then.'

Now I'm more lost. 'He was adopted?'

'Sorry. For a time, yes. I was only supposed to have him till they found a forever family for him. That's how it usually worked. And I wasn't supposed to have him long, because they put him up for adoption right away. Made the most sense, what with every-thing. And they found a couple very quickly. But it wasn't to be,' she adds. 'Their loss. My gain. They'd only had him a few months when the mother fell pregnant. So often the way, eh? And with twins, too. A heck of a decision to have to make, giving him up, but probably the right one in their case. So back he came, and I kept him. I couldn't let him go a second time.' She glances at me and smiles again. 'But that's probably a story for another day.'

She's stirring through the box now with her clumsy freckled fingers. And because the lid is now propped against my mug, it's hard to see over, but I glimpse greeting cards, various papers and a wodge of old photographs, held together in a thick rubber band. She frees the photos. 'Here you are,' she says, selecting one. 'That's his mum.'

She hands me a photo of a striking young blonde woman.

'And this, here' – another photograph – 'is his mama.'

I take them both. Absorb what they are telling me. What *she* just has. Mum and Mama. She watches me. 'Beginning to make more sense now?'

'Just a bit,' I say. '*Wow.* Okay. I've got it now. So, they're gay. Which is—'

'—why they needed a sperm donor. Exactly. They knew your husband, apparently. I believe Eva – that's the dark-haired one – was a colleague of his.'

I stare hard at the photographs. I can see Kane in the blonde one. But I recognise neither. I recognise nothing. Not least the suggestion – no, *god*, the reality – that David – *my husband* David – was their sperm donor.

How the *hell* didn't I know about this? I tap the blonde woman on the nose. 'So this one's his birth mother?'

'Correct. Her name was Kitty. Pretty name, pretty girl. You can see where Kane gets his looks from, can't you? He's bright too,' she adds. 'Very bright. As you'd expect. You want a top-up?'

'No, no,' I say. 'Thanks, but I'm fine. Well, a stiff drink right now definitely wouldn't go amiss.'

She chuckles. Strokes the cat. Seems to find this all amusing. While all I can think is: *how did I not know?*

'But David *knew* them, you say? But that's not how it works. Aren't sperm donors supposed to be anonymous?'

'Oh, yes, usually,' she says. 'But not in this case, apparently. Though I didn't know that at the time – when they first brought Kane to me, it was obviously just assumed that they'd gone to a sperm bank. David wasn't named on the birth certificate or anything. I only found out differently a couple of years back. That's why I assumed *you* knew. Assumed he must have told you.' She points to the pictures again. 'Eva, there – she was a doctor too. From what I've found out since, he did it for them as a favour. To help them out. Not for money. Just as a kindness, I suppose.'

I'm struck by the quaint term. A *kindness*.

A random act of kindness. A *bloody* random act of kindness. But at the same time such a *David* thing to do.

But for a 'friend' I didn't know. A 'friend' I didn't even know *about*. Why? Why the hell didn't he *tell* me? It wasn't as if he'd done anything that would shock me. Providing sperm for grateful couples was a big thing at med school. A nice little earner. At least for the boys. A means of amassing beer money, eking out paltry grants. Like signing up to test drugs, or to be infected with cold viruses. It was commonplace. Just a thing medical students did.

But he wasn't a medical student by then, was he? He was qualified. Working. And he was also married. To *me*. And I was pregnant with Tash. Why didn't he *tell* me? Because he thought I'd stop him? Because I'd worry that this *exact* situation might one day rear its head?

Because that conversation would almost certainly have happened. I'd have insisted upon it, in my rational, risk-averse, *responsible* way. Bottom line, if he'd told me, I'd have stopped him, no question. Because – *really, David, seriously?* – because of something like *this*.

And who the hell was Eva? The name rings no bells. The face sparks no memory. Obviously. So *obviously*. Because that was the way he wanted it. His secret. Their secret. Nothing to do with me, because I wasn't on their team.

A lump of overwhelming sadness lodges thickly in my throat. I tap the other photograph. 'So what happened to Eva, then?'

'Oh, she died as well,' Lacey says. 'Such a tragic accident. Lorry driver ploughed into them. Fell asleep at the wheel. They were on their way to Mayday hospital to visit Kane when it happened. He was premature, as I said, so they kept him in for a bit. They were shuttling back and forth every day to see him.'

She's been leafing through the box, and now she hands me a third photograph. The two women again, together, in a park, or a garden. And holding the hand of the blonde one, who is obviously pregnant, is a pretty little fair-haired girl of maybe three, maybe four.

And it seems Lacey hasn't done toying with me yet. 'That's Kane's older sister,' she says. 'Her name is Rachel.'

Thysania agrippina

The White Witch Moth

Rachel: from the Hebrew, meaning 'ewe'.
Rachel: from the Hebrew, meaning 'ewe' – meaning '*sheep*'.
I mean, I ask you. *Really?* Was that the best they could do?

Okay, so things I got when I moved to the first children's home:
A house 'mother' called Milly.
A Tamagotchi.
A rabbit. A bloody *rabbit*! If he'd been a rat, like I'd asked for – *ergo*, something with half a brain cell – I'd have named him Oberon. As it was, since he was a stupid rabbit, I named him Bottom. And they're like, 'Why?' 'Why Bottom?' 'Such an odd name to give a rabbit!' Christ, don't they know anything? 'Erm, bottom of the food chain?'

Erm, no. See, that's another thing. They can't get the staff.

Things I got when I moved to the second children's home:
A note on my file about an incident involving a rabbit.
A new house 'mother', name of Jade.
A place at a 'special' school. Ooh, get you. You're so *special!*
A boyfriend.

The main thing about Darren is that he is thick as shit. I know. A bit of a blunt instrument to describe the multiplicity of factors that have clearly contributed to his emotional development and academic potential having fallen so far short of that which could be hoped for (even given him having been born with Foetal Alcohol Syndrome on account of his mother being a lush), but there you go.

Where I am fourteen, Darren is fifteen-almost-sixteen. (Sixteen, in children's home terms, being more or less like the point where you get to win the lottery in that film *The Island*. You know – the one with Ewan McGregor and Scarlett Johansson, where you're bred to provide body parts and your organs get harvested.) He occupies the front bedroom on the boys' floor. Which is above the girls' floor, and directly above mine. Darren's main special skill is nocturnal absconding, which he does via his window, via the balcony in front of mine, which means I often get to see him making his nightly leap to freedom – which in his case means landing on the recycling bins, jumping the fence, and running to the park half a mile away, so he can do some skunk behind a bush with his 'friends'. Two of whom (I know this because I heard Jade talking on the phone to someone about it) are 'alumni' of this particularly fine 'university of hard knocks' – which, incidentally, I heard Sam (still my social worker, 'for my sins!') calling this place to some woman with an Audi, who came round for a strategy meeting at the last children's home, when he thought I was in the loo. I mean, *really*? Who comes up with this crap? Hashtag *dontputitonasweatshirtforgodssake.*

We have a deal, Darren and I, since I am the new girl. I don't dob him in, I don't get fucked up. I do dob him in, I do get fucked up. I have no idea what form me getting fucked up might take.

And, much against my principles, I've so far been on the 'don't dob him in' programme. Because much as I have an instinctive dislike of where this sits on the reward/punishment spectrum (surely 'don't dob him in, get something nice in return' is the more sustainable approach to interpersonal relations? But, hey, what do I know?) I have suspected since day one that Darren could be useful. He is, to quote the manual, something of a 'malleable, easily influenced' kind of knuckle-dragger, which means it's worth keeping him on side till I work out in what way.

Then – bam – yesterday, Darren got a laptop. Where I get birthday and Christmas cards from my sainted grandmother (ten-pound note and five-pound note, respectively – they follow me around like migratory birds) Darren has this mad bunch of generous relatives. None of whom want shit all to do with him, obvs, but, from time to time, and at, I imagine, the urging of his gentle social worker, stump up guilt-gifts for their part in his mother being such a basket case, and him languishing in a state-run shit-hole – sorry, children's home.

Darren has A LAPTOP. And, better than that, though Darren keeps on telling me that if I dob him in he will for sure fuck me up, I know something else – something that even he hasn't fully grasped yet. That, if I might be so indelicate, what Darren would *mostly* like to do is not so much fuck me up as fuck me.

Circa 4 a.m. A Wednesday, if I remember. Full moon.

[*Whispers.*] 'What the hell are you doing in my bedroom?'

'Couldn't sleep. Thought I'd come up and wait for you.'

'What the hell?' (I am in a T-shirt. I am cross-legged in his bed. MUFC duvet cover. Laptop on lap.) Then [*considers.*], 'Piss off, Rach. I'm fucked. Gimme that. Go to bed.'

[*Hands over laptop. Pulls duvet back.*] 'I already *am* in bed.'

[*Gapes. Slurs.*] 'What the actual *hell*, Rach? You *serious*?'

I am deadly serious. I prove it.

So now I have the precious rape card in the back pocket of my skinny jeans. *Ergo*, access to the laptop. Hashtag *hopeIdontgetchlamydia*.

But I digress. There are three kinds of white witch, give or take. This lepidopteran version, so called for whatever reason (it's also called the great grey moth and the ghost moth, among other things) counts 'having the widest wingspan of any moth – check *me* out!' among its talents. It's the albatross of the moth world. A moth that makes an entrance.

Then there's the white witch of pagan folklore. The good witch. The nice witch. The wafty, softy, *kind* witch. The witch who practises altruism (you'll know all about that, Julia), putting hexes (presumably) on ogres, sprites and, yes, *fairies*, and in doing so giving witchcraft a good, so *bad*, name.

Then, *of course*, there's The White Witch of Narnia. Enough said. One hundred years of winter. No Christmas.

No *Christmas*, Julia. Imagine that?

Ever.

Chapter 16

There are many, many houseplants on Lacey Harrison's kitchen windowsill. Seven or eight of them, of varying sizes, in terracotta-coloured plastic pots. A grey-blue succulent. A tradescantia. A couple I don't recognise. The closest is a spider plant, a big one, from which half a dozen baby spider plants tumble.

No, *spew*, I think. They spew from it. I cannot drag my gaze from them.

'I'm sorry,' Lacey is saying. 'It's a lot to take in, isn't it?'

The photograph in front of me swims back into focus. *Rachel. A daughter. Kane's older sister. Their firstborn.*

'So you're telling me this little girl is David's as well?'

Lacey nods. 'I think that's how it usually works with siblings. They store extra sperm so they can come back and have another child. Which they obviously did in Kane's case. Such a tragedy.' She nods towards the sunny little child beaming out at the camera. Jesus Christ. Is that Tash I can see in her smiling face?

'So, how old is she?'

'Twenty-four, twenty-five? She was coming up to five when Kane was born, I think. Difficult to get your head around, isn't it?'

I think she's talking about the revelation that these are my late husband's children. That this child was being born perhaps even as David and I were first going out together. But she's not.

'One minute you have your whole life mapped out before you,' she muses. 'Then, in a single awful moment, it's all gone. And that little one had the worst of it, no question. Terrible injuries. I remember reading the report. Bones broken, organs ruptured, epilepsy from the head trauma . . . No one thought she'd live. That's why they decided to split them up. They're usually loathe to part siblings, but since Kane was just a newborn they thought it would be better to make a clean break. Because even if she survived, it looked like his sister was going to be hospitalised for months. So they split them up. To give him the best chance of a new life. And her too, I suppose; it wasn't as if she'd miss him, was it? She'd never even known him.' She lifts the cat off her lap. Kisses it as she lowers it to the floor. 'I'd better feed this one, I think.'

She heaves herself to her feet again and crosses the small kitchen, where she opens a cupboard and pulls out a pouch of cat food. The cat, now miaowing plaintively, as if to hurry her along a bit, presses its flank against her legs as she reaches down to pick up the cat bowl.

'What's his name?' I ask. 'Or is it a she?'

She nods. 'She's called Sooty. She's going on fifteen now, but she's a rescue cat, a moggy, so she's got a few years in her yet, I hope. You have pets?'

'Not right now. I used to have a dog. A Jack Russell. I'm seriously thinking about getting another one.'

'You should,' she says, smiling again. 'I wouldn't be without her. Specially since Kane went off to university and the house feels so empty.' She glances back at me. 'But I suppose you'll know all about that, won't you?'

Such a big taboo, to admit that. Such a big, *stupid* taboo. And how would she know? For all she knows, I might be out partying every night. She doesn't though. Like Nick, she can see right into the truth of me. 'Yes,' I say. 'I do.'

I watch her carefully squeeze all the food from the pouch and find myself astonished that these children had no one. If anything had happened to David and me, there would have been fist fights for the right to take Tash.

That I just accepted this as normal suddenly weighs heavy. 'But wasn't there any family to step in?' I ask. 'I can't believe they would just give them up like that.'

'You wouldn't credit it, would you?' she agrees. 'But things were different then. And there was only a grandmother to fall back on. Kitty's mother, that is – Eva's parents lived in New Zealand – and there was no question of her taking him in. Or Rachel. She was in her sixties by then. And the grandfather was *very* homophobic. Very hostile. I think he and Kitty were more or less estranged by the time Kane was born. Though Mrs Sixsmith – Nancy, that's the grandmother – did at least manage to keep in touch with her for a while.'

I'm feeling overwhelmed by this maelstrom of people and events. 'So Rachel did recover, then? What happened to her after that?'

She places the dish on the floor and the meaty aroma of cat food fills the kitchen. 'She was in hospital and then rehab, over a year all told, I think. Then she went into care too. Though she was always a ward of court, of course. She went into foster care at first, I'm told, but she had a lot of complex needs – which made her challenging to care for, of course – so she apparently ended up being moved around a lot. Finished up in a children's home, sadly.'

Complex needs. Challenging. A children's home. *Damaged.* A new, chilling reality presents itself for inspection. 'And where is she now?'

'I have no idea. No one does. Though Kane did manage to find her – well, in actual fact, she found *him*, via the grandmother – it didn't work out. They only met up the once – June last year, it was.

Just before he finished second year at uni. He'd never expected to hear from her, not after all that time, but she got in touch with him out of the blue. Even went all the way down to Southampton on the train – that's where he's studying – to meet up with him. He was so excited, bless him, but, to be honest, I think it was more curiosity than anything on her part. After that, she really didn't want to know. They were supposed to meet up a second time but she didn't turn up. Waited hours, he did. He didn't want anything to do with her after that. But I can understand why she didn't. Must have been hard for her, seeing how well things worked out for him. Perhaps it was all too much. Though, to be honest, I can't say I'm sorry she's disappeared.'

If she has.

The cat attended to, Lacey puts the pouch in a pedal bin, and returns to her seat again, every small action as slow and deliberate as if performed on the moon.

'Why do you say that?' I ask.

She peers at me from over the box lid, and I know we are on the same page. 'Let's just say I've spent a very long time in fostering,' she says. 'And from what their grandmother told me, it was always going to be a fool's errand. She did live with her for a while, apparently – this was when she had to leave the last children's home – but . . .'

'So you've actually met the grandmother?'

She nods. 'Yes. Once I realised Kane was going to do it whether I wanted him to or not, I managed to track her down through social services. We went to visit her just before Kane started university. Desperately sad, it was. She looked, well, you can imagine, can't you? Haunted. Honestly, a shell of a woman. Racked with guilt, obviously. I don't think she can ever have got over it. But then, how could anyone?' She shakes her head. 'I have no idea how she manages to live with it. Being so tormented, wondering what you could have done differently. To know your own flesh and blood has languished in care in the way she did.' She shakes her head sadly. 'Anyway, that's how Rachel got his contact details. He left them for her to pass on just in case she got in touch at any point. It's also how we've come by all this stuff. Which has been lovely for Kane, of course. In that regard, at any rate. I suppose it's at least been good for him to know where he came from. Here—'

She hands me something else she's pulled out. A small pen-and-ink drawing in a cheap Ikea frame. 'Kitty was a professional artist,' she says. 'And a rather good one, as you can see. Specialised in natural history work. Illustrations for scientific journals; books and articles and what have you. This was obviously back before everything was on the internet. Posters as well, apparently, museum merchandise. That kind of thing. That's one of hers.'

It's a line drawing of a moth. Fantastically intricate. Almost photographic in its detail. 'Hang on,' I say, as the image jumps out at me. 'Isn't this the moth Kane has tattooed on his wrist?'

'Well spotted,' she says. 'Had that done not long after we went to see Mrs Sixsmith. I wasn't very happy about it at first – things you hear about some of these tattoo parlours – but he had it done at uni, and he was of age, of course, so there wasn't much I could do about it, was there? Still,' she adds, straightening her right leg and wincing, 'it made him happy. And it could have been worse. At least it's discreet. Size of the ones some of his friends have . . .' She tuts. 'But what's done is done. And if that's the last of the whole business, I'll consider we've got off pretty lightly. And I'm hoping that now your husband's gone – with all due respect, of course – that this really will be the end of it, too. Like I said, I never wanted Kane to start digging around in the first place. Not so much trying to find his sister, but certainly your husband. I mean, why would he care? And why should he? But he'd turned eighteen so he had a right to. A legal right, as it turned out, since they changed the law. So, what could I do?'

A startling thought occurs to me. Is this it? Or might there be more Kanes and Rachels? Was David sowing seed far and wide? I dredge a number up from med school. Ten families maximum. You could only make ten families. More than ten skewed the gene pool.

'And so he found him,' I say. 'But how? Isn't there some sort of official process to be gone through?'

'Oh, I imagine so. Usually. If it's come from a sperm bank. But no. In this case, again, via his grandmother. She had all her daughter's personal effects. And among them was a whole file of paperwork about your husband.' She makes a little 'tsch' sound. 'Heartbreaking, it was. They'd obviously every intention of telling them who their father was when the time was right. There were photographs of him, notes about him . . .'

The idea creeps me out. Did *he* know this? My gut instinct is no. 'And you saw all this, did you?'

'Oh, yes,' she says. 'Kane's grandmother went through it all with us. They'd compiled a whole dossier on him. Name, profession, background – all that kind of thing. I don't think there was *ever* any thought of getting in touch with him. I really don't. It was just giving them the facts, so they knew where they came from. Everyone wants to know where they came from, don't they? So it wasn't difficult to track him down. Kane literally found him that same evening. Just by going on Google. Not that I was comfortable with any of it, as I said. I mean, what good would come of getting in touch with him? I'm sure it was the last thing he was expecting. There was *you* to consider. You *and* your daughter. I mean, having some stranger come into your lives that way? I very much doubt that was part of the arrangement, was it? As you say, sperm donors expect the right to anonymity, and rightly so. So if I'd had my way, that would have been that. Believe me, I tried *very* hard to talk him out of it. Call an end to it.'

'So he found him. And then what? Did he write to him?'

'He sent him an email. Via his hospital, I think. Just saying who he was, and how he'd come by his details. And a few weeks later – this must have been January time, January *last* year – he emailed Kane back and agreed that he'd meet him.'

January *last* year. So, pre-dating the phone bills. Pre-dating the MacBook. Pre-dating those messages. This has been going on *that* long. 'And when did that happen?'

'Around Easter, I think. That's right. Yes, because Kane was home from uni. Yes. Easter last year.'

A year and a half ago. A whole year and a half ago. The levers click and clank as balls plonk into place. 'And then what?'

Lacey picks the watch up, her expression now thoughtful. 'He was incredibly kind to him. That's the worst of it. And the last thing I expected. He wanted to help him out. Help with money and so on. God only knows *why* he thought he had to, but there you go. He did.'

Perhaps because of this, I think, eyeing her swollen, stumbling fingers. Perhaps because of Kane's number in the lottery of relative privilege. David was always banging on about privilege, wasn't he?

Me and god. We both *know* why. We *get* it.

Money talk is ugly. And I don't care about the money anyway. I say, truthfully, firmly, *loyally*, 'That's because that's the kind of man he was.'

'I realise that,' she says, misreading me. 'I'm sorry. I didn't mean it like that. He was clearly a very decent man. It was all just so totally unexpected. And so *unnecessary*. I didn't want anything from him, I promise you. It was never about money. *Never*. We were fine as we were. We still are.'

'I understand,' I say. And I almost add, '*Really.*' But I stop myself because I read her eyes, which are already saying, 'Believe me, you do not.'

She runs her hand over the box again, her fingers lingering on the appliquéd felt letters. 'Though I'd be lying if I didn't tell you it came at, well, let's say a difficult time. I'd had to give up work.' She opens her palms, her meaning clear. 'And Kane was all for throwing the towel in – giving up his uni course. Coming home. Getting a job. What with the ridiculous rent on his student accommodation – well, you'll know.'

I nod.

'But I couldn't have that. I'd have sold the shirt off my back before I allowed that to happen . . .' She stares at her hands for a long moment. I have the strong impression that she's trying not to cry. 'Look, the truth is that I don't know what kinds of conversations they had, back and forth, but your husband – *much* against my wishes – well, let's just say that all talk about him giving up stopped. Which was *not* what I wanted. I would have managed. I always have—'

'It's *fine*,' I say. 'I understand that.'

'But, you know, Kane's take on things was rather different from my own. As far as he was concerned if his— if your husband wanted so much to help him, why *shouldn't* he be allowed to? If he wanted to be part of his life – and Kane's adamant that he did – then, well . . .' She spreads her hands again. 'Well, who was I to stop him?' She sighs heavily. Shakes her head. 'It really knocked Kane for six, you know, finding out he died.'

Tell. Me. About. It, I think. *Tell me and Tash.*

I don't say that. She surely already knows it. But what else *doesn't* she know? If this conversation is anything to go by, a lot. 'But that's what I don't get,' I say instead. 'David died back in

205

February. So why was Kane at our house in Wales all this time later? If he knew David had died, what was he doing there last month?'

She looks at me sharply. 'He just wanted to see the place for himself. I mean, why wouldn't he? He was in the area, so he just thought he'd walk up and see it.' She holds my gaze. 'He wasn't doing anything wrong.'

I wonder if those words have come directly from the horse's mouth. *Kane, what were you doing there? Mum, I just wanted to see the place.* I wonder if she believes what she's telling me.

'But he ran away from me. That's how he ended up getting himself in such trouble. Did he tell you that?'

She shifts in her chair again, and I see more discomfort tweak her features. 'Not in so many words,' she says. 'He doesn't remember a great deal of what happened. They say it's because of the brain injury. But I'd already guessed as much anyway; I know he wouldn't have wanted you to see him because you weren't supposed to know about him having found your husband.' She picks up the watch. 'Much less about this flipping thing. Why on earth he took it camping with him I don't know.' She leans towards me. 'Look, I can't speak for your husband, but that much I do know. That was part of the deal. That you didn't find out. You *or* your daughter. Not till he was ready to tell you, anyway. Which, to my mind, was just asking for even more trouble.' She sits back again. 'And I was right, wasn't I? I'm a great believer in the truth, Dr Young, so none of this sits well with me, believe me. Nothing against your husband, as I say, but – well, look, it's really not for me to say, is it? It just is what it is. And, hopefully, now you *do* know everything, it can be over with. Done.'

'*Done?*'

She looks shocked at my surprise. 'Well, isn't it? Isn't that for the best? That we leave it at that?'

In other circumstances she would have a valid point. Perhaps it *would* be for the best. Say goodbye. Draw a line. Like Kane, perhaps – cite a convenient brain injury?

But not *this* circumstance, when there is so much I still need explained. When I am still fearful of things about which she clearly knows nothing. When the words Nick saw on the beach are so chillingly present. When one half of the double-act my dead husband helped create is AWOL.

I'm sure I'm right in my instinct there are no answers to be had here. And since asking the questions might even stop me finding out, I think quickly and agree that it might. 'Will Kane let me visit him though?' I ask. 'I'd still like to see him.'

'Oh, I dare say,' she says. 'He's no reason not to, has he? Not now the cat's out of the bag. Plus, you saved his life, didn't you? If nothing else, he needs to thank you properly.'

'I didn't,' I tell her. 'If I hadn't disturbed him, hadn't gone after him, he wouldn't have run away and fallen, would he?'

She dismisses my protestations with a wave of her hand. 'That's irrelevant. You only did what anyone would have. And if you *hadn't* gone after him, he would almost certainly have died. Now, then. How about another cup of tea before you go?'

I stay half an hour more in Lacey Harrison's overheated kitchen. Drinking tea, hearing stories of all the children she's fostered. Of her sadness in never having had any of her own. Of how she'd wanted to adopt Kane, but realised she couldn't afford to, because once she became too disabled to work, it would be her fostering wages that would keep them afloat. Finding out that she's on her own now, since her husband walked out on her – before Kane was returned to her by the couple who didn't keep him, but just after her initial diagnosis of MS. Unlike David, she tells me, he was a deeply unlovely man.

By the time I leave her, I have – I *think* – some clarity, some understanding. More than she does, because I have information she doesn't, so I understand exactly why David didn't tell me Kane had found him. Know him well enough, *knew* him well enough – decent, kind, *empathetic* David – to understand that, when he died, he was still on that journey. A path he'd clearly trod carefully, proceeding with caution, making (oh, how he loved them) all his cost-benefit analyses, trying to work out how and when to take that massive leap of faith, and dare to introduce his secret son into his daughter's life.

And also, of necessity, to come clean with me.

So I wonder. Lacey Harrison talks about guilt, but I wonder. Guilt. Of course, guilt. Integrity's unwelcome bedfellow. It would have appalled David to have to lie about so much, for so long. Must have ground against the very core of his being. Yet he'd still done it. And, apart from our one big 'expedient untruth' I had never known him lie before. Had the one enabled – predicated – the other?

Had *I* given him a son, perhaps he might have acted differently, but as it stood, he'd been gifted the very thing I hadn't given him, and at a time when our marriage was already expiring. It was that big a thing. That compelling a prospect. That seductive an adjunct to his – and Tash's – future. So he was going for it.

But what has he unleashed?

It's fully dark when I leave, the street settling for the evening. The birds roosted, the workers home, the night animals stirring. Moths and gnats are hurling themselves at Lacey's carriage lamp.

'Oh, by the way,' I say, turning on the front path as I remember. 'Kane's friend Lewis? His was the other number I managed to get from his phone. I spoke to him over the weekend, and he's really keen to hear from Kane, so I promised that if I got hold of him I'd ask him to get in touch. Maybe you could let Kane know when you go in tomorrow?'

'Lewis . . .' Lacey says. 'Lewis . . . oh, of course. The boy from Wolverhampton. He's one of the crowd Kane went back to Wales with. Lovely lad. Yes, of course. Makes you think, though, doesn't it? What a difference a day makes. If he'd only left with the rest of them, instead of hanging around for that flipping party, we wouldn't even be here now, would we? Anyway, no problem. I'm getting a phone for him tomorrow, as it happens. An old one a friend's letting him borrow, bless her. So if you speak to him again let him know Kane'll be in touch soon.' She smiles. 'Then I'll finally get some peace off him. Kids and their phones, eh?'

And because there's been so much to try and process, and my head is already stuffed to bursting, like my handbag, I'm back in the car and about to drive off before I fully digest what Lacey has just told me: that Lewis had been there. Been *back* there, in September. Was *one of the crowd Kane went back to Wales with*.

But I know that's not right. Lewis told me he was on holiday with his family when Kane nearly died up on the Down. That no one had even *seen* Kane since their holiday back in August.

Kane – still on that fool's errand, perhaps? – *has* lied to her.

Rothschildia zacateca

Rothchild's Silk Moth

Silk moths are members of the Saturniidae family, as in-yer-face a bunch of lepidopterans as you're likely to see. They are emperors. They are regal. They are *royalty*. They are big and they are bright and they have many-splendoured wings. They are so amazing that they even have *windows* in their wings. Can you imagine that? Little peek-a-boo windows, fashioned by mother nature. Another sleight of hand to fool would-be predators.

And, of course, silk moths make the larvae that spin the silk that spawned the Silk Road. Soft as silk. Smooth as silk. Silken.

Silk rocks because silk's, like, the Range Rover among fabrics. Which is why stuff made from silk is, like, 'Whoah, *dang*, that's classy.'

But.

Question: What's the thing you can't make a silk purse out of?
Answer: (All together now.) A sow's ear.

See, that's the thing you didn't realise, Sam. That I *heard* them. Jade, that policeman, the skinny bitch from social services, and bloody   Todd-I'm-the-area-manager-and-I'm-simply-not-*having*-this bloody Smith. I am *not making this up*. Swear to god, Sam. I *heard* them. And that's exactly what they said, Sam. About *me*.

So what did they expect? What did *you* expect, Sam? That I'd just suck it up? Just sit there and take it? Just accept that's how they see me? How you *all* see me, truth be told, Sam. As the wonkiest bit of veg in that right-on wonky veg box that gets delivered. Damaged goods. Seconds. A scrappy remnant.

Let me tell you, it's bloody hard trying to find a way to deal with that kind of anger. And, for Christ's sake, it was only a shitting window. A *window*. A piece of sodding property.

I am in Shards. Fragments. Splinters.

I AM IN BITS.

Bits which cannot be put back together.

Chapter 17

Nick says, 'Ah, so you can't keep away, then' when I call him and tell him I'm coming back down at the weekend. And I suspect that's as true for him as it is for me. I can almost sense his nose sniffing the air in search of mystery.

As it would be, because I then gift him mine. It takes me a full twenty minutes to tell him everything I've learned, and at the end he says, 'Wow. So he was their *sperm* donor. *Wow*. I mean, I know that's a thing, but, still, I mean – what are the chances? That scenario never even crossed my mind.'

'Mine neither.'

'Well, clearly. I'm not sure it would cross anyone's, would it? And then what happened after . . . *Christ*, that is one hell of a story. And at the risk of being ripped to shreds by the sharp end of your tongue, can I have first dibs at being the one to tell it?'

He's not at risk. Because his levity falls on fertile ground. Having shared what I've found with him I have a sense of catharsis, of having laid several persistent ghosts to rest. But what I now have is a spectre and a new set of compelling questions. This Rachel – has she really disappeared?

'The story isn't finished yet,' I point out. 'Kane lied to his mother. I have a strong sense that there might be a great deal she doesn't know. Plus, she doesn't know where this Rachel is and thinks Kane doesn't either. What if he does, though? What if she's involved in all this too? What if they're very much still in contact? In secret?'

'Sounds feasible. And would explain a lot – not least the message on the beach.'

'Exactly. It doesn't take much of a leap of imagination, does it? Her childhood sounds absolutely horrendous.'

And her adulthood? What of that, given she knows what she knows now?

'When are you seeing him?'

'I don't know yet. Lacey said she'd text me. Soon, I hope. And in the meantime, I'm going to see if there's anything else I can find out. Something I've missed in David's paperwork. Perhaps he gave Rachel money too. Or, more to the point, perhaps he didn't.'

'Ah, I get your thinking. And if he didn't, you think she might have waged some kind of war on him?'

'She might be angry enough, if that's the case. Wouldn't you be?'

The rest of the week leaves little room for me to wonder. With two colleagues off sick, work is almost all-consuming, and with so much else crowding my brain there is barely a moment to chew over the ramifications of David's long-ago act of kindness, much less scrabble to make sense of events that still don't.

By the time I reach Rhossili, then, just after lunchtime on Saturday, it's discombobulating to feel as if I've never been away.

It's also raining hard, sluicing down, and as I turn right onto the track to home, and the bay fully reveals itself, the sea, outperformed, is now boiling with rage. As a view, it's spectacular. Elemental eye candy. But as clouds thunder past, low and dark, like spooked bison, I'm happy to view the showreel from the comfort of a warm kitchen, not least because I've neglected to remember to bring a hooded coat.

But possibly not just yet. Because no sooner have I parked the car and run inside the house than the house phone begins trilling. It's Megan.

'Oh, thank goodness. You *are* there. I didn't think you would be.'

'Yes, I've—'

'Listen. Are you free?' she says. Her voice is high and urgent. 'There's been another incident – can you *believe* it? Another one! An accident. Out on the worm.'

A weight presses down on me. I am so done with accidents. 'What kind of accident?'

'I'm not sure, but serious, I think. They've already called an ambulance. But it's going to be an hour yet, apparently, so they sent the woman down for help. Just on the off chance. They—'

'What woman?'

'The man's wife. It's her husband who's hurt. He's in a bad way, apparently, so I said I'd at least try you. Could you drive up and see if there's anything you can do, do you think?'

Because there's nothing else for it – bar refusing, which is not an option – I tell Megan yes, grab my jacket and car keys, and head back out into the rain, which, impossible though it seemed five minutes ago, is even heavier.

So it's not surprising that, bar Megan, who is now peering out through her kitchen window, there doesn't seem to be a soul about. Even the stoic, ever-open little gift shop has closed, and any walkers out there (despite the weather, there's little doubt that there will be some) will have already taken shelter in the Worm's Head Hotel.

I glance in wistfully as I drive past, trying to see through the driving rain. But there's such a lot of weather amassing between me and the causeway that all I can see now is a shifting grey veil.

I have to stop again at the gate by the National Trust shop – the route beyond is prohibited to all but emergency vehicles – and having driven through and closed it, dousing myself further in the process, I clamber back in again and set off towards the worm.

The veil clears a little as I drive, but the wind is even stronger, driving clusters of sodden sheep to find shelter among the gorse. Even with just the merest sliver of window open to try and clear the condensation, I can still hear their frightened, frantic bleating. And they're right to bleat – if the afternoon ends without at least one being swept over the cliff, it'll be nothing short of a miracle.

Soon the roof of the watch station takes shape within the squall, and, wondering anxiously if the human incident is similar in nature (though if so, what could I do? The tide's almost in and the causeway will be submerged now), I park the car tight behind the back of it, to gain a modicum of shelter, then once again stagger out, into the teeth of what, out here, is an even angrier gale. This is not, I think miserably, feeling my breath being ripped from me, exactly the sort of afternoon I'd reckoned on. Furthermore, I still can't see any people.

But perhaps they are inside now, I think, as I round the small, single-storey building, which, despite what people call it, is no longer an official Watch Station. That was closed long ago due to cutbacks. Instead it's now run by an army of volunteers, who, as well as keeping watch – it's still a dangerous patch of coastline – provide maps and tide charts, up-to-date weather information, and, for those who might want it, and many people do, a wealth of knowledge on the local flora and fauna.

I push the door open but can already see through the glass that the room's empty. Has whoever is on watch gone to help? I cast around again, peering out through the wide seaward window, bracing myself for what looks like the need to venture further towards the cliff edge, where there's a long switchback path down to the causeway below. A very, very long way below.

But they must have, so I suppose I must too. I flip my errant collar up again and am just heading out when I hear the roar of a hand dryer.

A few moments later, a middle-aged man appears.

I don't recognise him. It's clearly mutual. In fact, he looks shocked to see me. 'All right, lovely?' he says. He has a mug in his hand. 'What on earth are you doing out in this weather?'

'I'm Julia Young,' I explain. 'I was told there'd been an accident? That you needed a doctor?'

'An accident?' His back straightens immediately. 'Where?'

'I don't know. I was just told to come out to the worm. Maybe somewhere on the path down to the causeway?'

'Well, I don't know about that,' he says. 'I've seen no one since lunchtime.'

He's already put the mug down and now reaches for his walkie talkie, then makes various connections to various other volunteers, and it's soon obvious that no one knows anything about any accident on the worm. Or anywhere else along the Gower coastline. 'I mean,' he points out once he's switched off his walkie talkie, 'who'd be so daft to be out in this?'

Still, for good measure – refusing to let me go out and join him – he dons a cap, a heavy jacket and a fluorescent-yellow cagoule, and sets out to make a foot patrol of the area, just in case.

I peer out, but can see little else but glimpses of hi-vis. The rain's moving in sheets now, a wind-whipped liquid murmuration, and he's soon completely lost to me in the murk. It's a good fifteen minutes before he returns – equally stupefied, and now as sopping wet as I am.

'Not a sausage,' he says, as rivulets of water stream from cagoule to lino. 'Who told you all this, lovely?'

'My neighbour did. Megan Williams?' He nods. He would. Everyone knows Megan. 'She said the woman knocked at her door, looking for me. She said you'd suggested it.'

'*Me?*'

'Yes, apparently.'

'Well, one of them's definitely got their wires crossed, I reckon. So where is she now, then?'

'The woman? I have no idea. I assumed she'd be here. And that's a thought. What about the ambulance? She told Megan they'd called one.'

'Well, let's hope not, eh? Heck of a way to come for nothing.' He tuts. 'Not to mention a criminal misappropriation of valuable resources.'

'Quite.'

He lifts his cap and runs a hand over an almost-bald pate. 'Quite indeed. Well, I'll have to write it up, obviously,' he says. 'But I'm jiggered if I know anything about it.' Then he frowns at me. 'You've not walked all the way out here in this, have you?'

I shake my head. 'No, I drove,' I say. 'My car's parked just round the back.' I shrug. 'Oh, well. No harm done. I suppose I'll head off, then.'

'Sorry, lovely,' he says. 'I really don't know what to make of it – bit of a wild goose chase, it looks like. Some wires definitely crossed somewhere. Either that, or someone's been playing silly buggers.'

'Looks like it, doesn't it?'

'Well' – another frown – 'it's certainly been known. More's the pity. Still, no harm done, as you say.' He pauses, then frowns. 'Hang on. I just realised. I *knew* I knew you. Aren't you the doctor from the Old Rectory? That business a few weeks back?'

I nod. 'And I was hoping not to make a habit of it.'

He sticks a hand out. 'Well, I'm honoured to meet you, Doctor Young,' he says, pumping mine. 'I wasn't on duty that day, but I saw it all on video. You're the toast of the village, you are. He's one lucky lad.'

I agree that he is. I'm beyond trying to explain now, because there isn't any point. It's in print now, therefore it must be so.

But *this*? I sprint back round to my car, dodging sheep droppings and rabbit holes, and as I climb back inside and the wind slaps the door shut, I'm certain. This wasn't bad luck. This was *organised*.

Chrysiridia rhipheus

The Madagascan Sunset Moth

When is a colour not a colour? When it's devoid of pigment. Perceived, rather than actual. The result of optical interference, due to insect physiology; to the microstructure of *Chrysiridia rhipheus*'s scales. In other words, when it's a *lie*.

Jeez. The Madagascan sunset moth is also perfectly named, isn't it?

'What you up for?'

'Couple o' tabs of your best Madagascan Sunset Moth, please, dude.'

But be warned, drug enthusiasts. Don't drink when you're dropping. Or, bang*doooooozy*, you will SO be off your face. You will see things, and hear things, and taste things, and crave things. You will travel so far – so far *in* – that you will start to unravel.

And note: the word 'ravel' does *not* mean the opposite. For reasons best known to itself, it *also* means *un*ravel.

I know a lot about this, Julia.

You will, too.

But – where are we? Ah, yes, Tennyson Road, Portswood, summertime, late, bordering on early. We are all *royally* wasted. And Lewis is spouting shit about me. About how *messed up I am*, as per. Lewis, of the stupid hair, the nasal laugh, the irritatingly excellent connections (oh my, what would Mummy say if she knew he did *drugs*?) – and because Lewis is, like, *the* authority on just about every bloody thing (so *he* says), who am I to argue? And since I'm two spliffs in (plus line of coke, plus half a tab), can I be bothered? No, I can't.

And he's on my case, because that's what students always are, aren't they? Because they believe the lie that student loans = clever. So they get *on* it. And on it, and on it, ad nauseam. I've read this. I've seen that. I've done my homework. I've done the legwork. I've researched a whole essay on the subject, as-it-happens. Which will prove to be so *fabulous* that I will definitely get a first.

'So I know stuff,' he says. (We're talking the usual meaning-of-life bollocks.) 'And what I know is that *you* are *seriously* messed up.'

And l laugh. Because he's right.

But – point of order – he's also wrong.

He has such a poorly evolved, flaccid little cerebral organ, bless him. Where he sees chaos, I only see order.

Chapter 18

There's still no sign of anyone as I drive back past the car park, though, judging by the fog on the hotel bar's windows, even if they're not out, there are still plenty of people about. Could the woman who spoke to Megan be in there?

I discount my first idea, to call in there and make some sort of announcement. I have no idea who I'm looking for, after all. And if someone is playing another game with me (Rachel?) would they be likely to show themselves? No. No, it's Megan herself I need to speak to. And she to me, it would seem, because she's at her front door before I'm even out of the car. She's obviously been looking out for me, keen for news.

'Oh, lord, Julia,' she exclaims, as I squelch up her front path. 'You're absolutely soaked. Oh dear, come on in out of the rain. So what happened? Is everything okay? Was he very badly injured? I've kept a look out but no sign of the ambulance yet – well, unless I missed it. You want a cuppa? I'll put the kettle on. Come on. Come on in.'

'Better not,' I say, nodding downwards towards my muddy boots.

'Pop them off, then.'

'No, it's fine. I'll only drip all over your floor.'

She doesn't argue. Megan's home is the exemplar of the boutique B & B circuit. Her domestic standards are as legendary as her cakes.

'Goodness, though,' she says instead. 'Who on *earth* would go out there in this kind of weather in the first place?'

'No one, by the looks of it.'

'*Exactly*. Just *so* irresponsible. Why, oh why—'

'Megan, that's my point. There was nobody *there*. No accident. Nothing. The guy at the watch station checked the entire area.'

'*What?* But it was him that sent her down to me.'

I shake my head. 'No, he didn't.'

'But she said—'

'He knew nothing about it. He radioed round, too. There hasn't *been* an accident.'

'Are you *sure?*'

'One hundred per cent.'

'But she was in such a *state*. And look at *you*,' she adds, doing so again. '*Honestly*. You're *sure?* That makes no sense. She told me it was him who told her to come down and ask me. *Specifically* to ask me to phone *you*. So I assumed he must know you. So, what's happened to her?'

'I don't know. I didn't see anyone. Neither did the guy at the watch station. He's seen no one all day. There was definitely no accident.'

'But why on earth would she say that there was, then?'

'I have absolutely no idea,' I lie. 'He thinks someone's been playing silly buggers.'

'What? That's *shameful*. Why on *earth*—'

'So, what did she look like, this woman?'

She purses her lips. 'Hmm. Hard to say. I couldn't see a lot of her, to be honest. She had a beanie on and was wearing one of those waterproof ponchos with the hood up. Scrunched tight, like this, to keep the rain out.' She puts her fists to her chin. 'Big round glasses. I remember that, because they were steamed up on the inside. Late twenties, early thirties? Just, *why*, though? Why would anyone *do* something like that?'

It's very little to go on. In fact, it's nothing to go on. But all the while she's been speaking, my mobile's been buzzing in my pocket. 'I only wish I knew,' I say, as I pull it out. Two banners. A missed call. A text from Nick. *Okay if I head over in, say, half an hour?* 'I'd better go,' I say to Megan. 'I've got a couple of important calls to make and I'm already behind. But if you think of anything else, let me know, yes?'

'Yes, of course. Oh, but wait. Let me fetch you some flapjacks. You're wasting away, Julia, *honestly*.'

Or, more likely, I've shrunk in the wash. Though the rain's eased off a little while I've been standing in Megan's porch, I still enjoy another soaking as I run back to the car, warm Tupperware – the flapjacks are fresh from the oven – tucked safely under my jacket.

But as I drive down the track, I see light on the horizon. A strip of determined brightness edging the storm clouds away. What I don't see, however, is the far side of the house. So it's not till I've showered, changed, and am back down at the sink, filling the kettle, that I see something odd in the garden.

I put the kettle back on its rest and push my feet into wellingtons and, since it's still drizzling, take David's old Barbour from its hook and slip it on before opening the back door. The grass has grown at least a foot since I last cut it. It's because of that, and the rain, that it's immediately obvious that a trail has been trodden down across the lawn.

It runs diagonally, and I follow it the short distance to the corner, to where our old rosemary bush, grown leggy over the summer, fills the space at the intersection of two of the dry-stone walls. It's one of the few shrubs that's survived here and provides shelter for a carpet of thyme, covering the spot where we buried Tigger five years ago.

It's the grave itself that I'm now drawn to, the small concrete stepping stone that marks his final resting place. It's tucked almost under the bush now, but still clearly visible. As is what's on it, which I first mistake for a pile of dead leaves. Though from where? There are few deciduous trees here.

I crouch down to take a closer look, and now I see what I'm looking at. It's not leaves – it's a pile of dead carnations. Not the stalks; just the peanut-shaped dun-coloured heads, each one topped with a frill of wilted petals. They are arranged in a heart shape, some still carrying an echo of their previous pale pink.

They are the carnations I threw in the compost bin last time I was here. The flowers Jonathan and Verity bought me.

'There you are!' I twist on my haunches to see Nick standing by the gate. 'Odd time to be gardening, but I suppose it takes all sorts. Sorry – didn't mean to startle you. Just thought I'd check, since you didn't answer the door.' He looks at me quizzically as I rise to my feet again. 'You okay?'

'Come over here,' I say, beckoning him to join me. 'See what you make of this. I've just had the *weirdest* experience. And now this.' I point to the flowerheads. 'Someone's been here and put those there while I've been on a bloody goose chase to the worm.'

He crosses the lawn, follows my finger. Crouches down to inspect the gravestone. 'That's where our dog is buried,' I explain. 'What the hell is this about?'

'Well, *something*, evidently,' he says. 'What kind of goose chase? A wild one?'

'A highly orchestrated goose chase. That much I am absolutely sure of.'

I fill him in as we go back inside and stamp the wet off our boots. 'But you know what strikes me most?' I say. 'That this has obviously only just been done. As in just this afternoon. The flowers would have blown away if it had been done any earlier. Almost certainly while I was up at the watch station, and that poor man was running around all over the place looking for an accident that never was. *Why?* The house has been sitting empty for almost a fortnight. The woman – assuming it *was* her – could have got into the garden at any time to put those dead flower heads on Tigger's grave. Why wait till I'm here, just to make sure I'm *not* here? What's the point of that?'

'To *prove* a point, perhaps? That you're being watched? In which case . . .'

He spreads his palms. 'Rachel?'

It's at this point that my phone pings and, since it's sitting on the kitchen table, I can see the text is from Lacey Harrison.

Just 2 let u know, u can visit Kane on Monday eve in hospital, if that suits. Visiting hrs. 6 till 8. Let me know and I'll tell him. Hope yr well. Thx. Lacey H.

'And that,' Nick says, 'is I guess when you are going to get some answers. In the meantime, want to come to mine?'

I do.

Calyptra thalictri

The Vampire Moth

Creatures of the dark, moths aspire to the light.

Leave a light on and you'll see:

They will find you.

The lightest of the light places anyone can live is a place called Western White Privilege. Naturally, it has its rulers and they live in a high citadel, which, in turn, is called Western White *Male* Privilege. Bloody men. I remember Gran saying that often. Bloody men. And, in this case – rare as hell, this – Granny nailed it. Because with Calyptra – blood-sucking moth genus within the Calpini tribe – it's exclusively the males who get to do it.

They don't suck blood because they want to consume it, particularly. (Gastronomically speaking, they're fashionably fruitarian.) No, it's a bit like the pre-drinking sessions so beloved of fatuous undergraduate retards across the land; tanking up on blood is what gets them the girls.

Go Wiki it if you want a science lesson, but, to *precis*, it's another of those natty evolutionary adaptive processes. The more blood you suck, the more sodium you get on board. And the girl moths need the salt to pass on to their babies, so – hoo-di-hoo – the savvy males latch on to any passing mammal and then they go for it, using their hooked tongues to pierce the skin, and then the hooks *on* the hooks, so the host (such a word, 'host') can't so easily brush them off and stamp them into dust before they're full.

Which nets them more females to pass on their mammal-sucker genes to. *Et voilà*. Bo selector.

Sucking men, eh?

God, I'd hate to be old. God, I'd *detest* being a wrinkly. Creaky joints. Pissy pants. Saggy tits. Knackered teeth. But the thing I'd hate most about being geriatric is the sheer amount of shite you'd have stuffed in your brain. All that clutter from the olden days; bread and pull-it. Dig for victory. Don't spare the rod. Darn your socks. Know your place. Spit and polish. Mind your manners. Respect your elders.

Do as you would be done to.

Still, Gran has space. Lots and lots of it these days. Since my bastard grandfather, who I never had the pleasure of despising in person, popped off to the betting shop in the great beyond to lay an each-way bet on hevs or hell. LOSER.

'Well, it certainly *seems* feasible,' Sam says. And he needs it to be. For the next three years, till I'm eighteen, he's still the fun face of the council, who are still *in loco parentis*. I have been ejected from the children's home (and another school, funny that) but am still very much part of his caseload. Case load. What kind of crap label is that? I'm a case and I'm a load. And I am HEAVY. But if I can stay here (Just for a bit, pleeease. Just till I get on my feet, pleeease) I will lighten that load at a stroke. He can offload me to Granny's!

I can see his face, though. I know exactly what he's thinking. He's thinking, 'shit the bed, this is some creepy crib!' He's looking at my gran and thinking, ser-eeee-ous-ly? He is thinking reeeeeally? Will this old bird even cope *for two minutes*?

She says yes. He says hmmm. They have had some big meetings. A Strategy Meeting. (Again, I am not allowed.) A pre-pre-placement meeting. (I am allowed at the end bit. I am sweetness personified. I am casing the joint.) A pre-placement meeting. (I mean, *lordy*. Check this out. I am *being placed with* my own grandmother. She is being CRB checked. *Ha!*)

So. Tonight, I will sleep *in my dead mother's bed*. And my grandmother (Happy Birthday, Happy Christmas, Happy *life*. Sorry I couldn't make it but you know how it is) is taking that very belated but all-important step towards the celestial penthouse. She wishes to be saved. She's not a gambler.

Cue an itsy, bitsy, completely *banging* bit of freeeeedom! She doesn't, as the saying goes, know what's hit her. Yeah, she signed up for it, but the 'it' bit hits her like a juggernaut. A juggernaut at speed, me (I do like my drugs, see), so, in Granny-time, my presence is like a fast-forward blur.

If Grandma had a vid-eeee-o it would be knocked off from down the market, because Grandpa was a mean sod as well. She didn't – not least as far as I knew – and I still hold that against her. But if she *did*, it would be on permanent fast-forward – whirrrrrr, click, click, whirrrrrr – as my best years (from fifteen to seventeen – they were *vintage*) flash past. Watch them go (well, only in your mind's eye – this is ancient, cheap technology), all those little snapshots, curated, like an Instagram feed, thoughtfully captioned and hashtagged, as per.

The boyf! What a night. Hashtag *yolo*. Hashtag *sexgod*
Well, when in Rome . . . hashtag *harveysbristolcream*
New Threads. Hashtag *jackwills* hashtag *labellove* hashtag *wardrobegoals*
Parrrrrtayyyyyy! Hashtag *Parrrrtayyyyy!* Hashtag *Parrrrrrrteeeeeeeee!!!!!*

Whirrrrrr, click, click, whirrrrrr. I am finally *living*! Though just shy of seventeen now, I'm no longer shy or sweet. I am sour, like an acid drop. I am bitter, like grapefruit. I am *testing*, like a Friday night chicken vindaloo. And Gran's language betrays her. She cannot fully *own* this. This whole rule-the-roost, I'm-in-charge, do-as-I-say-or-else lark. Her terrible dilemma (and, oh, it's *that* hard) being the matter of 'doing the right thing' versus the real thing she is faced with, i.e. ME.

I am the daughter of her daughter. I am her precious living link. Her telomeres are short now, but her genes live on within me. Her exhausted old brain cannot deal with the contradictions. Her conscience weighs heavy. Her heart is tired and weak. She is simply, indisputably, *no match for me.*

Sam's, like, Christ. (Not like Christ.) Taking drugs in her *house?*

Sam's, like, seriously, kiddo, if you want this to *work* . . .

Sam's, like, *enough*. Have respect. Where's your gratitude? *Jesus*.

Sam's like, *seriously*. (Yup, again.) This should be a matter for the police.

Sam's, like, god, Rachel. I mean it. How *could* you? Surely you wouldn't steal from your own *grandmother*?

Why, of course I would, *moron*.

She *owes* me.

Chapter 19

Croydon University Hospital, whose sliding doors I am currently passing through to visit Kane Scott, is also the hospital where, had David and my respective careers not whisked us off to another part of London only a few weeks earlier, my daughter would also have been born. In fact, had Tash been conceived just eight or ten weeks before she was, I might even have been attending my first ante-natal appointment while Kane's mother was giving birth to him in the maternity department next door. A point about which David, his moment of altruism long since forgotten, was almost certainly oblivious.

Lacey has given me a ward name, but no more, presumably because she doesn't think I'll need one. And though navigating hospitals is one of my incidental life-skills, it takes me several goes to find my way to the corridor I want.

It takes me no time at all to find Kane, however, as he emerges from a side room at the same time as I enter the ward, a golden wraith in grey tracksuit bottoms.

He glances across at me, then shuffles off in Nike sliders, presumably back to his bed. He hasn't recognised me, clearly. But, then, why should he? Given his head injury, any memories he made of me before his eyes flickered shut are probably still as shrouded in fog as Rhossili Down was that morning.

Knowing what I do now, I also see him through a different filter. Just as David must have done when he first came face-to-face with him, I automatically do a whole-body scan, looking for points of recognition. I don't call out to him. I simply follow him. Take in his pronounced limp, his bearing, the slope of his shoulders, the marked loss of muscle mass from his already skinny frame, the way his hair, already long, has grown even longer, bar the wide strip of stubble that has been carefully mown – reverse Mohican-style – up the back of his head.

With his blonde hair – as fair as his father's was dark – he looks almost Jesus-on-the-crucifix messianic. And something shocks me. The fierce, almost maternal urge to protect him that mushrooms up inside me as I follow him. I don't know where it comes from because we don't share any genes. But the feeling's as profound as it's disturbing.

A nurse breaks the spell. 'Can I help you?' she asks crisply. At which point he turns around and I see comprehension dawn on his face.

'I'm visiting Mr Scott,' I say, gesturing towards him. And now, as our eyes meet, I properly see it. Just how much like David this boy really is.

And he is lovely. No question. Objectively. Aesthetically. And I wonder again at that first moment of contact. What emotions he stirred in David when they met. How did *he* feel when he saw him? I think I can guess: *This is my child. This is my son. And he is beautiful.*

And I wonder what might have happened had our marriage still been happy. Would David have brought him home? Presented him for inspection? *Look, Jules. This is my son. And he is beautiful.*

'Ah, Kane,' says the nurse. 'Yes, he did mention.' She smiles across at him. 'Okay, love?'

He nods, a blush staining his pale cheeks, then beckons me to follow him, limping ahead to the bay in which he's berthed. He points to the chair – standard NHS issue again, this time in blue – and clambers up awkwardly onto his bed. The chipped tooth makes him seem more childlike than ever. A goofy Adonis.

'So, here we are, finally,' I say. Brightly, because his discomfort and embarrassment in my presence is so palpable. He is, and I suppose with good reason on more than one front, a deeply reluctant visitee.

I shrug off my jacket and plonk myself down in the chair. 'Thanks so much for seeing me,' I add. 'I'm sure your mum's told you how worried I've been about you. That was quite a scare you gave me. How are you? On the mend now?'

'I think so,' he says politely. Then, as if remembering his script, adds, 'Thank you for everything you did for me. I . . . well . . . if you hadn't been there . . . '

'I only did what anyone would,' I reassure him. 'So there's no need to thank me. So. How are you feeling in yourself?'

'Not too bad,' he says. 'Bored. I just wish they'd let me go home.'

'Which they will soon, I'm sure. Once they know you're fully fit.'

'I feel okay *now*.'

'I'm sure you do. You look well. But you still have quite a limp. Are they working you nice and hard with your physiotherapy?'

He nods. 'Just a bit . . .' Then completely dries up.

I'm short of words too now, having so quickly reached the juncture where the next step would be either, 'Right, then! Let's examine you,' or, 'There we go. See you in a month. Goodbye. Next!' But with neither option available, and the silence growing awkward, I am uncharacteristically struggling to supply the next chunk of small talk.

And I know why I'm faltering. Because this whole thing is farcical. Because the elephant that's been trailing me into the room since I got his mother's text has pitched up, demanding attention. I don't know what conversations Kane's had with his mother since I saw her, but my hunch is that he's hoping this will prove relatively painless. That I've simply come to say hello, to wish him well, to accept his thanks. And hopefully – and again, I have no idea if he's spoken to his friend Lewis – that will be all I have to say, and then I'll go.

But I know he's been quietly assessing me since I arrived, and is looking ever more anxious as a consequence. Is he (the epitome of lucky, according to pretty much everyone) already anticipating that he won't be that lucky?

So I dispense with all the bland conversational supplies I'd packed for the journey, and plunge straight on to what we really need to talk about.

I lean forward in the chair. Clear my throat. Watch him stiffen. 'Kane,' I say gently. 'Look. About that day. As in why you were there, at my cottage in Wales. I know what you told your mum isn't the whole story.'

I wait, and it's a while before his gaze flickers up to me from beneath his froth of curly fringe. His fingers pick at handfuls of blanket. 'What have you said to her?' he asks finally. His voice is lower now, anxious.

'Nothing, Kane. *Nothing.*' He relaxes only slightly. 'But I spoke to your friend Lewis before I went to see your mum. And I know he wasn't with you, because he'd already told me. Yes, the first time, but not the second. So I just want to understand why you told your mum he was.'

Another anxious glance. 'You didn't tell her that, did you?'

'No, I didn't. It didn't even register till I'd left her, to be honest.' I note the look of relief when I say this. 'And since you obviously don't want me to, unless I have good reason to I won't. But my late husband has been dead for nearly seven months now, and I know you knew that too, Kane, so why?'

Again, he doesn't answer immediately, and I sit back a little, anxious not to seem as if I'm interrogating him. 'At first,' I add, 'I thought you'd broken in and stolen his watch. But I know that's not true. I know he gave you your own watch. So why *were* you there? Had you been there before? I mean, as in *before* the summer? *With* my husband? Was there something else of yours at the house? What?'

The seconds stack up again. We both watch a trolley rattle past. 'I just—' he begins. Then he stops and exhales heavily. 'Okay,' he says. 'Has mum told you about Rachel?'

Finally, I think. We are at last at the crux of it.

'Your sister?' I say. 'Yes, she has.'

'She's not my sister.'

Noted. 'Sorry. Of course not. Anyway, what about her?'

'I was supposed to be meeting her there.'

So, another lie: his sister, who his mother thinks has long since disappeared. Who he has allegedly had nothing more to do with. And I see that we are about to go further. He sighs again, and it's such an emphatic, sharp expulsion that it lifts the curtain of fringe right off his face. He's made a big decision, I realise. He's about to cross the Rubicon. And, despite that sigh, I can tell it's more in relief than resignation that he's plunged into those dangerous waters. That a weight has been lessened.

But what does she have to do with all this?

'Meeting her for what?' I ask him.

'It was her who wanted to break in,' he tells me. 'Not me. Her. It was *her* plan. I would never do that. *Never*.'

Because I believe he's the boy his mother described to me, I believe him in this also. I tell him so. 'But why? What was she after?'

'She wasn't after anything.' He looks surprised by the question. 'She just wanted to smash the place up. That's why I brought my watch with me. To try and stop her. Persuade her not to. It's worth *tons*, you know.'

'I do.' So I'm right. She is obviously bent on revenge. Was obviously there, watching. Has *been there ever since. Watching.* 'So what happened?' I ask him. 'Me showing up?'

He shakes his head. 'No, no. It was *her* who never showed.'

The picture on the jigsaw box starts coming into focus. 'But why do you think she didn't turn up? I mean, if it was her idea . . .'

'I don't know.' He spreads his palms. 'Maybe she saw you or something. Maybe she knew you were around.'

Which makes something else occur to me. That he *hadn't*. But then, perhaps he wouldn't have. I'd arrived late the night before and put the car in the car port. From where I'd seen him, assuming that he'd not ventured round that side of the house yet, it's possible that he wouldn't have seen it. Or perhaps he had, and was anxious to know where she was in case I saw *her*. Either way, it's a very disturbing thought.

As is another. Was it *she*, and not Kane, who was sending things to Tash? 'And our house in London?' I ask Kane. 'Had you been there as well? As in recently?'

He nods. 'But she never showed there either.'

'But you were meeting there for the same reason? To break in and do damage?'

'Not *me*. I *told* you.' His voice is reedy now, petulant. I'm not surprised. He has clearly been leading a double life, and then some. 'I was just trying to *stop* her. Just trying to do something to get her to leave me alone. Leave *you* alone. Give her the watch to sell. Get rid of her. She's a nightmare. You don't *realise*.' He looks at me through frightened eyes. 'Seriously, you don't realise. She's *obsessed*. Look, you mustn't tell my mum about any of this,' he adds, urgently. 'She'd *freak*.'

I'm sure she would, given what she's told me, but I don't want to push it. I'm too struck by how terrified he looks. 'So where is your sist— sorry, Rachel. Do you know?'

He rubs at the moth tattoo on the inside of his wrist. The indelible connection to the mother he never knew. 'I have no idea,' he says. 'Honestly. She could be anywhere. She hasn't contacted me since.'

'Well, have you any idea how I can try and find her? The phone number you had written on your hand, for instance. Was that hers?'

He nods. Tells me he wrote it down as his phone was almost out of charge, just in case.

'Have you tried it?' he asks me.

'Yes, of course. But it just rings and rings.'

'It would. She's probably dumped it. She does that. She goes through phones. Specially if she thinks someone she doesn't want to knows her number. Which is, like, basically, *everyone*.'

'Which she obviously would think,' I say, 'if she's seen any of the appeals.'

'Oh, she would have. She'd have looked. She'll know about it, for definite. And she'll know you're on to her. That the police might be involved. That's probably why she's decided to leave us alone now.'

I'm just about to correct him – relate some of the things that have happened – but the fear in his eyes makes me waver. 'I hope that's true,' I say instead, 'but I think I need to find her.'

'Why, though?'

'Because it sounds as if she's sick, wouldn't you say?'

'She is *so* sick,' he says, and his voice is emphatic. 'She likes messing with people. Spying on them. Hurting them. She gets a kick out of it. I *told* you – you don't realise what she's like.'

Perhaps. But I'm beginning to. Even more than he knows. 'And you've definitely not heard from her since you planned to meet her?'

'No, I *told* you.'

'What about on social media? Facebook?'

'You won't find her on Facebook. On anything. She doesn't do social media.'

I find that hard to believe. 'Seriously?'

'*Seriously*. She never lets anyone take her photo and she *always* covers her tracks. She's been in trouble with the police, so she's obviously completely paranoid. And if she doesn't want to be found, trust me, she won't be.'

'So how were you in touch with her?'

'Just by phone.'

'And you don't know where she lived? As in when you were first in touch with her?'

He shakes his head. 'No idea. First time I met her was in a pub in Southampton. She sofa-surfs. Moves around a lot. The only person I know she keeps in touch with is her grandmother.'

As in *his* grandmother. Nancy. 'Who you went to visit with your mum, yes?'

Another heavy outbreath makes his fringe do a Mexican wave. 'And I *so* wish I'd never.'

'But she might know where she is now, mightn't she? Where does *she* live?'

A beat. 'I don't remember.'

'But you just said you went to see her.'

'It was dark. Just some flat in Norwood.'

'South Norwood? Upper Norwood? West Norwood?'

'I don't remember.'

Don't or won't? 'But your mum might? Could we at least ask her?'

He looks mortified. So, yes, then. That'll definitely be a *won't*.

'I *told* you,' he says. 'My mum mustn't know about *any* of this stuff. You mustn't ask her. You mustn't tell her. I've given her enough grief already. And I can't put her through any more. I *can't*. Plus, Rachel doesn't know where we live and I want to keep it that way.'

And for the first time since I chased him up the Down in the fog, I feel a welling of anger at this naïve, vulnerable boy. *Yes*, I think. *But she does know where I live. Where* we *live.*

And you led her to us.

Pyrrharctia isabella

The Isabella Tiger Moth, or Woolly Bear

Compare and contrast. Ah, that old essay staple. Compare and contrast how developed societies put structures in place to foster social mobility, with particular reference to current child welfare provision in the UK, using examples to illustrate your points.

Example one: Kane Scott. With your lovely, lovely foster mum. Example two: Rachel Scott. A child of the system.

That's a thing. I mean, seriously. I am an item in a category. A care kid. A file on a DSS computer. A fat file, growing fatter – a statistic in itself. The sort of statistic they try to keep hidden. A weeping sore, without anyone to weep for it.

Does that make *you* weep, Julia? Just throwing that out there. Does it? Once you've downed enough champagne? Sat around in enough armchairs, putting the world to rights with sufficient socialists?

Let me see . . . hmmm . . . I'm guessing not. Because people who cry over all the world's orphans – *actually* cry, snot an' all – well, it's my contention that they'd be seen as a bit dippy, a bit wet. A bit OTT. A bit disin*genuous*.

I mean, yes, feel free to grab your phone and text DONATE10, DONATE20, BLOWAMIGHTY50!!!! (Specially if in company. Definitely then.) But you know what? I mean, yes, they might well be *in extremis*, all those barely saved, shivering infants of all those poor, desperate, drowned refugees. But, hey, just don't go *overboard*. Okay? Virtue signal all you like, but for god's sake, don't snivel.

So, Gran. She's a liar. She's a pants on fire liar. ALL MY LIFE, I had no idea. Not a single sodding CLUE. Let's see what I did know. That my parents were toast. That they were smashed turned to mangled turned to dead turned to ashes turned to ashes turned to dust turned to stardust.

Which left mini-me with (sob) no one bar dear old Grandma and Grandpa, and dear old Grandpa said Grandma couldn't keep me. End of. (Seriously, you think I didn't know that? Of course I knew that, you stupid old trout. And why'd you want to defend the bastard anyway?)

End OF. I was FIVE. And I was already drowning. Up the creek, paddle-less, white-water rafting. Clinging on, a human dinghy, being bounced off the rocks. Bounced to Will and Trude. Bounced to Cherry. Bounced to Millie's 'house' and Jade's 'house'. Bounced – boing! – to YOU.

And after everything, in the end, when it *mattered*, you bounced me too, Gran. You knew what you were taking on. You could have rolled with it, couldn't you? I made you cups of tea, didn't I? I even oiled your fetid ulcers. I was good for you. I was company. I gave you something to fucking *do*.

But even *you*, Gran. Even *you*. After everything you *owe* me.

You kicked me out. Shame on you. Shame on you.

Gotta hand it to her though, that gran of mine. I mean – haha! – what's she *like*, eh? Like she's got some pretty crazy shit going on, that's what. Like, *seriously* crazy shit. Bat-shit crazy shit. Because, she's like, out of the blue, three years later, *here's the thing, love*.

Just like that. I'd only phoned to tap her for some cash, SO I CAN MAKE A PISSING LIFE. And there she is, kapow! Just like batman. Just like that.

Just. Like. That.

Just. Like. *This*.

'Here's the thing, love, I know it's going to be a bit of a shock for you, love, but your mum, love, when she died, love, well, she'd just had another baby, love.'

And I'm, like, *seriously*? And *are you kidding me*? And *what the actual fucking FUCK*?

'And his name, love, is Kane, love. He'd like to meet you.'

Example one: Kane Scott. Who has metamorphosed into a beautiful tiger moth. Look at him! Kane Scott, who is loved! Who is *flying*!

Example two: Rachel Scott. Who has been condemned to stay a caterpillar. Forever over-wintering. Forever *crawling*.

No ticket for the cocoon stage. No *wings*.

Would it surprise you to know I hate you, Kane? It shouldn't. And, frankly, how stupid *are* you? And how stupid was *she*? (Case for the defence, m'lud. Mrs Sixsmith is a sixpence short of shilling. Mrs Sixsmith, in her defence, m'lud, thought she was doing something *help-ful*. Mrs Sixsmith, you see, m'lud, bore a great weight of guilt, m'lud, and on account of having watched multiple episodes of *Long Lost Families*, genuinely thought her actions would be of *benefit*, m'lud.)

Still, your loss. My gain.

A 'nice boy'. That's what she called you, Kane. She thought you would be 'good' for me. She thought – bless her heart – that if I met you, you would 'help' me. You wouldn't even have to do anything – can you imagine such power? Such breathtaking omnipotence? Just by taking breaths, just by *existing*, just by *being*. Just by getting up every morning from your fetid student bed, opening your mouth (nose, whatevs), and *breathing in and out*.

She thought (this, note, her central conceit – ha!) that you could *save* me.

Still, Southampton. Not a bad place, in a worn-out, bombed-to-fuck-in-the-war sort of way. Lots of green space. The sea. The Isle of Wight ferry. 'We should so take a trip there!' Remember me saying that? 'Go for a picnic to Blackgang Chine together, brother and sister! How nice would *that* be?'

No. Me neither.

*Point of order. I went there. First children's home outing. As in first children's home which took us out on an outing. Last children's home outing, too. *Cuts*. (Second children's home. Fuck off. Go and make your fucking beds.)

Still, you were sooo sweet, Kane. So sweetly *nervous*. (Fair play. So would I have been. Because I *know* me.) But at the same time, so full of it. Well, once you'd downed a pint of cider. Full of it and full of shit. But, at the same time, it was good shit. (The lord looked at the firmament and saw that it was *good*.) Oh, boy, you were so gloriously loose tongued. So *excited*. And I thought, on the train back – when I first found *you*, Julia – I thought, well, how very handy. How very *nice*.

Chapter 20

Christmas has come early to London. It always does these days. A creeping, seeping menace in bright, bejewelled clothes, shrieking 'embrace me!' from every shop window.

We have yet to address plans for this Christmas. This Christmas, this second 'first' – the first being Tash's birthday – in what will be a year of further traumatic milestones. This gaping festive sinkhole in our road to recovery. Which we must do. In some form or other. At home? At the cottage? At a ski resort somewhere? Skittering over ankle-breaking ice on too-early slopes? Right now, that feels the safest, least-worst option. *To be away.*

The weather, at least, is still doggedly autumnal. Refusing to join in and play jingle bells. As if to underline the point, there's been a downpour between my leaving work and emerging from Sloane Square station, so when I step out, it's to find pavements which are Mary Poppins glossy, shimmering with the reflections of all the automatic car headlamps, even though it's only one in the afternoon.

I see Tash before she sees me and feel a familiar heaviness settle on me. I know what it is, too. Not just the truths I have to tell her. It's the weight of just how much I wish for her. She has the hood up on her parka and the crown of vulpine fur framing her face makes her look like a character out of a Tolstoy novel. Or a

Russian princess. Or even an oligarch's mistress. The latter, I decide, given that she's ticking all the boxes; sheltering outside Peter Jones, and scrolling through some feed or other on the expensive mobile phone I bought her for her birthday.

She is a 'have' rather than a 'have not', and that weighs heavy too. Not her fault. Not anyone's. Just a fact of modern life, fraught with consequence.

I make my way round the square to her, playing hopscotch across the puddles, seeing her too, in my mind's eye, not in autumn, but late summer – the blowsy back end of that complicated August last year. I see the ghosts of all three of us – mum, dad and only daughter – gathered in the same spot for a very different reason – to celebrate her A-level results. Whereas today, after three days of logistical rearrangements, I have dragged her from her studies and coaxed her to London so I can shift the ground beneath her feet face-to-face.

She hugs me to her, the fur wet against my cheek as we embrace. Then steps back and sticks her hand out.

'Look at this!'

'Look at what?'

She waggles her fingers. 'At *this*, d'oh! My ring!'

For one astounded second I think she's about to tell me she's got engaged.

'It's Mamgu's,' she says, before I can close my open mouth again. 'She gave it to me last week. Isn't it stunning?'

It is indeed stunning. Another 'have'. This time forged from gold, set all around with tiny diamonds.

I compose myself. Exchange astonishment for a dismay I have no right to feel. 'Wow,' I say, regrouping. 'Yes, yes, it is.'

'Exactly. I *know*! It was Gran's eternity ring. Mamgu said she'd decided it was time she passed it on to me. Oh, and it's worth shedloads, apparently, so she said to make sure I speak to you about adding it to the insurance? And did you know? Grandad gave it to her when he got home from the war, and she never took it off again. They had to cut it off her after she died. See? See the join? So look, we match.' She grabs my hand. Where my own mother's wedding ring sits. Which will be hers as well one day. *One* day.

Why *now*, Laura? I feel derailed, wrong-footed, shut out, excluded. Then berate myself for indulging such childish emotions. Because that was almost certainly the intention.

'It's beautiful,' I tell her. 'Make sure you take good care of it.'

'Oh, there's no danger of me losing it,' she says, tugging at it with her other hand. 'Now it's on, I can't get it back past my knuckle. How does *that* work? Still. It's going nowhere, so no worries on that score. So, did you book somewhere? I'm absolutely *starving*.'

She slips her arm through my own, ostensibly jolly; ladies-who-lunch jolly. A little bit too jolly. I know she is not quite herself.

I've booked a table at the same little Italian restaurant we went to last time, which is tucked away in a little lane just behind the King's Road. I dithered about doing so, because she'd been so happy that day, and I'm worried about overlaying happy memories with fraught ones – wary of overwriting a cherished playlist on a cassette tape.

My own memories are more mixed. Coming, as it had, not long after David and I had reached our decision, we were a little like politicians fronting a fractious coalition; still feeling our way into how things would need to be, 'going forward'. How tediously businesslike we both were.

We needn't have worried. With the necessary self-absorption of the not quite fully formed adult, Tash saw only what she wanted to, basked in what *was* true – our mutual happiness for her. If she'd had the smallest inkling that any shards of her foundation stone were shearing off, I would have known.

But her innocence then makes today harder. How do you begin a conversation that will have at its end the admission that you have been lying to your child, and for so long?

But because I know she's already voiced the thought to Laura, I don't waste time skirting round it. Even before our starters arrive, I have already put her mind at rest about her father having an affair.

'It was nothing like that,' I reassure her, once I've confessed I already know about her fears. 'It wasn't another woman. It was Kane Scott he'd been meeting up with in secret.'

Her relief is immediately, tangibly, even surprisingly, obvious. 'I can't *believe* it,' she says. 'You mean, all this time I've been worrying about *nothing*? God, I've been that stressed about it. Like you wouldn't *believe*. Wondering if I should say something to you, wondering if I should just leave it. And then when all this all started happening I was so sure you'd find something. Once you started digging around and everything, I was *so* convinced you would. And all for nothing. *God*, so it was *him* all along! Mum, I *agonised* about telling you about that watch not being Dad's. And as soon as I did tell you, I really wished I hadn't. Because of *course* you'd start digging around, wouldn't you? And I so nearly said something when you wanted Dad's password. But then I thought how could I? How could I *do* that to you?'

I'm confused now. 'Do what?'

'Tell you about *Dad*. Well, what I *thought* I knew about Dad. God, Mum, I can't tell you, this is *such* a relief.' She raises her glass. 'We should drink to that, shouldn't we?' It's not a question.

We duly plink glasses. I try to corral my runaway thoughts. Which are now bolting in all sorts of directions.

Unlike my daughter's, clearly. 'So, then,' she says brightly. She's now very much herself again. 'What *is* the watch all about, then? If Dad wasn't involved with someone else, then who the hell is Kane Scott?'

Easier ground. For the moment, at least. 'Brace yourself, okay?' I say. 'He's Dad's son.'

Her eyes open wide now. '*What?* But you just said—'

'His *biological* son.'

'So, like, he's my actual *brother?*'

'Half-brother. But only genetically. He never knew Dad.'

Now it's Tash who's confused. 'What? I don't get you.'

'You've heard of sperm donation?'

She nods. 'Yes, of course I have. But you mean that's what Dad did? Sperm donation? *Seriously?*'

I note a couple of heads turning as the waiter sashays back and places salads in front of us. Mostly beetroot, in pale shades. Not dissimilar to the bright spots now blooming on Tash's cheeks. I wait till he's gone again. Lower my voice a little. 'Yes, seriously. Back when he was young, Dad was the sperm donor for a friend he used to work with. A doctor friend. She was gay, and she and her partner wanted to have children. And with Dad's help, they did. First a girl and then a boy.'

Tash has speared some beetroot, and it now hovers mid-way to her mouth, a translucent crescent. 'So I have a half-sister as *well?* You mean there are two people walking around who are *related* to me? Dad's *actual* children?'

'I know. You couldn't make it up, could you?'

'Mum, seriously. Are you even sure it's *true?*'

I tell Tash about Lacey Harrison. How there is absolutely no doubt. And curiously, despite her shock at discovering she has two biological siblings, what David *did*, now she understands it, doesn't seem to faze Tash at all. In fact, she seems to find it all rather lovely. And though objectively I understand the leap science has made since then, I don't think I've absorbed just how nonchalantly the young must view this sort of thing. My experience of IVF is just a small part of the story; assisted reproduction is now an everyday event.

As are road accidents. As are deaths. As are children going into care. Tragic though it was, that particular road accident was no different from any other. Common currency once again.

So, again, though she is rapt, Tash is far from incredulous. Though by the time our mains arrive I'm wading into far deeper waters; explaining what I know of the chain of events after the accident. Of Kane's childhood with his foster mother, of all the questions that travelled with him, and the perhaps inevitable realisation that he not only wanted, but *needed* to find out where he came from.

'Okay, I get all that,' Tash says. 'But how did he find Dad? How did he even know who he was in the first place? I thought that sort of information was confidential.'

'It was then. It isn't now. But because Dad did it as a favour for a friend it doesn't matter either way. They kept all his details, so that when they were old enough, Kane and his sister would know a little more about who their biological father was. I doubt they ever thought about things working out the way they have. If they'd still been alive, I'm sure they'd have dissuaded either of them from even looking. And perhaps they'd have no inclination to, either. As it is . . .' I push my plate away. 'Well, this is what we've ended up with. This is where we are.'

'But what about her? Kane's sister. Why didn't she just go to the same foster mother as he did?'

I tell Tash about Rachel's injuries, her epilepsy, her lengthy spell in hospital, the many physical and psychological problems she emerged with. Why her grandparents couldn't take her. How she became a ward of court. About her subsequent tortuous journey through the care system. 'At least what I know of it,' I clarify. 'Which is not a great deal. But what I *do* know is that she obviously has a huge axe to grind about how her life has turned out. She wants what Kane has – or had – and she believes, rightly or wrongly, that she's been denied it. That's why he was hanging around the cottage that day. He was supposed to be meeting her there.'

'To do what?'

Now I hesitate. I don't want to terrify her. Just keep her safe. 'I don't know.' Not quite a lie. I have only Kane's account to go on. 'All I know is that Kane planned to meet her to persuade her to leave us alone.'

Tash looks genuinely appalled. 'Leave us alone? What does she want from us? She doesn't even know us.'

Of all the things I hope for my only child it is that she never loses this. Naivety won't help her, but I don't think she's naïve. Just has a default belief in the goodness of most people, that will take her further than mistrust is likely to any day.

'This isn't about us, sweetie. Well, not personally. Just a case of what we have and she doesn't, I imagine.'

'So where is she now?'

'I don't know. Kane thinks she's given up now. But listen, that card you got? The message about Dad and so on? I'm more and more coming to the conclusion that it was her who might have sent them. She knew about Dad for a while before he died. Which means she almost certainly knew about us, too.'

'What, like as a practical joke?' she asks.

And then some, I think. 'Kind of,' I say. 'Though more malicious than jokey, I'm afraid.'

'But, Mum, I don't get it.' Tash is away now, on another tangent. 'Why didn't Dad just tell you in the first place?'

'I suppose because it didn't seem that important at the time. This all happened before I met him, don't forget, and perhaps he thought no more of it.' Another lie, of course. Because I still don't accept that. David had the recall of a savant on a game show.

Whether it was because he thought it didn't matter, or because he did, makes no difference. Either way, what it didn't do was slip his mind.

But Tash is already shaking her head.

'I don't mean that. I mean why didn't he say anything about being *found* by them? Specially if the girl is such a headcase. Why on earth would he keep that a secret?'

The waiter returns then, looking disappointed as he clears our far from empty plates, the picked-over food grown unappetising while we've been busy dissecting everything else. We both order espressos, and, as I watch him go, I form get-out-of-jail-free sentences in my head. *I have no idea. Because he didn't want to worry us. Because he thought he should deal with it himself.*

But I'm here to tell the truth, aren't I? So I must. 'Because at that time, Dad and I . . . well, sweetie, the truth is that we weren't in, well, the best place. We'd hit a bit of a sticky patch, as you'd already guessed. What with Dad's work, his post in Cardiff . . .'

Tash reaches a hand across the table and places it over mine. 'I *know*, Mum,' she says. 'That's the thing. The whole *point*. That's *exactly* why I did the thing you always said I mustn't.'

'What?'

'Added two and two and made *five*. About his seeing someone. And now it all makes sense. God, I'm *so* glad I was wrong, Mum. I mean, he's gone now, so perhaps it doesn't matter, but . . .'

I take my other hand and place it over hers. And I decide. That this will *do*. It makes sufficient sense for her. Does she *need* to know she counted correctly? No. She's closed the book now. There is no further need for chapter and verse.

Our coffees arrive and Tash downs hers in two swallows. All this time, I think, and she's been as much in knots as I have. Wondering if she should confess her own imagined secret.

That *would* have hurt me, terribly, had our circumstances been different.

She no longer has to worry about it. That's more than enough.

'Exactly,' I say. 'It's history. It's done. Though one thing – I don't want you going to the cottage for the time being. Not on your own, not till I've managed to track this Rachel character down.'

'You think she's dangerous?'

'I don't know. Maybe "dangerous" is a bit strong. But I do think she's sick. Anyway, just to be on the safe side, okay?'

'Okay,' she says. 'Weather's pretty rubbish now, anyway.' She glances at her watch. 'Do we have time to go shopping?'

I accompany Tash on the tube back to Paddington. It's an insane thing to do on a Friday afternoon in central London; if I went straight back to the hospital, where my car is still parked, I'd already be on my way home. As it is, I'll now be sitting in a jam for much of my rush-hour journey. But it will at least kill extra time which I'd only spend fretting. And if I do pop back into work first (which I will; there are a couple of in-patients I need to check on) by the time I'm back in Clapham, Tash will be almost home too. She'll at the very least have got as far as Swansea station.

I also want to take her back to Paddington. Yes, she's relaxed now she's lightened the load on her shoulders, but she still has lots to carry – in her head, if not her backpack, as she only bought a bracelet – so the least I can do is help her carry it as far as I'm able. If I had my way, she'd stay over and travel back tomorrow, but there's a party tonight (there is always a party) and perhaps her friends, and the many distractions and diversions of her student life, will prove a better environment in which to process everything than brooding about it all at home with me.

It proves the right approach, too, because I've not long got indoors and made a coffee, when her name appears on the incoming call screen.

I'm ready to be interrogated; now she's had time to think, I imagine she'll have lots of questions. But I'm wrong. She's not phoning to ask me anything. She's calling because she has something to tell me.

'Listen, Mum,' she says. 'You were right. About that Rachel girl being sick. Because you won't believe what I've just found. The grossest thing. I mean, *seriously* gross.'

I am immediately on edge again. 'What? Where are you?'

'At the cottage.'

'At the *cottage*? What on earth are you doing there? I told you not to go there on your own!'

'I'm not *on* my own. Jonathan's with me. He's been in Cardiff, so I picked him up from Swansea station so he could come with me.'

I curse myself. Why didn't I spell it out more clearly? 'But what are you doing there? Tash, I told you not to go there.'

'Mum, *chill*. Jonathan's here with me. I told you! I realised on the train that I was missing one of my textbooks. One I need for an assignment. But, listen – get this for creepy. Someone's pinned a dead moth to the front door. And I mean a really *huge* moth . . . You know, like the ones they have in Thailand? I'm talking *that* big. It's enormous. Almost as big as a *bird*.'

She is at the cottage. And there is a dead moth pinned to the front door. 'You've not gone in there, have you?'

'*God*, no! Of course not – not now. No *way* are we going in there. Jonathan's as spooked as I am. We're back in the car now. I took a picture though. I'm going to text it to you. Hang on . . . Okay, it's sent . . . Have you got it?'

My phone pings. 'I've got it.'

And up the image pops, beneath the glowing 'return to call' bar. And though it's hard to sense the size I know a big moth when I see one. I also recognise it as a hawkmoth.

But not a common or garden hawkmoth. A very distinctive hawkmoth. It has a pattern of a skull and crossbones on its back. A death's head.

Acherontia atropos

The African Death's Head Hawkmoth

Well, of COURSE it is. Don't you read? Don't you go to the mooovies? *The Silence of the Lambs*. Cracking film. Cracking *moth*. A moth who is named, if you didn't know, after one of the three Fates, or *Moriai*; *Atropos*, whose job description reads 'cutter of the thread of life'. Nice.

    Nice. But let's set aside all thoughts of fictional serial killers for a moment. Don't be scared. I have no desire to kill anyone. At least I don't *think* I do. Not now. Isn't that a thing, Julia? I know! Would you credit it? I'm not that stupid, either. I understand about golden eggs.

    Whatever. Ah, but honey. I am very fond of honey. At least, I assume I am. What do I know of your land of milk and honey, after all? Only that I would very much like to *taste* it. And sometimes, as they say, needs must.

This is one clever moth. It's – ahem – the bee's knees. It likes honey. Honey which sits in cells, sealed with wax, within a honeycomb, within a beehive, with bees guarding the entrance, so it's a pretty safe place for a honey stash to beeeeeee.

But *Acherontia* – the bee robber – has a particularly clever trick up its striped sleeve. Despite its size, it can sneak into a hive unremarked and unmolested, because it can mimic the scent of the very creature it aims to steal from. It can make itself *smell* just like a bee.

Oh, and guess what else, fact fans? Eep, eep! It squeaks! It squeaks in my head endlessly. Never shuts up. Just squeaks and squeaks and squeaks and squeaks and squeaks. It goes, 'honey money! Honey, money! Lovely filthy lucre honey money!'

It wants money, honey. It has no higher purpose.

Ah, but here's the thing, Julia. I do.

Chapter 21

'Kane, I need your grandmother's phone number.'

'I told you, I don't know it.'

'I'm sorry, but I don't believe you.'

'But I *don't*. She never gave it me. Look, I can't talk, okay?' His voice is a low, defiant hiss. 'I'm in my bedroom. I'm back at *home*.'

'So ask your mum, then. I've had enough of this.'

'But I *told* you. Look, I really can't talk—'

'I don't care where you are. I need to track Rachel down, and if you won't give me your grandmother's number, then I'll have to ask your mum myself. Kane, it's important.'

'What's happened?'

I tell him.

'*Shit*. God. She is *sick*. See? I told you. She—'

'So do I ask your mum or will you?'

'*No*. Look, I think I can tell you where she lives at least. Hang on.' I hear a door being closed. A chair squeaking. Clicks on a keyboard. 'Let me just bring up Google street maps. It's Upper Norwood. Definitely. Near the television mast up on Beulah Hill. Ah, here it is. I think I can describe it for you at least.'

He gives me a street name. 'It's on the left, as you're going up the hill. I don't know the number but it's about halfway up, and it has this old-fashioned letter box right outside it.'

'Letter box?'

'I mean postbox.'

'What, a red one?'

'Yeah, yeah. Standard postbox, just a really, really old one. I remember Mum pointing it out. You can't miss it. It's right there. Literally right outside the house. And it's the bottom flat on the right. Down a little flight of steps. Like a fire escape. Look – I'm sorry, okay. Really sorry. You know, for landing all this crap on you. If I'd known . . .'

'Kane, it's done. Don't apologise. What's done is done now.'

Except it's not. I have a hunch that it's only just beginning.

My first instinct is to write Nancy Sixsmith a letter and ask if she'll agree to me visiting her. But I stumble immediately at the first, obvious, hurdle. I still have no address, and though I tap her name and location into a number of websites, it soon becomes obvious that she has no online presence. Neither does she seem to be on the electoral roll. I consider enlisting Nick then – I'm sure he could trace her in an instant – but that, too, feels inappropriate. An invasion of her privacy. So when, by Wednesday, there's a half-chance of getting away from work on time, I decide to drive there and try my luck instead.

Kane's instructions prove easy to follow. Though it's a dark, moonless night, and the road is very long, there is only one house that fits the bill. On the left, as he described, with a high privet hedge, and, right there, on the pavement, the Victorian postbox, with a top like a minaret. The hedge is neatly clipped, the house behind similarly well groomed; warm-hued and respectable under the light of the adjacent street lamp.

Back when it was built, it would have functioned as a substantial family home, with plenty of room below stairs. Now it's flats, six of them, three on each side, and, just as Kane told me, in what would once have been the sub-basement, the bottom two have their own separate front doors.

I head down a short run of iron steps. The frosted glass panel to the side of the door has two stickers fixed to it. One, circular and peeling, says Neighbourhood Watch, and the other – a yellow rectangle which looks like a parking ticket – says no hawkers, no salespeople, no agents, no cold callers, no canvassers, no charities, no religious groups.

And, presumably, no strangers. I step down, rather than up, into the small open porch. There is no bell that I can see. Just the door knocker attached to the letter box, which squeaks as I lift it. I knock twice, not too loudly. It's almost eight and now I'm standing here my folly becomes more obvious. If I were her, at this time of night, at her age (which, even if she had her daughter in her teens, must be great) would I open my door to a stranger? I hang on to the fact that at least I'm not a male stranger, but if I were an elderly lady, living alone, would I let me in? No.

I hear movement though. Was she expecting someone? There's a wash of light as an internal door opens, and a form appears in the hall.

'That you, Jack?' I hear a voice say, from the other side of the door. 'You're early. Where's your key?'

'No, I'm Julia,' I tell her, through the nearest glass panel. 'Julia Young?'

In response, I hear a chain being shunted into place. The door then opens, even if only by the three or four inches the chain allows, and a white-haired woman peers out at me through tortoiseshell-framed glasses.

'Oh,' she says. Her eyes narrow. 'Where's Jackie?'

So she *was* expecting someone. 'My name's Julia,' I begin, smiling. 'I'm not—'

'Is she sick?' she asks.

'No. I mean, I don't know. I—'

'Who are you, then?'

'My name's Julia,' I say again. 'Julia *Young*. You don't know me. I was hoping—'

'Are you from the police?'

'No, no.' I keep the smile in place. 'Not the police. Nothing like that. My name's Julia Young. David Young was my husband?'

'*David* Young?'

'Yes, David Young. I was hoping to speak to you about your granddaughter Rachel.'

I widen the smile, but I can tell from the way her eyes also widen behind the glasses that the name has had an unwelcome effect. That, scared as she is of me, I've apparently now invoked a greater fear. Her gaze darts behind me then, and I automatically look back as well, up the steps. There's no one there. Did she expect there to be? She closes the door a fraction. There's just an inch of her showing now. A single milky eye. 'What d'you want with her? What about her?'

'I was hoping you might be able to tell me where I can find her,' I go on. 'As I say, my husband, David . . . Look, I'm so sorry to turn up here out of the blue – and so late – but I'm just really anxious to speak to you about Rachel, because—'

'What about her?' she snaps again.

'I'd just like to speak to her. She's—'

'She doesn't live here anymore. I don't know where she is. I haven't clapped eyes on her in years. Anyway, what do you want with her? What's she done?'

Her tone is defensive enough to add 'this time' without her having to say it. I have a strong sense that she's said this, or a version of it, many times. 'It's not what she's done,' I say. 'Not exactly. It's more what I'm worried she *might* do. I've been talking to Kane – Kane Scott, her brother? And I'm concerned that . . .'

'Who d'you say you were again?'

'Julia Young. My husband, David, was Rachel's biological father, and—'

'I know *that*,' she says. The door opens a fraction wider again. 'Do you have any ID?'

I reach into my bag. 'Of course. Yes. No problem. Here,' I say, as I retrieve my driving licence from my purse and hold it out for her. A tiny hand comes through the gap and snatches it from me. I note translucent fingers. A pair of rings. Pale frosted fingernails. Then the door shuts, and stays shut, so I wait. Some twenty seconds pass. But just as I'm wondering what to do next I hear the chain rattle again and the door finally swings open.

She looks both at me and behind me, then flaps a hand irritably. 'Well, come in then, if you're coming, before you let all the warm out.'

So I step out of the chilly night. But into what?

Where Lacey Harrison, enriched by love, was plump as a new cushion, Nancy Sixsmith is just as she was described to me, a shell, insubstantial under a cream blouse and mustard checked skirt, both of which look much too big for her. They look clean and fresh but have clearly seen better days. My ball park calculations of her age, logical in their parameters, have failed to take account of the biggest, most brutal factor. That this woman lost her only daughter in such appalling circumstances.

Lacey was right. Some vital life force must have died in her that day. And whatever powerful act of will saw this woman survive that, she must have been stretched to breaking point by everything that happened after. The immediate loss of a grandson – did she even get to see him? – and perhaps the even greater loss, of her grand-daughter to the care system. I cannot begin to imagine what that must do to a person.

There is still so much I don't know, and as she leads the way into a little front sitting room – once again, heated to a sub-tropical temperature – I can only hope she will be able to tell me some-thing useful. Something that will quell my growing fear that I have opened the lid on something much more disturbing and frighten-ing than a simple jigsaw of an unlikely family tree. It's an impres-sion not helped as I enter the tiny space, to be assailed by the sense that it's not even a real room, but one of those creepy room set reconstructions you find in museums that recreate the past. The ones children trudge past on school trips, bored and irritable, hold-ing clipboards. Time stopped here a good while ago.

'I don't have long,' she says, as she hobbles back to the seat she recently vacated. It's a threadbare wing armchair, in an institutional shade of green, with a seat cushion long-moulded to accommodate her tiny frame. The arms are greasy with use and age. The television is blaring – one of the soaps, people shouting – and a TV listings magazine is open on the floor in front of a spindly legged teak cof-fee table. She reaches for an oversized remote as she lowers herself back into the chair. 'I've a carer due,' she adds, as she turns down the volume. Her scalp gleams pink beneath a fuzz of white hair.

I also see, as she lifts it carefully onto a squat upholstered foot-stool, that, beneath tan pop socks, one of her legs is swollen and heavily bandaged.

'Of course,' I tell her, opting for a perch on the edge of the remaining armchair, whose seat sags so far it could almost be a commode. Once her husband's? Judging by the state of it, I suspect so. 'I was just hoping you could help me try and get hold of your granddaughter.'

'I wouldn't hold your breath,' she says. 'I told you. I've not laid eyes on her in years. She could be anywhere. She never stays in one place for long. And she only ever gets in touch when she needs money.' She expels air through thin lips. 'Which is probably why I haven't heard from her for so long – she knows I've none left.'

Her tone is bitter, and I'm not sure how to respond.

I opt for, 'I'm so sorry.'

'You and me both,' she says, looking sharply at me.

This home, like Lacey's, is full of framed images. But where hers were photographs, the images here are painted artworks, giving the cramped, subterranean space even more of a museum-like air. Watercolours, drawings, scientific-looking pen-and-ink sketches – the latter reminiscent of the one I've seen already. More moths. Many butterflies. Caterpillars, beetles, weevils. All kinds of winged and crawling insects, big and small. The sort of pictures and diagrams you'd expect to see in a natural history museum, hanging above display cabinets of dead, skewered specimens. Like the corpses I had to clear from their final resting place in my bathroom. Like the pupae. Like the moth skewered by a pin to the cottage door.

I cannot imagine surrounding myself with such images. Her daughter's art, then? Almost certainly. Why else? Her daughter's legacy. And though there appears not to be a single photograph of the woman herself in it, I realise this room is a shrine to her.

'So, when did you last see your granddaughter?' I ask.

'See her? In the flesh? I told you. Ages ago. Must be three years by now. Something like that. Probably more. I lose track. I only heard from her last year because she was off on one of her ridiculous hare-brained schemes again.'

'Schemes?'

She lifts a hand and flaps it as if she's flicking away a persistent wasp. 'Oh, I don't know. Some nonsense. Some painting course or other.'

'So, she's artistic, then? Like her mum?'

'Oh, *she* certainly thinks she is.'

But you don't, I think. 'So that's what she's doing now, is it? Painting?'

'I have no idea. I *told* you. All I know is that's she's bled me dry, that girl. *Dry*. But if you do find her, you can tell her the same as I told your husband – that's *it*.'

My mouth opens in shock. 'You've spoken to my *husband*?'

'Yes, and like I told him, I don't have anything left *to* throw away. She's had all my savings, all my jewellery . . . She'd have the shirt off my back if she thought she could sell it at a car boot. No, I'm done with her. And you'd do well to have nothing to do with her either.'

'When was this? I mean, when you spoke to my husband?'

'When he came here? Oh, last year sometime . . .' She chews her lower lip. 'September? October? I don't remember. As I said to him at the time, I'm done with her. I *mean* it. I'm not getting involved.'

She looks agitated. I sit back a little, trying to still my racing thoughts. So David came here as *well*?

'I understand that,' I say. 'But I really do need to find her. Because from what Kane tells

me—'

An irritable-sounding 'pfft' escapes her lips. 'From what he tells you . . .' she parrots back at me. 'So I suppose you're about to tell me no good's come of any of it, are you?'

Yes. Without a smidgen of a doubt. 'No, not that exactly,' I say. 'But I'd be lying if I said I wasn't worried. She's been . . .' I am at a loss as to how to put things diplomatically. This woman is her grandmother, after all. 'Well, Kane's put me in the picture a little about what's been happening, and from what I've found out for myself, various things that have happened, and a conversation I had with Kane's foster mother, it sounds as though she has some quite profound mental health problems.'

She rolls her eyes, and so emphatically that her whole face tilts heavenwards, stretching taut all the hollows and folds in her neck, and rendering her cheeks a sickly yellow beneath the ceiling light. It's a frosted glass bowl, full of real insect corpses. Everyday collateral, which, in this setting, feels anything but. 'I'd be surprised if she didn't,' she says. 'Amount of drugs she's taken. That was the last straw, it really was. I gave her so many chances. Anyway, what's she done? Taken your husband for a ride now as well, has she? I told him he was on a fool's errand, thinking *he* could do anything to help her.'

I feel her irritation crackling between us. 'He's my *late* husband now,' I correct her.

The effect is electric.

Though I'm not sure why I'm shocked. Because why would this woman know about David's death? But I find her response – from world-weary to horrified in an instant – shocking in itself. Because why would anyone respond like that to merely hearing someone's died?

Something else has also crept into her expression. As if this news, at least the *kind* of news, isn't totally unexpected. I'm not sure if I'm trying to make five out of four again, but I have absolutely no doubt that she has. 'He died of a stroke,' I add quickly. 'At work. Back in February. I had no idea he'd come to visit you, but I do know Rachel had found out who he was. And since his death . . . well, the truth is that David was helping Kane out financially and, perhaps understandably, from what he's been telling me, she's been badgering Kane since David died—'

'Trying to get her hands on his money too? Now, why doesn't that surprise me?' She looks up to the ceiling again, which is so low it makes the room feel like a bunker. An overheated bunker in which I suspect she spends a great deal of time. With all those creepy crawlies pressing in on her. It can't be healthy.

She seems lost in thought now. 'Mrs Sixsmith,' I try, 'look, if you can think of any means by which I might be able to track Rachel down . . . a previous address, perhaps? A friend she might have been in touch with? Or how about the course she wanted to enrol on? Did she tell you where that was? Because until I find her I'm not going to be in a position to try and help her, and—'

'*Help* her?' Another 'tsk' sound. 'You as *well*? Why would *you* want to help her? What's she to you?'

'Well, *obviously*, no one – I don't know her, do I? But I could at least try to urge her to *get* help. I know I don't know a great deal about her, but, as I say, it sounds to me as if she's quite severely mentally ill.'

Her mouth forms another frown between the clefts that run down either side of her nose. 'Huh,' she says again. 'Tell me something I *don't* know.'

Then her eyes crumple shut and I see her nostrils flare. And I realise she is fighting back tears.

I lean towards her across the low coffee table that separates us. 'I'm so sorry,' I say. 'I didn't come here to upset you. And if I can find her, and help her, I promise I will. But—'

Her eyes ping open again. 'Upset me? You honestly think *you* can upset me? You flatter yourself, dear. You have no *idea*.'

But I'm about to find out. And she isn't being honest about me upsetting her. I clearly *have*. At least cranked the handle on the lock-gate of her emotions, because it's through an unbroken stream of tears that she seeks to *give* me an idea, while I supply her from my travel pack of tissues. And, again, I have this sense she's been

267

here many times before, telling the same story and hoping for a different ending. Trying to justify what sounds completely justifiable but which, in her head, she simply can't.

It's the same story Lacey has already sketched out to me. One of wanting so much to help but being unequal to the task, and bit by bit, seeing that task grow ever harder.

'I know I couldn't care for her myself, but I kept in touch, always. Went to visit her in hospital. Every single week, I went. For a whole *year*. I even went to see her at one of those places they set up at the council. Awful place, it was. Like being in a padded cell. And her so *sick*. But then they moved her on again. They do exactly what they like, you know. You're not even consulted. You don't have any rights at all. Right out of London, to some specialist foster place that said they'd have her. And how on *earth* did they think I'd be able to get there? But they didn't care. They'd washed their hands of her – that's the truth of it, whatever *they* try to tell you. You don't know what they're like. They just didn't *care*.'

Because it's part of my job, I have long experience of dealing with dying patients' relatives. And just as the network of relationships in every life is different, so is the emotional response to every impending death. For a lucky few, it's simple. If it's someone who has loved, and has been loved, grief is profound but straightforward. For most families, however, it is anything but. There are few lives untainted by complicated relationships. Few deaths where they don't cast their own unique shadow. The put-upon. The absentee. The grudge-bearer. The resentful. The antagonist. The self-righteous. The *guilty*.

Nancy Sixsmith, I realise, has been grieving all her life, and not just for the child she lost while still so young, or the loss of her daughter's imagined future. She was also grieving for the future she had failed to give her daughter's *children*. The one ripped away from her within a matter of days, and the other – perhaps more cruelly, given that she already knew and loved her – erased from her life over a period of years.

I don't doubt it was more complex than Nancy Sixsmith imagines; that it was challenging to find care-givers in such a difficult, multi-factorial case. I wonder if she's fair to assume what she's assuming. But more than that, I wonder about the previous occupant of the armchair I'm currently perched on. The man Lacey described as hostile and homophobic. About just how much responsibility for this elderly lady's plight he must bear? How much of her weight of guilt should he be bearing?

I don't ask. I don't mention him. She doesn't either; in the emotional horror chamber she's currently showing me around, I suspect he has his own special place, safe behind a door she has decided to stop opening. And, as a consequence, she's shouldered his guilt as well.

Grief and guilt, in my experience, are a toxic combination. From a cross word that no one could have known would be a last word, to the terrible load carried – and I've seen this so often – by a person who knows that they never did enough; didn't help enough, didn't care enough, didn't cherish enough, didn't love enough. Who are condemned to limp on through life nursing a wound which will never heal because they cannot go back and change the past. Who know the worst words they can conjure are 'if only'.

I know grief fades eventually but where there is guilt in the mix, I also know how easily it takes its place. And, because her guilt is always hungry, it has nibbled at her, chewed on her, wolfed her down, gobbled her up. There is little else left of her. It has consumed her.

And it's now brought her to a place where she must wash her hands too. Piling yet more guilt onto the wealth of it already there. I wonder how many people in her life – who *are* the people in her life? – have attempted to stop the rot and sow seeds of hope in her. To help her find meaning within these four mausoleum walls.

That they've failed is all too evident. And I know I won't do better.

I still try, even so. 'It's no one's fault,' I tell her. 'It's just life. Bad things happen.' I place my hand on her tiny wrist, feel the brittleness of her bones. 'It's just the way things work out some-times. You couldn't *know* what was going to happen. How could anyone? I know it's easier said than done, but you really mustn't blame yourself.'

Tears are tracking down her cheeks, but her gaze now is unblinking. She knows as well as I do that my words are as empty as her life is. 'No?' she says. 'So tell me. Who would *you* blame?'

Since I have no answer to that either, I could not be more grateful to hear the sound of a key turning in a lock. Then of the front door opening, and the night air flowing in, a cheerful 'Nancy, love! Only me!' riding on it.

A smiling young woman in a purple tabard appears in the doorway. 'Ah,' she says, looking first at me, then back to Nancy, who is so obviously distressed. The smile drops. 'Everything all right, love?' she asks. 'You okay?'

I don't know what she has me pegged as, but there's nothing subtle about the suspicion with which the woman is now looking at me. But perhaps that's to be expected. I'm a stranger in an elderly lady's house. The sort of stranger who might be there selling double glazing, or spurious insurance policies, or disabled living 'solutions'.

Worse than that, Nancy is still sobbing – proper, shoulder-heaving sobbing. And, as I pluck the last tissue from my packet, I have no idea how to console her. I feel as if I've unleashed some-thing dark and cruel and evil. And that, now she's started, she might never stop.

'I'm Julia Young,' I say, rising from my chair and wondering whether to extend my hand to the woman. Since hers are full – keys in one, bag of tricks in the other – I opt not to. 'Mrs Sixsmith is upset. I—'

'I can see that for myself,' she snaps, glaring at me. She plops the keys into the bag and the bag down on the coffee table. 'Nancy, love, are you all right?' she says, bending down to comfort her. 'Is this woman bothering you? What does she want?' She turns back to me then, still glaring. 'Who exactly *are* you?'

'Julia Young,' I say a second time. 'I'm—' *What?* What exactly *am* I here? And how on earth do I begin to explain?

I open my mouth to try to. But Nancy Sixsmith clears her throat, and flaps the hand holding the tissue. 'It's all right, Jackie,' she says, as she dabs at her wet cheeks. 'She's just come to talk to me about Rachel.'

'Ah,' says the woman. And our eyes meet, and she nods. And I can tell that she's heard all this before. 'Ah,' she says again. 'I *see*. I'll go and pop the kettle on for a cuppa then.'

And because I feel as if I'm drowning, as if the air is being sucked from me, I repeat my promise, make my excuses, leave my phone number and go.

Attacus atlas

The Atlas Moth

And I give you . . . . Atlasss! The biggest
mothhhh in the worrldddddd!!!!!!

Atlas was a Titan.

Atlas was in a war.

The Olympians beat the Titans.

Atlas was punished.

Condemned to carry the world upon his shoulders
for ever more.

Oh, empathise away, *Daddy*. You gods gotta stick together, after all. But – point of order – it wasn't all heavy lifting and upper back pain. Even as he carried the entirety of everything, Atlas still managed to knock out a few kids along the way.

Funny how they do that, eh? Males?

So, I'm early for our Important Meeting. I always make a point of being early. The early bird tends to catch stuff the late-comers don't. Like the vibe. I love a vibe, me. I thrive on a vibe. And this vibe's so vibey, it's a vibe within a vibe. It vibes away inside my head. Pinging vibelets back and forth. I see them. I smell them. I taste them. I *feel* them. I absorb the knowledge of their complicity by osmosis.

Here's the thing, though. You had one job, *daddy*. To understand the principle that's at stake here. Two sperm. Two ova. Two embryos. Two foetuses. Two babies. Two offspring. Two *dependent human beings*. Who are, praise be (and please don't pretend you don't know this), born equal in the eyes o' the lord.

Equal. That's pretty key. That's the locus and the focus. That's pretty much the bottom line – the *numero uno*. That's the principle upon which rests the entirety of everything.

Highfalutin, huh? Well, of course. Though there is nothing highfalutin about my reason for being here. About my hashtag *2017slash2018goals*.

Still, I'm good, me. I'm conscientious. I'm not just an artist. I am a *thespian*, darling. An *artiste*. So I am always well rehearsed.

'Hi, Kane. Hello, David. It's *so* good to meet you. Though – *wow* – this is just so weird, isn't it? I mean, seriously. I mean, bonkers. I mean, god, like, when my gran said . . . Well, doesn't it do your head in? Just . . . Sorry, I'm just so *nervous*, I— Okay, yeah. I'll sit there, shall I? Sorry . . . Yes, very good, thanks. Oh, um . . .

oh. Um, thank you. Er . . . um, just a Diet Coke please? Great. *Thank* you. It's just . . . *god*, on the tube, I was, like, wow. I can't *believe* this. Sure you get that, Kane, don't you? I mean – what a mind-fu— I *mean*, hahahahaha, isn't this *surreal?* Like, all these years . . . and, well, yes . . . Oh, I have a job working at a deli. Yeah, it's great. Only temporary. It's not, like, for*ever.* But at least it pays the bills. Well, some of them, at any rate. I'm . . . oh. Yes, studying art. Haha. D'oh. Yes, hopefully. In the genes . . . Hahahaha. Yes, *god*, I *hope* so . . . You know, night school? A foundation course? It's one of the entry requirements. Yeah, yeah, okay so far . . . Oh, commercial artist, probably. I love fine art, but . . . No, exactly. No money in it, is there? Yep. I'm working on my portfolio. Doing a little performance art on the side . . . No, no, it's just a collective . . . It's . . . Oh, right. Okay. Um . . . gosh, such a big menu! Um . . . hmmm . . . you say three each? Well, um . . . gosh, I don't know. Maybe . . . Ah, sorry. I'm vegan. So, I . . . *Sorry.* No, it's fine, *honestly.* Um, perhaps the *patatas bravas?* Oh, of course. No – d'oh. Hahaha. Of *course.* No mayo . . . So, um, maybe the broad bean thing? And some olives. And maybe hummus? Hahaha. Yes, I do get that. A *lot.* But it's fine. I'm pretty used to it now. Plus it's cheap – Hurrah for tempeh! – so that's good . . . Yeah, it's pretty tough. What with all the fees and that. London prices . . . Trying to earn enough to *live*, let alone *save . . .* '

And so on and so tediously so forth.

But put your ear to the door, folks. Listen up. Listen *carefully.* Can you hear the snap of shears as they start cutting the crap? The snip of scissors as they cut to *the chase?*

You have money.

I need money.

You need to give me money.

You have given *him* money, *ergo* you need to give *me* money.

What part of 'you owe me money' do you not understand?
You had one job, *Daddy* Dave-god. You had *ONE job*.
Instead, you're sitting there offering me HELP?

Fade in:
INT: Generic urban tapas bar. Midweek. Midday. Half full.
  <u>DAVID</u>, coffee cup raised, part way to his mouth.
    Cue: <u>DAVID</u>

'The thing is,' he says. 'Rachel,' he says. 'Well,' he says, 'it's this.'
(Lowers voice.) 'I don't feel entirely comfortable about giving you
money. Yes, I know I've helped Kane out with his tuition fees and
so on, and it's right that I do likewise for you too, of course it is.
But in terms of actual cash . . .' (Winces slightly, looks at Kane,
pinches bridge of nose.) 'To put it plainly, I know you're a drug
user, Rachel, and while I'm sensitive to your situation, it wouldn't
be responsible of me to – either knowingly or *un*knowingly – fund
that.'
 I think: What the actual hell, Kane?
 I say: Nothing.
 'So, what I'm thinking,' Daddy Dave's saying (upgraded to
full-on Daddy Dave Operating System version 2.0 now) 'is that
the most helpful thing I can do for you right now is get you help.'
(Pregnant pause.) 'With that problem.'
 I think: What the actual HELL, Kane?
 I say: Nothing.
 I turn: Towards Kane.
 I feel: Murderous.

Daddy Dave sees my look. Which is my best look. My worst look. My 'I SO MEAN IT' death stare. The waiter flits past like a big black-and-white butterfly.

'I have been to see your grandmother,' says Dave, all low and firm and gnarly. Knowing (oh he's clever – did I mention our fantastic genes?) that 'been to see your gran' is secret code for 'you've been proper shopped, love', and that any and all jaunty responses I might fashion will be blown as chaff from the back of his combine harvester. Oh, and hasn't he been the busy one? Hasn't he harvested well?

And from somewhere in the mist, and it's red, now, proper blood-red, I hear him say the word 'intervention'. And the jaunty response I'm busy fashioning (well, a girl's gotta try) just won't come out of my mouth.

I am reduced. Even worse, SO much worse, I am *pitied*. And being pitied is not permissible. Being pitied, to use the parlance, is *insupportable*.

I do not know (and this a rare and dangerous thing) what to do next.

'I'm sorry?' I say eventually. (Sweetest voice, bat of lashes.) 'I don't know what she's told you, but she's clearly got her wires crossed.' (Glance at plate. Durr. Take note. I'm a sodding vegan, for god's sake!)

Daddy Dave glances at Kane again, the little weasel in his pocket.

I think: Bastard.

I think: Fzzzzzz. Error code 404.

'Listen,' Dave says. 'Look.' (Listen and look. Hark and heed.) 'I am sorry for your situation, Rachel, genuinely sorry. I want to help you.' (Sheesh! Does the man never LISTEN?) 'I know this isn't what you want to hear, but there's nothing to be gained by trying to deny it. I've thought long and hard about what best to do, and I genuinely want to help you with this.'

I look at Kane.

I look at Kane.

I look at Kane.

'I was thinking [full-on drone-mode] that perhaps finding you some counselling will be a – No, no, it's fine, Marco. Everything is fine. Thank you – a good place to start.'

I look at Kane.

I look at Kane.

I look at Kane.

Kane, who is frightened. Kane, who is properly shrinking into himself now. Like a slug someone poured a bunch of salt on. With his half of pissy shandy.

Like Alice with the potion, I drink his fear in, gulp it down.

'Rachel?' Daddy Dave says. 'Rachel, are you all right?'

'*Jesus*, Rachel.' Kane hisses. 'Stop it. David, let me—'

'*No*, Kane. I'll deal with this. Marco—' He lifts a finger and the lackey's there in seconds. 'Can I have the bill, please? Thank you so much.' Then to me. 'Rachel, do you need some air? I think we need to get outside, into the fresh air.'

He reaches into an inside jacket pocket. To his bulging, throbbing wallet. How much is in there, I wonder. How many crisp notes does he keep close to his beating, cheating heart? But it's a randomer, that little thought. A throwaway. A bagatelle. The big thought – the important thought – is a welcome return to sanity. I am going to get nothing but grief from this man. If this is Dad – if this is *dads* – you can keep them. Who the fuck do they think they are?

Be of good cheer, Moth! Other ways to skin cats are available. Oh, yes *indeedy*.

I am done here.

Some people make entrances. I prefer making exits. Exits are my forte. Exits define me. Exits are what I have been making *all my fucking life*.

Hmm, now. Let me see. There's still glassware on the table. Still Kane's glass, with drink in. Three tumblers, without. And a car-afe. No, a 'craf'. ('A *carafe* of tap water, please, Marco?' 'Yes, of course, sir. Right away, sir.')

A craf which will do very nicely.

So (you asked for it, you did, you know) cut to the scene:

When they make the movie, it will, of course, be shot in slow motion. Mood lighting. Portentous violins. Appropriately dark palette. There's Marco (ever present) shouting 'Noooooooo' as I lift the 'craf', then a cutaway to a reaction shot of Kane's horrified expression, which they'll have to do several takes to perfect. Then back to me – hey, I'm the star here! – as I raise it even further (by the neck, of course) then slam it down, centre table, for shardage to the max. Then 'ping!' (this the bonus) as it connects with the cruet, and a big lump, the biggest lump (for this is as it is ordained) flies up and hits Kane – 'smack!' – right in the kisser – all of it captured by a wide tracking shot.

'*Jesus*, Rachel!' (He won't help you, mate.) 'You've broken my bloody tooth!'

Then the – what's the word? Yes, *denouement* – as I make for the entrance. And Kane's bleeding. And Marco's, like, 'Someone call the pleeeece!'

And (no-sugar) Daddy David's, like, 'No, no, please. It's fine, Marco. I'll sort everything out.'

And he's, like, 'Really?'

'Yes, *really*. I'll pay for the damage.'

And, oh, yes, you *will* pay. You will *indeed* pay for the damage. Cue music. Cue closing credits.

[Ends.]

See, I know how to make an exit. And *you* need to listen. I *told* you.

I have been making exits *all my fucking **life***.

Chapter 22

It's gone ten, and I'm just putting my key in the door when I feel my handbag start vibrating against my hip. I'm still feeling shaken up, soiled by association. That I've been force-fed too many unpalatable secrets. And because I've given Nancy Sixsmith my number, and she's promised to call me if she can think of anything, my automatic assumption is it must be her. Or – fear grips me now – perhaps it's Tash.

I drop my holdall on the doorstep and fumble for my phone. It's neither. It's Kane Scott.

'Look, I need to tell you something but you must promise not to tell my mum, okay? It's about Rachel – look, I haven't told you the whole truth about everything, okay?'

'I know you haven't. Why didn't you tell me David had been to see your grandmother?'

'Because . . . because . . . Look. I just . . . Look, I just didn't want to . . . Look, the thing is, the reason I don't want you to tell my mum anything about Rachel is because I've got a caution from the police.'

He's firing words at me at such a rate that they seem to tumble over one another as if fighting to be first to leave a stricken aeroplane.

I ask him to hang on while I get inside and shut the door. Then yank up the handle to lock the dead bolts as well. The dark in the hall is absolute. I ping the light on. I need to hurry up and get a dog. Perhaps a German Shepherd after all.

'A caution for what?' I say.

'Possession.'

'Of drugs?'

'Yes. But it wasn't anything to do with me. Honestly.'

'They all say that, Kane.'

'No, *honestly*. It was *her*.'

'And when was this?'

'Last summer.'

'Just gone?'

'No, no. The last one. Towards the end of my second year. After she came down to Southampton.'

'So when you first met?'

'No, a couple of weeks later. She just turned up out of the blue. I thought I'd seen the last of her. She never answered my texts or anything, so I thought that was that. But she'd found herself a bar job, and a room.'

'You mean she *moved* there? To be near you?'

'Exactly.'

'Just like that?'

'Just like that. And I didn't realise what she was up to, not then. I mean, I thought it was a bit weird that she'd just turned up like that, but I just took it for what it was. You know, with what her gran had said about her, about how she moved around all the time. It was only when I realised the amount of drugs she was doing—'

'So what exactly happened? How did you end up with a caution?'

'We had a police raid at a party at ours.'

'Which she'd come to?'

'She *brought* them. Well, if not her – I'm not exactly sure if she did or didn't – definitely the guy she'd hooked up with. He was on Lewis's course. You know Lewis?'

'I know Lewis.'

'And he was another right cokehead. Not Lewis,' he adds loyally. 'I'm talking about his mate. No *way* would anyone else there have that amount of coke on them.'

'So you think she planned it? Tipped the police off?' I can't quite believe the words I'm saying. Can't quite believe this isn't the plot of a 1970s police procedural. That it's happened. That it's *real*. 'I mean, wouldn't she have risked getting arrested herself?'

'Oh, she did. We all did.'

'And were you charged?'

'No, thank god, me and my mates just got cautions. They had to arrest everyone, but they knew it wasn't us.'

'And Rachel? What did she get?'

'I don't know. They don't tell you. And she disappeared straight after. Just vanished. And at the time, I was just relieved. Just glad she'd gone away. And then she messaged me out of the blue again, about wanting to meet David. And I was obviously really anxious because of the whole drugs thing—'

'So you didn't want him to meet her.'

'Of *course* not. Not now I knew she was so . . . well, *wild*.'

'But you told him about her?'

'Course. How could I not? I'd started it all, hadn't I? If I hadn't tracked her gran down, she wouldn't have even known he existed. But now she did. And it was my fault. And she could find him herself easily enough, couldn't she?'

'And what did David say?'

'He wasn't happy.'

I'll bet, I think. *I'll bet*.

'He knew he shouldn't give her money. I mean, he thought he should maybe help her, but what with the drugs and that, he was no *way* going to give her money. And I felt bad about telling him, because it wasn't like she was doing anything wrong – not like she was causing any trouble or anything. Not then. And I just felt so *bad* about everything . . .'

'So you talked him into it.'

'It wasn't *like* that. I just – well, she wouldn't leave it, so it wasn't like it was going to go away, was it? Anyway, in the end he said he'd meet her.'

'*After* going to see your grandmother?'

'I never thought he'd actually *do* that. It was right out of the blue. He'd come up with this plan to get her on some drug rehab programme, and if he'd told me, I could have told him – she'd *never* go for that. But he never told me he even had, not before we met up.'

Tell me about it, I think. David, why didn't you just *tell* me?

'Okay. Hang on,' I say. 'Let me scroll back a bit here. Was this last November? I have all David's phone records and I know you met up with him in London. You told him you were sorry. Was that then? Was that when he met Rachel?'

It seems it was. Kane describes to me a fraught, ugly encounter. And, in the madness of all this, I find I'm not surprised to hear it. I know enough from Lacey, and now her grandmother, to accept Rachel's logic. Why on earth would she accept that kind of help from some patronising stranger?

'So what happened after that?'

'She was, like, go to hell, basically. And he was, like, fine. The offer's open. Let me know if you change your mind.'

'And she didn't have any further contact with him?'

'Not that I know of. And he told me if she threatened me to tell him right away. I think he realised by then that she might be dangerous.'

'And *did* she threaten you?'

'Not exactly. She was just on and on at me for money.'

'So did you tell David?'

Silence.

'Kane? Did you?'

'No, I didn't. Look, I *couldn't*. I'd landed all this shit on him, so I needed to be the one to get her off his back. I thought if I gave her money—'

'Christ, Kane. *You* gave her money?'

'A bit,' he admits. 'But she'd never leave off. She was, like, on and on that he was loaded. That she was *entitled*. That if she couldn't get it off him, then it had to come from me.'

'Hang on a minute,' I say. 'When we met you said she wasn't after money.'

'Oh, she's not *now*. It's gone *way* beyond that. She just – look, no offence or anything but she really hates you.'

'Hates *me*? She's never met me.'

'Hates you and Tash. I told you, she's crazy.'

But perhaps not so crazy. She's spent almost all her life being passed from pillar to post in care. To hate the *idea* of me – my family, my life, my cherished daughter, *her* life – oh, I can definitely see that.

'So you kept giving her money?' I say. 'Why Kane? Why would you do that? What did she threaten you with?'

'With *Mum* – that's why she tried to get me nicked in the first place. So she had it over me. So she could threaten to tell my *mum*!'

I can't quite believe what I'm hearing. It's like something out of Grange Hill. 'For god's sake, Kane! *How* old are you? Why on earth didn't *you* tell your mum? *And* David, for that matter.'

Jesus. *David, why the hell didn't you just tell me?*

'I don't *know*,' Kane says. His voice has changed. I think he's crying.

'But I *did*. In the end I did.'

'*When?*'

'Just before he died. She'd decided she was going to break into your cottage, smash the place up a bit, that kind of thing.'

'Unless you got more money for her?'

'Yes. And I was really properly scared now. I thought she'd do it anyway. She was really proper raging. High on something. I really thought she'd actually do it.'

So *that* was when he'd warned him. That nineteen-minute call. Their final exchange. One week and four days before David died.

Of a stroke, I think wretchedly. Of a critical mass of pressure in an already stressed system. An already genetically susceptible system. Oh, *David*.

'So you told him the truth? About the caution? About all of it? About what Rachel was threatening?'

'All of it.'

'And what did he say, Kane?'

'He told me he'd deal with it.'

'Just that?'

'Just that. I think he'd decided he should tell you.'

Not me. The contents of a text message crowd into my brain. *Tash*.

Daaaddyyyyy, re Friday, how exciting! Yes, indeed I can. Shall I book Jamie's Italian? Can't wait to seeeee you! Proseccccccco times! Woop!

He *was* going to tell Tash. But he never got the chance.

And it's been going on ever since. And is no longer about money. Perhaps it never was. Not at a deeper level. It's all about rage. A possibly psychotic rage, that now *I* have to deal with. But *how*?

'Kane?' I say.

'What?'

'It's okay. I will deal with it. Now gather yourself together. Dry your eyes. And *tell your mother the truth*. That's *not* a suggestion.'

Because Kane has no picture, I have only his description. Dark-blonde shoulder-length hair, medium height, medium build. No glasses. As far as he knows, no distinguishing features. *Or* tattoos.

I consider calling Lewis, then dismiss the idea. He's clearly out of the loop now. And even if he can give me more of a description, what exactly am I going to be able to do with it? Send Reg in? Print an identikit and pin it up on trees? Drive to Wales and start making house-to-house enquiries?

But, again, saying what? That someone's been playing practical jokes on me? Playing 'silly buggers'? Because how else would I describe it? And, more to the point, in a world full of tangible grown-up criminality, how else would the police respond to it than as nothing terribly important? *Of course, madam. Made a note, madam. Thanks for advising us. We'll be in touch.*

I feel, more than anything, completely impotent. What precisely *can* I do with what I know now?

But I do find out something. Buried deep in David's phone records. A call made a week before the lunch date that never happened. It's a call made to 101. To the police. So David was dealing with it, just as he'd promised, while I – and I scroll through my work schedule to confirm it – was sitting in a Trust meeting, oblivious to the storm clouds amassing over his life. That had almost certainly played a part in his premature death. *God, David, why didn't you just tell me?*

There is one thing I know I must do, and that's call Tash and warn her properly. Leave no room for misinterpretation this time. Tell her that she must not, under any circumstances, go back to the cottage. Go anywhere near it, in fact.

Though it's now past ten thirty, I take a chance and try Tash on facetime. I'm only half expecting her to respond, and I'm almost at the point of logging off when I hear the familiar metallic clang and my laptop screen shivers to life. And there she is, rosy-cheeked and pony-tailed in front of me, sitting cross-legged on the sofa in the sitting room in their house, obviously on her laptop as well.

She is wearing leopard-print leggings and a smile and has company. Either side of her sit Jonathan and Verity. They are all drinking something pink, from straws, out of what look like jam jars.

'Hey, Mum!' Tash chirrups at me. 'We're just watching *Made in Chelsea*. What you up to?'

'Going to bed shortly. But listen, sweetie,' I say. 'I'm just calling to tell you not to go anywhere near the cottage. At least till I know what we're dealing with.'

All three lean in, heads together, as if for a selfie. 'God, what has happened *now*?' Tash wants to know.

'Nothing new. Well, at least as far as I know – I haven't actually been there. I've just returned from seeing Rachel's grandmother, and found out a little more about her. And I don't want you running into her if she's hanging around there, okay?'

'Blimey,' Jonathan says. 'It's like something out of CSI!'

'I sincerely hope not,' I tell him.

'What did you find out?' asks Tash.

'Just that she has serious mental health problems.'

'What sort of mental health problems? Is she bi-polar or something?'

Even now, ever the fledgling psychologist, I think. 'I have no idea,' I say. 'I just know she's sick. Very sick. And with an axe to grind, apparently.'

'Against us?'

'Yes, against us. But probably against the whole world, truth be known. From what her grandmother's told me, she sounds really damaged. And obsessed with us, apparently.'

'So she *is* dangerous, then?' asks Verity. 'Tash said you thought she might be.'

'I don't know. I'm hoping not. But she might be – she's clearly ill. So I'm going to phone the police tomorrow, and report what's been happening – before anything else happens. But in the meantime, as I say, don't go there.'

Tash sucks on her straw. 'Mum, *you're* not going to go there, are you? Don't, okay, *don't.*'

I shake my head. 'Not right now. And certainly not alone. Though I'm not entirely sure what to do, so I'm hoping the police will be able to give me some advice. And maybe they'll have enough to go on to help them track her down before she *does* commit a crime.'

'Blimey,' Jonathan says again. 'It's more like *Minority Report* now.'

'*What?*' Tash asks. I sense she's more irritable with his quips than I am.

'You *know.* That Tom Cruise film where they can see crimes before they happen. So they can arrest them before they do them. Don't tell me you haven't seen it . . .'

'Just stay safe,' I say. 'Okay? Because one thing I don't have is Tom Cruise on speed dial.'

Though I do have Nick Stone. It's too late to call him, so I text him.

He calls me back immediately. He's out walking the dogs, he says, down on the beach. So he can give Freda a proper run out, off the lead. He tells me all seemed to be well at the cottage last time he checked. That it's the starriest night he's seen in ages.

I tell him London is overcast, a bit like my current mindset. 'So, do *you* think I should call the police?' I ask him, once I've filled him in. 'I'm not entirely sure what to say to them.'

'Yes, of course. If you're worried. Which is what I think I'd be. Listen, do you want me to put some feelers out too?'

'No, no. It's fine. I just don't see what they'll be able to do. I mean it's not like she's committed any sort of crime, is it?'

'Doesn't matter. You're being stalked, and they have a duty to take that seriously. Just call 101 and tell them what's going on, so they record it. And, listen, d'you want me to go back up and double check the doors and windows?'

'Would you? I've told Tash not to go anywhere near it, obviously, but would you? If you're happy to? It would really put my mind at rest.'

Which is nonsense. Because of course it won't. If he finds nothing, it means nothing. And if he finds *something*, then what? How can I deal with a hypothetical something when I have no idea what that something even is?

Cyclophora punctaria

The Maiden's Blush Moth

The maiden's blush moth is a fusspot. A little Lady Fauntleroy. A creature of impeccable habits. A creature who believes her own hype. And like the best Instagram Influencers, she pushes an agenda; to become the pastel *prima donna* many lesser larvae aspire to, one must practise discernment, eschew inferior foodstuffs, and dine exclusively on the leaves of the mighty oak tree.

Lesser larvae, though. Do you like that? Such an elegant put-down. But here's the thing about larvae. Just as the 'ugly duckling' was always destined to be a swan, so, too, are they wonderful winged things in waiting. Oh, they might *look* ugly (though that's a value judgement you're bloody cretinous to make, frankly) but the beauty of a larva is in its focus, its drive, its commendable strength of character. It never falters. It cracks on and puts in the *work*.

Which is why, on the right day, on the flight day, it emerges – a little sleepy, a little wobbly, a little *recherche* – and pumps blood around the vessels that will unfurl its folded wings.

Always good to have a few New Year resolutions, right? (One hundred years of winter, no Christmas, etc. And shit-all else going on, after all.) Early bird and all that. Early bird and all *this*. Early bird indications having overwhelmingly suggested that there's absolutely no mileage in trying to flog a dead horse.

But there are many, many ways to skin a cat.

Chapter 23

The first thing I hear the next morning is the dustcart. And in my mind's eye, I can see Reg, out on his doorstep, making notes, making sure they are doing a proper job.

As I lie in the dark, the sounds clatter through the open quarter-light; the familiar whines and wheezes of the huge pneumatic levers, the rattle of recycling bins being bumped over kerbs, the thumps and clunks as the mechanism gulps down its breakfast. City sounds. Soothing sounds. Sounds that melt into the consciousness. *Gracious, Julia!* (Laura, once.) *How do you sleep with all that racket?*

Normally, without all this? Like a baby.

There is charcoal in the sky now. I can see it through the blind slats. But it's getting later every day and I know I'm entering my personal autumn equinox. The period that lasts for a full four and a half months, when I will wake up in the dark, leave for work in the dark – for a time, even arrive at work in the dark – toil under artificial light all day (despite the proddings of the well-being brigade, how many of us regularly leave the hospital?) and come home in the dark as well. Or, rather, dark tinged with sodium yellow.

But it's the only life I know. Do I want any other? And as if previously cued and waiting for the perfect moment in my thought process, my phone heralds a text message and photo from Nick.

Portuguese man o' war!!!!! The former reads. *Had to share. WOW. In other news, all still well at your cottage. And the surf is up. How are you doing? You OK?*

He's added flag and squid emojis (they have yet to add Physaliidae), and as I reply (*wow indeed. Thanks. Go and have a SURF. A little twitched, to be honest. A LOT frustrated . . .*) I manage to reclaim a little of my lost equilibrium, together with some scraps of my missing sense of perspective. There is a girl out there, somewhere, with a grievance against us. I will inform the police I have a stalker. I will make sure we are safe.

But how, exactly?

I wish I knew what to do.

David had a stalker once. Back when he was a registrar. Back when he still wore a white coat and had a pigeonhole. It started with a note, a folded page nestling on top of his pile of post one morning. Just two lines – *I really like you and I know you like me too* – on a page torn from a refill pad, narrow feint.

I particularly remember that narrow feint. That and the handwriting, which was childish, and the lack of punctuation; both of which took on a life of their own for me. With so little to go on (for several weeks, he was at a loss to know who was writing) you focus on what you do have, and I would study these by-now regular missives with a kind of obsessive pedantry, driven by a furious righteous anger. Who did she think she was? She, with her poorly formed letters, her loose relationship with punctuation, her sorry, vapid syntax, her feeble vocabulary. Did she seriously think my husband would look twice at a person who'd write *I know you've got a family but we should be together she'll get over you* and not see the screaming need for a full stop in the mix? Funny how a flaring of a long-mothballed emotion (romantic ownership, jealousy, some combination of the two) can manifest itself in such unlikely ways.

Though I didn't doubt David's fidelity for an instant. When he brought home the first note we'd both laughed about it, thinking it was some sort of practical joke. But as they began stacking up, the entreaties more bald, shrill and disturbing, we'd chew over how best to deal with it. By then he had an inkling. An outpatient receptionist he'd barely ever spoken to. Something a few discreet enquiries soon confirmed as highly likely.

My approach was to confront her – Tash was seven; how *dare* she! – but David's, characteristically, was empathy personified. Assuming it was true that she was 'troubled' – his consultant's PA's term for it – his concern was more for her; for the disciplinary ramifications. Don't worry, he kept telling me. I will deal with her.

But he hadn't. Not because he didn't fully intend to. Because he hadn't had to; one day she simply left – both her job and the area – leaving her last note in his pigeonhole: spurned by him, she was leaving to live with a new boyfriend in Scotland. And neither she nor it – the whole unsettling, potentially dangerous *Play Misty For Me* episode – was ever much remarked upon again.

He isn't here to deal with this. But he could have been. He should have done. *Why the hell, David, did you leave it so bloody late?*

I find a moment to call the police mid-morning – a chunk of time I really can't spare – and regret having done so immediately. It takes twenty minutes to report the crime that isn't a crime yet, and by the time I'm done, it feels even more pointless than it did when it was still only hypothetical. A form filling exercise, little more.

But what did I expect? That they'd put out an APB on her? Drop everything – like all the *actual* crimes – to look for her? Till she does something further, something more 'concerning' (a word they seem rather keen on), what else are they supposed to do?

And what, in the meantime, can I do?

'How about directory enquiries?' Nick suggests when I call to update him. 'You know her name and her rough age. Might be worth a shot.'

'Rachel Scott, though – how many of those must there be?'

'But it's a start. At least it's *something*. Tell you what – I'll have a go shall I?'

Which he does. It's on my phone when I pull it out after my afternoon clinic. A picture of a long list – some two dozen names and addresses scattered around Wales and London, of Rachel Scotts who appear to fit the age band. Could it really be that simple? Surely not. As the itinerant both Kane and her grandmother described to me, would she even be on an electoral roll?

But something else is there too. A missed call from Laura and, uncharacteristically, a voicemail as well.

'Is Tash away?' the message runs. 'Only I've been trying all afternoon and I can't get hold of her.'

And I know then that I am right to be so anxious. Because Laura never speaks to machines, so I know she must be worried, and Tash *always* answers her phone.

By the time I'm home, PhD thesis in hand – my homework for the weekend – rationality has the upper hand again. I've failed to get Tash either, but I have considered things logically. If she's not answering her phone, then she either has no juice in her phone battery, or an absence of signal. Plus, I recall Tash telling me about some big student bash that's happening tonight. It's now gone seven, and it could already be well underway.

I phone Laura and convey all this to her. 'Oh, well,' she says. 'If you get hold of her could you ask her to call me? We're supposed to be meeting for coffee tomorrow, and I was wondering if she could bear to come to the school Christmas Fayre with me. I've been roped in to man the cake stall because one of the teachers is sick. Some dreadful norovirus going around.' It's the most unsolicited information Laura has shared with me in a long time. 'Not like her, though, is it? I mean, where could she be?'

Not like her. No, it's not. So conscientious is my daughter in dealing with chronic maternal angst that were her phone dead she'd have used someone else's phone to text me – sometimes even before I would have wondered where she was. And in a place without a signal, she would *find* a signal. That is Tash. Being incommunicado for longer than the length of a lecture, or a movie, or a plane journey, *isn't.*

So when I've rung off from Laura, I try Tash again. And after that, send a group text to her, Jonathan and Verity. And am at least cheered to note that they are unresponsive too. Perhaps they're genuinely, unexpectedly, hobbled by a lack of signal – something I confirm when I check Instagram and establish that I was right – there is a big bonfire party happening on Llangennith beach, just behind the campsite, at the far end of Rhossili Bay.

This temporary salve allows me to eat dinner, and further Instagram postings – presumably from those with different mobile providers – allow me to get a little work done as well. I even manage to RSVP to a colleague's birthday invitation. And with an uncharacteristic, if not entirely honest, 'looking forward to it'.

But my instinct is becoming ever more insistent. And by the time I go up to bed, phone still eerily silent, I already know it's unlikely that I'll sleep, despite my long, tiring day.

I deploy mental mantras; she's at a party. With her friends. There is safety in numbers. I do not need to track her movements every single day. I am getting carried away and not being rational. I have evidence that she is somewhere where she might not have a signal. I have no evidence that she's in danger. I can drive down first thing. I am worrying about nothing. If I chant that enough times I will surely go to sleep.

And I do. But at 2 a.m., the silence invades my dreams. And with sufficient force to propel me to an instant awakening; a surge up to consciousness and my still-sleeping phone, its empty screen like a punch in the face.

Something is up. She needs me. I just know it. I throw on T-shirt and jeans, slide my feet into boots, head downstairs, grab my car keys and go.

It's almost five in the morning when I finally cross the Severn estuary, where the water, far beneath the bridge, lies under a bedspread of mist, bright white against the black dome of sky. I want to keep driving, but by the time I've cleared Bridgend, I know I need to stop at the next motorway services; with a full bladder and an empty tank I have no choice. It's nowhere near dawn yet. The sun won't be up till gone seven, and even when it rises, it will do so behind my back. Driving west is to be driving into a dense, inky darkness, which will have lightened only slightly by the time I get there.

Despite the earliness of the hour, the Sarn services are far from empty, people trudging back and forth clutching waxed cups of coffee, spewing crumbs as they take bites from pastries in paper bags. All but one of the pumps in the petrol station are occupied, and I pull in behind one of several white vans. Where are all these men – they are all men – headed so early? Who has plumbing needs, plastering issues, electrical problems, before the sun is even a suggestion at the bottom of the sky?

The cold slaps me in the face as I emerge from the car and seeps through my ill-considered clothes. The scrubby grass around the margins is hazy with dew and crane flies, and the air reeks of dying autumnal foliage. *Tash, where the hell are you? Why haven't you called me?*

I'm just emerging from the toilets when my phone starts to ring, and I rummage in my bag for it, embracing the inevitable – that I've been silly, that I'm worrying needlessly, that I've driven all this way for nothing. *Mu-um* – I can hear her chiding me – *you are bonkers!*

Please let me be bonkers.

But when I have it in my hand, it isn't Tash's face I see. The screen is black, and against it there are three familiar symbols. Three question marks.

???

I stare at them for a second or two, not quite making sense of it. Like going into labour and, despite having waited for it every minute, every hour, not quite being able to believe that's what the pain is.

It *is* what it seems. The mountain has come to Mohammed. Rachel Scott – finally – has come to me. But to say what? To ask for what? To *do* what? And where is she?

I swipe my finger across the screen and put the phone to my ear. There's a crackle of static, spits and pops – the signal's obviously fragile.

'Hello?' I shout into the noise. '*Hello?* Can you hear me?'

Then there's a whisper. A hiss. Another crackle. A tiny voice.

So tiny that when I recognise it, I don't quite believe it either. Yet I'm right. Inexplicably, I *am* hearing my daughter's voice.

On this phone.

'*Mum?*' she's whispering. 'Oh, thank god you're there. Mum, it's *me*!'

Ascalapha odorata

The Black Witch Moth

Point of fact, fact-fiends! That death's head hawkmoth in the film? It wasn't in the book. In the book it was *this* moth. The Black Witch moth, *Ascalapha odorata*. (Asca*lapha* odo*rata*. Asca*lapha* odo*rata*. Asca*laaaaapha* odo*raaaaaata*. Just like the spell out of *Bedknobs and Broomsticks*. Neat.)

The black witch moth, like the white one, is a moth of myths and legends. Down Mexico way, some say if it flies in, then if you're already ill you are surely going to die. In parts of the Caribbean, where it's known as the *Sorcière Noire*, to see one is to have an evil spell cast upon you. It's a lost soul (Jamaica), a Moneybat (Bahamas), and if you chance upon one and are resident in Hawaii, it's a dead friend who has come to say *aloha*.

Alo-fucking-ha.

It's all bollocks, obvs. (God, the crap people believe.) But what is true of this moth is that, along with light, obvs, it's unerringly attracted to the heady scent of soft, overripe fruit.

Sorry and all that, but there it is.

Chapter 24

I've known many shades of death. Terror though, not so much. I was scared during childbirth – of pain, of complications. I was distressed when I miscarried, for the babies I'd never meet. I was in a shunt in my car once, with Tash in the back seat, and for a short time – ten seconds? – I feared for her safety. But terror, up to this point, has largely been a stranger. It has never visited my life. Only my dreams.

But now it's here. Nipping at my heels as I sprint back to my car.

'Where are you?'

'In the garage, in the utility room.'

'You're at the *cottage*?'

'Mum, I'm safe. The door's bolted. Where are *you*?'

Tash's voice is such a tiny thing. Just a wisp of a whisper. *Retrieve key fob*, I think. *Keep your head straight. Press the button.*

'Sarn Services. Safe from what? Why are you there? I told you not to *go* there!'

'Mum, I *know* that. But I *had* to.'

Open door. Climb inside again. Shut door. Press ignition. 'Why? And where did you get this phone from? Where's *your* phone?'

Engage drive.

'She *smashed* it.'

Release handbrake. Press accelerator. Concentrate. Pull away.

'Smashed it? *Who* smashed it?'

'*Verity!*'

Ctenucha virginica

The Virginia Ctenucha Moth

V is for Violin. Volcano. Vulture. Vendetta.

V is for Vision. And VE-RI-TY.

Sod the name Rachel. I chose V. But not for Verity. (Which means 'truth'. Haha. *Please.* Give me strength.) No, V . . . [*Pause to split sides from laughing.*] . . . is for *Virgin.*

What else? I'm no accident. I am something *ordained.*

I'm the original Virgin birth, me.

From Wiki: Panning for gold often results in finding pyrite. Nicknamed fool's gold, it reflects substantially more light than authentic gold does. Gold, in its raw form, appears dull and lustreless.

In summary: *All that glisters is not gold.*

Tell me, what would you have me do? Were you in my shoes, what would your plan be? Come on, tell me.

Jesus, I could scream at the injustice of it all. You don't get it, do you? You never have, have you? You just don't realise. It could have all been so different. So *nice*. Sod that bastard husband of yours – aka my *daddy*. I already had things straight anyway. Things arranged for us all. I had everything in place for our happy-ever-after. Bells, whistles, klaxons – an I-DEN-TI-TEEEEE. But you made a bad call that day. A bad, *bad* decision. You shouldn't have got into your stupid car, driven to your shitting 'holiday' cottage in Wales, got your silly little board out (oh, forgive me, sweet Julia, but who the hell did you think you were impressing?), got in the sea (which, by the way, you should stop romanticising; it would kill you as soon as look at you), and paddled, and faddled, all the way out to sea – Julia, you surely realise: I WATCHED you.

And on that day, that *too soon* day – that day that was *my* day. My day to fly, finally. To prevail. To draw a line, get the watch, and be rid of the little shit. Have him never darken my shiny doorway into a new life again. To have something else ON him, because that's how it always works, see? And off you went and ruined it – saw him, and chased him, and lit the blue touch paper. And having lit it, you should have let him DIE there.

Let it lie.

Let it go.

Let nature take its course.

Let the fates square the circle so the circle could become a square again.

Let the natural order – of your dead husband's *genes* – be restored.

You could have loved me. You know you could. God, you're *such* a hugger; such a huggy hygge mummy. Such a heart-tease. And you didn't know it – you still don't – but I was the thing you *needed most*. Your yearning made flesh. A bright shoot of brilliant green. To square *your* secret circle.

Another, *better* daughter.

God, how you wanted. I know, you see. I *know*. You beat yourself up about it. Raged, screamed and wept about it. Cried yourself to sleep about it. Counted countless sheep about it. Agonised. Analysed. Reached all the wrong conclusions.

You could have had me. You would have loved me. But now you've denied me.

And now you will pay.

Chapter 25

Terror, I realise, is a terrible passenger. A back-seat driver who must be ignored at all costs.

Engage brain. Concentrate. Take the third exit.

'Sweetheart, listen,' I say, as I merge back onto the motorway. 'This phone. Where did you get it?'

'I *told* you. It's Verity's.'

Tash's voice is so indistinct now that I'm struggling to hear it. I twist the knob on the dash to increase the volume, but it makes little difference.

'Sweetheart, it can't be. This is Rachel Scott's number – the number Kane had on his hand. How did Verity get hold of it?'

'It *is* Verity's. I *told* you. It's her old one. Her *other* one. The one she takes to festivals in case she loses it or breaks it. Mum, I don't know what to *do*. How long are you going to be? *Oh, god.* I can *hear* her. *Shit*—'

'What's happening?'

'I don't know . . . Oh, god, I think she's in the car port. God knows what she's doing now. Mum, she's completely *lost* it. She's been acting weird for a couple of days now. Ranting on. Saying stuff . . .'

'What sort of stuff?'

'Mad stuff. Scary stuff. Violent stuff—'

My pulse pounds in my temples. 'Has she *hurt* you?'

'Not yet, but, Mum . . . *God* knows what she's going to do next. Someone gave her a pill at the party. Some drug. I don't know what, but she's lost the plot now . . . *properly* lost it. That's why I thought I'd better go with her . . .'

'Go where?'

'*Here!* Oh, god, Mum, come quick. She's gone *mad*—'

My sat nav says I'll be there in one hour and seven minutes. My head says the bolt on the utility room door is strong and true. My memory says the closest police station is in Swansea.

But my heart remains silent. It is strangled by terror. It cannot get a word out. But then it *mustn't* get a word out. It must *shut up*, because it's no use to me right now.

Inhale. Exhale. Eyes on road. Correct lane. Stay focused. 'Stay quiet, sweetheart,' I whisper. 'Not a sound, okay? *Listen.* I'm going to have to ring off now so I can call the police. And Nick Stone, because he lives literally *just around the corner.* Stay put. Turn your ringer off. Stay as quiet as a *mouse.*'

'Oh, god, Mum, what should I *do?*'

'Just stay where you are. Quiet *as a mouse.* Ringing off now. I love you.'

'I love you too, Mum. But, *Mum*—'

'Shhhhh . . . Just stay quiet, sweetie. *Silent.* I'm going to get help, okay? *Now.* Okay? *NOW.* I love you. Ringing off now. I love you. I'll call back. Ringing off . . .'

I know terror now, I think. Just like death, I have its measure. Terror is driving too fast in the outside lane of a motorway, with a finger hovering over a phone icon, on a touch screen, on a dashboard, to end a call. Terror is in the knowing, in the significance, in the *import* of such an action.

In taking *this* action. In ending *this* call.

I dare not think further – I can't afford to. I press.

I'm a scientist. I'm trained to measure. So I work in reverse order. And Nick, to my relief, answers his mobile immediately. And responds as anyone else would when phoned at 5.40 in the morning.

'Julia. What's happened?' he says blearily. 'Is everything all right? What's going on? You okay?'

'Oh, god, I'm so sorry to ask you, Nick, but could you drive over to my cottage? I think Tash might be in danger. I've just come off the phone to her. She's holed up in one of the outbuildings, and Verity's on some sort of rampage. She's taken drugs, I don't know what, but—'

'Verity? As in, hang on—'

'Yes. *Verity.* As in her *friend.* She's got her *phone*, Nick – she's got *Rachel Scott's* phone. Tash has managed to get Verity's phone off her, *and it's Rachel's.*'

'Christ, Julia. Look. Shit. I'm not there. I'm in Cardiff. But, okay, I'm on it. I'll get there soon as I can. Whereabouts did you say she's hiding?'

Cardiff. Oh, *god.* 'Don't worry, Nick. I'm already ahead of you.'

'Where are you, then?'

'Still an hour away.' *Shit. And inhale. And exhale. And drive.*

'Okay, so just get there. I'll call the police for you.'

'No, I'll—'

'Just *drive.* I'll call them. I can do it *en route.* You just get there, and—'

But the phone clicks. He's gone.

And when I try to call Tash again, she's gone as well.

I drive on into darkness, too fast, trying for furious; any emotion I can muster with sufficient intensity that it can wrestle me from the cold iron grip of my fear. Verity. *Verity.* I cannot get my mind around it. Kind, thoughtful Verity. Calm, capable Verity. *How?* How can it be? Am I still making five here? Could Rachel have sold her phone? (*She's like that, she goes through phones.*) Could Verity perhaps have bought it from that contact she knows at college?

But Verity has *lost it*. She has *properly lost it*. Verity, who doesn't lose things. Verity, who always keeps them. A cool head. A willing ear. My daughter, from sinking. But she has *lost it*.

I can't believe it, but that doesn't mean it isn't true.

I stab the console as I drive. *Phone. Calls received. Last ten. ???*.

Still Tash doesn't answer. It just rings and rings, no voicemail. How many times now have I tried this sodding number? I try it again. Still nothing. *Shit.*

But you told her to stay silent, didn't you? Stay focused. Concentrate. Inhale. Exhale. Keep driving.

I press my foot down on the accelerator even harder. Through junction thirty-eight. Thirty-nine. Forty. Forty-one. I mark landmarks. I crave them. The next one, and the next one. Margam Park. Port Talbot. Briton Ferry. Pontardawe.

Drive. Just keep driving.

Finally, I reach junction forty-seven and turn south. Then I realise that, soon, I will have no signal either, because I'm entering a mobile-phone dead zone.

I stab the console uselessly as I fly past the Harvester. Then the rugby ground. The railway bridge. The nursery, with its yellow paintwork. The traffic lights, which are green. Though terror has a hierarchy, just like anything else; I know I would drive through them even if they were red.

Oh, David. Christ, David. *Do you realise what you've done?*

A diet of horror films, partially of the serial-killer variety, might lead you to suppose there might be order to evil-doing – dastardly, pre-prepared scenarios playing out as the evil-doer orchestrates their life-defining moment in great and precisely tuned detail. Their show-stopping denouement. Screams, and gore, and carnage.

In reality, as I arrive, all is apparently calm and silent. Megan's house is in darkness, the village beyond likewise, and the gate to the track is shut. I jump out and open it, knowing I won't bother shutting it. Then jump straight back in and drive on down to the cottage, which sits in the landscape as if refusing to co-operate with my terror – like a house in a toy farm set, picture-book pretty, with its neat grid of stone walls, the sheep dotted in the pasture and, perched high above, Gower ponies on the hill, behind which the sun will rise on a perfect late-autumn day, jewelled with blackberries and dew-spangled webs.

It lies. There are lights on, though not the outside one. The light's spilling out from the back, over the lawn.

I skew-park and, as an afterthought, turn the car around before leaving it. Then, seeing nothing, hearing nothing, sensing nothing, I get out, and pad around the side of the barn, to the utility room.

I can see the door is open, and fear chokes my windpipe. She isn't in there. Where *is* she? I turn back towards the house.

It's only when I reach the side wall that sound finally reaches me. The sound of shouting – female voices – and then a single, guttural scream.

And as I round the house, to the back, pulling out my keys in case I need them, I finally see a glimpse of them, through the half-open kitchen blind. Tash and Verity. *No*, I correct myself. Tash and – it must surely be – *Rachel*.

Though logic tells me to be cautious, maternal instinct overwhelms me. So I barrel on in; through the back door, through the wet room and – after vaulting a fallen chair which is lying on its back like a dying insect – into the kitchen, where I'm almost upended. I don't know what I've slipped on, but as my foot shoots away from me, both girls' startled faces, as one, turn towards me.

As I grab the door to steady myself, I take in what I'm seeing – that they are locked in a grotesque, shifting, blood-spattered embrace. That my daughter is bleeding. From a wound on her forehead. And that Verity – no, *Rachel* – has one of my kitchen knives in her hand. A knife that Tash is desperately trying to evade. I have never seen a blade wielded in such a way, not in real life. My knife. My chef's knife. Which is so big, *so* sharp. I've seen far smaller knife wounds end lives.

I think I shout then, though I don't know what exactly I'm shouting; my focus is all on the distance between me and my daughter and the time it will take me to cover it. Which I do, grabbing for the corner of the kitchen table as I reach it, and heaving it bodily, hand and hip, out of my way, towards Verity. Things scatter – mugs and glasses, a gin bottle, my mother's sewing box – then clatter, fall and crash, smashing onto the flagstones, spewing shards.

'*Help* me!' Tash is screeching. *Why the hell is she back in here? Why didn't she stay out in the utility room, where she was safe?* 'Help me!' Tash screams again, as Verity draws both body and arm back. But my appearance has changed things; she is watching me. Intent on me. Is my arrival the icing on some sick murderous cake? Is her gaze darting towards me because she's realised what she can do now? Have me *see* her plunge the knife into my daughter?

It's enough of a misstep that I have a precious half-second in which to throw myself between them, shoulder braced against the blade. And as she swipes – she is still aiming it at Tash, albeit through me – I feel a hot sting of pain in my upper arm.

'Get out!' I shout at Tash, who is now clutching at my jacket. 'Get out! Go up to Megan's! Go on – go!'

She doesn't. Instead, she picks up a chair, and as the knife sings through the air once again, it smacks me on the other shoulder on its way past me, where, glancing off Verity's arm, it clatters down around her legs.

One of her knees buckles, and I realise she is as drug addled as Tash described. 'Get out of here!' I bark again. 'I *mean* it, Tash!'

'No!' Her voice is shrill but determined. 'I'm not leaving you on your own with her! She could *kill* you!'

And could have killed Tash. And *still* could. So I summon every ounce of strength I have, and as she regains her balance, I take a punt on my advantage, and smash my arm down on her wrist, sending the knife clattering to the floor.

She bends down then, to retrieve it, and as I sense Tash beside me, I see her foot kick out and make contact with Verity's thigh, which sends her back down again like a darted savannah animal.

'Go!' I bark at Tash again, as I kick the knife away from us. 'Go up to Megan's! Get *help*!'

Again, she ignores me, dipping down to retrieve the knife instead. 'I'm not leaving you on your own with her, Mum!' she shouts again.

Perhaps she's right not to, because Verity's rage has still not abated. Even as she hits the floor, she's already scrabbling to get to her feet again, and, recalling how much she hates me, I know if she had the strength she might try to kill me with her bare hands. It is almost too much to look at her, let alone take that in. I grab the nearest kitchen chair to shield me, breathing hard and grinding down, because I know that if I have to I will smash it down on top of her. I will be able to. And I will do, because this is *Rachel*.

But she senses it. Our eyes meet – she's now almost upright – and, suddenly, I *know* it; that she *knows* I'll do it. That I am strong enough. That I would kill *her* before I let her harm my daughter further.

And, hard up in the corner, between the Aga and sink unit, I watch her realise she has no route of escape.

She plucks the kettle from its stand.

'Put that *down*!' I say it firmly.

'V, put the bloody kettle down!' Tash shouts at her from behind me. 'Stop this! For Christ's sake! Let us help you!'

Help her? I am at a loss to know what's going on now. And even as I try to process Tash's words, I watch Rachel judging angles. And as our eyes meet again, I see something that I have never seen before. I see David. David's coolly appraising eyes.

She stares at me. Stares and stares. I can almost feel her brain whirring.

'Just stop,' I say. 'Now. Put the kettle down. This is over.'

'*Over?* You think? Oh, Julia, you're so *funny*. You really think you're in charge here? You really think you're the boss of *me*?' She laughs. She actually laughs.

'For Christ's *sake*, V!' Tash says.

'Shut up, you mindless *brat*!' Verity snarls. 'You mindless pathetic *twat*.' And though I can't see Tash's face, I don't need to. Her gasp is enough.

'Tash, go to Megan's. Get help. *Please*. Go now.'

'Yes, go now,' Verity parrots. 'Run away, little Tashy Tash. This isn't about *you*. It's not *all* about you, you know. Run along now.' She flaps a hand. 'This is between the *grown*-ups. Me and *Mumma*.'

'You bitch,' I hear Tash say.

'Yeah, yeah, yeah. Bitch, witch, what*ever*.' But to my astonishment, as she speaks, Verity *is* putting the kettle down. Carefully. Slowly. With great concentration. It slots back onto its base with barely a sound.

But just as Tash cries out – 'Mum, be careful! Watch her!' – she raises both hands in front of her – they are now bloody claws – then launches herself at the chair back with a swift, almighty thrust, shoving both it and me backwards against the kitchen table.

'Fuck you, then!' she yells. 'You have destroyed every fucking thing, Julia!' And before I can regain my balance, she's already pushed past me and, swatting Tash aside, staggers out into the night.

As I blunder to the window, and Tash lurches to the sink and vomits, I see a flash of turquoise and a ripple of black cloth, growing smaller, and Verity – no, *Rachel* – is gone.

Finally, I exhale properly. Unbunch my bunched muscles. Take in great gulps of air as I try to make sense of – to even *believe* – what has just taken place here.

Tash continues to heave over the sink and, still peering through the blind slats, I automatically pull her hair back from her face. The acid smell of bile rises up, prickling in my nostrils, as I inspect her wound, mightily relieved to see it's only flesh deep, the blood doing its job, already congealing. I reach across Tash, whose bloodied fingers grip the sink edge, white-knuckled, and turn the taps on, spraying water over both of us.

'All this blood,' I say, my fear rising a second time as I look around me. There is blood everywhere. Smears, splats, sprays and *pools of it. Jesus.* 'Christ. Are you hurt anywhere else, sweetheart?'

Tash's head moves from side to side beneath me. 'No. that's all *her* blood. She – shit—' I feel her shoulders heave and shudder, and she says no more.

I gather her into my shaking arms, and hold her tight, so tight, *so* tight, against me, staring out at the empty garden, the empty distance, the pewter sea, the yawning dawn.

Seconds pass. Still I hold her. The bulk of her. The fact of her. She is okay. I try to still my heart. She is okay. She is okay.

It's Tash who breaks the silence, stiffening against me, straightening. 'Mum, we have to go after her.'

'*What?*'

'She's hurt. We have to *find* her.' Then, clearly reading my astonishment as something other, something harsher, 'Mum, we *have* to!'

And in that instant I realise – Tash *hasn't* realised. Not fully.

I point to the window. 'That's *Rachel* out there,' I say. 'Rachel. Don't you *realise*? Verity *is* Rachel. Her phone. The phone you called me on? It's Rachel's.'

'*What?*' she parrots back at me. 'But she—'

'*Is Rachel,*' I say again, watching her cast her gaze around her. See the thought process that, given her addled state, has up to now failed to happen. See the conclusion, as easy to reach as it is painful.

'Oh, god, Mum,' she says. 'Verity is Rachel? But—'

A door bangs, scaring both of us. I feel giddy suddenly. Is she back? Then I gape as my sister-in-law appears from the wet room.

I do a double take. *Laura?* Why the hell is Laura here? She's in her heavy coat and purple scarf and ankle boots, over mis-matched socks. She looks like she's dressed in a hurry.

'Oh, my *Lord*,' she says. 'What on earth has happened here?' Her handbag hits the kitchen table with a whump.

Tash runs to her. 'Oh, Mamgu, I'm so sorry,' she says, hugging her. 'I didn't mean to frighten you. I'm okay now. It's all okay now. I'm so sorry to drag you down here. I'm fine—'

'Fine? This is fine?' Laura homes in on Tash's forehead. Her shaking hands. 'This is *fine?*' she says a third time, nodding next towards my jacket. I twist my arm. There is a bloodied rent in the leather which is a good five inches long. I shrug my arms free of it to see my top is also ripped. I can't feel it, but there is a wound tracing a line down my upper arm.

'Oh, god, Mum, you're hurt *too!*' Tash says, rushing back to me. 'Let me see.'

'It's nothing—' I reassure her by rubbing at the row of tiny blood beads. 'See? Just a scrape.'

'Just a *scrape*?' Laura squeaks. Her headteacher voice is on leave now, I notice. She looks pale. Bewildered. Frightened. Imagination in overdrive.

As is mine, and I respond to it. We could all still be in danger. I run around, to the hall, to the wet room, to the windows. Locking everything lockable. Making safe, battening down. But Tash is having none of it. 'Mum, we *have* to go and look for her.'

'Look for who?' Laura asks.

'For *Verity*,' Tash tells her, her voice shrill and scratchy.

'As in Verity, your friend from university? Are you telling me it's your *friend* who did all this?'

'Yes,' says Tash. '*No!* Mum, seriously, we need to go and try and find her. She's—'

'Absolutely not,' I say. 'You are going nowhere. She was trying to *kill* you.'

'But—'

'Tash, for god's sake! She was attacking you with my chef's knife!'

I see Laura's eyes bulge. I grab a chair. Suggest she sits on it. I can't believe the words that are coming from my daughter's mouth. Except should I? Because she doesn't know the half of it, does she? She still sees this – despite everything – as her friend 'losing the plot'.

'Mum, she's injured.'

'She didn't look very injured to me,' I point out.

'But she *is*. She's been cutting herself. That's how all this started. Where else d'you think all this *blood* came from? She was using your sewing scissors till I managed to get them off her. Shit—' She begins looking round the kitchen, her hair swinging wildly. 'Where are they? Oh, god, she must have grabbed them when she left!'

I feel exasperated. Confused. Fizzing with too much adrenalin. My mother's sewing scissors. Out of bounds throughout my childhood, in all and any circumstances. Don't you *ever touch* those scissors. They are too big. Too sharp. I see the needlework box again, upturned on the floor now, the foxes, hounds and horses still leaping across the lid.

And all around it, I now see, is the detritus of some sort of frenzy. Some sort of crazed attack on our photograph collection. Pictures ripped out of albums, pictures cut and ripped up; some into many, many tiny pieces. Tash's childhood, so carefully documented, now laid to waste. And for all that it's a blizzard – of paper, card, and *rage* – I realise I'm gazing upon the aftermath of something that now makes perfect sense.

'Is this what brought you here?' I ask Tash.

She shakes her head. 'I just didn't dare let her go. She took some drug. I don't know what. It sent her crazy. She was hallucinating. And when I caught up with her, *here*, she was all over the place, so I brought her in, to get her water. And she just—' She spreads her hands. 'She just totally, totally lost it. Stamped on my mobile, started turning drawers out, started screaming and crying and threatening to stab me if I stopped her . . .'

'Which is when you locked yourself in the utility room?'

Tash nods. 'I just grabbed her phone and ran for it.'

'But why on *earth* did you come out again?' I can barely say it now. 'She could have *killed* you!'

'Because I thought she might kill her*self*. You don't *get* it, Mum. I *told* you—'

A rap on the door. Sharp and firm. Then the sound of the letter box being lifted. 'Anyone in there?' It's Nick's voice. 'Is everyone okay?'

I run to let him in. He has his hand around Freda's collar. 'Nobody hurt?' He looks past me. 'Where is she?'

'Gone.'

'And she's hurt,' Tash adds, joining us. 'We have to find her.'

'On it,' Nick says. Then he nods back towards the open front door. 'You know there's a whole bunch of people up the lane, don't you? Your friends, I'm guessing?' he adds, turning to Tash. 'Your neighbour – Megan, is it? – she's looking after them. She's going to tell the police where to come. Shall I—'

'Go out to the worm,' Tash says. 'You know the worm? That's all she kept going on about.'

'On it,' he says again. Then, without another word, he's gone.

'Going on about?' I ask Tash as we return to the kitchen. Laura's pulled the blind shut and has the kettle in her hand. If she's noticed the blood caked all over it, she isn't saying so.

'I'm going to make a pot of tea,' she says firmly.

'Going on as in how she was going to jump off the head,' Tash is saying. 'As in fly off it. She kept on about how it was time for her metamorphosis or something. Shit,' she adds. 'God, Mum, that *moth*! That's what she was *saying*! When she was stabbing herself. That she was cutting her way out of her cocoon!'

'*What?*' Laura squeaks.

Cocoon, I think. *Cocoon.*

'Mum, she might even be bleeding to death! If she's got those scissors still . . . Mum, you need to go and make sure she's okay. You *have* to.'

She is looking at me in a way that no longer leaves room for argument. And she is right. If there is a life at stake – any life – that's exactly what I must do.

'Go,' Laura says. 'See what you can do. Tash is safe with me.'

I pull my jacket back on, yank a drawer open, and stuff my pockets with pads and bandages. 'I know she is,' I tell her. And I do.

When I get back outside there is light on the horizon, and as I run up the track I see the silhouettes of several people

– presumably the ones Nick was talking about. And as I near them, I spot Megan (I'd recognise that floral poncho anywhere) who is clearly shepherding them into her house. They wear the hollowed-out expressions of newly arrived refugees, but though I'm desperate to know what sequence of events has brought them here (has everyone taken something? A bad batch of drugs, perhaps?) I make no move to follow; one crisis, one trauma, at a time. And when I wave to Megan, her answering thumbs up makes it clear that she has everything in hand anyway. Nick must have spoken to her on his way back up.

I also realise he must have taken his car. It would be far quicker than walking out to the worm, after all, not to mention giving him at least a fighting chance of intercepting her.

I realise I'd be mad not to do likewise. So I run back down to the cottage to collect my own car, then head out to the mist-shrouded promontory. I take the same route to the causeway I did last time I was here, grateful that the dawn is at last breaking, bright and clear, shunting the mist out to sea.

But how to follow him when I can't see him – or Verity, or Freda? Tash might have been sure she would head for the Worm's Head, but would she? Might she not save herself the trip? There are treacherous locations aplenty all around: the sheer cliffs down to the bay, where half a dozen people have lost their lives in as many decades, and the paths round towards Fall Bay, with their vertiginous drops. But since it seems symbolic, from what Tash says, I carry on out to the watch station – famous landmarks are, tragically, always seductive.

I pass the watch station (no one on watch – it's still too early) and pull up alongside Nick's car, next to the sign that marks the path down to the causeway, which warns 'danger' in the sort of shouty typeface that leaves no room for doubt.

And it's right to. Twice a day, every day, it is no place to be. And that will soon be the case. The tide is out but heading in, the sea still polished pewter striped with ribbons of pale foam, as the sets come rolling up and in, to inundate the beach. And away, to my right, at the far end of the bay, the muddy dawn light is pierced by an intense orange glow; that of the bonfire that has been burning since yesterday.

Like a moth, the thought comes to me. *To a flame.*

Biston betularia f. carbonaria

The Black-Bodied Peppered Moth

So, if you don't know about this dude, where the hell have you *been*? He might sound like a wanky pasta dish from that *cucina* you rate in Clapham, but he's actually another version of our old friend the peppered moth. And the embodiment, literally, of Darwin's theory. His very existence proves evolution by natural selection. He is a *mutation*, and as a consequence, he has survived.

If you know your basic school curriculum as well as you should, you'll also know that this version – this dusky Vulcan Bomber of the moth world – evolved during the Industrial Revolution when coal became the energy source *du jour*. You probably also know how it goes. You conform to type – you know, flitting about in your usual peppered get-up – then it's 'Uh-oh, I'm in Bradford!' Or Manchester. Or Sheffield. Where the walls – thick with soot – offer fuck-all protection. *Shit*. And then you're eaten. While the carbon-coloured version survives.

Yes, that's right; the one who's different, the one you discriminated against, the one you *sneered* at. And then he hooks up with a babe moth and his genes are passed on. And, before you know it – and I *know* you already know this, Julia – those black moths are turning up everywhere. They have *prevailed*.

Science tells us that human evolution happens over a much longer timescale, which is why they study genetics using fruit flies instead of people. But the principle still stands. That's the thing you need to get your head round. That for some, in some places, at some point, for some *reason*, it's a simple process. Mutation or death.

But. Point of fact. As with metamorphosis, there are no shades of grey, just sacrificial lambs:

You have to die to let your *species* mutate.

Chapter 26

It's as I swing my gaze back around to the worm that I see him. Spot the tomato-red jacket as he bobs across the causeway, picking his way through the jumble of limpet-encrusted rocks which form the route out to the body of the worm. And ahead of him, camouflaged against the bleached limestone of the distant foreshore, I also see Freda, a good hundred yards ahead of him, moving confidently, and, by the look of it, on her telescopic lead.

I jog down the first part of the track which will take me down there, glancing up intermittently to follow his progress, my hair slapped against my face by a strengthening breeze. Offshore, I think automatically. The best kind for surfing.

I'm almost down at the rocks myself when I finally see Verity, her turquoise hair – her clever *camouflage* – bright against the green. She has already crossed the causeway and is heading up the grassy hill which will take her up, along and down again, towards the serpent's rocky shoulders. Does she know where she is headed? Has she been here before? Something about the way she's running tells me yes.

I call out, but my voice is immediately swallowed. He doesn't look back – if anything he's moving away faster. But not as fast as

Verity, who is lengthening the distance; wherever she plans to fly away from – or off – she is now on surer ground and picking up speed as she makes her flight towards it.

I head on out gingerly because I'm not in my walking boots, and the rocks beneath my feet are slick with bladderwrack and algae. I'm having to watch every step – I could twist an ankle at any moment – so I'm almost halfway across before I dare to look up again, to find that Nick's stopped and is now doing something with Freda's lead. He's reeling her in, I realise, shortening the distance between them, and making better progress now he's cleared the wet causeway.

He leans down to her neck then, and it's clear what he's doing: he's unfastening the lead from her collar. And, with a gesture I don't see or hear, he lets her go.

What did he tell me it was, the speed his dogs can run? Was it thirty miles per hour? Certainly faster than any human, however fleet of foot. Freda canters off up the slope with astonishing speed. Towards *Verity*. I still can't quite believe it.

Freda has almost caught up with her before Verity turns around and sees she's closing in on her. She's too far away for me to make out the detail of her expression, but the body language is as clear as the sky now is above her, the watery sun finally heaving its way over the Down and bathing the worm in a pale, wintry brightness.

For a moment, I feel panic. *Does* Verity have the scissors? Might she lash out? Might she stab Freda? Might she still get away? The fear is thankfully short-lived, though. Despite all that careful retraining, Freda does exactly what she's trained to – leaps up, clamps her jaws round Verity's forearm, and brings her down. And to my great relief she stays down.

It takes me a good ten minutes to cross the rest of the causeway and haul my tired body up the slope. My legs are leaden and sluggish after almost five hours of driving, and I'm struggling with the steepness of the gradient. That, and trepidation. As I near the spot, high on the hill where I watched Verity fall, I see that Nick, who I'd thought was kneeling down beside her, tending her, is doing nothing of the kind. He is sitting on her.

I stumble up the last few yards, using clumps of grass as handholds, and it's only now – on hearing my laboured, noisy breath – that Nick turns arounds and spots me.

'I'm sorry,' he says immediately. He is straddling her, on his knees. Holding her wrists in his hands, across her stomach. He has to swivel his torso one hundred and eighty degrees to see me. Beneath him, her legs move alternately, like pistons – as if doing a legs, bums, and tums class in her dreams. 'I had to make the call. There was no way I was going to reach her.'

I realise he's talking about letting Freda off the leash. She's sitting on her haunches just above him now, watching me clamber up the hill, her tongue hanging from her jaw, raising steam.

I have barely the breath to speak yet. I shake my head and gulp some air in. 'No, you were right to,' I say, as I scrabble around to kneel beside them. With so much on, and her clothes streaked with blood and god knows what else, it's hard to see the extent of Verity's injuries. I can see bloody holes in her leggings, rips in her T-shirt and in her long black cardigan, streaks of slobber on her sleeve where Freda clamped her in her jaws, but I suspect she is beyond feeling any pain. Her colour is good though, and she's struggling, which speaks volumes. That she's conscious at all is half the battle already won, even if a very curious kind of conscious – almost an altered state, because, despite the thrashings of her body, Verity's head is perfectly still, almost as if her neck bones have fused. She's staring straight up at the sky, unblinking, unseeing. Or, at least, seeing something I can't.

And she's muttering. Barely audibly. But repetitively and clearly. *Enter moth. Enter moth. Enter moth. Enter moth. Enter moth. Enter moth.*

I squeeze her arm. There is a weeping, blistered graze on her cheek. New. Perhaps a burn. *Enter moth. Enter moth.*

'*Verity?* Can you hear me?'

She blinks once, then turns towards me. Her legs stop their drumming. Then she smiles a beatific smile and starts intoning again. '*If we shadows have offended, Think but this, and all is mended: That you have but slumbered here, While these visions did appear. If we shadows have offended, Think but this and—*'

'*Verity.* Can you hear me? It's Julia.' I touch her forehead. She shrinks from my hand as if I've prodded her with a branding iron. '*—and all is mended: That you have but slumbered here, While these visions did appear . . .*'

'What's she saying?' Nick asks. 'You think she's tripping on something?'

'I think so,' I say. 'She's almost certainly having some sort of psychotic episode. It's Shakespeare,' I add. 'She's quoting bits of Shakespeare. Verity. Rachel. *Rachel.* Are you with us? It's *Julia.* I'm here to help you. Can you hear me?'

I gently cup her face and turn it. And now Verity has gone. Finally, I am looking into the eyes of Rachel. Her pupils are black holes. Enormous. What's going on in there? But eventually, something clears, and she seems to focus on me. 'Julia,' she says. 'Lovely lovely lovely lovely, Julia. She who never had *so* sweet a changeling.' She blinks. 'Did you see me? Do you *see* me? *Can* you see me?'

'I saw you. Shhh, now. Yes, I can *see* you.'

'Can you can you can you? Now I'm out of my cocoon?'

'Shhh,' I say. 'Yes. And we need to get you down off here so we can sort out all your injuries. You're hurt, Rachel. Can we do that?'

She nods. A single inclination of her chin. 'Lovely lovely lovely lovely, Julia.'

'D'you want to get off her, Nick? Let's see if we can get her up, shall we? We need to get her down from here before the causeway's submerged.'

'Shit,' he says, glancing past me. 'You're right. We need to hurry.'

Rachel lies motionless, staring up at the sky, while Nick clambers off her. '*Shit, you're right,*' she says. '*Get her up. Shit, you're right. Better hurry. Get her up, get her down. Better hurry. Better hurry. Enter Peaseblossom. Mustard-seede, Cobweb and Moth. Enter Peaseblossom, Mustard-seede, Cobweb and Moth. Enter—*'

'Come on, sweetheart,' I tell her. 'Let's sit you up. Can you manage that?'

'Can you? Can you can you? I have to go now. Lovely, Julia.'

'Lovely, Julia,' I agree. 'And, yes, we do have to go now. Here, take my hands – that's right, slowly now. Up you come.' She lets me pull her up to a sitting position, bloodying my hands with her own. Then, with Nick's help, unsteadily, to her feet, where she sways.

'I have to go,' she says flatly. 'I have to go, Julia. It's time to fly now.'

'Yes, you do,' I soothe. 'We all do. And we're both going to help you.'

I am supposed to be a good listener. I *am* a good listener. But I clearly haven't listened well enough or hard enough. Because just as I thread an arm through the crook of her elbow and gesture to Nick to do likewise, in that tiny chunk of time, she has all she sees she needs. And when we begin moving – Freda is already loping down the hill ahead of us – she makes a movement so propulsive it leaves both of us staggering, flinging our arms off, whirling around, and sprinting further up the hill. *Shit*, I think. *I should have seen that coming.*

'Christ!' Nick lurches backwards and only just keeps his footing. But I'm in a better place, slightly higher, on slightly flatter ground, slightly closer, and I am able to go after her like a runner off the blocks. And, though I'm no runner, I'm strong again, where she *must* be weakening. So I have no need of Freda as I thunder up the slope behind her. I am powered now by a chemical cocktail even more potent than hers: five parts terror (my new friend), five parts sheer bloody-mindedness. I will *not* have her kill herself. Not on my watch.

But in less time than it takes me to visualise an image of her broken body, I realise I have misjudged both her and myself. For as the gradient begins to steepen, up to the edge of the worm's shoulder, I realise my legs are weakening, whereas she (inexplicably, given her probable blood loss) is actually speeding up. Metre by metre she is getting away from me. Getting closer to the edge. What on earth *has* she taken?

I see where she's heading, too. The Worm's Head, just as Tash said. *Where there be dragons.* I will my legs to pump harder.

I glance behind me, too, to see Freda flashing past me, a sudden blur of cream, panting hard. Nick's not far behind, either, but still too far behind. If the dog can't bring her down again, we're done for.

But in that moment, turning back to the sea, I know we're already done for. Because the black shape, too far ahead of me, has now stopped. As has Freda, about a metre or so behind her.

I feel hope drain. Though I can't quite see the lie of the land there, I know even well-trained ex-police dogs have their limits. She has stopped because there is no safe way for her to go on. Rachel must have made the leap onto the jumble of jagged rocks.

So Rachel is safe now. And she knows it.

I see it in the way her whole body seems to straighten. In the way she stills herself. Readies herself. Gives herself a moment. Seems so oblivious of Freda's urgent barking. Because she is.

She then unfurls, like a moth – no, a *butterfly* – from a pupa. Lifts her arms to shoulder height, tips her head back as if in wonder, then crouches. Then, as if wholly unafraid, she finally makes her leap.

As if she knows, beyond doubt, that this *is* her time to fly.

Before she plunges off the cliff edge, the very last thing I see is the air – the dawn, the *sky* – beneath her feet.

Chapter 27

Clapham, London, late November

'So, what are you going to do for Christmas? Are you going to go away?'

Nick is in my kitchen and I can feel his silent scrutiny as I conjure his favourite coffee – I nipped out to the corner shop specially – from my not-quite-as-swish-as-his coffee machine. I've taken two days' annual leave; I still have a lot more to use up. A lot to *fill* up, for that matter. In the business of making a new life. For now, though, I still have a thesis to finish marking. Which has given up calling to me in favour of sending up flares.

But Nick is here. So it can wait. At least for an hour or so. He is here, for the most part, to meet up with an old newspaper colleague later. Some commission or other, about which he's quite excited. And for the smaller part – my cautious interpretation, at any rate – to pop in and see me on the way.

'Just to Swansea,' I tell him. 'We're going to spend the day with my sister-in-law. Snow cover will be rubbish anyway. We're going to go in March. You?'

He takes the coffee. Sips it gingerly. Sets it down again to cool a bit.

'Not a clue,' he says. 'It's not my turn to have Nate this year, so we'll see.'

He looks so sad. I want to say *it's just a day*, but I stop myself. We all reach that understanding eventually. Even me. Hopefully he'll do so a little quicker.

'Well, if you're home on Boxing Day,' I say instead, 'I'll be around if you want a surf lesson.'

'No fear,' he says, and so quickly that I feel silly for having offered. It's a new thing, this whole negotiating of new relationships. But his smile is encouraging.

'No, you've got that all wrong,' I point out. 'You have to *feel* the fear and do it anyway.'

'Aren't you all done with fear for a bit?'

'Some kinds. For Tash, at least. Well, as far as I'm ever able.'

'So she's back in uni okay?' he asks.

'She is.'

'Must be tough for her. A lot to process.'

'She's doing okay. At least that's what she tells me. Fingers crossed that's the truth. I'm keeping an eye on her. Well, a covert eye, obviously. It's going to take time, I'm sure, but she'll get there.'

'And Kane?'

'Far as I know, ditto. He's back in uni too now. They bounce back, don't they, kids? Well, at least some of them. The lucky ones . . .'

We both know who I'm talking about.

'I still don't get it,' he says. 'I mean, how did she manage to construct this whole other identity and maintain it for so long?'

'That's just it. She didn't. Apart from the guarantor for the house lease, which she got around by paying her rent up front, she didn't even need to. She had a passport in her own name. She used her gran's house as her home address. She was Verity to her friends, but in everything official – everything *legal* – she was still Rachel Scott. It was even on her debit card. And no one ever noticed.'

'But what about uni?'

'She never pretended to be at Tash's uni. She told her she was at Swansea Met. Though she wasn't – she'd enrolled on an art course at a local college, just like her gran said she'd planned to, and had a part-time job in a little coffee place down at the Mumbles – and all this even before Tash started uni. Can you believe that? And she met Jonathan during freshers, and started seeing him soon after, which is how she was able to get close to Tash.'

'Hang on – didn't you say she didn't meet David till last November?'

'She didn't. This all happened *before* that. She moved to Swansea pretty much as soon as she'd found out who we were.'

'To construct her new life,' he says. 'Incredible. And no one twigged? No one noticed she wasn't on the course she was supposed to be on?'

'Clearly not. But you know what kids are like. They all took it at face value. As did I. But why would I not? It's really sobering, isn't it? We spend so much time worrying about identity theft, yet she was able to just rock up and insert herself into Tash's life without anyone so much as batting an eyelid.'

'But you have to ask yourself why. What was her plan? She must have had one originally. Not a death wish, from the start. Surely not.'

'Oh, she did have a plan at first; I know that much from Kane. She wanted what he had – what she felt she deserved too. And I believe him about the business of her wanting to threaten David, try to scare him into giving her some money too. Instead of' – I use finger quote marks – '"help". After that, though . . .' I shake my head. 'His death obviously changed everything. He was no longer there to threaten, was he? And by that time – and even more so as a result of it – she'd really begun to immerse herself in Tash's life, wholesale. And perhaps – and this does chime with what I've been told subsequently – she'd decided to embrace her new identity, at least in the moment. Who knows what might have happened had I not discovered Kane that day? It's conceivable that she'd still be friends with Tash – still be Verity. It was right there in the sand, wasn't it? Because it *was* me who went and ruined everything, wasn't it?'

'Bit harsh,' Nick observes.

'But still true, I think. I know it's pointless to hypothesise about the workings of such a damaged mind, but I think a part of her genuinely thought she could make a new life as Verity. Just as long as she made sure we never found out who she really was. Which I well and truly scuppered, didn't I?'

'Thank god. She could have killed him. You can't blame your-self. You didn't ask for any of this.'

He touches his wrist as he speaks. 'How's your arm doing?' I ask, remembering.

He traces the line of the scar on the inside of his forearm; legacy of his run-in with my mother's sewing scissors just before I reached them, which he'd never said a word about. Not till hours and hours after. Not till after the air ambulance had come, and the police, and the coastguard, and then had gone again, along with Rachel's broken body. Not till the next day, when I'd spotted the blood seeping through his shirt. Funny to think of those precious sewing scissors, now lying, unloved and rusting, out on the worm.

In the bigger picture, it's also the legacy of his run-in with *me*. We've all of us been bashed about a bit, one way or another. 'Fine,' he says. 'How's yours?'

'Fine,' I say. 'How are George and Freda?'

'Fine again,' he says. 'You know, you should—'

'I've already got my name down.'

'For a puppy? A German shepherd?'

'A German shepherd. The very acme of insanity. Tash is beside herself with excitement about it.'

'Good,' he says again. 'You won't regret it.'

'I hope not. Because I've just cleared out my regret cupboard. I needed room to repurpose it. It's now a hindsight one instead.'

'Which is a wonderful thing. Listen. Do you have plans for later?'

'I thought you had a meeting.'

He shakes his head. 'It's tomorrow.'

Our eyes meet, over our coffees, and for just that fraction long enough to confirm that, as of now, I have no other plans.

Except to live. To appreciate the privilege.

Kallima inachus

The Dead Leaf Butterfly

Was anything, ever, all at once, quite so beautiful and so clever? So shimmering an example of the majesty of Mother Nature? So peerless a confection of biological form and function? Because the dead leaf butterfly doesn't just *look* like a dead leaf – when it senses it's in danger, it also *acts* like a dead leaf by flying erratically, closing its wings, and then dropping to the forest floor. And staying down there, out of harm's way, till the danger has passed.

Only then, when it's safe, does it unfurl its wings and fly.

It's what's known, in science circles, as a *survival strategy*.

AUTHOR'S NOTE

I have long had a fascination for moths. Butterflies too – I'm a committed foot soldier for the annual UK Butterfly Count. But it's the night-time lepidoptera that I find myself drawn to, since playing a part, albeit a small one, into research around *biston betularia*; a moth which, as Rachel notes early on in *Can You See Me?*, is the modern exemplar of Charles Darwin's theory of evolution by natural selection.

It was back in the late eighties that I first encountered the peppered moth and a huge number of other nocturnal insects besides. As part of my degree, I was studying genetics and evolution, and my cohort of students were the last group to be tasked with the rather thrilling-sounding job of setting up moth traps in our gardens. Our role was to gather data on the two forms of the moth as part of a UK-wide study of their distribution.

I duly set the trap and went up to bed, leaving several thousand watts of halogen light flooding the back patio. In the morning I was not disappointed. No invertebrates were harmed during my tiny bit of science, obviously, but, boy, were they cross. No sooner had I gingerly lifted a corner of the trap lid than I was up close and personal with scores of angry insects; and what a diverse and pretty haul I'd lured in there. Peppered moths, yes (the pale kind, since I lived in the south of England), but cinnabars and tiger moths, swallow tails and emeralds, and three kinds of hawkmoths – one of them larger, and by some distance, than any moth I'd ever seen in the wild. There were also lacewings, and flying beetles, and (I shudder to recall this) the scariest arachnid – a giant harvestman – that I'd ever encountered, and which promptly made a dash for freedom up my arm. It's true: the crawliest creatures *are* the creepiest.

My piece of science accomplished, I thought little more of it until a few years ago, when I learned from my son's teacher fiancée, Hannah, that the evolution of the peppered moth – including statistics to which I personally contributed – is now on the UK primary school curriculum. I was tickled by that. And also inspired. Perhaps this novel was always meant to be.

ACKNOWLEDGMENTS

The writing of a novel is a largely solitary occupation, but, thankfully, most of the rest of the process is not. Quite the opposite, in fact; it's refreshingly collaborative, even if some of the collaborators don't ever twig that their chance words, shared anecdotes or dark, fascinating secrets end up, in some form, in my books.

Happily, most do know, so I'm able to thank them. Andrew Lownie, my indefatigable agent and friend, without whom my ghostwriting career – much less this novel – would not exist. My editor Jane Snelgrove. What can I say? Wow. You have truly helped this novel to grow and evolve, and in ways I might never have worked out by myself. Katie Green, who's done so much to prune my often rampaging prose, and the whole team at Thomas & Mercer.

Julie Shaw. You'll know why. Dave Wardell. You will too. Cairan Jones, for the insider info. My fabulous friends, for indefatigable support and for listening. And listening and listening. And, moving on to those who aren't strictly speaking 'those': the Natural History Museum, London (always my favourite museum), the area of outstanding natural beauty that is the entire Gower coastline and The Old Rectory, in which much of this novel takes place. (And is both a real and, I hope, happy place.)

Finally, just as it takes a village to raise a child, so it takes a family – of the understanding, tolerant, patient, *best* kind – to support the creation of a novel. It's not just me who has lived for years with what you have just read. So has my husband, Pete, my now-grown children, Luke, Joe and Georgie, plus Charlotte, my daughter-in-law, Hannah, my nearly-daughter-in-law, and the youngest of the clan, my grandson Rex. (To whom this is dedicated and who can read it in – um – around seventeen years.)

Thank you all for your forbearance. I love you squillions.

ABOUT THE AUTHOR

Lynne Lee was born in London and began her writing career as a teenager. She has been a full-time author since the mid-1990s, writing romantic novels, short stories and ghostwriting bestselling books. *Can You See Me?* is her first psychological thriller and is written under a pseudonym.